BROKEN TRUST

A LAST RESORT NOVEL

NATHAN BIRR

Published by BEACON BOOKS, LLC

Cover Images Copyright ©
fl1photo/iStock

Scripture quotations are from the ESV® Bible (The Holy Bible, English Standard Version®), copyright © 2001 by Crossway, a publishing ministry of Good News Publishers. Used by permission. All rights reserved.

ISBN: 978-1-7321373-3-2 (hc)
ISBN: 978-1-7321373-4-9 (sc)

www.nathanbirr.com

To Mark and Bonnie . . .
I'm more grateful than you know
for your love, godly heritage, and
for welcoming me into the family.

ONE

The rugged, craggy peaks of the Teton Mountains resembled the teeth of an inverted saw piercing the vast Wyoming sky. Ray Eastwood knew this from photographs; by the time he crossed the Continental Divide and descended into the valley on its western side, darkness had fallen. Anything the lights of Ray's Chevy Silverado pickup didn't directly illuminate was obscured. Including the Tetons. For all Ray could see, he might as well have been back home in South Dakota. Eastern South Dakota, not the Badlands and Black Hills and "great faces" carved into granite that made the state a tourist destination. Ray hailed from Sioux Falls, a nice enough city, but one that was out in the middle of nowhere. Absolutely nowhere.

The darkness was accompanied by mist, something between drizzle and fog. Just enough that he had to keep flicking the windshield wipers on and off. Not nearly enough that he could leave them on without them squeaking as they bounced across the glass. At least the need to reach for the lever every minute or so helped fight off drowsiness. No sense running into a buffalo or elk this close to his destination.

Ray had left home at seven that morning, a dozen minutes before sunrise. He'd crossed four hundred miles of South Dakota, the miles outnumbering the trees about two to one. Then he'd entered eastern and central Wyoming, a place so barren it made South Dakota look like a rainforest. It had been a lot of ground to cover and with not much to distract him but the occasional pronghorn standing out among the sage. He could have used a distraction, something to take his mind off recent events. Instead, all he'd seen was a visual reinforcement of his loneliness.

He'd had an early lunch at the famous Wall Drug Store, along with a cup of their much-advertised five-cent coffee. After that, his left knee had started to stiffen up, as it did now and again. He'd stopped at a solitary rest area south of the Black Hills near the border, then again in the town of Lusk, Wyoming, to fill up on gas and get something to eat. After eight and a half hours in the car, his knee had really been bothering him—a high school football injury that liked to remind him he wasn't all that young anymore, now thirty-one. He'd taken a break in Casper, then grabbed dinner in Riverton before passing through the Wind River Reservation and climbing slowly toward the Continental Divide. It had been warm and sunny on the east side, summer refusing to give way to autumn, despite the calendar's insistence. As the sun had set, however, it was as if a curtain had been pulled across the sky, shrouding the horizon. Darkness had made the effect complete, and Ray had yet to spot the famed, iconic peaks to the west.

Something darted across the road, and Ray instinctively reached for the brake pedal. His high beams only caught a flicker of movement. It was far too small to be big game, probably just a fox or coyote. Ray sat up a little straighter anyhow, then nudged the wipers on again with a sigh.

He saw a sign for the Jackson Hole Airport and knew he was getting close. From research on the internet and a refresher looking at a road map—an actual paper, fold-up roadmap—while stopped in Riverton, Ray knew the basics. Bounded by the Teton Range on the west and the Gros Ventre Mountains on the east, and bisected by the aptly named Snake River, Jackson Hole stretched fifty miles north to south. It was anywhere from eight to fifteen miles wide. Three highways—U.S. 26, U.S. 89, and U.S. 191—ran concurrently through the valley from south to north, with U.S. 26 branching off east in Moran toward Riverton. U.S. 89 and U.S. 191 continued toward Yellowstone National Park. All along the route, turnouts provided stunning views of the Tetons. Ostensibly. During daylight.

At the northern end of the valley, the road was known as John D. Rockefeller Jr. Memorial Parkway, a designation applied to the section connecting Grand Teton National Park to Yellowstone National Park. At the southern end, the three highways formed the main drag through the town of Jackson. The primary municipality in the valley, Jackson was a haven for tourists, including many celebrities. It served as a base camp for hikers, climbers, rafters, wildlife enthusiasts, art-lovers, shoppers, and general sightseers. In the winter, skiers flocked to the valley, many of them staying at Teton Village, many staying in Jackson. The city was famous for its Town Square, located where the joint highway turned west. Surrounded by touristy shops, galleries, and restaurants, the Square was framed at each corner by large archways constructed from elk antlers. Ray had seen photographs of them too.

Jackson was also home to Ray's cousin Graham Stoddard. The son of Ray's mom's sister, Graham had long tried to cajole Ray to come visit him in "God's Country." Ray had never known Graham all that well, and what he did know didn't include much of anything to do with God. Graham had always been what Ray's mom referred to as a free spirit. (Ray's dad called him a fruitcake.) He was good for an afternoon or weekend at a family gathering. He told some amusing stories. He played the amicable life of the party well. But he and Ray were never going to be pals, and so Ray had been hesitant to spend his hard-earned money or precious time visiting Graham. Plus, he'd never spent more than a Friday-to-Sunday in his general presence. A whole week of just the two of them might be more than he could take.

But stocking away his every last penny wasn't suddenly quite so paramount. Ray now had untold amounts of time, and a week's vacation to burn. More than anything, he needed to get away, get out of Sioux Falls for a while. And he certainly wasn't headed to the Caribbean by himself.

Despite the darkness and full-blown drizzle, Ray became aware of a steep incline to his right. He knew it to be the East Gros Ventre Butte, one of a pair of ridges marking the southern end of Jackson Hole. They stretched northward into the valley for several miles, angled just a little bit to the east. East Gros Ventre Butte formed the west and north boundaries of Jackson, so Ray knew he was almost there. Then the speed limit dropped, and a small green sign announced the town border. It listed the population as 9,577 and the elevation as 6,209 feet—a mile and change—above sea level.

Across a small creek, a town appeared out of the darkness. A couple of motels. A Dairy Queen. Then a visitor center on the left and a Chevron on the right. At almost nine o'clock on a rainy September night, there was nothing to differentiate Jackson from any small Western town as Ray coasted through the first traffic light. Nothing to suggest this was a tourist mecca.

Ray's Silverado didn't have GPS, and he wouldn't have used it if it had. He'd have used a map had his hotel's confirmation e-mail not given directions. He'd opted for a hotel because Graham lived in a tiny apartment—space was at a premium in Jackson—and because spending a week with his cousin was stretching it for Ray; sharing quarters would be too much.

Operating by memory, he turned left on Gill Avenue, then south on Willow Street, then back west for half a block on Broadway. (East of the Town Square, it was just Broadway, not also U.S. 26/89/191.) The Jackson Hole Inn was located on the south side of the street, with a narrow alley leading around to parking in the back. It was a small place, maybe ten or twelve rooms, two stories tall. It had been available and reasonably priced, considering. Graham had also recommended it, although what local knew anything about the quality of hotels in their hometown? Following the e-mailed directions, Ray parked in a cramped lot between the hotel and the adjacent building. After thirteen hours of driving, a couple more of combined stops for food and fuel and to stretch his legs, a time change, and too much physical and mental isolation, Ray shut off the Silverado's engine for good.

Reaching to the passenger seat, he grabbed the strap of the large duffel bag containing a week's worth of clothes, toiletries, a couple of books, his laptop, and a few packs of beef jerky in case he got the late-night munchies and Graham had become a Vegan. He hefted it onto his shoulder as he got out, tentatively testing his left leg as he always did subconsciously before trusting his weight with it. As it almost always did, it held.

He entered the lobby from a door off the parking lot, expecting to see game mounted on the walls, a bearskin rug or a coffee table supported by the legs of an upside down poly-resin bear, or moose antler switch plates and penholders and other similar forms of bric-a-brac. There was none of it. The walls were wood paneled. Three straight-back chairs and an end table were nondescript, as was the unlit lamp on the table. The immobile ceiling fan was just a ceiling fan. And the check-in counter was void of any clutter. The only indication this wasn't a roadside inn in Indiana was a painting of the Tetons at sunset above a small copy machine on a back counter.

The room was empty, so after waiting approximately one minute, Ray rang the bell on the counter. From a back room to the left, a woman appeared. She was tall, heavy, with short grayish-white hair and lots of wrinkles. Maybe in her fifties. She smelled of cigarette smoke, although the only thing between her lips was a mostly full set of yellow teeth. The smell emanated, in all probability, from where it had been trapped by a bulky gray sweater. It was mangy, an alpaca or a llama or something. Probably had cost several hundred dollars at one of the local stores, if Jackson was like any other tourist town.

"Can I help you?" the woman grunted in the garble of a lifelong smoker.

After hours of silence, Ray found his voice. "Reservation under Eastwood."

She turned and thumbed through several papers sticking out of an upright file sorter. She pulled out a sheaf of them that were clipped together. "Ray?"

He nodded.

"Staying a week?"

He nodded.

"Just need a credit card for incidentals."

It took two minutes for her to run the card, print off a receipt, and walk through hotel policies. Then she dropped a key onto the counter. It was an actual key, brass, attached to a standard circular ring that was in turn attached to a chubby ceramic moose. It stood two inches high, just as wide counting the antlers, and was wearing a pair of overalls. Someone had hand-painted "Jackson Hole Inn" onto the front flap of the overalls.

"Second floor," the woman said. "Second door on your left."

Ray nodded, still looking at the key, imagining it in his pants pocket. He'd borrowed his sister's car a few times, and her keychain not only contained more keys than a school janitor's but also had all sorts of fobs and ornaments attached to it. The conglomeration weighed a ton and didn't even fit in Ray's pockets. Fortunately, she carried a purse the size of a small overnight bag, a purse in which even her keys managed to get lost.

"Oh, and this is for you," the woman said as Ray palmed the room key. She unclipped a card-sized envelope from the papers she'd pulled and slid it to Ray. "Came in the mail today."

Ray frowned as he turned the envelope with his hand. It was addressed to Ray Eastwood at the Jackson Hole Inn, Jackson, WY 83001. No return address. Not even a name. Postmarked from Salt Lake City, Utah, the day before.

Ray picked up the envelope with the hand that held the key. Nobody but Graham, Ray's sister, Ray's parents, and a few coworkers knew he was coming to Jackson. And none of them lived anywhere close to Salt Lake City.

"Thank you," Ray said to the woman, who had already refiled the rest of the papers and started to shuffle back to her room.

He went back outside and climbed stairs immediately on his left. A covered walkway led to two rooms on the left before making a ninety-degree turn to the right and providing access to four more rooms. Beneath them, at ground level, opening to the parking lot, were four more. Maybe a fifth was tucked beside the lobby, looking at the street. Ray couldn't remember how many doors there had been.

He stopped and looked at the second door on the left. It was plain, green, with a small shelf attached below the peephole. The shelf was just big enough to support an exact replica of his keychain moose. He looked back at the first door and saw it had a similar shelf, holding a small ceramic bison. No numbers on either door. He sighed.

Ray unlocked the door and flipped on the light. The room was simple if not Spartan. The bathroom was immediately to the left. It was standard but clean and big enough for a grown man. Some weren't. The room opened to the left beyond the bathroom, featuring a queen bed (no kings had been available) under a giant photograph of a moose in a still river, head lifted to display an enormous rack of antlers, droplets of water falling from his beard. A nightstand contained a push-button phone and clock radio, red letters displaying the time as 9:03. Across from the bed was a dresser with a picture tube TV. Next to the dresser sat a chair, not unlike those in the lobby, and a round table. In the opposite corner were another chair and a lamp that cast yellow light over the room.

Ray set his duffel on the bed and walked to the curtains. He pulled them back to reveal a small—by hotel standards—window. He slid it open, letting some fresh air into a somewhat stale room. At least it didn't smell like cigarettes. Or alpacas. And while it was nothing special, the room was fairly typical. Clean. Reasonably up to date as far as color scheme. Not too tacky. No gap between the bottom of the door and the threshold. It would do.

A car slushed by on the wet street, then all was silent. Ray was sick of silence, so he picked the remote off the dresser and turned on the TV. It worked. There was a hotel guidebook on the dresser, and it probably contained a list of channels. Instead of searching it, he thumbed the channel button on the remote until he came to ESPN, currently airing college football highlights. He lowered the volume and tossed the remote on the bed, next to his duffel. He dug his cell phone from his back pocket and sat down.

He'd told Graham he'd call him when he got in, expecting it to be late. Then again, he doubted nine o'clock constituted late on a Saturday for Graham. But Ray wasn't up for anything after a day of driving, and he hesitated to call now for fear that Graham would want to grab something to eat or hit a club—Did Jackson have nightclubs? It must. Where else would the celebrities hang out? And Graham had never been the kind of person to take no very well. He would nag and plead and "come on, dude" until a person gave in and drove to Wyoming for a week.

Ray swiped and tapped to his contacts and called his cousin. He put the phone on speaker, set it down, and turned his eyes to the TV. Southern Miss had apparently stunned top-ranked Alabama, and the talking heads were breaking down the upset.

The phone purred four times, then clicked. Graham's voice came on. "Hey, it's Graham. I'm either working or chillaxing or my phone's buried under my butt and it's too loud in the bar. And in all honesty, I never listen to voicemails, so just hit me back later if you don't hear from me. Out."

"It's Ray. I just got in. Call me if you get this by nine-thirty," he said, looking back at the clock. "Long day, so I'm going to hit the rack. If I don't hear from you, I'll call you in the morning. Out," he added, then tapped the red circle to end the call.

The football replays looped as an "expert" phoned in to give his opinion of the monumental shocker. Ray bumped up the volume a few decibels only because he hated having to strain to hear. He stood to extricate his car keys from his pocket, then tossed them on the dresser where he'd set down the moose. Beside it was the envelope, and Ray's curiosity got the best of him. He reached for it, then sat back on the bed, feeling a frown on his face as he studied the handwriting. It leaned toward sloppy, which didn't do much in the way of narrowing it down. The envelope was heavy, even for a card. And it wasn't Ray's birthday—wasn't close. He frowned some more, then realized he wasn't going to deduce anything this way. He slipped his finger under the flap.

The phone rang.

Not his cell phone, but the room phone, on the nightstand beside the clock radio.

He set down the envelope and looked at the phone as it rang again. Graham had his cell number. So did Ray's sister and parents. He glanced down at his cell phone to make sure he hadn't missed a call. He hadn't.

The phone rang a third time.

Maybe it was the lady from the lobby, calling to see if he could spare a light. As with the envelope, Ray realized staring wasn't going to bring about results. He scooted back on the bed, reached around his duffel, and snagged the receiver with a long arm just as it rang again.

"Ray Eastwood."

"You're Ray?" The voice was feminine. It was loud. And it was coming from someplace loud.

"I am."

"You're Graham's cousin?"

"That's right. Who's this?"

In reply, Ray heard distant voices. Male voices. And music. Hip-hop music. The feminine voice said something he couldn't hear, then something louder.

"Hello?" he asked.

"Yeah, I'm here," she said. "You're Ray's cousin Graham—I mean Graham's cousin Ray?"

"Yes. Who's—?"

"Shut up."

"Excuse me?"

"Not you."

Ray rubbed his forehead. It had been a long drive. He waited, trying to pick up the background noises. It sounded like a bar or a nightclub or a party.

"Hello?" she said.

"I'm here. Who is this?"

"Heidi."

"Who's Heidi?"

"I'm Heidi."

He didn't think she was playing Abbott and Costello with him, but he couldn't be sure.

"What can I do for you, Heidi?"

"Where are you right now?"

He licked his lips.

"Oh right, I called your hotel. Duh, blondie." She giggled.

Ray waited.

"Graham said you were coming."

"Is Graham with you? Is this one of his gags?"

"Graham isn't here."

"Do you know where he is? He didn't answer his phone earlier."

"No, he isn't here."

"Where is here?"

"What?"

"Where are you?"

"I'm at Rattle."

"What's Rattle?"

"Rattle is a bar."

"Where?"

"Sitting at the bar. I'm on a cell."

Graham had always had an affinity for practical jokes, like the time he put laxative gum in Ray's sister's purse. It was even money he was sitting beside Heidi, at a bar named Rattle or otherwise, busting a gut as she strung Ray along.

"Heidi, why did you call me?"

"I'm looking for Graham."

"He isn't here."

"I know."

Ray sighed.

"Are you coming down here?"

"Why?"

"To help me figure out what happened to him."

A man's voice said something, then laughed.

"Knock it off, Sandy," Heidi said. Back into the phone: "Just get down here." Before Ray could reply, she clicked off.

He sat there holding the phone for several seconds, then placed it back on its cradle. There was still a very real chance Graham was running some sort of welcome-to-Wyoming initiation. Even if not, Ray had no idea who Heidi was, and she sounded drunk. He really wanted to turn out the lights and go to sleep.

But he didn't like the phrase "figure out what happened to him." And he couldn't shake the frankness that had found its way through Heidi's potentially inebriated confusion when she'd asked for help. So he stood, grabbed his keys, and headed down to the lobby to ask the cigarette smoking, alpaca wearing lady where he could find a bar named Rattle.

TWO

Ray didn't drink, and therefore didn't frequent bars, and therefore only knew of them what he saw on TV. Rattle fit the mold pretty well. It wasn't bright inside, by any means, but it wasn't overly dark. The air wasn't mountaintop clear, but it wasn't tinged with blue haze either. The music was loud—still hip-hop. A tiny, unoccupied dance floor was in the middle of the room. Tables and booths surrounded it on three sides. On the fourth, to the left, a bar ran the full length of the building—forty feet or so. Behind it were stacked a variety of bottles of alcohol, glasses in various sizes and shapes, and above them, a mounted, stuffed rattlesnake. It was the biggest Ray had ever seen. A pair of TVs flanking the snake showed sporting events, an MMA fight and a Wyoming Cowboys football game. Nobody in the place seemed to be paying particular attention to either. Nor to Ray. A few cast glances his way, probably the way they did every time the front door opened.

He walked forward. In bars on TV, the worst way to find someone was to walk up to the bartender and ask for So-and-so. It was also the best way to get shown the pavement in the alley behind the bar by a couple of stiffs. Ray figured that was overdramatized for TV. And on TV, the So-and-so was usually a criminal informant or a mob bagman or something like that. Not a dingbat who could barely hold her own on a phone call.

Ray'd had about ten minutes to think as he'd followed the smoky alpaca lady's directions to Rattle. It was located on the west side of town, where the main highway curved south again. It was situated in a strip mall between a sub shop and an auto parts store. The building was one of the few in town that didn't have a sleek, urban vibe or a woodsy, rustic appearance. (Even the Jackson Kmart looked like a giant log home.) But Ray didn't think Rattle, the sub shop, or the auto parts store made any of the tourist brochures.

With ten minutes to think on the way over, he'd replayed his conversation with Heidi. He was almost positive she was drunk, and therefore he couldn't take anything she said about Graham too seriously. Twice, he nearly turned around and went back to bed. But he knew he wouldn't sleep until he at least probed her "figure out what happened to him" remark.

Ray counted eleven people seated at the bar. Four were female. Two were obviously with someone. Another was forty if she was a day, and Heidi hadn't sounded thirty, much less forty. So he walked toward the remaining female, seated alone at the far end of the bar. She had long blond hair, straight. It fell over a pink shirt that hung off one shoulder to reveal a black strap. He couldn't tell if that was intentional or not. She rested both arms on the edge of the bar, loosely holding a longneck bottle between them, her eyes staring through the wall behind the bar.

Ray straddled the stool next to her. "Are you Heidi?"

She looked his way for several seconds. Her face was blank. Without speaking, she lifted the bottle and tipped it back. She leaned back on her stool to drain every last drop, and Ray thought she was going to fall. He was content to let her.

Somehow, she kept her balance, rocking back forward and clanking the empty bottle on the bar. She turned her head and signaled for the bartender, who was several patrons down.

"You're Ray."

He nodded.

"How about you buy me another beer?"

"It looks like you've had enough."

She huffed. "Graham's not here."

"We covered that much on the phone."

She looked at him.

He looked at her. She was attractive, in a purely physical way. A pretty face, curves in the right places, the hair. But the messy drunk look did nothing for her, nor for Ray. And he preferred a woman who could carry on a simple conversation without prompts. Or, at least, he had. It'd been a long time since he'd thought about what kind of woman he preferred.

"What I mean is, Graham's not anywhere. He's missing."

Ray frowned. "What do you mean 'missing'?"

Heidi looked at him like he was the drunk.

"He's gone. Not here. Nowhere. Missing."

That cleared it up.

The bartender set another longneck on the bar in front of Heidi, vapor rising from its open top. He looked at Ray, who shook his head.

"Where should Graham be?" he asked when the bartender left.

"Where you're sitting, trying to get fresh with me." She burped.

"Are you and he dating?"

"More or less." She turned on the stool, wobbled slightly, and extended a hand. "I'm Heidi."

Ray looked from the chipped polish on her fingernails to her wide blue eyes.

"Right," she said. "You already know that." She pointed to her head. "Blonde."

"What do you say we get out of here?"

She managed a lopsided smile. "You work faster than Graham."

"You have a tab here?"

"Yeah, right."

She spun her stool around and reached for her purse on the adjacent stool. That's when she fell to the floor.

Ray's mom had raised a gentleman, so he helped her up by the elbow, then stood awkwardly as she dug through her purse, nearly losing her balance in the process. She wore three-inch heels, which had to be hard enough when sober, along with ripped black pants of indeterminate material. They were tighter than Ray's skin.

Heidi wobbled again as she slapped some bills on the bar, leaving them next to her mostly full longneck bottle. Ray took her elbow and helped her to the front door. Outside they stood under an awning that spanned the entire building, including the sub shop and the auto parts store. It was still drizzling, and the temperature couldn't have been fifty degrees. Ray wore the clothes he had traveled in, blue jeans and a blue South Dakota State Jackrabbits sweatshirt over a plain T-shirt. He was not warm. Beside him, Heidi shivered and shrugged her shirt over the bare shoulder.

"Do you have a jacket?" Ray asked.

Heidi shook her head.

"Did you drive?"

"I just live a couple blocks that way."

"I can drive you. I'm parked right over here."

He led her to the Silverado and helped her into the passenger seat. When he climbed behind the wheel, he saw she had dropped her head back against the headrest, her eyes closed. He started the engine.

"I may throw up in your truck."

"Are you serious?"

She nodded slightly. "Maybe we should walk."

He would survive if she would, and it beat spending his Sunday morning detail-cleaning his truck. So he killed the ignition and they got back out. Heidi took several deep breaths, then started across the parking lot on unsteady ankles.

"What makes you say Graham is missing?"

"For one, he doesn't answer any of my calls or texts."

"Since when?"

"The last two days."

Ray had called Graham the night before, just to verify plans, and had gotten that annoying voicemail greeting. He hadn't left a message and had sent a text instead before starting out that morning. Neither the call nor the text had been returned, but that didn't really surprise Ray.

"When was the last time you talked to him?"

"Whatever three days ago is. What's it, Saturday?"

Ray nodded. They turned on a sidewalk, headed east along the side of the building. Heidi held her elbows in her hands and shivered. Ray thought about offering her his sweatshirt, but he didn't want it to get puked on any more than his truck.

"And he didn't come home from work the other night," Heidi said.

"You live together?"

She huffed. "I wish. You know what rent is in this town?"

Ray said nothing.

"My roommate is a weirdo, so I hang out at his place a lot. He didn't come home from work. All night."

"What night?"

"I don't know. Thursday?"

"Where does he work?"

"A couple places. A little bistro called Metro, over on Glenwood, and at the Bar Something-Something ranch."

"Graham works at a ranch?"

"They take tourists out into the woods to eat dinner or something. Saps," she muttered under her breath.

"Which job was he working Thursday?"

"The ranch. Every night till nine or ten."

"You remember the name of it?"

"Bar H-9 or Bar 4-H or something. Ask me when I can see straight."

They turned onto a narrow street, one without sidewalks. It was cracked and uneven. It should be an adventure.

"How long have you and Graham been together?"

"Beginning of summer."

"When's that?"

"What am I, an almanac?"

"Graham says it snows into May. I don't know what you call summer out here."

"Call it May," she said. "We've been on and off."

"Not too serious then?"

She shrugged. "Why?"

Graham had not mentioned Heidi, not mentioned that he was seeing someone, not mentioned that she often hung out at his place to avoid a weirdo roommate. Ray didn't tell her that.

"He told you I was coming?" he asked.

"Last weekend, said his cousin Ray was coming from South Dakota. I thought you'd be chewing on a piece of straw or have a wad of tobacco in your mouth or something."

"Sorry to disappoint you."

She shrugged again. "That's my apartment." She pointed at a nondescript, two-story building across the street.

"Any chance he flaked out?" Ray asked. "Forgot I was coming and went somewhere for a long weekend?"

"Where? There is nowhere for about a billion miles. He's not camping on the side of a mountain, that's for sure."

Ray shrugged.

"Besides, he's missed like four shifts now. He wouldn't do that."

"He say anything off or unusual?"

"No. But he's been acting weird lately."

"Weird?"

Heidi successfully negotiated a trio of concrete steps leading to the front door of the apartment. "I don't know. Like something was on his mind. He usually doesn't shut up, but he's been quiet."

"He say what it was?"

"No."

"How long?"

"A week maybe."

Ray nodded. He'd like to ask Heidi these questions when she wasn't bombed, see if her answers changed at all.

"Thanks for walking me home."

"Thanks for not puking in my truck."

Heidi smiled. She dug into her purse for keys. They were not attached to a ceramic moose.

"You go to the police?" Ray asked.

She huffed. "The Keystone Cops? No. And it hasn't been forty-eight hours."

"You said he didn't come home Thursday night."

She stared at him. "So I can't do math. Whatever. No, I haven't gone to the police."

He nodded.

"I need to go pass out," she said.

"Can I have your number?"

She glared at him. "You do work fast."

"In case I need to get a hold of you."

She continued glaring for a moment before breaking off and digging into her purse again. She lost her balance again and sagged against the railing. When she found her phone, they exchanged numbers, then said goodbye.

Ray walked back to his truck in the Rattle parking lot. He didn't know what to make of Graham's disappearance. He didn't know what to make of anything Heidi said. He doubted she was lying, but it was more than possible she was mistaken and confused. Graham had always been a flake, bouncing from job to job, and Ray could see him blowing them off for some other "adventure." He couldn't see him blowing off his cousin's visit. Unless he'd forgotten, which was one of those things Ray could see.

He decided to get a good night's sleep, see if Graham returned his call or answered his phone in the morning, and figure out what to do then. Graham was a "free spirit," but he wasn't the type to get in serious trouble—to disappear like people did in the movies. Better chance he viewed his and Heidi's relationship as off again and didn't have the intestinal fortitude to tell her. Ghosting, Ray was pretty sure it was called.

Fifteen minutes after leaving Heidi, Ray was back in his hotel room. He plunked the ceramic moose and room key on the dresser and, out of curiosity, tuned the TV to the Wyoming game. They were behind 21-3.

With a deep sigh, he lifted his duffel bag off the bed. That's when he saw the card-sized envelope. Curiosity trumped tiredness, and Ray sat down and tore the envelope open.

He frowned as he pulled out four—no five—postcards. Who mailed postcards in an envelope? With a last look inside, he set the envelope aside and shuffled through the postcards. The first was of the Jackson Town Square, featuring an antler arch. The second showed a cowboy on a horse roping a calf. "Jackson Hole Rodeo" was scrawled over the image in sweeping letters. The third showed a large brown building tabbed as the Jackson Lake Lodge. On the fourth, a tree-covered hill and a fiery sunset were both reflected in a perfectly still lake. The final postcard contained a cartoonish map of Jackson Hole, with certain features like Grand Teton and a grazing buffalo depicted prominently.

Ray frowned some more. He flipped the postcards over. On the back of the cartoonish map someone had hastily written several phrases:

Betsy Garner's grave
Woody's ranch
TSS
2265 N Fish Cr
Moran from east of Oxbow
Find the triangles

The phrases meant nothing to Ray. They were penned in the same script as the address on the envelope. He turned the postcard back over and searched for anything identified as Oxbow, TSS, or Woody's ranch. He saw nothing. Mount Moran was one of the peaks north of the Tetons, Ray was pretty sure, but it wasn't on the map. Nor were any obvious triangles.

He sorted through the other postcards. None had any writing on the back. The tree-covered hill was identified as Signal Mountain, and each of the four had brief snippets printed on the top, describing the image on the front. No mention of any of the places written on the back of the fifth.

Ray tapped the postcards into his palm. He was clueless. Had Graham sent them? Had he gone to Salt Lake City for the weekend? Is that where he was? If so, why? And why the postcards? Recommending places for Ray to visit, things to do? Who was Woody? Who was Betsy Garner? What was at 2265 N Fish Circle? What did triangles have to do with anything? And if not Graham, who had sent the postcards? And why?

None of the ideas that popped into his head made any sense, so he set the postcards on the dresser next to the ceramic moose. He would see what the newness of morning brought in the way of insight. And in the way of a missing cousin.

THREE

Ray had spent four years in the United States Army out of high school, and, in addition to equipping him for a career as a data analyst, the Army had given him three things. First, he'd come away with a greater appreciation for freedom and for the price to preserve that freedom. Second, he'd learned the value of discipline. His parents hadn't been lax by any means, but the military was a different animal. Third, he'd figured out how to sleep anytime and anywhere, and how to wake up whenever he wanted without an alarm clock.

So without bothering to set the alarm on the clock radio by his bed or leave a wake-up call with the smoky alpaca lady, Ray awoke at precisely six-thirty. It was still dark as he showered, shaved, and dressed. Having long grown weary of the tedious morning routine, he typically spent that twenty or so minutes in prayer. Lately, that had become something of a chore, as more and more Ray felt like it was an entirely one-way conversation.

Nobody in Ray's family, nobody in his church, nobody he had grown up with had ever claimed to hear God audibly speak to them. That was reserved for missionaries and special cases like Abraham or Moses. But the pastor in Ray's church growing up and a sweet, single, middle-aged woman at his current church talked about "hearing" God's voice and "sensing" His direction. Ray had no idea what they meant. Sure, he felt the occasional prompting or suggestion, but nothing that resembled a voice, nothing overt. And weren't those promptings and suggestions largely attributed to a life of being raised by Christian parents and attending a Bible-believing church or even basic intuition? Those things could still be the work of the Holy Spirit, but they weren't what Ray would call God speaking to him. Could that be what his former pastor and the sweet, single, middle-aged woman meant by "hearing" and "sensing"? He didn't think so.

It had been suggested, once upon a time, that maybe the issue was that Ray wasn't "in tune" with God. But he didn't know what to do about that. He did have faith—he trusted in Jesus Christ's death on the cross as payment for his sins—Ray was "saved." He prayed, read his Bible—when he remembered to pack one for vacation—and went to church. He supported various mission and rescue organizations financially, in addition to tithing to his local church. He met a couple times a month with a few buddies from church as part of a Bible study/accountability group. How else was he supposed to "tune in"? God hadn't "called" him to some full-time ministry, to sell all he had and give to the poor. Had He?

It had been subtle, but Ray had felt a strain in his relationship with God in recent months, and outright frustration for the last several weeks—since Labor Day Weekend. Why didn't God speak to him—audibly or otherwise—if He did to others? What was Ray missing?

He was fully dressed and groomed, and his prayers drifted off with a quick request for health and safety for his family, the usual conclusion. Ray powered on his phone. No message or text from Graham. He would wait to call him until a little later when there was a better chance Graham wouldn't sleep through the call. Scooping his keys and wallet off the dresser, Ray headed outside.

The morning was dark and cool. The sun had not risen yet, Ray didn't think, because the gray blanket overhead was darker than it was light. At least it was dry, almost crisp, even. Forty-five degrees, max. He wore a thick blue and black checkered flannel shirt, and figured that as long as he kept moving, he would stay warm.

Ray set out along the sidewalk headed west, toward the Town Square. He passed a block and a half of shops and galleries, all closed at seven a.m. Most of the shops faced the street, but several opened onto small courtyards set back from the sidewalk. He passed a woman in yoga pants and a bright jersey pullover, earbuds blasting loudly enough that he could hear the music. Then a couple walking hand-in-hand, snuggled as close together as possible while still walking. They were young, clearly in love. Probably honeymooners. Ray kept walking.

The Town Square occupied a block to his right, filled with an assortment of pines and deciduous trees whose leaves had turned shades of yellow and orange. Seeing the square—in particular, seeing the elk antler arches at the four corners—reminded him of the postcards.

Who sent postcards in an envelope? Ray wasn't aware of the going price of a postcard stamp, but he knew it was a lot more than one-fifth of a standard stamp. Could it be somebody was just that cheap? But who? He went through the list of people who knew he was in Jackson.

There was Graham, who jumped to the top of the list because his "disappearance" and sending five random postcards with mysterious writing on the back were both out of the ordinary, although Ray couldn't see the connection. And Graham had the personality to do something strange like send Ray postcards in an envelope. But why?

Ray's sister, Cathy, lived in Omaha where her husband worked at the University of Nebraska-Omaha. It was one of the top research universities in the nation, oddly enough, and he was pursuing his Masters while working as a research assistant. That kept him plenty busy, and two kids with a third on the way kept Cathy occupied. She was not a mysterious person, although plenty quirky. But where would she have gotten Jackson Hole postcards?

Same question for Ray's parents, who lived in Huron, South Dakota. Ray's dad, stereotypically enough, managed a Ma & Pa hardware store. If they sold any postcards, they were of dead presidents and weird rock formations.

Several of Ray's coworkers fit the quirky, practical joking type, but postcards were a lame practical joke. There was just no explanation Ray could think of that made any sense.

The Salt Lake City postmark threw him too. He didn't know anybody in Salt Lake City, had never been there. Was it possible that all mail from Jackson was routed there, a couple hundred miles and a state away? Had Graham or somebody else with easy access to Jackson Hole postcards sent them from Jackson to Jackson, would they have had to travel all the way to Utah first?

Ray had no answers and kept walking. Beneath him, the sidewalk had been replaced by wood planks. The awnings and overhangs of the shops were supported with Y-shaped posts, some out of actual logs. Had the storefronts not been displaying expensive artwork and hawking tourist T-shirts, and not been adorned with unlit neon signs, Ray might have believed he was back in the Old West.

The sky had lightened, and Ray figured the sun had risen behind the wall of clouds. They were now just a light gray. They had depth, looked as if they could open at any minute and unleash rain. Or snow. It wasn't quite that cold, but it was close.

A circular sign up ahead in the recess of a large building reminded Ray of the one at Fisherman's Wharf in San Francisco. He'd seen pictures of it too. Only this circular sign had a rose instead of a crab in the middle, and no spokes like a ship's wheel. A vertical sign behind it caught Ray's attention, advertising JH Coffee Roasters.

Unlike most of the places Ray had passed, it was open. He ducked inside. Compared to the sleepy streets and sidewalks, Jackson Hole Coffee Roasters was bustling. Patrons sat at tables and booths, talking and clanging silverware on plates as they ate. The smells of eggs and sausage and potatoes competed with the rich aroma of freshly roasted, freshly brewed coffee. The coffee won.

Ray approached the counter, beneath large silhouette murals depicting cowboys by a fence and a buffalo hunt. He ordered a large Kona blend coffee and a pastry to go and exited to the sidewalk.

He checked his watch. Not quite 7:15. It was still too early to call Graham. Ray hadn't looked into any local churches, in part because he was on vacation, in part because he expected to be with Graham and thus not in church, and in part because he figured everyone out here worshiped the sun or the moon or a certain species of tree. So he turned and headed back toward the Square.

The antler arches really were something. They stood a dozen, maybe fifteen feet high. They were several feet thick, made of hundreds if not thousands of elk antlers intertwined to form an arch under which several people could walk side-by-side. The antlers had faded over the years and were almost white. Dangling from the center of the arch, over the sidewalk entering the Square, was a moose antler with the words "Jackson Hole, WY" stamped on it.

Ray strolled through the arch and sat down on a metal bench that was cold through his blue jeans. He warmed with a sip of steaming, aromatic coffee. It was delicious.

Four sidewalks entered the Square, one from each corner, and intersected around a statue of a cowboy on a horse atop a stone pedestal. Plaques were set into the stone, but Ray couldn't make out what they said from where he sat. The cowboy held to the saddle horn with one hand while the other waved a hat. The statue bore a close resemblance to the University of Wyoming's sports teams' logo.

Like the town, the Square was quiet. A few people traversed it. A man in a beanie, sweater, way too tight pants, and no socks or shoes sat cross-legged on a blanket across the way. An old woman in a parka sat on another bench while her Golden Retriever strained at a leash. She focused on her phone, not the dog. A slight tremor of wind shook loose a hundred leaves across the park, and they fluttered to the ground.

Ray took another drink of coffee and tried to figure out what was bothering him. Back in the coffee shop, he'd felt a sudden sense that something internal wasn't quite right. He'd been reading the menu, surrounded by the noise of a coffee shop, and hadn't paid it much attention. By the time he had his coffee and pastry, it had taken a backseat to the environment around him. It wasn't anything major, just enough of a trigger to garner his attention again now.

Another drink. A smell? A sound? A sight? A person? It hit him as the warm coffee slid down his throat. The woman who had served him. Annabelle. Her name had actually been Susie or Sarah or something run of the mill. Not a lighthearted, imaginative name like Annabelle. She hadn't really looked like Annabelle either, not overtly. But it could have been something as simple as the way a loose strand of hair fell out of her chignon, the way her eyes brightened when she smiled, or a mannerism as she handed Ray his coffee. Maybe it was her perfume, which he couldn't even remember, or maybe it was nothing more than Susie or Sarah being a blond woman of normal height and weight, just like Annabelle. It could have been anything. Many times previously, it *had* been anything.

Ray sighed. He looked at his watch. He'd made it fifty-two minutes into Day 20 without thinking about his ex-fiancée.

∧   ∧   ∧

Ray ate his pastry and walked through the Square, then north on Center Street. He passed life-sized statues of a bull elk, leaping whitetail deer, a bull moose, and a black bear in the parking lot of a gallery. He continued north, no destination in mind, and sipped his coffee. When he got to the next street, he stopped. Center Street ran into a parking lot, so he turned around. He checked his watch. Five minutes till eight. Close enough.

He called Graham, got the same frat boy greeting, and left a brief message asking where he was and to please call as soon as possible. He did not mention Heidi. Next, he sent a text, having long ago learned in a world where everybody had a cell phone, for whatever reason, some people only texted. He walked back toward the Square, looking beyond it at the wide paths through the trees on the mountain south of town. He couldn't remember the name, but it was a ski resort. Sun King or Snow King or something like that.

Graham did not return the call or text. Ray walked back to the motel and pitched his empty cup in the wastebasket in his room. Then he thumbed through his phone contacts and found the number Heidi had given him on the steps of her apartment the night before. He dialed and listened through four rings before her voice came on. "This is Heidi. Leave a message."

Ray did not leave a message. He disconnected the call and promptly called again, on a hunch. After three rings, he heard a pitch change in the dull background hum. Then a groggy, "Yeah?"

"Heidi? It's Ray Eastwood."

She made some sort of an indiscernible noise.

"Did I wake you?"

"Ugh. It's eight . . . fifteen—eight-fifteen? It's eight-fifteen in the morning on a Sunday, and I'm hungover. Yeah, you woke me. What do you want?"

"I take it you haven't heard from Graham."

"I haven't heard anything."

"Do you have a key to his place?"

"What?"

Ray paused. He doubted she hadn't heard him.

"Yeah, I have a key. What, you want to play detective?"

"Before I involve the police, I want to know if there's a reason to be alarmed."

Heidi sighed. It may have been a muffled curse.

"Can you meet me there?" he asked.

This sigh was more of a groan. "Give me time to at least take a shower."

"How's nine o'clock?"

"Fine. Ugh."

"Where does Graham live?"

Heidi stumbled through directions, and when Ray asked for an address, she said she didn't know the address. She just knew where it was. The more she talked, the more confused Ray became. He began rifling through the drawers in the dresser and nightstand looking for a phonebook on the off chance Graham was listed.

"I think it's on Simpson Avenue," Heidi said. "You know, like Bart Simpson."

23

"What kind of car do you drive?"

"I don't. I walk or get a ride."

"How about I give you a ride? Save us both some trouble."

"Whatever."

"I'll pick you up at nine."

"Okay."

"Do you drink coffee?"

"What?"

Ray waited again, sure the issue wasn't her hearing what he'd said.

"Are you asking me out or something?"

"It's a cold morning. It's early. I'm going to grab some coffee. You want a cup?"

"Whatever."

She terminated the call without saying goodbye. Ray lowered his phone and shook his head. Then he looked down at the Gideon Bible he'd found in the nightstand drawer. He pursed his lips. He didn't open the Bible.

At twenty to nine, Ray left his room and got into his Silverado. He found a parking spot across the street from Jackson Hole Coffee Roasters and patronized them for the second time that morning. He left with two large to-go cups of the Kona blend and headed for Heidi's apartment.

He arrived five minutes early and waited in the truck, parked by the side of the road. Heidi came out two minutes after nine. She wore gray sweatpants and a light blue and purple zip-up sweatshirt half zipped over a white shirt. Her hair was piled in a wad behind her head. She looked somewhere between angry and stoned.

Ray leaned over to open her door. "Good morning," he said as she climbed up into the truck.

She muttered a, "Morning," back.

"You have the key?" he felt compelled to ask.

She held up a lanyard and shook the key attached to it back and forth.

He extended one of two cups of coffee to her.

She looked at it, then him. "Thanks."

"Careful, it's hot."

She didn't drink any as she guided him to Graham's apartment. Ray figured they were several blocks south and west of the Square, meaning it would have been quicker to walk there from the hotel than drive to Heidi's and back. Such was life.

The building was rectangular, two-stories tall, with two rooms per level on either side of a central hallway. Eight in all. The central hallway was accessible from the street or from a parking lot around back. Ray and Heidi entered from the street and took the stairs to the second floor, back left room, facing southwest. Apartment F, for what it mattered.

Without knocking, Heidi unlocked the door and pushed it open. Ray followed her inside.

The apartment was a mess. Clothes on the arm of a sofa-sleeper that was still unfolded. And unmade. Clothes everywhere, in fact. They were joined by empty beer bottles, dirty plates and bowls and silverware, an open pizza box with two crusts sitting on the counter that served as an eating area in the small, studio apartment. Just one room. Two if you counted the bathroom, which Ray had no interest in seeing, given the condition of the rest of the apartment.

"What a pig," Heidi said.

"Is it always like this?"

"To varying degrees."

The apartment looked unkempt, not tossed or ransacked.

"What are we looking for?" Heidi asked.

"Anything out of place."

She raised her eyebrows.

"So to speak. Is anything missing? Is anything here that shouldn't be?"

"Like everything," she said, kicking a PlayStation controller out of her way. "I'll check the bathroom."

Ray nodded, gulped some coffee, and set out for the galley kitchen. He hesitantly opened the refrigerator, expecting to be knocked over by a smell. The refrigerator contained a lot of beer, some pop, half a gallon of milk, lunchmeat and bread, some staples like ketchup and ranch dressing. No fruits or vegetables. He closed the door and checked the freezer. It was mostly empty, in need of defrosting, containing a few frozen pizzas and TV dinners and some Fudgesicles. Ray didn't know they still made Fudgesicles.

Beside the refrigerator was a coffeemaker. The pot was a quarter full of cold coffee, and there were soggy grounds in the basket. Next to the coffeemaker was a toaster. It and the counter around it were covered in crumbs. The sink had dishes piled in it and a few clean ones in a rack beside it.

Ray figured an ace detective would analyze the washed dishes, the unwashed dishes, the position of various items in the refrigerator, and conclude what Graham had eaten and when. They could probably do the same with the clothes and bottles and cans scattered around and recreate his movements for the last few days. All Ray could tell was that his cousin was a slob.

"Nothing in the bathroom," Heidi said. "Unless you count toothpaste stains on the side of the sink."

"Anything gone? Toothbrush, razor or shaver?"

"You haven't seen Graham in a while."

"Why's that?"

She held her hand several inches beneath her jaw, open with her fingers spread as if holding something in it. "He's got a full lumberjack. Blacker than coal. I don't think he's shaved since I've known him."

Ray nodded.

"But nothing's missing that I could tell."

"You were here Thursday night when he didn't come home?"

"I know what you're thinking. Why didn't I clean up?"

Ray said nothing.

"Because I had just worked a twelve-hour shift and I'm sick of picking up his crap. So I crashed on the bed and watched TV."

"Did you eat or drink anything?"

"I had a beer. I put the bottle in the recycling bin like a human when I was done."

Ray nodded.

"And since you're about to ask, I fell asleep waiting, woke up to pee, and woke up again in the morning. He wasn't here, and I went home to change and go to work."

"Why were you at Rattle last night?"

"Where should I have been?"

He shrugged. "Seemed like you were drowning your sorrows."

"It was a Saturday night, and I had nowhere to go, nothing to do. My boyfriend wasn't around. Sorrows might be a little strong, but yeah, I guess you could say that."

"You said the last time you saw him was Wednesday, right?"

"No, I said the last time I talked to him was Wednesday."

"What'd you talk about?"

She looked straight at him. "My cycle."

Ray said nothing.

"I was late. Until Wednesday. I called to let him know he was off the hook."

"You talk about anything else?"

"Nothing much."

"He didn't say anything unusual?"

"Like that maybe he was going off the grid? No."

"Do you know where he was?"

"Sitting right here," she said, nodding at the sofa sleeper.

"He tell you that?"

"I could hear his lame video game in the background."

"So he was here Wednesday night. What time?"

"I don't know. Ten. Eleven. I waited till I knew he'd be back from work."

"And that was the last time you talked to him?"

Heidi nodded.

"Do you know that he went to work on Thursday?"

"Why do you ask?"

"It seems he disappeared sometime between Wednesday when you talked to him and Thursday night when he didn't come home. But that's an almost twenty-four-hour window." Ray stroked his jaw. "Any of his clothes missing?"

"Serious?"

Ray waited.

Heidi broke first and turned to a dresser on the far wall, next to the bathroom door. She ransacked it for thirty seconds. "Doesn't look like it, but I don't exactly keep track of his underwear and socks." She shook her head. "What, you think he packed up and left?"

"It's a possibility, but it doesn't look like it."

"So what then?"

"Two options. It's clear Graham's missing—"

"Told you that last night."

"So we can either go to the police, which would be prudent. Or we can talk to someone at this ranch he worked at and see if he showed up for work on Thursday, work our way back to the last time someone saw him."

"I can help with that."

He looked at her.

"A friend of mine works with him. Let me call her."

Ray didn't say that would have been a good idea forty-eight hours ago. He didn't say anything. He just took a drink of coffee and followed Heidi out of the apartment.

FOUR

Heidi needed to put something in her stomach, so she arranged for Ray to meet her friend Diane outside Our Lady of the Mountains Catholic Church. Diane was a devout Catholic and attended the ten a.m. mass there. For a friend of a friend, she agreed to arrive a few minutes early to talk to Ray. So he dropped Heidi at her apartment so she could make herself some breakfast, told her he'd call if he heard from Graham, and then drove back to within two blocks of Graham's apartment to the church.

It was a unique building, constructed in the log cabin motif of so many Jackson structures, and dressed in fieldstone. The defining feature was a bell tower evocative of a European castle or a Venetian spire. Ray stayed in the truck so as not to look like a creep and get busted for loitering. Heidi had given him a description of Diane, and he figured he could spot her when she arrived.

The sky was still overcast, but the clouds appeared to be thinning a little. There was no blue sky yet, but at least it hadn't rained either. Ray spent a few minutes pondering why someone—presumably someone named Jackson—had formed a settlement on this side of the Gros Ventre Buttes instead of on the other, in full view of the Tetons. Then he wondered which lady the church was named after. He didn't know much about Catholicism, but he heard names of a lot of churches that confused him. Then again, that wasn't limited to Catholicism.

A tall woman with reddish-brown hair got out of a tan Mazda and looked around before starting toward a ramp leading to the far corner of the church. Taking one last swill of now lukewarm coffee, Ray got out and hurried across the street and up the sidewalk toward her.

"Diane?" he called.

She stopped and turned toward him. She was in her early thirties, Ray guessed. Thin glasses, hair in a low ponytail. Very cerebral. She was dressed like most churchgoers these days, which was to say, casual—a sweater, blue jeans, flat-heeled dark shoes.

"You're Heidi's friend, Ray?"

He nodded, figuring they were using the term "friend" loosely. He extended a hand as he approached. "Thanks for taking time to see me."

"Heidi said you had questions about Graham Stoddard."

"That's right. He's my cousin."

She nodded, said nothing.

"I arrived yesterday, supposedly to spend a week with him. But I haven't been able to get a hold of him since I arrived, and Heidi said he didn't come home from work Thursday, and she hasn't seen him since. I thought maybe you could tell me if he showed up to work on Thursday and what his mood was like if so."

Diane had bit down on her tongue halfway through his explanation, and she now released the pressure. "Yeah, he *came* to work Thursday. But he left early."

"How early?"

"We take the customers out around six o'clock. Usually get them back by eight-thirty or so. That night Graham was on parking detail as they arrived, then was scheduled to work the store when we got back."

"The store?"

"We sell some memorabilia, things to remind people of their visit to the Bar H-9. You know how it goes."

"Sure."

"It's an easy gig, parking and shop detail. Easiest assignment there is."

"Was that what Graham always did?"

"It varies from night to night. Every now and again, somebody has to come late or leave early, and the owners are pretty flexible. It's a good place to work."

Ray nodded. "You said he *came* to work and was *scheduled* to work the store."

"Yeah. We came back on the wagons, and he wasn't there. Jasmine, the other girl who worked the store, said he just never showed. We never saw him again."

"Where would he have been between parking detail and store detail?"

"Riding fence. It's our term for cleaning the restrooms, picking up any stray trash, basic straightening up."

"Did any of that get done?"

"Come to think of it, now that you mention it, no."

"So he could have disappeared anytime between when the wagons left and when they returned?"

"Pretty much."

"Would anyone else have been there with him? Jasmine, maybe?"

"No, she had a role to play in our 'drama' but got back early to help in the store."

A handful of people passed them on their way inside from the parking lot. Diane crossed her arms, presumably for warmth against a sudden breeze.

"Just a couple more questions."

"Sure."

"Was Graham scheduled the last two nights?"

Diane nodded.

"And he never showed?"

"Nope."

"Had he been acting weird beforehand? Did he say anything, was his behavior erratic?"

"I really don't know him all that well. We work together, but we don't socialize." She shrugged. "I didn't notice anything."

"Okay. I appreciate your time. I won't hold you up anymore."

"No problem. I hope he's all right."

"Thanks. If you think of anything else, would you give Heidi a call? She can reach me."

"Sure thing."

They said goodbye. Diane headed in to worship, and Ray returned to his truck. Diane's information had narrowed down the window of time when Graham had disappeared but didn't give any indication of what had happened to him. Had he blown off the rest of his shift for some reason? Had he been kidnapped? Had he saddled up and ridden off into the sunset?

Ray drove to the Jackson Police Department a few blocks south of his hotel. He didn't know what else to do. Graham's mom—Ray's mom's sister— had died a decade ago, when Ray was in Afghanistan with the Army. Graham's dad had split long before that, and Ray couldn't remember the last time he'd seen him. He had no way to track him down. And Graham had no siblings. There was no one else to call, nowhere else to check. And waiting hadn't worked so far.

A sign on the door informed him that business hours were 8-5, Monday-Friday. He was directed to the lobby of the Teton County Jail, across the parking lot. There he spoke to a deputy and said he wanted to file a missing person report. The deputy, a square-jawed man with a buzz cut, looked at him with one eye closed.

"Is something wrong?" Ray asked.

"What's the name?"

"Mine or the—"

"The missing person."

"Graham Stoddard."

The deputy nodded. "You're the second one today. Have a seat, please, and someone will be with you in a few minutes." Ray sat, and the deputy picked up a phone and spoke in hushed tones Ray would have had to strain to hear. He didn't strain. The deputy put the phone down. "Just a few minutes," he reiterated.

Ray nodded. And counted. It was two minutes precisely when the door opened, and a man entered from outside. He was as tall as Ray, six-foot, and a bit heavier—probably close to two and a quarter. He wasn't fat, just big. Thick. He wore blue jeans, loafers, and a button-down shirt. His hair was black tinged with gray. Ray guessed him to be mid- to late-forties.

He offered a hand. "I'm Detective Will Celek, TCSO."

"Ray Eastwood," he said, shaking the hand.

"You're here to report a missing person, Graham Stoddard?"

"That's right."

"Why don't you come on over to my office."

Detective Celek led Ray back outside and across the parking lot to the Teton County Sheriff's Office. He explained that it wasn't uncommon for the Sheriff's Office to assist with investigations, particularly on the weekend. Then he asked where Ray was from. He asked why he was in Jackson. He asked what his connection was to Graham Stoddard. By the time Ray told the detective that Graham was his cousin, they were seated in his cubicle in the Sheriff's Office.

The cubicle was cluttered, but in a way that suggested to Ray that Detective Celek knew where everything was. Celek sat in a chair beside two blank computer monitors. A framed photo showed a middle-aged woman and three younger men—Celek's wife and sons, presumably. Diplomas and certificates and awards on the wall assured visitors, like Ray, that Detective Celek was competent. Just the way he carried himself suggested that, loafers and blue jeans aside. It was, after all, a Sunday.

Celek looked across the desk at Ray. "Tell me what's going on."

Ray did. He recounted his last twelve or so hours, adding in details about his plans to visit Graham, the last time they'd communicated, and his attempts to reach him Friday night and Saturday morning. Celek listened without saying much until Ray mentioned going to Graham's apartment.

"You were in his apartment?"

"His girlfriend had a key."

"What's the girlfriend's name?"

"Heidi. Don't know the last name."

"Did you touch anything?"

"Sorry, we did. The door, refrigerator. Not much."

Celek sighed. "I don't suppose it matters. He disappeared from work, so it's not like we're going to find a kidnapper's prints at his apartment or something."

"You already knew he was missing?" Ray said.

"His boss called us this morning, about an hour ago. He said Graham skipped out on the last half of his shift Thursday night and hadn't shown up the previous two nights—that is, previous to today. He tried calling him yesterday and this morning and was worried that maybe something had happened to him. He said it wasn't like Graham to miss work."

"He say anything else?"

"Not really. Just that nobody he talked to at the ranch had heard from Graham, knew where he was, that sort of thing."

Ray nodded.

Celek reached for a folder on his desk. He opened it far enough to get his hand inside and withdraw a sheet of paper. He placed it in front of Ray on the desk, on top of some other papers. It was a printout of what looked like a security camera feed of a van in a parking lot, in the aisle. The image was black and white, and the van was a lighter shade of gray, probably white or silver. It was a standard work van, no windows on the back. "Jackson Hole Cleaners" was stamped on the side of the van, along with a logo of what appeared to be an anthropomorphic vacuum cleaner.

"What's this?" Ray asked.

"Shot of the ranch's parking lot about a quarter after six on Thursday night."

Ray nodded.

"That van was reported stolen Friday morning. The owner showed up to work, found one of his two vans wasn't where it was supposed to be, and called the police. We found it thirty minutes later parked in a lot in the middle of town. No prints, no trace of anybody or anything, nothing missing. Odometer showed about twenty more than the end of day log on Thursday, which would account for driving from the shop to the Bar H-9, and a little bit more." Celek shifted his frame in the chair. "Since nothing was missing and he had his van back, the owner said it was no big deal. Probably kids joyriding, which he said happened once before. He didn't have security cameras in his lots, the police had no leads, so that was pretty much the end of it. Until this morning."

"Did the Bar H-9 send that over?"

"Sent their surveillance videos." Celek spun in his chair and shook his computer mouse back and forth, activating the two monitors. "They have a couple cameras around the ranch, but this is the only one of the parking lot. Check this out."

Ray leaned forward as Celek tilted one of the monitors toward him. Celek called up an open video file, slid the scrubber back a short way, and clicked play. The security feed was zoomed out from the photo of the van, showing twenty or so cars in a gravel lot. The timestamp in the lower right corner read 18:13:09—about a quarter after six.

A man in jeans, a plaid shirt, and a cowboy hat walked from left to right into the picture. He had a thick dark beard, a "full lumberjack."

"That's Graham," Celek said. "He was on parking detail greeting people at the front gate. According to the boss out at the Bar H-9, he was to stay there until a quarter after, by which time the wagons are long gone, and any latecomers are pretty much out of luck." He had paused the video and now clicked play again. The Jackson Hole Cleaners van drove into the picture from the right and stopped in front of Graham, blocking him from view. The timestamp read 18:13:44.

It ticked slowly on. Nothing happened. The driver in the van didn't move as far as Ray could tell on the somewhat grainy feed. Ten seconds. Then fifteen.

"What's he doing?"

Celek said nothing.

At 18:14:06, twenty-two seconds after it stopped, the van accelerated smoothly and steadily and drove out of the picture on the left.

Graham was nowhere to be seen. He had not emerged from around the back of the van. He had not appeared beyond the van, hadn't cut through the parked cars perpendicular to the direction the van faced.

Ray sat back. He took a deep breath. "They took him."

"It would seem so. I sent two deputies to Jackson Hole Cleaners about five minutes before you showed up. They're closed today, but the owner was going to meet them, given the circumstances, to let them check the van again. But it was clean Friday."

"What about the other vehicles?" Ray asked.

"What about them?"

"Can you get reflections in their mirrors or windshields to verify what happened?"

"Not with the quality of this feed," Celek said. "Plus it was overcast, so no strong reflections like on a bright sunny day."

Ray sighed.

Celek went over a few questions about Graham, and Ray provided what information he could. Celek assured him they would do all they could, and Ray believed him. But unless someone had seen where the van stopped before the parking lot where it had been found—assuming it had stopped elsewhere—and unless Celek and his deputies stumbled upon that person, Ray didn't particularly like their chances.

"It's also possible he went voluntarily," Celek said. "It would be odd, ducking out on the rest of his shift in a cleaning van, but it is possible."

"Yeah," Ray said. "Possible."

He thanked Detective Celek for his time, and they both promised to be in touch. Then Ray exited to the parking lot and returned to his truck. Blue sky had broken out in a few places, but it was still mostly overcast. And it was still cool.

Ray got into his Silverado but made no move to start it. Graham had been kidnapped. This wasn't another case of him being a free spirit—he hadn't shirked work or gone on a bender or something. Nor was his absence all a misunderstanding, a schedule conflict or something else he and Ray would laugh over later. No, he had been kidnapped, snatched from the parking lot. Ray took several deep breaths, trying to believe it was really true.

Even given that revelation, his visit with Detective Celek left him with more questions than answers. Assuming the van had been used to kidnap

Graham, why that van? Did the kidnappers have an "in" with Jackson Hole Cleaners or something else that made it an easy target? And why hadn't they returned it—Why leave it in a parking lot? Was that their rendezvous with a second getaway vehicle? Unlikely, considering it would have been during daylight, during the heart of the dinner rush, when a parking lot in the middle of town would be fairly conspicuous. Ray thought about getting out a map, computing mileage from Jackson Hole Cleaners to the Bar H-9 to the parking lot, subtracting that total from the twenty miles that had been put on the odometer, and calculating how far the van had gone. It would narrow down the search a little.

He left that for Celek. He seemed more than competent and would have the resources to follow that line of inquiry. Ray didn't, but he did have something else. He had five postcards with cryptic markings on one of them. He hadn't mentioned them to Celek, an oversight, but decided to play that hand out a little bit before possibly diluting Celek's investigation with random information that Ray wasn't even sure was pertinent.

Ray started the truck and drove back to the Jackson Hole Inn, only because he had left the postcards on the dresser there. He unpacked and powered up his laptop, frowning at the postcards while it booted. An antler arch at the Town Square. The Jackson Hole Rodeo. Jackson Lake Lodge. Signal Mountain.

The Jackson Town Square was obvious, an icon. Same with the Rodeo, perhaps. Was there something that made the Jackson Lake Lodge stand out from any other inns and lodges and hotels in the area? What was the significance of Signal Mountain? What kind of signal? Why no Tetons? Why no other landmarks or iconic locales? Why nothing written on the back?

Ray looked at the other postcard, the one with the cartoonish map of Jackson Hole on the front. The Town Square was highlighted on it, with an antler arch, no less. Signal Mountain was also indicated with a pair of binoculars. Nothing about the Rodeo or the Jackson Lake Lodge.

He flipped it over.

Betsy Garner's grave

Woody's ranch

TSS

2265 N Fish Cr

Moran from east of Oxbow

Find the triangles

He carried his laptop to the table by the window and spread the other four postcards out in front of it. The fifth, with the map, he turned upside down.

Find the triangles

He scanned the four postcards, looking for triangles. He saw none. He flipped over the postcard with the map and looked for triangles. He saw none. Unless he counted a mountain. They weren't depicted particularly triangularly, but they could count. He didn't think that was it, however.

Ray resorted to Google. He read the history of the antler arches, first built almost sixty years prior. Several had been replaced since, and he watched a time-lapse video of the process. Fascinating but not helpful.

He visited the Jackson Hole Rodeo's website. The rodeo ran Memorial Day through Labor Day and thus had been over for three weeks.

Labor Day. Ray shook that thought away.

Nothing on the website meant anything to Ray. Nor was anything triangular. Same was true of brief research on Jackson Lake Lodge and Signal Mountain. He sighed.

It was eleven o'clock. Twelve noon back in Huron, where his parents lived. He called them most Sunday afternoons, usually a little later in the afternoon. At noon, they would likely still be at church or out to lunch with friends. He tried calling his sister, Cathy, but got her voicemail. He didn't leave a message.

Ray turned his attention to the postcard with writing on the back. He entered "triangles Jackson" into the search engine, then added "Wyoming" to the end of it. He got nowhere.

He searched on "Woody" and "Woody's ranch" and "Woody Jackson." He got nowhere.

He typed in "Betsy Garner." He got nowhere.

His last search was for "TSS Jackson." Google's top result was the Teton Science Schools. Leaning forward, Ray clicked on the link. According to the website it linked to, Teton Science Schools comprised three campuses in northwest Wyoming and Idaho, one of which was in Jackson. It taught more than twelve thousand youth and adults per year by immersing them in nature, a method called place-based education. The Jackson Campus occupied nine hundred acres just west of Jackson, with its cluster of buildings in a ravine in the West Gros Ventre Butte.

Ray had no idea what he would find, or if the school would be open on a Sunday, but he had nothing else to do. Because it beat sitting around waiting for Detective Celek to find a lead, Ray decided to check out the school.

FIVE

Ray drove west through town, feeling as if he'd already crossed Jackson a dozen times that morning. While driving, he called Heidi. She was finished with breakfast and sounded better. He told her about the meeting with Detective Celek, about the Jackson Hole Cleaners van.

"So he was kidnapped from work?"

"It looks that way."

"Who would want to kidnap Graham?"

"I have no idea."

She sighed. "What are you going to do?"

"That's why I'm calling. Can you send me names and numbers of some of his closer friends, people he may have confided in or tipped off in some way?"

"I guess. He doesn't have a lot of close friends."

"Any particular reason?"

"He's busy. And he's sort of friends with everybody he meets."

Ray knew what she meant. Graham was a socialite. The type who would have a hundred friends but no *best* friend.

"Let me look," she said. "I'll text you a few numbers."

"Thank you."

Where the concurrent highways jogged south, they intersected with Wyoming 22, which headed west to Wilson and then through a mountain pass to Idaho. Ray followed it for only a mile before turning onto Coyote Canyon Road. It led into a ravine—presumably Coyote Canyon. Ray drove past a gravel parking area on the right, then around a loop that led right up to a cluster of buildings. Three vehicles were parked in stalls along the right of the loop, and Ray became the lone occupant of eight short-term spaces just around the loop.

He shut off the truck and got out. Ahead, the hillside rising in front of him was nothing but brown grass and grayish green sage. Looking behind him, the hill was dotted with pine but otherwise the same. To his right, young aspens flanked a walkway between the buildings. They were sleek yet fit with the terrain, featuring open joists and plenty of glass to let in natural light.

Ray approached the first building on the left, identified as the welcome center. The doors were locked, and he'd expected nothing less. He walked a hundred feet between the buildings, saw no sign of any people. There was a pair of hiking trails on the property, and he guessed hikers explained the three vehicles he had seen. The campus looked deserted. It was Sunday.

Find the triangles

There were triangles everywhere if he looked at the buildings and imagined lines connecting trusses to walls, or one building to the next, or a sidewalk to the main walkway. But there were hundreds of such triangles at any location. That couldn't be what the postcard meant, could it?

Ray walked back to the stairs leading from the welcome center to the parking lot. He stopped and surveyed the scene—back behind him at the two rows of buildings, to the tops of the hills on either side of the ravine, to the trio of cars in the parking lot. He had no idea what he was looking for, why someone had written TSS on the back of a postcard and sent it to him. For that matter, he didn't even know this was the right TSS. Surely those letters stood for something else too. A name. A corporate entity. A stock exchange abbreviation. Who knew?

With a sigh, Ray reached for his phone, shielding the screen with his hand. He'd felt it vibrate in his pocket a moment ago, and looked to see that Heidi had sent him a text. It contained three names and three numbers, plus a short note: *Sorry, all I have –H*

Three was better than nothing, and Ray dialed the first number as he walked back to the truck. It was for Kris, and Ray expected a woman but got a man. He sounded high. It took nearly a minute for him to process that Ray was looking for Graham, and he couldn't recall the last time he'd seen or talked to him. Ray thanked him and quickly ended the call.

He got into his truck and dialed the other two numbers before leaving the parking lot. Neither Elijah nor Lee answered, and Ray left brief voicemails asking for a callback.

He had only had a pastry for breakfast, and that over four hours ago. Heidi had mentioned that Graham worked at a bistro named Metro. Figuring he might as well kill two birds with one stone, Ray found it on his phone and set a course back to town.

Metro was located a few blocks from the Town Square and was everything Ray had feared. Seating was at bistro tables, most of which were beside giant panes of glass that faced the street on either side of the front door. Farther into the restaurant, a pair of delicatessen display cases spanned a diner-style soda counter, only it served kale smoothies and vegetable juices instead of malted milkshakes, according to the menu board above it. Everything on the menu was preceded by the words "organic" or "artisan." Non-GMO and gluten-free made plenty of appearances too, as did assurances that the food was sustainably-sourced and fair-trade.

Leafy greens and various shoots dominated the menu. Ray ate his vegetables, but he didn't necessarily get excited about it. He preferred a good steak, burger, or pasta dish. The closest he found at Metro was a turkey and cheese panini. He ordered it without the avocado and red onion, earning him a frown from the lady behind the counter. The snake tattoo that crawled up her neck and wound around her ear (visible because the hair was shaved on that third of her head) earned her a frown right back from Ray.

He wasn't there just to eat, so he asked if she knew Graham Stoddard.

"Sure. He works here."

"Have you seen him lately?"

"Just got back from a wedding in Rock Springs. Haven't been in since Thursday. He was here then till about three."

"He seem off to you at all?"

The woman frowned again. "Off?"

Ray explained that he was Graham's cousin here to visit and that he hadn't been able to locate him. He didn't explain that the Sheriff's Office was looking for him too or about the van in the Bar H-9 parking lot.

"He was quieter than normal, but we all have our days." She handed Ray his change—$13.50 for a panini. "Somebody'll bring that right out."

Ray thanked her and found an empty table in the corner. The music was terrible. "Kiss Me" followed by "This Love." He tried to ignore it, along with an Oriental scent from some reed diffusers on the table, and figure out what he was going to do.

Ray was not a detective. He was not going to outwit or outhustle Detective Celek to find Graham. He was a data analyst, but when the data was five postcards and nonsensical writings on the back of one of them, he was hamstrung. He could quiz a few coworkers and friends, but they weren't likely to know something Graham's girlfriend didn't. Bottom line, Graham was missing, it would appear kidnapped, and Ray had no idea where he was, who had taken him, or why they had done it.

So did he hang out in Jackson by himself for a week? Go on some hikes, maybe book a wildlife expedition, buy his coworkers Jackson Hole T-shirts and coffee mugs? Did he sit in his hotel and watch cable while waiting for news from Detective Celek? If the dire warnings issued on the crime dramas he watched were true, the first forty-eight hours were the most critical, and they had already passed. Did he go home?

He decided to give it at least the rest of the day. See how he felt in the morning and decide then.

A young guy in skinny jeans so tight they hurt Ray to look at brought his panini and about eight homemade veggie chips. He wore a flannel shirt with the sleeves rolled up above his elbows, and it was loose only in comparison to the pants. His beard could have been painted on, and his hair was swept across his head from right to left, emphasizing the fact that it also went from brown to blond in the same span. And Ray wasn't sure, but he might have been wearing eyeliner.

"Excuse me," Ray said.

"Yes?"

"You know Graham Stoddard?"

"Yeah. Why?"

"I'm his cousin, and—"

"You're Graham's cousin? From North Dakota?"

"South Dakota."

"Yeah, he said you were coming to visit. Where is he, anyhow?"

"That's what I'm trying to figure out. Nobody's seen him since Thursday."

"Yeah, he missed his shift Friday. Hanna was pretty upset."

"His boss?"

The guy nodded. "She said if he misses another shift, he's fired."

"When is he scheduled next, do you know?"

"I don't. I can check."

"Would you mind?"

"Not at all."

The guy was gone two minutes, in which time Ray sampled his panini. He'd just as soon have a Whopper, but it wasn't bad.

"Tomorrow," the guy reported. "Ten till four."

"Thanks."

"No problem."

"You and he close?"

"He has a girlfriend."

Ray raised an eyebrow. "I meant are you guys friends, more than just coworkers?"

The guy shrugged. "I suppose."

"Have you talked with him much recently? Did he seem different, paranoid, did he say anything that struck you as unusual?"

"No, I don't . . . I don't think so. Nothing comes to mind."

"Okay. Thanks."

"Sure thing."

Ray inhaled the panini and left.

It was twelve-thirty. The sun was actually shining, although plenty of clouds still coated the sky. If he was going to wait until morning to figure out his long-term plans, that left him an afternoon to kill. He wasn't going to spend it in his hotel room or tracking down more coworkers who didn't seem to know Graham all that well. Diane, the lady with the snake tattoo, and the guy with the eyeliner all knew him but only kind of-sort of. Of the three friends Heidi had mentioned, one wasn't clearheaded enough to be of help, and the other two hadn't returned Ray's calls.

He headed north out of town, crossing the small creek—Flat Creek—he had crossed when entering town an eternity ago the night before. On his left, the brown, lifeless East Gros Ventre Butte was dotted with a few clumps of green but was otherwise barren. On his right, a flat marsh stretched for maybe a mile before the hills rose up to the sky. The marsh extended north as far as the eye could see. It was an odd sight, in a mountain valley, and a sign told him it was the National Elk Refuge. Funny, he didn't spot any elk.

The road ascended slightly, and as Ray crested the small ridge, a sense of anticipation came over him. Then the butte fell off, and the vista opened up. Over a field of drab sage, Ray spotted the magnificent Tetons. Specked with snow, the dark gray granite knifed into a blue sky so pure and vivid it seemed almost otherworldly. The clouds no longer blanketed the landscape but were a mere accompaniment, casting spots of shadow on the jagged ridges and ravines. Ray was not easily impressed, but the view was breathtaking.

His phone rang. Spying a turnoff just ahead, he slowed as the phone trilled a second time. Then a third as he braked and veered into the turnoff. A brown sign hanging from darker brown log supports announced he was entering Grand Teton National Park. The phone rang a fourth time as Ray stopped out of the flow of traffic.

"Ray Eastwood."

"Ray. It's Lee Hunnicutt, Graham's friend."

"Lee, thanks for calling me back."

"You having trouble finding Graham?"

"I am."

"You check that weird café over on Glenwood?"

"I did."

"Because he works there a lot of mornings and afternoons, then out at a ranch in the evenings. He somehow got a gig taking folks on an authentic chuck wagon dinner experience. Funny, he hates horses."

"Lee, it's more than I can't find him. He's missing."

Lee paused. "Missing how?"

"I talked to his girlfriend, Heidi."

"They're still together?"

"Sort of."

"Hmm. Yeah?"

"She said he never came back from work Thursday. I talked to a Detective Celek at the Teton County Sheriff's Office, and he showed me video footage—"

"Whoa, the Sheriff's involved?"

"The Bar H-9 called when he missed a couple shifts, this after not finishing his Thursday night shift."

"Whoa."

"About six-fifteen Thursday he was walking across the parking lot. A van pulled in front of him, parked there for twenty seconds, and when it was gone, so was he."

"Whoa," Lee said again, this time barely audibly.

"Heidi gave me your name. I was hoping you might have spoken to Graham lately and would know something—anything."

"I talked to him . . . Monday morning. We had coffee. He seemed fine, I guess."

"You guess?"

"He was a little less talkative than normal. I didn't think much of it. Thought maybe he had something on his mind or maybe it was just a Monday, you know?"

"He didn't say what might be on his mind?"

"No. It'd been a few weeks, so I asked about Heidi, and he was kind of noncommittal. I kind of got the feeling they were on the outs, and maybe that accounted for his mood. I didn't press it."

Ray remembered Heidi's words when he'd asked if she and Graham were dating: "More or less."

"What can you tell me about their relationship?"

"Not much," Lee said. "They were like a country song. It was even odds if they'd get married someday or kill each other."

Ray said nothing.

"I don't mean it like that," Lee said. "I just mean they fought as much as they loved, you know?"

"How well do you know Heidi?"

"Barely. We've hung out as a group a few times, and I've seen her at Graham's once or twice. She's fine."

Trying to read a voice over the phone wasn't easy, but Ray sensed no hostility in Lee's words.

"Anything else about Graham strike you? Anything he said or didn't say? Anything he did?"

"I can't think of anything," Lee said after a moment. "No."

"Okay. If you do, maybe give Detective Celek a call. He's working the case."

"What are you doing?"

Ray took a deep breath. "Trying to figure out how to fill a week in Jackson."

"That should be easy, bro."

Ray thanked Lee and ended the call. He turned his head left, past the Grand Teton National Park sign and to the actual mountains beyond it in the distance. He could just go solo, spend the week in the area as planned. He'd traveled for business before—to seminars and conferences—and had spent nights or extra days by himself in various locales. Vacationing alone wasn't great, but it beat sitting at home alone. And Ray was going to have to get used to being alone.

He felt a twinge of guilt even thinking about vacation under the circumstances. But it wasn't as if he and Graham were that close. Had he learned of Graham's disappearance while back in Sioux Falls, he wouldn't have likely done much of anything except pray and hope. And truth be told, had he been back in Sioux Falls, he wouldn't have even learned of it. He and Graham spoke maybe once or twice a year, and had it not been for a somewhat knee-jerk reaction to his breakup with Annabelle and having a honeymoon's worth of vacation time and money suddenly available, that wouldn't have likely changed.

As he stared at the row of mountains gradually rising from left to right and culminating in the apex of Grand Teton, Ray's thoughts drifted to Annabelle. They had planned a trip to Jamaica—pristine beaches, tropical breezes, exotic waterfalls, steel drum bands. He'd been excited about romancing his new bride, but also traveling to some far-off place, just the two of them.

He imagined she was in the passenger seat with him now—maybe on an anniversary trip out West, or maybe on a getaway just because they could. They would hike in the foothills, searching for wildlife, her with a jaunty ponytail flaming behind her. Or maybe they'd come in winter and ski the Tetons, then take a famed sleigh ride through the herds of elk that made Jackson Hole their winter home. Ray's mind drifted to romantic evenings in the lodge, with a fire crackling in the hearth . . .

He shut off the fantasy. It wasn't happening. He and Annabelle weren't going to Jamaica or Jackson or the Mitchell Corn Palace. They weren't going hiking or traipsing through waterfalls or cuddling in front of a fireplace. They weren't doing anything.

She was gone. It was over. And Ray knew he had to move on.

Six

Annabelle Foster had walked into Ray's life by chance—a chance that seemed like a divine encounter. He had showed up late for church one morning, at the early traditional service that was usually pretty full. This week it had been more than pretty full. It had been packed. Spotting an empty seat in the middle, he'd turned into the row, edged past a few singers, and arrived at the vacant seat at the same time as a beautiful blond woman in a long, silky sundress.

Beautiful failed to describe Annabelle's appearance in the same way blond was an inadequate descriptor of her hair. It was a color like Ray had never seen, almost as if it was imbued with light—a dazzling, sparkling radiance that shone through each follicle to give the waves of hair that splashed onto her shoulders a golden luminescence. That radiance, that luminescence, was matched by a cherubic smile—not at anything or in response to anything. Annabelle's face was just angelic by default.

Ray was not easily smitten and, in fact, was pretty casual around the opposite sex. But Annabelle had taken his breath away. It was clear she'd spotted the vacant seat as well, and they both stopped. Despite being stunned by her appearance, Ray had kept his quick wit and used brief hand signals (the congregation was in the midst of "In Christ Alone" at the time) to concede the seat to her. Annabelle had sagged her shoulders in quiet acceptance of and gratefulness for the gesture, and then Ray had backed out of the row.

He'd stood in the back of the sanctuary all service, not even thinking to head to the overflow balcony seating. In truth, he hadn't thought much at all during that hour. Instead, his mind had been consumed with the mysterious woman—one he'd never seen before at church. He kept replaying her beauty, from her soft eyes, warm smile, attractive figure both modestly concealed yet strikingly apparent in her sundress. He'd felt like a teenager all over again, and more so after the closing of the service when his efforts to spot her in the crowd revealed she was walking directly toward him.

She'd come to thank him, with a voice like an angel's harp. Ray had heard his dad's words in his head—"Make hay while the sun shines"—and did something he never did: he spontaneously asked this woman, whose left hand was absent of any jewelry, if she'd have coffee with him. To his surprise, she smiled wider and said, "Yes."

Coffee led to another coffee, then a casual dinner. Within a month, Ray and Annabelle were dating. Within a few months, they were deeply in love. Not only was Annabelle externally beautiful—be it with hair styled and in a silky sundress or in jeans and a T-shirt with hair up while watching the Broncos with Ray—but also internally. Her heart burned with a desire to love God more and to serve Him better. She was generous, compassionate, smart yet occasionally eccentric in a cute little schoolgirl sort of way. Her playfulness checked Ray's more reserved demeanor, and her sense of adventure kept everyday life from getting monotonous. She surprised Ray with little notes and treats and packages of Rolos—Ray loved Rolos. She found activities that interested both of them, or showed an interest in things Ray liked. She continually challenged him to seek Jesus, to grow in his faith. She was the best thing that had ever happened to him.

Over the winter, their relationship deepened. She met his parents, and he met hers. They took a weekend trip to Omaha to see Ray's sister. Jason and Cathy had only one spare bedroom, so Ray slept on the couch in the living room. Saturday night, Annabelle had been unable to sleep and had crept out to the living room. They'd stayed up all night talking on the couch and then made Sunday breakfast for everyone. That was the moment when Ray knew he wanted to spend the rest of his life with Annabelle.

He proposed in the spring, with blessings from Annabelle's father and his own folks. They talked about a summer wedding—the following year—but neither wanted to wait to begin their life together. They settled on the second Saturday in October, in the fall. It was a short timetable for a wedding, but both agreed the wedding was just the kick-off. The lifelong marriage was the end game.

The summer flew by in preparation and anticipation. And temptation. Ray and Annabelle were both committed to remaining sexually pure before marriage, but as their love grew deeper and their relationship more intimate, it naturally drew them together physically. It didn't help that it was summer, meaning Annabelle's long legs and slender arms were always on display. It took a lot of prayer and a lot of self-control, but Ray survived. Annabelle knew the strain it put on him, and felt it too, and confided in him what a "wonderful example of a committed man of God," he was. Even so, he couldn't wait for the second Saturday of October, when Annabelle would be fully his. Or for the week in Jamaica, waterfalls and beaches aside.

A car horn sounded, and Ray snapped to attention. He quickly appraised the situation and realized he was drifting into the center lane on U.S. 26/89/191. He swerved hard back into his lane as a sedan whooshed by.

He exhaled twice, rubbed a hand over his face and through his hair. A mile ahead was another pullout, and Ray exited the highway. This time he turned off the car and got out.

The air was as warm as it had been all day, with the sun beating down on the valley floor. Ray continued to take deep breaths, walking around the truck and studying the terrain in all directions. It was something to behold.

His thoughts returned to Annabelle. It had been three weeks, now, and he couldn't keep from flashing back to what had been. Nor could he keep from imagining what might have been. He was getting marginally better at shutting out the thoughts, the memories, the daydreams. Usually. Just the previous week, he'd completely zoned out in a meeting at work. In the midst of a series of graphs and pie charts, he'd found himself picturing Annabelle walking barefoot on a Jamaican beach, a long sundress fluttering in the breeze, tendrils of hair trailing her as she tucked a flower behind her ear. It was weird, more Hawaiian than Jamaican, and Ray was not the daydreaming sort. But Annabelle had had that effect on him. His boss had pulled him aside after the meeting and suggested maybe he take some time off. Two days later, after Ray had talked with Graham, his boss had okayed a week's vacation on short notice.

That had been Friday, eight days before Ray had left for Wyoming. Graham had sounded fine then—typical Graham. He'd been fine on Sunday when Ray had called to confirm plans. They had texted a few details Tuesday morning, and that was the last they'd communicated. Nothing had ever suggested to Ray that anything was wrong in Graham's world—anything that would lead to his disappearance. Then again, maybe nothing had been wrong—nothing Graham could discern.

Ray got back into his truck. He had no idea really where he was going. Just driving. He reached for a map, then remembered he didn't have one. He knew the general layout of the area from memory. And he could probably pull up something on his phone. But Ray hated scrolling and swiping and zooming with his fingers. Plus he just liked holding a map in his hand, kind of like people who preferred flipping pages in a physical book to swiping on a screen. Usually, when you entered a national park, you passed a checkpoint and were given a map. But Ray had driven from Moran all the way to Jackson last night, traversing some twenty-five miles of the park in the process, without ever passing through a checkpoint.

He got back on the highway and continued north, without the aid of a map. Sooner or later, he knew, a road journeyed west, closer to the mountains and Jenny Lake, forming a loop with the highway. Maybe he'd find a checkpoint there. Last night, after all, it had been too dark to see much of anything.

It wasn't two miles farther on that a sign announced the turnout to Jenny Lake and a visitor center. Ray slowed and took the exit onto Teton Park Road. It descended slightly, crossing the sage flats down into the river valley. A bridge led over the Snake River, flanked by lodgepole pines, yellow- and orange-leafed aspens, and flaming cottonwoods. With the Tetons as a backdrop and the blue sky overhead, it was downright majestic.

At a four-way stop, Ray turned left toward the visitor center. He had no trouble finding parking, then hiked to the timber-sided Craig Thomas Discovery and Visitor Center. Out front, a giant bronze moose reminded Ray of the one he'd seen near the Town Square in Jackson. He was starting to wonder if the only wildlife he'd see in Jackson Hole would be of the bronze variety.

The visitor center was new and impressive, with high ceilings and plenty of glass looking out at nature. There were more bronze animals inside, as well as stuffed "real" animals. There were also bronze people—explorers, Native Americans, park rangers. Ray wandered for a few minutes, studied a raised relief map of the park for a few more. Being self-sufficient, he didn't question the rangers on duty, but took a park map and headed outside to look it over.

He sat on a rock bench in the sun, beneath panes of glass that formed the visitor center's west wall. For a moment, he ignored the towering Tetons ahead of him. He pinpointed Signal Mountain to the north, due west of where he'd entered the valley in Moran. Not much farther north was Jackson Lake

Lodge. Looking around some more, he also identified Fish Creek Road, ostensibly what was meant by "*2265 N Fish Cr*" on the postcard. If he wanted, Ray had an afternoon's worth of sites to visit. What he'd do there . . .

The cover of the map showed the Tetons, obviously, and the aptly named Snake River winding in the foreground, down in a clearly defined ravine. It was reminiscent of the famous Ansel Adams black-and-white shot, and Ray had a mind to see the view for himself. "Snake River Outlook" was marked on his map, either on the way to or from Signal Mountain and Jackson Lake Lodge. He sighed. He really didn't want to spend the afternoon trying to decipher someone's dubious directions.

"Can I help you find something?"

Ray looked up to see a woman standing six feet from him. She wore the typical drab green trousers of a National Park Service park ranger. They were perfectly starched and creased. Her brownish-gray short-sleeved shirt bore the NPS "arrowhead" patch on the left sleeve and a gold badge on the left breast. The iconic campaign hat covered brown hair pulled back into a tight ponytail. She was in her late twenties or early thirties, about Ray's age. Her face was friendly—either naturally or by Park Service directive. Ray immediately liked her voice. It was neither girlish nor masculine, and she spoke with a directness evident even in a six-word question.

"No, thanks," he answered. "Not really."

She smiled. "Not really meaning but sort of?"

Ray bobbed his head but said nothing.

"I'm Lauren Waite," she said, extending a hand. Ray set down his map and stood, which drew a raised eyebrow and a fractional widening of the woman's smile.

"Ray Eastwood."

"What brings you to Jackson Hole, Ray?"

He took a breath. "Vacation, in theory."

"In theory?"

"It's a long story."

Lauren raised one eyebrow. An invitation.

"You don't have something official to do?"

She shook her head.

Now Ray's eyebrow went up marginally. He gestured at the bench, and they sat down. He explained why he'd come to Jackson, to visit his now missing cousin. He explained meeting Heidi at Rattle the night before, then searching Graham's place that morning. He explained talking to Detective Celek and the surveillance video showing Graham's disappearance. And he explained the postcards, the writing on them, and the mystery of where they had come from.

"I can help you with that one," Lauren said. "All Jackson mail goes to Salt Lake City."

"So they were mailed from Jackson."

"Or anywhere in the region."

He nodded in concession.

"What's your cousin's name?" Lauren asked. They'd been talking about five minutes, so far undisturbed on the patio.

"Graham Stoddard."

She frowned. "Does he by any chance work at a trendy bistro a few blocks west of the Square?"

"Yeah, Metro. You know him?"

"I had lunch there a few weeks ago with a friend, and a guy named Graham was our server. Big beard, kind of a swept-over hairstyle?"

"Apparently. I haven't seen him in a while. You remember your server's name?"

"He stood out. It was a slow day, and he pulled up a chair and joined us at our table."

Ray frowned.

"It was fine," Lauren said. "After ten minutes, it felt like we were old friends."

"Yeah, Graham always could make friends with the wall."

"I think I'm offended."

Ray winced. "Sorry."

"I know what you mean, and yes, he struck me as the type. He had us in stitches telling us about the time he got lost in the Mormon Tabernacle as a kid."

"Been there myself."

"Lost in the Mormon Tabernacle?"

"Enraptured by his stories."

She grinned and shifted her posture. "So the postcards—that why you're looking at the map?"

"I guess. I've got nothing much to do, no real avenue to find Graham. So I thought I'd see some sights and maybe check out the locations. Not that I know what I might find or even what I should be looking for."

"Other than triangles."

He nodded.

"Mountains are sort of triangular, but aside from that . . ."

"Yeah."

"You think Graham sent them?"

"I guess that's the assumption, just because there's absolutely no other explanation for them."

"Why would Graham send you postcards?"

"No idea."

"What was on them again?"

"The Town Square, the Rodeo, Jackson Lake Lodge, and Signal Mountain. Then the last one was a map of the entire valley." He looked at her. "Why do they call it a hole anyhow? It is the whole valley that's considered Jackson Hole, right?"

Lauren nodded.

He waited.

She shrugged. "Jackson Valley doesn't roll off the tongue too well, does it?"

He wondered if she was serious until a thin smile broke out.

"The town was named after an 1800s beaver trapper named Jackson. He was one of the first white men to winter in the valley. Trappers like Jackson and mountain men used to refer to valleys that were completely surrounded by mountains as 'holes.'" She shook her head. "Nothing more fascinating than that."

Ray nodded.

"Your first time here?"

He nodded again.

"Well, then you have to see the view from Signal Mountain."

"Yeah?"

Lauren nodded. "There's a road," she said, pausing as Ray retrieved the map. He held it between them, and she tabbed a spot with her finger and continued. ". . . leading up here to the summit. There are actually two overlook spots. Breathtaking."

"Yeah?" he said again.

"Yeah. And the architecture and views from the Lodge are worth the visit too."

"Then I guess I have an itinerary."

"Are you single, Ray?"

He turned his head, his eyes narrow.

"I don't see a ring on your finger. But you have a girlfriend back home?"

Ray slowly shook his head.

"The reason I ask is that I don't want this to be awkward."

"A little late for that."

She smiled. "I mean this—what I'm about to say."

Ray waited.

"If you want some company, want a local to guide you and show you the best views and spots, I get off about five or five-thirty. I haven't been to the top of Signal Mountain in quite a while, particularly with the fall colors, and I always love seeing the Lodge. Plus I'm intrigued by these postcards and why Graham or someone sent them to you."

Ray said nothing.

"Now, if you were married or had a girlfriend, that offer might seem a little forward."

"A little awkward."

"Exactly."

He nodded.

"No pressure. But the offer's on the table."

"Is that SOP for a park ranger?"

"Offering to serve as a personal guide for a relative stranger? No."

He nodded.

"I have the night off," she said. "I love spending time in the park, love helping others enjoy time in the park. And given your circumstances, trying to find your cousin . . . I'd like to help."

Ray looked at Lauren. It was unorthodox, certainly, her offering to go with him. It wasn't something he'd do, were the roles reversed. But he could use some company. He was tired of being alone with his thoughts. And he wasn't going to call up Heidi and ask her to join him. He didn't know what measure of help Lauren could provide because he didn't know what he was even going to do at Signal Mountain or Jackson Lake Lodge. Truthfully, he hadn't really decided to go there until talking with her. But maybe another set of eyes, another person to ponder the words on the postcard—maybe it would make a difference—especially if that person was familiar with the park. If nothing else, it'd keep him from being alone all day. Again.

Ray slowly began to nod. "Okay. Yeah, why not?"

Lauren smiled.

"Five or five-thirty?"

"Make it five-thirty. Give me a chance to change out of my ranger duds."

"Okay."

"Since we're headed north, I'll meet you here?"

"Okay."

She stood. He did too.

"You don't have to stand on ceremony for me, Ray."

"Noted."

"That said, it is appreciated." She smiled. "I'll see you at five-thirty."

"Five-thirty."

She turned and walked toward the visitor center entrance, then stopped and looked over her shoulder. "If you've got a camera, Ray, bring it."

He nodded.

"I promise, you won't be disappointed."

SEVEN

Once again, Ray was lost in his thoughts as he traversed the highway, this time headed south back to Jackson. He had most of an afternoon to kill and would be seeing the sights later with Lauren. So for now, he decided to work off the theory that Graham had sent the postcards. Maybe there was a way for Ray to deduce what had happened to him—what had led to his disappearance.

He still didn't know what to make of Lauren Waite and her offer to help. Nor of his acceptance of it. He was pretty sure it didn't have anything to do with her being an attractive female. Ever since falling for Annabelle, he'd felt as if he was in a vignette. Everything around him blurred. He noticed other women, sure, noticed they were attractive. But it never felt relevant. He was with Annabelle.

Now, since Labor Day, other women were theoretically relevant again. But while he noticed them, he still felt if he was in a vignette, as if the edges of his vision were blurry. Only there was no one in the center of his vision any longer.

Back in Jackson, Ray found a parking space on the north side of the Square. Since he had several hours to kill before "investigating" with Lauren, he decided to buy the requisite souvenirs. Postcards for the folks, a Jackson Hole sweatshirt for his sister, coffee mugs for a few of the guys at work. Maybe stuffed moose antlers for Cathy's kids. Ray was not a shopper; he was a buyer. Get in, get out. So souvenir shopping wasn't his thing. But they'd never forgive him if he came back empty-handed.

He started south along Cache Street, on the opposite side of the street from the park, past several galleries and the Million Dollar Cowboy Bar. Its neon lights and the cowboy on horseback sign atop the roof were reminiscent of old-school Vegas. He walked a block and waited for the light. To his left, a pair of horses stood in the turn lane. They were hitched to a red and yellow stagecoach that looked just like the Wells Fargo coach from the commercials. A driver in a denim jacket and a cowboy hat was waiting for a fare, and he nodded at Ray, who then turned and crossed Broadway.

On the corner was a store called Shirt Off My Back. Ray remembered it from his morning walk, and he ducked inside. It had a lot of shirts, some coffee mugs, some postcards. None of the shirts jumped out at him as Cathy-ish, but he did pick up a mug, then checked out the postcards.

"Looking for anything in particular?" the clerk behind the desk asked. She was young, had an accent, sounded Eastern European. If a guy from Suburbia, South Dakota, could judge such a thing.

"Not really," Ray said. He stopped, an idea hitting him. He turned away from the postcards, quickly paid for the mug, and headed outside. There he called Heidi.

"Heidi."

"It's Ray Eastwood."

"You find Graham?"

"No. Do you happen to have a picture of him on your phone? A recent one?"

"I suppose. Why?"

"Could you text it to me."

"What, are you asking around town or something?"

"Yeah."

"For real?"

"For real."

"Okay. I'll send you one."

"Thanks."

He ended the call, debated for one moment, and turned west. His theory was that Graham had sent the postcards. (Why was a mystery, one he and Lauren would work on that evening.) If so, he had to have purchased them from somewhere. With Graham's photo on his phone, maybe Ray could jog the memory of a shop owner or clerk who had seen Graham, and maybe they would remember something he had said or something else he had bought with the postcards. And maybe that something would provide Ray a clue as to what had happened to Graham. It was a long shot, but since he had time to kill and was going to visit the shops anyhow . . .

His phone buzzed. He looked to see a picture of Graham, a goofy smile on his face as Heidi kissed his cheek with one eye turned toward the phone she presumably held. He did have a lumberjack's beard, albeit groomed. Jet black. His hair was cut in the pompadour comb-over style Ray saw frequently. He looked happy.

Ray entered something called Mangy Moose Emporium. It sold more knickknacks than Shirt Off My Back, and Ray looked for something for his mom. He settled on a miniature elk antler photo frame. A little kitschy, but she'd like it. Then he searched the postcards, looking for the particular ones Graham had sent. No luck. He questioned the cashier anyhow, but she didn't recognize the photo. He thanked her and left.

He seriously considered another stop at Jackson Hole Coffee Roasters but passed. He checked out a couple more shops with no luck on the souvenir front or the finding Graham front. At the end of the block, the shops petered out. Ray turned around and headed back the way he had come. He crossed to the north side of the street and walked past the Wort Hotel, Barker-Ewing River Trips, and a couple shops that didn't interest him.

The stagecoach was still at the intersection, the driver still waiting for a fare. Ray nodded at him this time as he crossed back to the south side of the street. He entered Lee's Tees and found more of the same. He realized that the stores largely sold the same shirts, same hats, same coffee mugs, same trinkets and baubles. He found a pink shirt with moose antlers for Cathy, then found some overpriced Wyoming-themed toys in the basement for her kids. He decided his dad could use the coffee mug from Shirt Off My Back and his coworkers didn't need gifts. Not at these prices.

He checked the postcards. There were several showing the antler arches, including one that matched the one he'd received. He turned the rack and spotted the Signal Mountain postcard too. Those were the only ones, but as he paid for his items, he withdrew his phone and asked the cashier if he'd seen Graham.

The cashier squinted. "He looks familiar."

"Maybe Thursday afternoon?" Ray's assumption was that Graham had purchased and mailed them hurriedly. Otherwise, he would have been more descriptive. Then again, Graham was a little wacky.

"I wasn't here in the afternoon."

"Could have been anytime last week."

The cashier shrugged. "Couldn't say. I see a lot of faces."

Ray nodded, and they finished the transaction. On the way out, he saw another employee and asked her if she'd seen the man on his phone. She recognized him, knew his name was Graham, knew he worked at Metro. It was a small town. But she hadn't seen him in at least a few weeks. Ray thanked her and left.

In the Jackson Mercantile, almost back to his hotel, Ray struck gold. The other three postcards.

A giant elk guarded the front door, and the interior was filled with mounted animal heads and bodies of every type. Wolves, foxes, coyotes, wolverines, bears of several species, elk, deer, and the largest moose head and rack Ray had ever seen were hanging over the counter. There were plenty of shirts and mugs and assorted souvenirs too. But Ray's focus was on the postcards.

"Can I help you?" the cashier asked. A man about Ray's age, wearing a ball cap, the start of a beard.

Ray showed him the photo of Graham on the phone. "You happen to see this guy last week? He bought five postcards."

The cashier gave Ray an "are you serious?" look. Then he studied the photo again. "Yeah," he said. "Thursday afternoon?"

"Maybe."

"Yeah, I remember. He practically tore the rack apart."

"He say anything?"

"Nothing I recall. He just bought the postcards and ran."

"Ran?"

The cashier shrugged. "He left in a hurry's all. Why?"

"He's my cousin and nobody's seen him since."

The same "are you serious?" look crossed the cashier's face.

"You know about what time on Thursday?" Ray asked.

"I don't know. Four, maybe. Three?"

"He look paranoid, look like somebody was following him?" Ray was grasping at straws.

"Not that I noticed."

"He buy anything else?"

"A stamp."

"One?"

"Regular stamp too, not a postcard stamp."

Ray was sure there was something else he should ask, but he didn't know what. So he thanked the man and left. He stood outside, next to the elk. Graham had bought the postcards Thursday afternoon, before heading to work at the Bar H-9 and before disappearing, likely in a Jackson Hole Cleaners van. Why? Had he known something was about to happen to him? If so, how? And why hadn't he gone to the police? And why hadn't he called Ray instead of sending him a cryptic message on the back of one of five postcards? Had he only had time to write a little? Was the message incomplete?

Ray returned to the Square and walked north on the opposite side of the street. He browsed a few more shops to kill time and asked a few more people if they had seen Graham. They hadn't. He exited on the northeast corner of the Square, across from Moo's Gourmet Ice Cream and the bronze elk and deer and moose and bear. And across from one of the antler arches, the one in the postcard, Ray was pretty sure, judging by the backdrop.

He looked for traffic and crossed the street. He stopped and looked at the tangled antlers, faded white by the years. The arch rested on a foundation lined with stone and offering a seat to passersby, guys waiting for their wives in the jewelry and clothing shops, ladies waiting for their guys in one of the stores selling antique guns or displaying big game, and anyone else who needed to take a load off. Ray stood. He looked around. Why a postcard of here? Because it was iconic? Because it was central?

The arch, the Rodeo, Signal Mountain, and Jackson Lake Lodge. What was the common denominator?

He thought of the words on the fifth postcard, the one with the cartoonish map.

Betsy Garner's grave
Woody's ranch
TSS
2265 N Fish Cr
Moran from east of Oxbow
Find the triangles

Six lines. No direct correlation with the other four postcards. What triangles? He was tired of thinking. And somewhat tired in general. He sat down after all, on the ledge to the inside of the arch. He looked left into the park, along the sidewalks that bisected the greenspace. To the wood fence separating the grass from the sidewalks that ran along the street. The sidewalks were composed of wood planks, except for right at the corner where concrete allowed for a curb and a ramp to the street.

Out of nowhere, he saw it. Where the arches cut off the corner of the park, the sidewalk widened to fill the extra space. Looking at it from Ray's perspective, or from above, one could see a triangle with one corner at the intersection of the two streets, and the other two corners at a point where a line parallel with the arch intersected the street.

Was that what was meant by "Find the triangles"? By that sort of reasoning, there were triangles everywhere. The four quadrants of grass in the square were triangles, bound by external sidewalks on one side and the sidewalks that bisected the park on the other two. Was that what Graham had meant?

It didn't make much sense to Ray and left him with a lot of questions. Foremost among them, so what? He'd found the triangles. What did that have to do with anything?

Ray thought about mentioning the postcards and the triangles to Detective Celek. He thought about how TV detectives always handed someone a business card and told them to call if they thought of anything, no matter how irrelevant it may seem. He thought about how rarely TV accurately portrayed real life. And he thought about Detective Celek's eyebrows racing up his forehead when Ray told him.

He stayed sitting under the arch.

He thought some more, about his visit to Teton Science Schools' Jackson Campus and how he could have envisioned triangles there too had he been of a mind to. He thought about the Rodeo and where he might be able to visualize triangles there. He thought about Signal Mountain and Jackson Lake Lodge and investigating them for triangles with Lauren. He thought for a brief minute about Lauren's presumptuous offer of help, pondering her motive. Was she just that helpful? Just that civic-minded? Just that bored?

Then he thought about how early he'd have to leave the following morning to get back to Sioux Falls at a reasonable hour.

EIGHT

According to the app on Ray's phone, sunset was almost two hours away. It would be sooner on the valley floor, what with the Tetons towering over it. For now, the light was a little dusky but still vibrant. The morning clouds and morning cool were gone. It was a beautiful afternoon turning to evening.

Mostly due to boredom, he was about ten minutes early. He parked in the same lot at the Craig Thomas Discovery and Visitor Center and strolled toward the building. He and Lauren hadn't specified an exact meeting spot, so he returned to the patio where they'd met that afternoon. He sat down.

Grand Teton, the tallest mountain in the range, topped out under 14,000 feet, which didn't even put it in the top fifty in the U.S. But with its sharply protuberant peak, prominence above the Snake River Valley, and the lack of surrounding foothills, it appeared much taller. At least to Ray. Now that the rain and clouds were gone, the view didn't disappoint. Perhaps the only thing on this trip.

"Hey, Ray."

He turned from the mountains. Lauren now wore reasonably distressed blue jeans and a maroon knit pullover under a beige utility jacket. Standard athletic shoes. Her brown hair was down, brushed, and looked much better without the campaign ranger hat. Truth be told, so did she. She carried a backpack over one shoulder, holding onto the strap with her hand. The other hand held a pair of silver-rimmed aviator sunglasses.

"Hi, Lauren," he said, standing.

"You didn't change your mind," she said.

"You expecting I would?"

"A strange woman invites herself along on your sightseeing junket, yeah, kinda sorta."

"Well, when you put it like that . . ."

They both smiled.

"You eat yet?"

Ray shook his head.

"If you're still planning on heading to the Lodge, you can't beat grabbing a bite at the Pioneer Grill and eating on the patio overlooking the Tetons."

"You talked me into it."

"Ready?"

He nodded and followed as she turned and started for the parking lot. She walked quickly, with purpose, yet not hurried. Ray could appreciate that.

"What do you drive, Ray?"

"Chevy Silverado."

She made a face.

"You disapprove?"

"The road up Signal Mountain is pretty narrow. But it's paved. That should work."

He nodded.

"If you don't mind me riding with you."

"If you don't mind the smell of beef jerky."

"Intoxicating."

He nodded and pointed her to the truck. She tossed her backpack on the floor before getting in and peeled off her jacket after getting in. "It's clean," she said as Ray started the ignition.

"You're surprised?"

"Most guys I know who own pickup trucks don't keep them clean."

He said nothing.

"Best way," she said as she buckled her seatbelt, "is back on 191 north."

"Okay."

He exited the parking lot and turned east, away from the park gate. He still hadn't had to buy a park pass. With Lauren riding shotgun, maybe he wouldn't need to.

"Tell me about Graham," she said as they drove north, surrounded by nothing but sage on either side.

"Graham the cousin or Graham the missing person?"

"Either."

"I don't know Graham the cousin all that well. We didn't see each other very often, but we got along. Your ten minutes at lunch seem like a pretty accurate snapshot."

"If you don't know him that well, why'd you come to visit?"

Ray pursed his lips. Thought of Annabelle and honeymoons that weren't. "He'd been asking for a while. I had time, had the money."

Not untruths.

Lauren nodded.

"It's odd," Ray said.

"What's that?"

"I feel like I should feel more bothered by the fact that he's missing. And I am. He's family, and I like him. But if I'd gotten a call a month ago telling me Graham had been hit by a bus, it wouldn't have rocked my world." He looked at her. "Does that make sense?"

"It does."

"That's probably too cold and uncaring. That's what my . . ." He raised his eyebrows.

"Your what?"

"Girlfriend would have said."

Lauren paused. "'Would have' as in past-tense girlfriend? Because you told me you were single."

"I am."

She nodded.

"Cold, maybe," she said at length, "but because of the distance, not because you're uncaring."

He shrugged.

"If I may be so bold as to judge you after five minutes."

Ray said nothing.

"Tell me more about the postcards."

He did. He recounted his afternoon, his idea to show Graham's picture around, discovering he'd been to the Jackson Mercantile and bought postcards and a stamp there.

"So he was the one to mail them."

Ray nodded.

"But no idea why?"

"None."

"And there was a message on the back about finding triangles?"

Ray recited the words from memory, and also mentioned finding triangles—so to speak—at the Jackson Town Square.

"You think that's what he meant?" Lauren asked.

Ray shrugged.

"And if so, why?"

Ray shrugged again.

She asked more about Graham's disappearance, and Ray brought her fully up to speed on all he knew. While he talked, she looked at him—or at the mountains out his window. He couldn't be sure which. He looked at her occasionally too, when the winding road didn't demand his attention. She sat in a way that let the seat envelope her, as if she was in a cushy Papasan chair, not the passenger seat of a Silverado. She was very relaxed. With a stranger. Ray was relaxed enough too, he supposed, but it was different as a guy. Although, maybe not in Wyoming.

"Stop!"

"What?"

"Quick, pull over."

He did. Before he had the gearshift in park, Lauren had ripped off her seatbelt and opened the door. She practically jumped out of the truck, before Ray could ask why. He watched her round the front of the truck and followed her gaze across the road, toward the mountains.

That's when he saw them. In a vast field of prairie grass were more than a hundred bison. Maybe two hundred. None of them were particularly close to the road—the nearest were maybe fifty or sixty yards away. Most weren't moving, either eating grass or standing in place. A few roamed. Two butted heads, kicking up clouds of dust as they circled, charged, backed off, and repeated.

Ray waited for a car to pass, then opened his door and got out. He moved to stand beside Lauren, just off the roadway. The two bison butted heads again.

"So this is where the buffalo roam."

She looked at him with a smile, a recognition of how unoriginal that was.

"I was wondering if I would see any wildlife here."

"Wait a few months till the elk outnumber the residents of Jackson."

"So I've heard."

Lauren crossed the road. Ray followed.

"Don't be scared," she said, noticing his hesitance.

"Aren't park rangers supposed to tell us to keep our distance?"

"Hundred yards for bears and wolves, twenty-five from everything else. Including bison."

"You ever seen any moose?"

"All the time."

"Really?"

"In the right time and place. Early and late in the day, in creek bottoms and river beds. Yeah."

"Bull moose?"

Lauren nodded.

"Grizzlies?"

"A few."

"Close?"

"One hundred yards." She winked.

One bison turned, took a few steps toward them. He was well over twenty-five yards away. Probably honing in on a clump of grass, not distant observers.

"We should get going if we're going to eat and make it up Signal Mountain by sunset."

"You halted the convoy."

"I did."

They crossed the road and got back into the truck.

"What's life like as a park ranger?" Ray asked. "Not all guided tours and warnings about wildlife distance, is it?"

"There's plenty of that—giving talks and demonstrations and leading tours and whatnot. But it's pretty varied—one day I'm at the visitor center, the next out in the field, the next working as a cashier, the next on some unique project. I like the variety."

"How long have you been doing it?"

"Going on nine years now, six here at Grand Teton."

"Where before that?"

"Craters of the Moon in Idaho."

"Long-term plans, to be a park ranger?"

"For now."

He nodded.

"What do you do back in . . . where are you from?"

"Sioux Falls, South Dakota. I'm a data analyst."

"What's that mean?"

"Numbers, numbers, and more numbers. Finding trends, predicting future trends."

"In what field?"

"We're a private company. We hire out to all sorts of businesses—insurance, manufacturers, restaurants."

"Long-term plan?"

"I guess."

They were to Moran Junction, and she instructed him to turn left and follow 191. Not stay on 26 back toward Riverton, Rapid City, and home.

"Can I ask you something?" Ray said after they passed through a checkpoint. Lauren's ranger pass got them in for free.

"Sure."

"Aren't you concerned getting into a truck with a complete stranger?"

"No."

"Why not?"

"A lot of reasons. You have kind eyes."

He looked at her.

"Windows to the soul."

"Really?"

She nodded.

"I could be a serial killer."

"Are you?"

"No."

"Okay then."

"That's it? I have kind eyes?"

"My mom died when I was nine, so my dad raised me. He taught me to ride a horse, shoot a gun, and drive a tractor, all before I went to my first school dance. I went to a small, rural school that didn't have girls' athletics, so I played pick-up games with the boys. In college, I took a self-defense class, so I know how to physically incapacitate a man twice my size in a matter of seconds. I've had nine years of park ranger training, which includes surviving in a wide range of scenarios. Long story short, I can take care of myself."

He looked at her but said nothing.

"Plus I believe God is watching out for the sparrows, much more me. Doesn't mean I should live recklessly, but it does mean I don't worry about the little things, like the off chance you are a serial killer who I couldn't incapacitate in a matter of seconds."

He looked at her but said nothing.

"And to top it off, I saw your CDs," she said, pointing at an organizer attached to the passenger visor. "Nobody who listens to Third Day worries me."

"Fair enough, I suppose."

"And the eyes do matter, Ray. You can tell when you look at somebody. At least, in my experience."

He looked at her eyes. They were blue. Pretty typical. He didn't notice eyes all that much. Except for Annabelle's. They had . . . sparkled. A terrible cliché, but one that was true.

"So do you do this a lot?" he asked.

"What's that?"

"Spend your free time riding around with guys with kind eyes?"

She turned and exhaled. "Not lately."

He said nothing. Some things were better left unprobed.

^   ^   ^

The turnoff to Jackson Lake Lodge was as innocuous as any. A two-lane road led through some trees and more sage, with a side road leading to a service station and medical clinic on the left. They passed a swimming pool, also on the left, followed by a large parking lot. To the right, several narrow roads diverged under a canopy of trees. The roads led to a series of small cabins. They looked modern if not overly luxurious.

Lauren directed Ray to turn into the last row of parking spots on the left. It was September, and the crowds had thinned, meaning people could again find parking at lots and turnouts. The summer months were crazy, she said, and the total solar eclipse that had passed right over Jackson Hole a few years ago had been a nightmare. Pun intended, she said.

They parked and got out. The Lodge was mostly obscured by pines. They followed a sidewalk that led under a massive carport and entered the building through one of two sets of glass doors.

Ray had visited some national parks, and a lot of the lodges were made to look old and rustic. Dark wood, low lighting, very American frontier. The Jackson Lake Lodge was bright and modern. The front desk was on the right, the concierge on the left. The floor was paved with smooth fieldstone. Real, Ray thought. Lauren led him straight ahead and up a long flight of stairs. A sign above them said it led to the Upper Lobby, with shops, restaurants, meeting rooms, and a lounge.

The lobby itself was a site to see. Marble floors. Neat fieldstone walls adorned with large paintings of wildlife. High ceilings supported by open rafters. Lit wood fireplaces in the near corners. Plentiful seating areas arranged around curio cabinets containing Native American artwork, pottery, and knickknacks.

Despite it all, Ray's eyes were immediately drawn to the far wall. It wasn't so much a wall as a bank of windows, some thirty feet high. They looked out on the deck and patio, and beyond them, a marsh called Willow Flats. Lauren informed him of the name as he stood by the window and stared across the flats at the Teton Range. Directly ahead was a somewhat conical peak appearing about as high as the Tetons to its left. Jackson Lake was also visible beyond the flats. Not a bad view.

Lauren had turned around, facing the lobby. "The rafters," she said.

"Huh?"

"They are full of triangles."

Ray turned around as well. The dark brown lumber braces of the rafters formed a series of triangles. They were nothing that would stand out, unless one had triangles on the brain.

She shrugged as Ray looked at her. "If the angles of a park and a surrounding sidewalk count, why not this?"

"It doesn't make any sense."

"Some food for thought?"

"You mentioned the Pioneer Grill?"

"The Blue Heron's a nice lounge," she said, pointing to their left. Then, with a nod ahead and to the right, she said, "But the Pioneer Grill has a to-go window, and the patio beckons today."

"That it does."

He ordered a pulled pork sandwich with sweet mustard barbecue sauce. She ordered a chicken sandwich, hold the onions. Both ordered fries. Because the autumn evening air was bound to have a chill, Ray ordered a coffee. She made it two. They went Dutch. Their wait was short, and they took their dinner out onto the deck and down to the patio, where they shared a wooden bench overlooking the flats and the mountains. They were alone, save for a few passersby who paused to gawk at the view.

Ray noticed Lauren bowed her head and closed her eyes before eating. A prayer. It was a habit he'd long ago given up, mostly because it had become just a habit.

The sandwich was great. So were the fries. Coffee too.

"Tell me what was on the postcard again—the one with writing."

"Six lines. '*Betsy Garner's grave.*' '*Woody's ranch.*' '*TSS.*' '*2265 North Fish Creek.*' '*Moran from east of Oxbow.*' And '*Find the triangles.*'"

"Well," she said, covering her mouth with the back of her hand as she swallowed, "that's Moran right there."

"Where?"

"The big—" She looked at him. "—triangle right in front of us."

"Any idea what Oxbow is?"

"Bend in the river a few miles back. Scenic overlook."

"With a view of Moran?"

She thought for a moment. "Yeah. A good one."

"A triangle."

"As much as any mountain. And just as vague as the other triangles."

He nodded. "TSS I interpreted as Teton Science Schools."

"That makes sense."

"I visited. No triangles. Not in any overt way, I mean."

"Overt like rafters and sidewalks?"

"When you put it that way . . ."

"So the writing on the one card doesn't seem to specify anything on the other four."

"Not in any overt way," he said with a crooked grin.

Lauren raised an eyebrow. "He couldn't find postcards of those places, so left another clue?"

"Or didn't have time. But what clues? What do triangles have to do with anything?"

"I don't know," she said, gazing off at the mountains.

Ray took a bite of his sandwich.

"Betsy Garner."

"You know her?"

"No. I know the last name Garner, and I know of a Woodrow Garner. They might call him Woody."

"Then why doesn't it say Woody Garner's Ranch?"

Lauren shrugged.

"For kicks, who's Woodrow Garner?"

"He's a wealthy businessman who has a spread on the western banks of the Snake River. I don't know where or how he made his money, but he has a lot. And he has his hands in a lot of Jackson Hole businesses. Owns shops and stores and restaurants, or owns the subsidiaries that own them, or owns the land and property and rents it out to the shops and stores and restaurants. Eight-figure net worth."

Ray counted the zeroes. Tens of millions.

"I don't know much more than that, and that is only what I've heard as scuttlebutt and gossip over the years. Jackson Hole's a big place, but it's small too, if you know what I mean."

"Think there's a chance he knew Graham?"

"A chance. Not sure how."

"His landholdings include the Bar H-9 or Metro?"

"The Bar H-9, I doubt. And from what I hear about him, Metro wouldn't be his place. I suppose he could own the property and rent it out, but I don't know."

Ray nodded.

"Never heard the name Betsy," she said and took a bite of her sandwich.

"Is Woodrow married?"

"I think so."

"But not to Betsy."

She shrugged.

"Could be his mom, sister, daughter," he said.

"Or another Garner. It's not the least common of names."

"No."

"It said '*Betsy Garner's Grave*'?"

Ray nodded.

"I went to school with an Audrey Garner."

"In Jackson?"

"Um-hmm. I grew up outside Boise, but we moved here when I was fifteen. Dad worked at the Elk Refuge for about a decade."

"He still live around here?"

"Moscow."

"Russia?"

"Idaho."

"Audrey any relation to Woodrow?"

"I don't know. We weren't best friends or anything."

"She still live around here too?"

"She works at a gallery in town. Might own it, in fact."

Ray sighed. "This feels like a lot of chasing around, and I still don't know what we uncover. Sidewalks, rafters, a pointy mountain."

"You mentioned Graham's girlfriend earlier. You talk to her about the postcards?"

Ray shook his head. "I'm not sure I've talked to her yet when she was fully sober."

Lauren nodded.

He had finished his sandwich and ate the last of his fries. She wasn't far behind, and when they were done, they took their coffees and walked. First, they deposited their trash in specially designed, bear-resistant receptacles. They were common in the parks.

They walked north, slowly, sipping coffee. Ray and Annabelle used to take long walks. Slow walks. Hand-in-hand walks. He still missed Annabelle, missed her hand in his, her fingers intertwined with his. He tried to remember their last walk. That is, their last walk before *the* walk.

"You okay?" Lauren asked.

"Huh?"

"You look like you were in a trance."

Ray tipped up his cup, took a full gulp. He shook his head. "No. Yeah, I'm fine."

They walked a little more.

"Thinking about Graham?"

"No."

Lauren said nothing. Some things were better left unprobed.

They had climbed a little, such that they could look back and down at the dark brown exterior of the Jackson Lake Lodge. They were surrounded by sagebrush interspersed with wildflowers. The view of the Tetons was, if anything, better than before as the sun sagged toward them. The jagged peaks looked like they might impale it. The sky was traced with wisps of clouds. The air was cool but not cold. It was a perfect evening.

"What time did Graham buy the postcards?"

They had stopped to admire the view. Ray looked at Lauren, her face glowing in the fading sunlight. He hadn't really paid it much attention before, but it was a pretty face. High cheekbones, button nose, dimples when she smiled. It was a carefree face. But also a serious one, at least right now. She had something on her brain.

"The clerk didn't know," Ray answered. "He guessed three or four."

"And what time was he at work?"

"I don't know. According to his coworker, they take people out on the wagons at six, and he was on the security camera at six-fifteen. But I don't know when he'd have to arrive."

"So two to three hours at most."

"Why, what are you thinking?"

"The cashier said he seemed in a hurry. That would fit with writing such concise notes. Question is, was he pressed for time because he was late for work or because he thought someone was chasing him?"

"I'm guessing the latter. If he was just late for work, he could have waited and bought postcards or mailed postcards another time."

"Not if he wanted to make sure they got to you by the time you arrived."

"Which he'd only have to do if he thought something was going to happen to him."

"In which case, why did he go to work at all?"

Ray shrugged.

Lauren's posture sagged.

"And why postcards? If he had some sort of message for me, why not text, why not call?"

"Postcards can't be hacked. Tapped. Traced."

"No, but somebody could have intercepted and opened his mail."

"If they knew about it. Maybe he thought someone was electronically eavesdropping."

"Who?"

"Or maybe he wanted something on record in case something happened to him." She bit her lip. "That's a lot of maybes and speculation."

"And still doesn't give us a clue as to what the message he left behind means."

"We haven't solved it all either. We haven't visited all the places. Maybe when we do, something will click."

Ray picked up on her use of "we."

Lauren looked down at her watch, visible with her sleeves pushed to just below the elbow.

"Should we get going to Signal Mountain?" he asked.

"Sunset is in half an hour," she said. "I don't think we'd make it."

"How far is it?"

"Right there," she said, pointing over the lodge at a tree-covered hill. "But the road to the top is at the southwestern end, and it's slow and meandering."

Ray nodded. He already knew not to question Lauren on park geography.

"Then I guess we can enjoy the view for a few more minutes."

She nodded. And they did.

Then she asked, "You have plans for the rest of the evening?"

NINE

Lauren held up her coffee cup and shook it back and forth. "I'm buying, and I'd kind of like to see the postcards."

"You want to see them?"

"I'm a visual learner. And thinker."

Ray did not have plans for the rest of his evening. And Lauren had proved good company thus far. So, while it still seemed a little strange, he had no objections. Plus, if Lauren's blue eyes were any indication, she wasn't a serial killer either.

They walked back down the trail, back through the lobby of Jackson Lake Lodge, and back through the parking lot to Ray's truck. The parking lot was entirely in shadow. Back on the road, shadow was interspersed with radiant sunlight, depending on the frequency and height of trees. Shortly after getting on 191, Lauren had him turn off onto Teton Park Road.

The road headed into the setting sun, then curved as it approached an earthen dam that kept Jackson Lake at bay. They drove over a bridge that spanned the outflow of the lake, the Snake River. The view from the bridge was spectacular. Ray was learning the view was always spectacular. Then they entered the trees.

Occasionally, they caught a view of the lake. But mostly it was trees for several miles. Lauren indicated the Signal Mountain Road turnoff. It led deeper into the trees.

When they finally emerged into another meadow of sagebrush, it was on fire. The sun was a ball of orange just above the mountains, which were bathed in its glow. Tendrils of clouds reflected an untold number of colors. And the Tetons loomed straight ahead, growing closer by the second.

Lauren leaned over and punched on the radio. She looked up, her hand on the dial. "You mind?"

"Only if you listen to lousy music."

"I don't."

He nodded.

She scanned the dial for a few minutes. The mountains grew. The sun sank. She left the radio on a country station and thumbed through Ray's CDs. She selected an old NEEDTOBREATHE album. *The Reckoning.* She slipped it in and rolled her window down.

The mountains grew larger. The sun disappeared behind them. The road turned, more southward, then a little east of south. The band sang "Drive All Night," and it was an appealing sentiment. Lauren put on her jacket. And asked, "How long have you lived in Sioux Falls?"

"Since I left the Army."

"You served?"

"Four years."

"Thank you."

He nodded.

"Where before the Army?"

"Huron."

"I'm sorry, did you just say Urine?"

"H-U-R-O-N."

"You didn't say H-U-R-O-N."

"The H is silent."

"Not sure whose idea that was, but it wasn't a good one."

He smiled.

"What's in H-uron?"

"Dad runs a hardware store. We moved there when I was ten."

"Where from?"

"Reliance."

"South Dakota?"

He nodded.

"Sounds like a town on a Western."

"About the size of it, too. Dad ran a third-generation family farm outside of town but got sick of the hours, vagary of the seasons."

"Why'd you join the Army?"

He looked at her, at her brown hair blown by the wind through the window. At her inquisitive eyes. They were getting hard to see in the dusk.

"Three reasons I typically hear," she said. "Love of country-slash-patriotism. Free college. And some variation of needing to get my act together."

"A little of the first, a lot of the second, and in retrospect a little of the third too."

"Did you go overseas?"

"Afghanistan."

She said nothing.

"How about you? What made you become a park ranger?"

"I love the outdoors. I love being out in God's wide-open wilderness, seeing all that He made. I like animals, but not in the I-want-to-cuddle-kittens-and-baby-giraffes sort of way. I want to see bison butting heads across a field of sagebrush or watch two elk tangle in a meadow."

"Speaking of, any elk left in this park?"

"Just keep your eyes on the road. Had a tourist from Tennessee last week who plowed into a cow at fifty-five. It wasn't pretty, for the elk or the driver."

"Noted."

"And I like helping people. That's part of my job, at least some days."

"That's admirable."

She shrugged.

They were to the checkpoint just west of the Craig Thomas Discovery and Visitor Center parking lot. When they arrived, she pointed out her car, a tan Ford Focus hatchback sitting by itself in the corner. "You still up for coffee?" she asked as Ray parked behind her car. She unbuckled her seatbelt and looked at him, letting the belt slide slowly back toward the door.

"I am."

"You familiar with Jackson Hole Coffee Roasters, just west of the Square?"

"Intimately."

She narrowed one eye.

"I visited them twice this morning."

"You want to go elsewhere?"

"It's good coffee," he said.

"The best in town."

"Works for me. I'll get the postcards and meet you there."

"I'll get us a table."

She got out, and Ray waited until she had unlocked her car. Then he drove off.

The sun had set, at least behind the mountains, but the distant ridgeline to the east was still colored a pinkish orange. Ray turned south on 191, NEEDTOBREATHE still singing on his radio.

He thought about the last twenty-four hours. His arrival, the postcards, Heidi in the bar, searching Graham's place, Detective Celek, running around looking for triangles, and then Lauren. He didn't know what to make of much of any of it.

Ray was back in Jackson in fifteen minutes, to his hotel in twenty. He dug the ceramic moose out of his pocket to let himself in. As soon as he saw his bed, he was suddenly tired. But he didn't dawdle. He found the postcards, stuffed them back in the envelope, placed it in his back pocket, and set out again.

He walked the two or three blocks and found Lauren waiting at a table by the window. Her jacket was over the back of her chair. Two mugs of steaming coffee sat on the table. Her hands cradled one of them.

"I took the liberty," she said.

"Let me guess, you could tell by my posture that I take it black."

"And because you ordered black at the lodge."

"That too."

"And if you wanted something else, I'm good for two cups."

He took the envelope from his pocket and dropped it on the table. Then he sat down.

"May I?" Lauren asked.

He nodded. She opened it. He sipped his coffee. Good as the morning's brew.

She sorted through the postcards, first looking at the images on the front. Studying, as if searching for people on the sidewalks around the antler arch or for an elk against the tree line in front of Signal Mountain. She read off a majority of the places listed on the cartoonish map. "The Square, Snow King Resort, the two buttes, the Elk Refuge, Teton Village, the Snake River, Jenny Lake, various peaks, Signal Mountain, Jackson Lake, a couple overlooks."

Ray drank coffee.

She flipped the postcard over and read the six lines on the back. Twice. Then paused for a drink from her mug. She set it down but held it in her hand, three fingers through the handle, one beneath it, thumb around the other side. With her other hand, she tapped the postcard on the table. Thinking.

Then she turned it over.

"Got something?"

"'*Find the triangles*,'" she said.

"Yeah?"

"Maybe . . ."

She took another drink of coffee. Set the mug down and let go. Then put the postcard down, face up, facing Ray. She looked at him. "There are, what, a dozen or so places featured on here?"

He nodded. More were labeled, but a dozen were indicated by cartoon images of an antler arch, a skier, a bugling elk, and so forth.

"Common geometry, you have three points, you can connect them to make a triangle."

He nodded again.

"'*Find the triangles*.'"

"But which ones? Which points do you connect?"

She sighed. "The other four postcards aren't all identified on here, but some are."

"The antler arch and Signal Mountain."

"And none of the places written on the back are."

Ray shook his head.

"It was a thought."

"A good one."

She sighed again and sat back. "How long are you in town for?"

He raised an eyebrow. "Somewhere between an early breakfast and the weekend."

Her eyebrow called his raise.

"Truth is, I don't know what to do. Graham and I weren't best friends, but the plan was to spend the week with him. I feel kind of dumb vacationing by myself for a week, especially since something has clearly happened to him. But, part of me also wants to stay and try to get to the bottom of things. Assuming there's a way to do so. I don't know. I've already paid for the hotel through the week, and nothing's waiting for me back in Sioux Falls. I guess I'll poke around a few more places tomorrow, take it day by day."

Lauren waited a few seconds. "I don't work tomorrow."

He looked at her.

"All week in fact."

"You have off all week?"

"I typically take a week of vacation around this time of year to enjoy the park on my own schedule and own pace. Sometimes Dad comes out here with me, or I go see him. But this week, I have nothing on the agenda."

Ray said nothing.

"So if you want a sidekick, a second pair of eyes, or just somebody to talk to . . ."

Ray said nothing.

Lauren squirmed in her seat but said nothing.

They each took a drink of coffee.

"Why?" he finally asked.

"Why?"

"You said this afternoon you had the evening off, liked helping people, were intrigued by the postcards."

"I did, I do, and I am."

He nodded. "But now you're willing to give up your vacation to help me?" He shook his head. "That doesn't make sense."

"Doesn't it?"

"No." He leaned forward. "Forgive the bluntness, Lauren, but what's your angle?"

She too leaned forward. "No angle, Ray. I'm a thirty-one-year-old single woman with no family in the same time zone, no boyfriend, no true soulmate girlfriends, and I see more four-legged creatures than two-legged ones on the average workday. Now I have a week of free time because I had to use it or lose it by the end of October, and as much as I love traipsing around the park, I quite frankly get tired of doing so by myself."

She leaned a few inches farther forward. "So when I heard your story, I thought to myself, Lauren, see if you can help the guy. If nothing else, it'll kill an evening. Turns out, you're not bad company, you've already admitted you're not a serial killer, and I am still intrigued and still like helping people."

"You forgot my kind eyes."

"I didn't forget." She smiled. "So that's my angle, so to speak. Take it or leave it."

Ray took a swallow of coffee. He sat back. She didn't.

"Okay," he finally said. "I'll buy that."

"Buy it?"

"That you don't have an angle. That you're authentic."

"I try to be. But it does rub some people the wrong way."

He thought there might be more to that comment, but he didn't pursue it.

"I appreciate authenticity," he said. "More people could stand to be a little more authentic."

There was more to that comment too, but she didn't pursue it.

Ray looked down at his nearly empty mug. Nodded at hers. "Buy you another round? The evening's only half dead."

Lauren's dimples reemerged, and she extended her mug to Ray.

^   ^   ^

Ray and Lauren closed down the coffee shop. They talked about childhoods, respective lives in South Dakota and Idaho then Wyoming. About the Army, losing a mother, and the quirks of extended families. It was deep conversation for people who had met that afternoon, but maybe not given their mutual appreciation for authenticity.

Annabelle did not come up.

At nine, they parted ways with plans to meet up the following morning and check out some of the other locations specified on the postcards. Ray walked back to the hotel, breathing in the crisp, cool, evening air. Jackson was quiet after dark, off season, with most of the shops and stores closed. Better than shoulder-to-shoulder pedestrians and bumper-to-bumper traffic.

Ray locked himself in his room and immediately set about unhooking the key from the ceramic moose keychain. It had been digging into his leg all day, especially when he sat, and he wasn't going through that again tomorrow. Then he called his sister and apologized when he remembered she was a time zone east of him, and thus it was twenty after ten, not twenty after nine.

The kids were in bed and her husband, Jason, was buried in a book, so Cathy didn't mind. She asked how his trip was going, and he told her about Graham. She was stunned and listened quietly as he explained the basic details.

"So what are you going to do?" she asked when he was finished. "Are you staying in Jackson?"

"For now. I met a lady park ranger, and she and—"

"A lady park ranger?"

"Is that politically incorrect? A lady who is a park ranger?"

79

"How did you meet a lady who is a park ranger?"

"By chance."

Cathy was quiet.

"She'd met Graham once, and was intrigued. She and I are checking out a few of the places on the postcards."

Cathy was still quiet.

"It's late," Ray said. "I should let you go."

"What are you doing, Ray?"

"What?"

"Playing detective with some woman you just met this afternoon?"

"I have to do something."

"Ray, I know it's been hard on you these last few weeks—"

"Cathy—"

"But this isn't like you."

"Isn't it?"

"No. You don't even talk to your mailman."

"Nobody talks to their mailman. Nobody who has a job anyhow."

"I mean on Saturdays."

He frowned. Cathy made less sense after nine or ten at night. He'd forgotten that when he called.

"I'm not following you," he said.

"Are you trying to fill a void with some sort of adventure or accomplishment or a pretty face?"

"I never said she was pretty."

"Is she?"

"Yes, she's pretty."

"See."

"There's nothing to 'see,' Cathy. We went to look at Jackson Lake Lodge, one of the places on the postcards. We grabbed dinner, then had coffee and brainstormed."

"Dinner and coffee?"

"It was dinnertime. And you know how I drink coffee."

"Somebody's getting defensive."

"A natural reaction to somebody getting offensive."

"Ray, I'm just looking out for you."

"I know, Cathy. But there's nothing to look out for."

She sighed.

"I'll call you tomorrow, update you."

"Be careful, Ray."

"Good night, Cathy."

He tossed the phone on his bed and sat back. He frowned. He didn't think he was trying to fill a void. What he was trying to do was find Graham. Figure out how to spend the rest of his week. Lauren was helping with the former and possibly the latter. That was all.

He got up to brush his teeth and get ready for bed. Cathy read too many novels and watched too many made-for-TV movies. Strangers falling in love, kissing on horseback, that kind of nonsense. And that's probably where she got the idea that he was trying to fill a void. Novels and made-for-TV movies were filled with pop psychology mumbo-jumbo and filling voids.

Besides, his void was unfillable.

TEN

Lauren knocked on Ray's door at precisely eight-thirty Monday morning. She wore the same athletic shoes as yesterday, similar if not the same blue jeans, and a teal, purple, and white checked shirt over a white T-shirt and under an unzipped dark brown leather jacket. Her hair was down, past the shoulders, a little wave. Her silver aviator sunglasses pushed it back like a headband. She held two to-go cups of coffee, large, each wreathed in a tan sleeve bearing the words "Jackson Hole Roasters." Steam swirled out of drinking slits in the lids.

She smiled. "Morning."

"Morning," he said, stepping out and closing the door behind him. He took the cup in her right hand, which she had extended toward him. "Thanks."

"You eat?"

"I did."

"Shame. I have donuts in the car."

"I didn't eat that much."

She'd offered to drive since she knew the area. So they walked down to her car, the tan Ford Focus hatchback, parked out front. It was sunny but cool, almost frosty. Autumnal. Ray had left his jacket behind, opting for a zip-up hoodie instead. "Army Strong" was stamped on the front in bold letters. The sweatshirt was a decade old.

"I've been thinking," Lauren said as she backed away from the curb.

"Yeah?"

"Before we head for Signal Mountain, we should swing by the Rodeo grounds."

"Okay."

"Look for triangles."

"Makes as much sense as anything."

She shoved the gearshift into drive, and off they went. Lauren made a hard right at the first intersection, Willow. Ahead of them, Snow King Mountain loomed large against a blue sky. Swaths of grass—ski runs—carved through a carpet of pine trees. No snow yet.

"You mentioned donuts," Ray said.

Lauren smirked and turned in her seat, reaching back with one hand. Her other kept the wheel nearly straight.

"I can grab them."

"I . . . got it," she said, lurching back forward with a small paper sack. She course-corrected as she sat up and handed the sack to Ray. "Take your pick."

"Thanks."

"Brain fuel."

He selected a chocolate-covered long john and extended the open sack to her. She'd picked up her coffee, which she set between her legs, and reached in for the remaining donut, a glazer.

"I called Detective Celek this morning," Ray said after taking a bite of his donut.

"Yeah?" Lauren said. She looked his way and smiled.

"What?"

She reached out the hand with the donut, extending just one finger, to wipe a smudge of chocolate from the corner of his mouth. Something of a forward gesture. One might say, authentic. Ray took a drink.

"And?"

"I mentioned yesterday they were going to check out the van again, from Jackson Hole Cleaners."

She nodded.

"Nothing. No prints. No DNA. No clues."

"You're sure he was taken by it?"

"That's the theory. Pretty odd for that van to show up at the Bar H-9, idle for half a minute in the parking lot, then leave, and at the same time that Graham disappeared from the security camera."

"I suppose." She took a bite. Then set the donut on her leg and took a swig of coffee. "They could have vacuumed it out. I mean, they'd have had the equipment."

He nodded.

Lauren turned west on Snow King Avenue. They drove through several blocks of residential neighborhoods and then came upon the Teton County

Fairgrounds. Three decks of bleachers faced an open dirt area. Beyond it was a large, single story structure. A barn or stalls. Then came the grandstands and livestock pens encircling a dirt oval. Then a large, red barn. More stalls. Lauren drove almost to the end of the block before coming to a break in the curb and a wood fence that separated the sidewalk from a mostly dirt parking lot. It was nearly empty, just a few pickups and horse-trailers, one SUV, one old beater of a car. She parked close to the barn, and they sat there, finishing their donuts.

"Can a park ranger get us access to the fairgrounds?" Ray asked, reaching for his coffee.

"I'm not a park ranger today."

"What are you?"

"Whatever it takes to get us access to the fairgrounds."

They got out of the car, both holding their coffees. Ray thought they looked like tourists. That or very casual cops.

"I see squares," she said as they approached an open doorway. It was big enough for horses to enter. Big enough for a truck, actually. It was square-shaped. "Rectangles," she added, nodding at windows high in the walls.

Ray nodded.

They entered through the square doorway and had to adjust their eyes to the relative darkness. The floor was dirt, groomed, mostly cordoned off by metal fencing to form a riding area. That was evident because a single rider trotted a brown horse around the perimeter. Ray was not a horseman and didn't know one breed from the other. The building smelled, although not bad. Just like hay and dirt and a little bit of livestock. A green tractor with a bucket was parked off to one side, beyond the fencing. There was a Coke machine, a few stacks of rubber containers, some miscellaneous items Ray couldn't identify from a distance. Mostly it was just open dirt, maybe two hundred feet by one hundred. A nice area to work a horse. A lousy area to spot triangles.

The horse and rider made the far turn and came their way. They slowed and stopped in front of Ray and Lauren. The horse snorted. "Hi there," the rider said. He was a male, maybe a little younger than Ray, thin as a rail. He wore jeans and chaps, a plain T-shirt, and a Colorado Rockies baseball cap. Cowboy boots, of course. "You folks looking for something?"

"Just looking," Ray said. It was the standard brushoff he gave to eager sales associates at Hy-Vee, but realized it sounded pretty stupid in this environment. So did the guy. He frowned.

"That's a beautiful horse," Lauren said, leaning her arms on the railing.

"This is Maisy. I'm Coop."

"Ray and Lauren," she said.

Coop nodded.

"She yours?" Lauren asked

"Yes, ma'am."

"You keep her here?"

His eyes narrowed maybe a fraction. "I do."

"Do you happen to know if any of the Garners keep a horse here?" she asked.

Ray looked at her. She looked at him. Coop looked at both of them and shifted in his saddle. "The Garners?"

"Specifically Woodrow Garner?"

"Um . . . yeah, they've got a permanent stall here. Not far from mine."

"Can we see it?"

Now his eyes narrowed for sure. "Who are you folks?"

"Would you believe we're undercover cops?" Lauren asked.

"Does Jackson have undercover cops?"

She shrugged. And smiled wide. "I'm just kidding, Coop. Ray's visiting from South Dakota, and his cousin suggested we come here. He also mentioned Woodrow Garner, so we thought maybe he meant to check out his horse. I love horses, Coop."

"Yeah?"

Lauren made several slow head nods.

Ray kept his mouth shut.

Coop shifted in the saddle again. "The stalls are in the building on the far side of the fairgrounds. You can exit through that door. You'll see it."

"Are the stalls marked?"

"Theirs is. A big plaque above it with the horse's name."

"Which is?"

"Isosceles IV."

Lauren glanced at Ray out the corner of her eye, as he did at her.

"Thanks, Coop." She waved just her fingers. "Bye, Maisy."

Coop and Maisy cantered or galloped or trotted off, and Ray and Lauren headed for the exit door Coop had indicated.

"I'm starting to have my doubts about you," Ray said as they exited the barn.

She lowered her shades. "How's that?"

"Your authenticity."

She looked at him.

"'His cousin suggested we come here'?"

"He did," she said. "Sort of."

"'He mentioned Woodrow Garner'?"

"Roundaboutly."

"'We thought he meant his horse'?"

"Okay, so that one was a stretch. But I was right."

"You were. And it was good thinking."

"It was a hunch. Certainly better than 'we're just looking,'" she added with a wink.

The open-air building housing the fairgrounds' permanent horse stalls was about a hundred yards away across open ground. There was a grass field to the left and the pens and chutes and grandstands of the rodeo ground to the right. Beneath them, the ground was hard dirt.

"So what do you think the odds are it's a coincidence that Woodrow Garner keeps a horse here and the horse is named Isosceles?" Lauren asked when they reached the stalls.

"I guess Graham is using the term triangle pretty loosely. Makes me wonder if we should be looking for more than just geometry."

They had no trouble finding the stall Coop had referenced. Isosceles IV was large and black and looked like the type of horse Ray saw every May when he watched the Kentucky Derby. He stood calmly in his ten-by-ten stall, paying no attention to his visitors. He let Lauren stroke his shoulder. He snorted softly. Then he turned and munched on some hay.

"I'm guessing he's what we're supposed to find," Lauren said.

"Yeah."

"Something wrong?"

"Just wondering how Graham knows about Woodrow Garner's horse."

"Maybe he knows Woodrow Garner."

"It'd be surprising if Garner's who you say he is. Graham's a nobody."

"He works at the Bar H-9. Horses there, horses here. Maybe that's the connection."

"Maybe."

She tapped his elbow. "Head for Signal Mountain?"

"Might as well."

Lauren flipped down her sunglasses as they again stepped out into the sunlight. It reminded Ray of how brilliant a morning it was. There was something about mountain air—it was thinner, and maybe that accounted for it. Somehow, it was just fresher. More invigorating. At least when it was sunny.

They took the now familiar U.S. 191 (Lauren didn't bother using all three route numbers, so Ray saw no point in doing so either) north out of Jackson, past the National Elk Refuge, and beyond East Gros Ventre Butte to where the Tetons were again visible. It wasn't as if Ray hadn't seen mountains before, although it had been a long time. But he couldn't take his eyes off them.

"Scenic route?" Lauren asked when they reached the Moose Junction turnoff.

"Why not?"

"It's actually quicker anyhow."

She hung a left, and they set a course straight at the mountains. They crossed the Snake River, passed the visitor center, and continued on the Teton Park Road. They retraced the path they had taken back to town the previous night, past the Jenny Lake Visitor Center, Ranger Station, and Store. Lauren announced there was some pretty good hiking around Jenny Lake, in a way that suggested they should maybe go for a hike. Ray nodded in a way that agreed on the maybe part.

"You think there's a chance the Garners are connected to all these locations?" Ray asked as they entered the trees, sorely limiting the views.

"How?" Lauren asked.

"I don't know. But we've got a rodeo connection through their horse, we've got the obvious connection if '*Woody's ranch*' means Woodrow Garner's ranch—"

"Seems like a fair bet."

"And Betsy Garner, whoever she is, is clearly connected. That's three of nine."

"Okay, but how are they connected to a mountain or Jackson Lake Lodge or one of the antler arches around the Square?"

Ray shrugged. "You said Woodrow has his hands in a lot of Jackson area businesses. Any chance that includes the Lodge?"

"It's on government property, managed by the Park Service."

"What about food vendors, merchandise, IT contracts? Maybe they own a cottage there."

"Maybe. But to what end?" She looked at him. "I mean, why did Graham send you a list of places they are somehow connected to?"

"I don't know."

Lauren slowed, signaled, and turned onto a narrow, albeit smoothly paved, two-lane road. It was tightly bordered on both sides by hundreds of tall, thin pine trees.

"Could he have suspected the Garner family or Woodrow was after him in some way?"

"After him?"

"He was in a hurry, sent a cryptic message, then disappeared." He shrugged. "Seems to suggest paranoia that was legitimate."

"And you're asking me?"

"You know them better than I do."

"I don't know them," Lauren said. "I've heard a few things."

"Still more than I know," Ray said, resting his elbow on the doorframe.

The road meandered but didn't climb. Lauren had hooked up an MP3 player, saying radio reception in the park was spotty. Her selection of music wasn't lousy either, running the spectrum from '80s rock to Lauren Daigle.

"There's a view from the top of this?" Ray asked as they continued to drive through solid forest, ascending slightly. The speed limit was 20, and Lauren wasn't speeding.

"Just you wait."

They curved a few times and caught brief glimpses through the trees of Jackson Lake.

"When was the last time you saw Graham?"

Ray exhaled, thinking. "Would have been late summer before last. No, the summer before that. Big family reunion."

"He lived here a long time?

"Mmm, four or five years. He's a drifter."

"We collect quite a few of them around here. A lot of them stop drifting."

"I can imagine."

After a few more minutes, Ray began to see thinning in the trees. They rounded a snug hairpin turn with a few parking spots and a trailhead, and Lauren announced it was the Jackson Lake Overlook. Then she said, "Close your eyes."

"What?"

"Just close 'em."

With a shake of his head, Ray did.

"You don't get carsick, do you?"

"We'll see."

He could almost hear the dimples.

"Yeah, well, the view is a lot better at the top if you don't spoil it first."

"You're the tour guide."

It was only a couple of minutes—and another hairpin turn—before Lauren told him to open his eyes. He did as she parked in another small lot. This one had a pit toilet and another trailhead. They got out and started toward the trailhead. It climbed a small rise above the parking lot and led to a paved overlook bounded by a simple wood fence. The view was unrestricted for one hundred eighty degrees, revealing a panorama of the entire valley.

Ray leaned on the fence and marveled. To his left, rolling hills and distant mountains rose and fell in unending ridgelines. Panning to his right, he saw the Snake River cutting through a dense forest and then a wide meadow of sage. Here and there, a few trees poked up from the otherwise carpet-like field, similar to one that blanketed the mountainside beneath Ray, with sage and wildflowers running from the valley floor to just feet from where Ray stood. The far side of Jackson Hole was rimmed with a ribbon of white, topping the distant mountains. The town of Jackson was hidden by Blacktail Butte, way off in the distance beyond another wide-open meadow. Turning a little more to his right, Ray saw the Teton Range rise slowly from the horizon until the promontory of Grand Teton, so close it almost seemed as if Ray could reach out and touch it.

"Told you," Lauren said from beside him after several minutes.

"Yeah."

She tucked a loose strand of hair behind her ear. "Kind of makes you never want to go down."

"Kind of."

Ray took in the view for a few more minutes, not thinking at all about Graham. Then he turned around and leaned on the fence. He turned to Lauren, whose eyes still roved over the valley. "They should cut down a few of these trees," he said. "Make it a three-sixty."

"I'll make sure to mention that," she said with a soft laugh. "You know how the Park Service loves chopping down trees."

"Plant a few in eastern Wyoming to atone."

She gave him a playful glare before returning her eyes to the panorama.

"That or bring a drone up here," Ray said. "What a view that would be."

Lauren said nothing, a faraway look in her eyes.

"I say something?"

"No. It's nothing." She sighed. "My ex had a drone. Obsessed with the thing."

"Ex? You were married?"

She laughed. "Not even close."

Ray let it pass. Let a few minutes pass. "I don't see any triangles," he said. "Unless we're counting mountains."

"No."

"Maybe a 'Woody Garner was here' Xed into the fence? That's about what we're down to."

"Wanna check out the Jackson Lake Overlook?"

"Let's do it."

They trekked back to the car, which Lauren put in second gear to coast down to the lower parking lot. She did not make Ray close his eyes, and he looked out her window at the view as they descended. He did not get the heebie-jeebies, but the road was barely wide enough for two vehicles. With no guardrail, there was nothing to slow a vehicle from plummeting through the sagebrush down to the valley below. He didn't get the heebie-jeebies, but he would have preferred Lauren keep two hands on the wheel.

From the lower parking lot, another narrow, paved trail led through a small strand of trees and along the edge of the slope. It offered more of the spectacular views of the valley to the left. Although it was a short walk, Ray felt the strain from the altitude, roughly 7,500 feet. At the end of the pavement, a plaque labeled the various peaks visible in the distance. Ray memorized a few names and followed Lauren. She had shed the jacket before getting out at the previous lookout, and her teal, purple, and white checked shirt complemented the various shades of green and blue in the trees, mountains, and sky.

The path was now gravel, interspersed with brush and wildflowers. Lauren stopped suddenly, and Ray nearly bumped into her. The vista was breathtaking. Grand Teton, Mount Saint John, Mount Moran, Eagle Rest Peak, with blue sky above and beyond and the turquoise waters of Jackson Lake—rimmed by unending pine forest—in the foreground. But that wasn't what had caught Lauren's eye.

Instead, she was looking down and off to the side. When Ray drew even, she pointed.

Twenty feet off the path, angled almost in line with the ridge, was what resembled a giant, crude arrowhead. It was a rock, maybe six feet from one point to the next, rounded slightly on top so that it rose a couple feet above the surrounding terrain. From a distance, it gave no indication of being manmade, yet its three points were unmistakable. A natural triangle atop Signal Mountain.

Lauren turned to Ray, ignoring hair dragged across her cheek by the breeze.

"Ray. This is starting to get interesting."

ELEVEN

"Well," Lauren said, "I think Woody Garner's off the hook on this one."

They were halfway down Signal Mountain, and neither had spoken since getting into the car.

"That rock's been there since Noah," she added.

Ray said nothing.

They had wandered off the path and checked, in case Woodrow Garner had chiseled his initials inside a triangle on the side of the massive rock. He hadn't. There were no chisel marks, nothing to indicate anyone had helped shape the granite. Centuries of rain and wind and erosion had smoothed out the corners, but Ray guessed only marginally. It took a while for wind and rain to alter the shape of granite.

"I can't believe I missed it," she said. "I've been up here how many times and never saw it."

"I'm sure you saw it," Ray said. "You just weren't thinking about triangles, so it wasn't relevant."

She bobbed her head in concession. Ray contemplated the places he and they had visited. Teton Science Schools. The Jackson Town Square. The Fairgrounds. Jackson Lake Lodge. Now Signal Mountain. Why had Graham sent them on a wild goose chase, and how was their chasing ever going to uncover what had happened to him?

"You want to visit Oxbow Bend?" Lauren asked as they neared the bottom of the road.

"Are we close?"

"A few miles. Back toward the Lodge."

"Might as well."

She turned north on Teton Park Road, back across the dam with the views of Jackson Lake, then east toward Moran. "There's Oxbow Bend," she said, pointing to a paved turnout overlooking the Snake River. "Which means '*east of Oxbow*' is the next turnout."

It was only a quarter of a mile, and they sat in the car and looked through the windshield. The tree-covered Signal Mountain blocked the three Tetons, but not Mount Moran. It rose prominently over the surrounding peaks. Perfectly triangular. It could have been viewed similarly from almost an infinite number of locations in the park. So why this one?

Ray sighed.

"What do you say we take a break?" Lauren asked.

"A break?"

"From chasing triangles. It's starting to wear on you."

"And do what instead?"

She shrugged. "See the park. It's a beautiful fall day for a hike."

He sighed again. "I feel bad, what with Graham missing."

Lauren said nothing.

"Something's happened to him, and we're long past the 'forty-eight hours' they say you have to find a clue."

"Who says that?"

"Every TV cop ever."

"Uh-huh."

They were silent.

"I don't know," Ray said. "This feels more like a hobby, anyhow. I don't know how finding these triangles will bring Graham back. If anybody can find him, it should be Detective Celek."

"You talking yourself into something?"

"Weren't you?"

"I was pitching an idea," she said. "I think letting this rest, getting some exercise, might help you think more clearly."

"Yeah?"

"Yeah. Don't you ever get confused staring at data and then come back with a fresh perspective?"

"No. I usually stare until my eyes burn and then I see it."

"Good way to go blind."

"Hmm, maybe."

"And you're right, Detective Celek is the pro. If . . ."

He turned her way. "If what?"

"I maybe shouldn't say it."

"That usually stop you?"

Lauren's eyebrows shot up, but then she grinned, planting her tongue in her jaw. "I was going to say, if Graham was really taken."

"The video evidence was pretty solid."

"The video evidence, as you described it, showed him disappearing behind a van. From what you've said, and from an admittedly very short sample at Metro, I get the impression that Graham is kind of . . . how do I—"

"A flake."

She nodded and repeated him. "Any chance he just left?"

"In a Jackson Hole Cleaners van?"

She shrugged. "What was he driving?"

Ray stopped. "I never thought of that. His car should still be there."

"Or he got a lift from someone."

"I should check that out."

"I'm sure Celek will."

"I suppose so. Probably already has."

"Either way, my question still stands. Any chance he 'flaked' and left, by any means of travel?"

"In the middle of his shift at the Bar H-9?"

She shrugged again.

"Without telling anyone?"

She shrugged a third time.

Ray sighed. "It's possible. He might have . . . He might have thought he found some Native American treasure and the triangles were clues on a map or else solved the riddle of where some pioneer was buried or—"

"You watch too much TV, I think."

"Yes, it's possible. Anything's possible at this point."

She put her hand on the gearshift, sliding it to reverse. "What do you want to do?"

He looked at the clock. Closing in on noon. "Get something to eat."

"Check. And then?"

"In theory, where would you hike?"

"In theory?"

He nodded.

"Jenny Lake. Great views, a waterfall or two, maybe some wildlife."

Ray thought of his knee, the one he'd hurt playing high school football. It hadn't bothered him since getting to town. He nodded again. "Lead on, Macduff."

She grinned as she backed up, then put the car in drive. "You know that's a misattribution, don't you?"

"I do now."

"'Lay on, Macduff.' It's from *Macbeth*."

Ray raised his eyebrows.

"What, didn't take me for a Shakespearean?"

"I'm just waiting for you to give me the act and scene."

She grinned again.

They drove a couple miles, leaving Highway 191 and journeying west on Teton Park Road.

"Act 5, Scene 8."

Ray looked at her.

She kept her eyes straight ahead.

"Act 5, Scene 8?"

Lauren nodded.

"I don't suppose you can quote it for me."

"Not verbatim."

"Who knew?"

It took about twenty minutes to arrive at the Jenny Lake Store, which shared a parking lot with the visitor center. The store was just what one would expect a western national park general store to be—log siding, porch facing the mountains, an assortment of snacks and drinks, souvenirs, and clothes for sale inside. Ray and Lauren bought a snack lunch of jerky, some fruit in cups, granola bars, and bottled water. Then they set out for the Jenny Lake Ferry Dock.

The trail around the lake was seven miles long. There was also a ferry across the lake that allowed hikers to walk approximately halfway around the lake and take the ferry back. Or vice versa. Neither Ray nor Lauren was up for a seven-mile hike, so they opted for the ferry. Since they had snacks to eat, they bought tickets and rode across the lake while eating.

The boat was small, single story, with open-air seating. It was mostly full, and Ray and Lauren sat near the back. The views were spectacular, as Grand Teton seemed to rise up out of the western edge of the lake. The breeze was cool, but abundant sunshine offset it. Ray figured it was five to ten degrees warmer than the day before, a result of the sun being out all day.

"Well, this is embarrassing," Lauren said as they disembarked on the western shore. They had discussed hiking up to see Hidden Falls or Inspiration Point, but opted instead to head back around the southern shore of the lake.

"What is?"

"I forgot bear spray."

"And you a National Park Service employee."

"I usually carry it with me. Part of the uniform."

"Are we going to need it?"

"Probably not. The trail's pretty active, even this time of year. And bears prefer early morning or late evening. We'll talk and walk. The noise will keep them away."

"Okay."

"And better ditch the food," she said, nodding at the bag of jerky in Ray's hand.

He tipped it toward her, and she took a piece. He then dug around for a few crumbs, ate them, and dumped the bag in the bear-safe trashcan. "Can they smell this on our breath?"

"We'll see."

The hike was not strenuous, and the views not as spectacular since the mountains were behind them and, in many cases, too close or blocked by trees. But it was still more scenic than Ray's neighborhood in Sioux Falls, that was for sure.

"So who is she?" Lauren asked a few hundred yards into their hike.

Ray slowed. "Who is who?"

"I don't know. But you have this . . . sadness hanging over you. No, sort of emanating from within you. Girl sadness."

"Hmm."

"It's your business, and if you don't want to talk about it, you don't have to. But I'm—"

"Authentic," he said.

"Yeah."

He trudged a few steps. "Her name is Annabelle."

"That's pretty."

"Yeah. We were engaged."

Lauren didn't ask, "What happened?" She just stepped over a rut, cracking a dry stick beneath her foot, and waited for him to answer the question anyhow.

"Three weeks ago—to the day, in fact, on Labor Day—she broke it off."

"I'm sorry."

"We went on this walk, down by Falls Park. Killing time before a barbecue with some friends. She said we needed to talk, and I figured it was about wedding details or how we were going to merge closet space or something. She said she couldn't marry me, that God told her 'This isn't My plan for you.' Then she quoted Jeremiah about plans to prosper her and whatnot. Then she took my hand, kissed my cheek, said she was sorry, and turned and walked away. I haven't seen her since."

They had stopped, facing each other across the trail. Lauren said nothing, verbally. Her eyes were misty, narrowed.

"At first, I thought maybe she'd change her mind. But she made it pretty clear this wasn't a whim, wasn't cold feet. God had told her not to marry me." Ray huffed out a laugh. "Funny, He didn't think to tell her that before she said yes, before we made plans, told all our family and friends."

Another couple appeared on the trail, and Ray and Lauren stood back to let them pass. When they were around the bend, Ray nodded after them, and they started walking again.

"I had a couple grand earmarked for a honeymoon, a week's vacation suddenly available, and a cousin who'd been begging me to come out to Wyoming and see him. I figured, why not? Sitting around my house alone every night wasn't going to get me anywhere. So here I am."

Lauren trudged beside him, looking down. Then she touched his arm. "Thanks for telling me."

He shrugged.

They walked some more.

"It's the weirdest thing," he said.

"What's that?"

"Some days, I can't tell if I'm sad because I still love her so much or mad because I hate her so much."

"I don't think that's weird at all. I think that's normal."

"Maybe. More than anything, I feel like I've been in a fog for three weeks. I don't know if I just haven't processed it yet, or if this is the new normal—life without Annabelle. I know I have to move on—it's what everybody tells me. But . . ." He sighed. "I had buddies in the service who lost arms and legs. They had to move on too, and they did." He shook his head. "But they were never the same. I wonder if that's going to be me, going through life maimed."

Lauren said nothing.

"Sorry you asked?"

She met his look. "No."

"Thing is," he said after a few steps, "it almost feels like the fog has lifted a little."

Lauren looked at him.

"I don't know if it's a change of scenery, change of routine, Graham and all that's on my mind with him." He looked at her. "Having some company, for a change."

She said nothing.

"Or maybe time is healing wounds after all."

They kept walking.

"So, this may sound a little trite," Lauren said. "Kind of like when Joe Pesci told Mel Gibson about his frog that had died."

Ray frowned.

"A couple of months ago, I broke up with my boyfriend. The drone guy. Turned out he and I had different ideas about some important things, like the sanctity of marriage. We weren't engaged, weren't even close, like I said, but I had thought maybe there was some promise—at first, before I realized we weren't in harmony on the stuff that really mattered. Anyhow, we'd been together for a few months, and . . . it hurt. And I was in a fog for a little while. But it did get better. It keeps getting better."

She ducked behind him for a few paces while the trail narrowed. Then she pulled even with him and said, "Now I know dumping a handsy boyfriend isn't the same thing as having your fiancée break off an engagement. But the principle's the same, I think, on a lesser scale. Or to put it another way, as Winston Churchill said, 'When you're going through heck, keep going.'"

Ray said nothing.

"He didn't say heck, but I don't believe in talking lightly about hell. Another topic for another day." She looked up at him, one eye squinting.

"I don't know what to make of you, Lauren. First Shakespeare, then *Lethal Weapon*, now Churchill?"

She shrugged.

"But thank you. I know you're right. It's just that when you're in . . . heck, sometimes 'keep going' seems almost impossible."

"I know."

They kept walking.

"My chance to pry a little?" he said.

"Fair enough."

"Did God tell you to dump your boyfriend?"

Lauren tilted her head. Wrinkled her nose. Squinted one eye again. "I guess you could say that."

Ray nodded. "Must be a woman thing."

"What's that?"

"When a guy breaks up with a girl—that is, if he has the courage to tell her and not just stop returning texts or calls—he shoots straight with her. When a girl breaks up with a guy, she passes the buck to God."

"I didn't pass the buck. I looked him straight in the eye and told him it wasn't going to work between us."

"Because God told you so."

"Because God very clearly outlined certain standards regarding sex and marriage and restricting certain behavior."

"You're talking about Bible verses."

"I am."

"But did He tell you to dump your boyfriend, specifically?"

"Not in an audible voice, if that's what you mean."

He nodded.

"Did He tell Annabelle, specifically?"

"I don't know about the audible part, but she was pretty clear God told her to break off the engagement."

"How did she know?"

Ray stopped.

So did Lauren.

"How did she know it was God telling her that?"

"Because she was 'in tune' with God." He looked at Lauren. "Her words. Her dad's, actually."

"I see."

"Annabelle often said 'God told me' this or that. I just took it as Christianese. You know, people are always feeling God's call and sensing His direction. They never just take jobs or make choices."

Lauren said nothing.

"I don't know. I just never had that happen to me."

They kept walking, heading almost due south, if Ray's read on the angle of the sun was right. The afternoon was silent, just the occasional whisper of wind through the grass or trees, the soft clapping of water against the shoreline, a bird or an insect. That and their footsteps thudding on the dirt, crunching on pebbles, snapping small twigs. It made Ray think of bears, and Lauren's lack of bear spray, and her suggestion that they talk and walk.

"Does God speak to you?" he asked.

She looked his way. "Every single day."

He nodded.

"Well, not every single day. Most days."

"Most days?"

"Yeah."

"Audibly?"

"When I read out loud."

He looked at her.

"The Bible. I read it most days. Some days I slack. And I usually don't read out loud."

Ray said nothing.

"That's not what you meant, is it?"

"No."

"Then the answer is no. I've never heard the voice of God. I've never heard the '*still small voice.*' But I don't know that I should expect to, either. God never promised to speak directly to people. Even in Bible times, it seems that it was incredibly rare. But we have something they didn't, His Word. If you want God to speak to you, Ray, read your Bible."

He said nothing.

"I don't know Annabelle or her father, so I can't speak for them. I wouldn't even if I did. But I've heard other people who claimed God spoke to them, in an audible voice or as they 'were silent before Him,' and I've always wondered, how do they know it's God?"

He said nothing.

"I knew I was doing the right thing breaking up with Jesse because he didn't share biblical standards on purity. It was right there in black and white. Did God tell me to dump him? I'd argue you that yes He did, through His Word."

"So when Annabelle said that God said, 'This isn't My plan for you' . . ."

Lauren shrugged.

"I've been trying to figure this out for three weeks," he said. "Longer than that, actually. Why would God give her specific instructions about marriage, but not give them to me? And why would He tell her we shouldn't get married but not tell me?"

"I don't think He would," she said. "I don't think He did."

Ray stopped.

"Not if it wasn't in Scripture. Not if it wasn't something derived from Scripture, like avoiding sexual immorality or being unequally yoked."

He nodded.

"If she—or if you or if I—can't take 'God's word' back to God's Word and authenticate it, how do we know it was God's word? The answer is, we can't."

He nodded again and started walking.

"Sorry, I didn't mean to preach. But you asked."

"I did, and you're authentic."

"To a fault."

He shook his head. "There's no such thing."

That's when the bull moose stepped out of the trees and onto the trail in front of them.

TWELVE

"It isn't normal, is it?" Ray asked.

"Is what?" Lauren asked. One hand was on the wheel, the other floating out the open window as they cruised through Jackson at twenty-five miles per hour.

"A moose wandering onto the trail in the middle of the day."

"You're still thinking about the moose?"

"Hard not to."

She dipped her chin in concession.

"I thought they were morning and evening creatures, like you said with bears."

"They are."

"So it isn't normal?"

"No, but I wouldn't call it abnormal, either."

The moose had been maybe thirty feet in front of them, plodding slowly, one long, spindly leg after the other. It stopped on the path, turned its head, and stared at them. Only for a few seconds, before continuing across the trail and down to the water's edge. But they had been incredible, terrifying seconds. Moose were huge, standing up to six and a half feet tall, plus the antlers. And this moose had a full set of tan antlers. As big as the ones on the moose mounted in the Jackson Mercantile. Maybe bigger.

Ray and Lauren hadn't moved for several minutes, watching the moose alternate between munching on pondweed and slurping lake water. He was at most a dozen feet off the path, and when he showed no signs of moving, Lauren suggested they backtrack and take the ferry back. Ray didn't object.

They made it back to the dock on the eastern shore a little before two-thirty and, on Lauren's suggestion, they headed into town. They had two objectives. First, a mid-afternoon snack at Moo's Gourmet Ice Cream, right on the Square. Second, a stop at Audrey Garner's shop to pick her brain, if she was in.

"Nice thing about fall," Lauren said as she turned onto Deloney Avenue, "you can find parking." She proved it by pulling into an angled slot two down from the northeast corner, where Ray had sat the previous afternoon and "discovered" the triangles formed by the sidewalks. It was also in view of the bronze moose and other animals along Center Street. The bronze edition had been somewhat tarnished by seeing the real thing.

They set out for Moo's. On the inside, it looked just like a hundred other ice cream shops. The selection of flavors was almost infinite but limited to twenty-four a day. It was homemade and organic, according to the signs (everything was organic, in Jackson, Ray had concluded) and it was served in a variety of cones and dishes.

"What's a huckleberry anyhow?" Ray asked, noting one of the flavors.

"It's like a blueberry. A little more tart. They're in everything out here."

"I've noticed. Makes me think of Val Kilmer in *Tombstone*."

Lauren shook her head.

"Hey, you're the one who brought up Joe Pesci and frogs earlier."

"You gonna order, or what?"

They left a few minutes later, he with huckleberry ice cream in a waffle cone, her with German chocolate in a dish. They headed west, across the street and along the sidewalk beside the Square.

"How long were you and Annabelle together?" Lauren asked.

He looked at her.

"Unless you don't want to talk about it."

"I don't, but that probably means I should."

"They say it's therapeutic."

Ray licked his ice cream. Tasted like tart blueberry. It wasn't bad. "Thirteen months. Engaged five and a half."

"Thirteen months is a long time."

"Felt like more. Felt like we had been together forever."

"How'd you meet?"

Ray recounted the story as they walked west, then south, toward Snow King in the distance. Lauren listened attentively, looking at him between bites of her ice cream. She didn't "aw" or tear up, which was good. She just listened.

"Jesse and I ran into each other skiing. Literally. When a decent looking guy wipes you out and then offers to buy you cocoa, what are you going to do?"

Ray shook his head.

They turned, past the stagecoach, this time with a cowgirl holding the reins, waiting for passengers.

"You ever been skiing?" she asked.

"No."

"No?"

"Tore up my knee playing high school football."

She lowered her chin but looked him in the eye.

"What?"

"That's not just a line you tell the girls, is it?"

"Want me to limp to prove it?"

"What happened?"

"I was chasing a running back when a lineman came out of nowhere and threw a cut block."

"A what?"

"Dived at my knees."

Lauren winced.

"All my weight kept going upfield, but my knee and lower leg planted into the turf and stopped. Never played another down."

Lauren stepped back and to the side.

"What?"

"You walk fine."

"It healed, and I made a full recovery. But every once in a while it still buckles or gives. So trusting all my weight on it while I speed down a mountain's never been on my agenda."

"Hmm."

"Plus I live in South Dakota. The nearest hill has four presidents carved into it."

They walked slowly, finishing their ice cream by the time they reached the Square's southeast corner. They crossed Center Street, cut between some parked vehicles, and approached a small storefront squeezed between a jewelry store and a shop selling leather goods. A wood sign hung over the entrance. It was engraved with gold lettering, spelling out "Panorama." The two small display windows on either side of the door housed landscape watercolors and oil paintings, sculptures of wildlife, and ceramic and blown-glass bowls and miscellaneous objects. The door was propped open, letting out the strains of soft flute music and the aroma of lavender.

Ray stepped aside and let Lauren enter first. The gallery was dark inside, with track lighting casting paintings and sculptures in a soft glow. Even though it was small, the gallery was open, with minimal items on display. Ray didn't need to see more to know it was out of his class. Glances at a few hand-written price tags confirmed it.

The checkout counter was little more than a small computer desk with a card swipe and a barstool behind it, situated halfway in on the left. A young woman sat half on the barstool. She was maybe thirty, max. She wore a long, festive skirt, flared at the bottom, a peasant blouse with three-quarter sleeves, and what Ray figured were expensive and very trendy wraparound sandals. Lots of beady, woody bracelets and a necklace to match. Her hair was blond, short and styled almost like a man's. A hipster man's, not any of the men Ray knew or hung out with. She wore rectangular-framed glasses, through which she was reading a novel. When Ray and Lauren entered, she looked up, smiled, and offered a soft, "Hi." Then she went back to the novel.

Ray looked at Lauren. She nodded. The young woman was Audrey Garner.

Lauren approached her. "Audrey?"

She looked up.

"It's Lauren Waite. We went to Jackson Hole High together."

"Yeah, I remember you. The basketball star."

"I wasn't a star."

Audrey dog-eared the page of her book and set it down next to a keyboard on her desk. "How are you?"

"I'm doing well. Is it true, that you own this gallery?"

Audrey blushed slightly. "Co-own, but yeah."

"Congratulations."

"Thanks. It's always been a dream of mine. Speaking of, did you go on to veterinary school?"

"No, I went to Boise State as an environmental studies major. I'm a park ranger."

"Here?"

Lauren nodded.

"Oh, wow. That's awesome."

Ray smiled politely and let them chitchat. Audrey wasn't a suspect, they weren't cops, and this wasn't an interrogation room.

"Is this Mr. Park Ranger?" Audrey asked.

"This is Ray. He's visiting from South Dakota."

"Hi, Ray."

"Hello."

"Audrey, we actually have a couple of questions for you, if you don't mind."

She furrowed her brow. "Questions?"

"It's kind of a long story. Do you have a few minutes?"

Audrey gestured at the empty gallery. "I'm made of time."

Lauren briefly explained about Ray's reason for coming, finding Graham missing, and the notes on the postcard. At the mention of Betsy Garner and Woody, Audrey's brow furrowed further. "We have no idea what Graham was referring to," Lauren said, "and we don't mean to imply that the Garner family had anything to do with his disappearance. We're just trying to put the pieces together. Truth be told, I wasn't even sure if you're related to those Garners."

"I am," Audrey said. "Woodrow Garner is my uncle."

"He is?"

She nodded. "He and my dad sort of had a falling out a few years back, so we're not close. Never really were, for that matter."

"What about Betsy Garner?" Ray asked. So far, he'd let Lauren do the talking. It was his cousin and his postcards, but it was her high school acquaintance.

"She was my grandmother. She died in 2005."

"I'm sorry."

Audrey nodded. "It was after she died that dad and Uncle Woody had their falling out. Uncle Woody accused my father of not buying into the family legacy."

Ray said nothing, not wanting to pry.

Lauren was very authentic. "The family legacy?"

"Their version of Manifest Destiny. Uncle Woody seems to think the Garner Family is the next Vanderbilt or Rockefeller or Roosevelt Family. Dad and Uncle Gerald didn't agree. Delusions of grandeur, they called it."

"Why'd he think that?" Lauren asked.

Audrey sighed. "Because the Universe told him so."

Lauren raised an eyebrow.

"I know, it's crazy," Audrey said. "Uncle Woody believes in Fate and Luck and all those things as if they're real entities, not just coincidences or odds. And he believes some cosmic power has ordained him for success."

Lauren looked to Ray, then back to Audrey.

"He believes Jackson Hole is special, that it is a place of high energy, a place where the universe is aligned. He about peed his pants when we had the eclipse a few years ago. He said it was a sign from the Heavens. Capital H."

"Is it true that he's heavily invested in Jackson Hole properties and businesses?"

"Uh-huh. They turn a profit too, which doesn't hurt, but every business he invests in, every piece of property he buys, has some special significance. High energy, a force field, whatever." She sighed. "It sounds like a bunch of *Star Wars* meets Harry Potter to me, but he's sold on it. And the thing is, he's brilliant. He's not one of these weirdos who gets naked to worship the sun on the solstice or something. Well, actually he might be. But he has an M.B.A. from Columbia, has run several incredibly successful businesses, is a shrewd investor, a people person. He's not a flake."

Ray frowned, trying to put the pieces together, trying to figure out how Graham tied into this. Lauren, apparently, was doing the same.

"Do you know Graham Stoddard?" she asked.

Audrey shook her head.

"He works over at Metro."

"I only went once. It's kind of pricey."

Ray let the irony pass, considering the numbers on tags on items at Panorama.

"Any idea how he might be connected to Woody?"

"No. No offense," she said with an eye at Ray, "but Uncle Woody doesn't typically associate with 'regular people.' He runs in circles way above shop owners, waiters, and other neophytes."

Lauren went through the places she and Ray had identified from the postcards—Teton Science Schools, Jackson Hole Rodeo, Signal Mountain, Jackson Lake Lodge, the Square, the view of Mount Moran from east of Oxbow Bend. Audrey was pretty sure Uncle Woody kept a horse at the fairgrounds but didn't know, as they didn't keep in touch. She admitted *"Woody's ranch"* probably referred to his place west of town. She revealed that Betsy Garner was buried in Jackson, but hers was just another grave. And she said she didn't know what was at 2265 N Fish Creek Road.

"What about triangles?" Lauren asked. "Is there any connection to Woody you can think of?"

"He worships triangles."

Ray and Lauren looked at each other.

"Literally?" Lauren asked.

"Maybe. It's all part of his belief. He thinks triangles have special power and meaning. I don't know what it is, something about Fate and energy and all that. They signify something—he'd have to tell you what it is, but yeah, they are incredibly important to him."

"Such as he might find special value in places with triangles?"

"I would imagine, yeah. His ranch is even triangle shaped. He specifically bought and sold extra portions of land, had them rezoned, went through a huge hassle about it all. It's like a religion to him."

Lauren looked at Ray.

"Does it have anything to do with Freemasonry?" Ray asked.

"Freemasonry?"

"They're big into triangles too, I think. The all-seeing eye in the pyramid on the dollar bill?"

Audrey shrugged. "No idea. I've never heard of them." She shrugged again. "Anyhow, what any of this has to do with your cousin, I don't know."

"Neither do we," Ray said.

"Uncle Woody's eccentric, but he isn't evil."

"We didn't mean to imply he was."

Audrey nodded.

"Thank you for being so open," Lauren said.

"Sure."

"It was good to see you again."

"Yeah, you too."

Ray offered his hand and thanked her as well, then followed Lauren out of the shop. They strolled slowly north, back toward Moo's. Neither spoke. Then Lauren stopped, leaning on the railing in front of a place called Jackson Hole Resort Store. The wood sidewalk was elevated a couple feet above street level. Thus the railing. They looked at the Square, the shadows cast by the trees only partial as thin, white clouds began to obscure the sun. Ray didn't know enough about mountain weather systems to determine if that meant a change in the weather or just a little less vibrant sunshine.

"So what do you make of that?" Lauren asked.

"I don't know."

"There's clearly a connection to the locations Graham specified, triangles, and Woody Garner."

"But what?"

"And what's the point?"

Ray exhaled. "I feel like I should know what we're missing, but . . ."

"We're missing it."

"Yeah."

Lauren looked at her watch. "I hate to run, but I should get going. I have a few errands to run and then a ladies' Bible study tonight."

Ray looked at her. "Thanks for your help today."

"Help?"

"With whatever it is we're doing. Chasing windmills."

"Sure. My pleasure."

"And for . . . just talking earlier. About Annabelle, about God."

Lauren eyed him. "My pleasure."

He nodded.

"I'll think about all this," she said. "Triangles and significance and special places."

He nodded again.

"If inspiration hits, I'll let you know."

"I appreciate it."

"Thanks for the ice cream, Ray."

"You're welcome."

She gave his arm a pat, the way a buddy would when ending a conversation. Then she walked behind him and toward stairs at the corner. Ray watched her cross the street, then waved as she got into her car. She waved back and drove off as if her rear bumper was on fire.

Ray sighed. There was too much on his mind. Graham. Postcards. Triangles. The Garner Family's "Manifest Destiny." Annabelle. Lauren's words of advice and wisdom.

He needed a way to clear his head. He needed a break.

He needed a vacation.

THIRTEEN

After Lauren left, Ray spent the next couple hours doing research, first on his laptop in his hotel room, then at the Teton County Library. It was a sleek, gray building on the western side of town, across from the RV park. By the time Ray exited the library at a quarter after six and set out to find dinner, he had a few more pieces to the puzzle.

Using the internet and several historical records, he pieced together a brief Garner genealogy. Audrey's father, Patrick, was the youngest son of Warren Garner. Woodrow was the oldest. Warren, who had married Elizabeth "Betsy" McSween, was the only son of Fredrick Garner, who along with his wife, Henrietta, had settled in Jackson Hole in the 1920s. It was not clear if Woodrow Garner had inherited his notions of a family legacy, his belief that Jackson Hole was "special," or his fascination with triangles from either his father or grandfather.

He had, however, inherited something else, so to speak. In 1976, Woodrow had married Zora James, the second child of Maverick James, the grandson of Bret James. Bret James, according to several sources, was one of the "founding fathers" of Jackson Hole. He'd arrived in the valley in 1890 with his wife—also named Elizabeth—and established multiple successful businesses, including B.S. James Freighting Company, a ranch with several thousand head of cattle, and a trading post. Over a century and a quarter later, the James family was still riding the success of their patriarch.

What, if anything, that had to do with Graham or his disappearance, Ray had no idea. It was historical context, but little else. Sometimes adding pieces to the puzzle only made it hard to fit them all together.

As Ray walked to his truck in the lot north of the library, the sun had disappeared behind a bank of gray, and the temperature had dropped ten degrees. Against his instincts, he stopped at Metro to pick up something to eat. While there, he tried to chat up a few more of Graham's coworkers, hoping to learn something he hadn't previously. He got nowhere. The woman who took his order had never heard of Graham—nor passed grade-school math classes, apparently. The man who served him knew of Graham but didn't have much interaction with him, as their shifts rarely overlapped. Same for a woman cleaning tables around him as he was finishing his meal. Made sense. Graham worked most nights at the Bar H-9, thus not with the people working nights at Metro. Factor in the number of seasonal employees and the transient nature of a restaurant's staff, and it was not a surprise.

Ray returned to his hotel before dark. He emptied his pockets, checked his phone to see if he'd received any texts or calls, and then prostrated himself on the bed. He flipped on TV, channel surfed, and settled on *Monday Night Football*.

He had virtually no interest in a game between the Dolphins and the Bills, and his mind drifted. He replayed the day in his head, particularly the conversation on the Jenny Lake Trail with Lauren. He was somewhat surprised, as he thought back, that he had opened up with her about Annabelle. Surprised that it hadn't been more painful. That he, for the first time in three weeks, didn't feel terrible to the core.

He thought about what she said about God speaking, through His Word. He wondered what Annabelle's rebuttal would have been to that. He wondered what her father's rebuttal would have been. He wondered what his former pastor or the sweet, single, middle-aged woman at his church who "heard" God's voice and "sensed" His direction would say. Didn't God "call" pastors and missionaries? Weren't Christians the world over following His leading and prompting about life decisions? What about the conviction of the Holy Spirit? Did Lauren not believe in that? Was this all a matter of semantics, of different meanings to words and terms?

Speaking of Lauren, there was something about her. Something he couldn't place his finger on. Something that . . . almost bothered him. No, bothered wasn't the right term. He liked her well enough, enjoyed being with her, enjoyed her insight. But something . . . felt unsettled inside him. Was it her straightforward "authenticity"? Was it her desire to help a stranger she met by chance at a National Park visitor center? Was it her strong convictions about God and Scripture—and the fact that Ray had been a little cool about both of late?

A Bills receiver got loose for a long pass, which distracted Ray. He sat up a little, deciding to get out of reflection mode. Lost in all the thinking, all the chasing across the valley, the hikes and conversations and ice cream and history of the Garner Family, was the fact that Graham was missing. Had been for four days, plus. Ninety-six hours—more like ninety-eight by now—and counting.

Ray felt impotent. He was unable to accomplish even the simple thing of figuring out the message Graham had left him, let alone figure out why he'd left it. He stood and paced around his room, ignoring the game on TV, the hum of the built-in heater under the window. He went over everything again—the postcards, the words on the back of the one with the cartoonish map on the front, the places he and Lauren had visited, the triangles—everything from a horse named Isosceles to shapes in the rafters—and the conversation with Audrey in her gallery.

What was the deal with triangles? Woodrow Garner obviously felt they had some significance, something almost spiritual, something odd. Maybe something even a little OCD, at least if shapes in rafters and the layout of the sidewalk made places significant to him. But did they, or were these places significant to Graham, irrespective to Woodrow's spiritual and geometrical beliefs? Or did he also buy into the triangle nonsense? Was he a "disciple" of Woodrow Garner? Had he been paranoid and thought Woodrow Garner was after him because of something having to do with triangles, one way or the other? And whatever the case, why did he send Ray a cryptic message?

Find the triangles.

Ray stopped walking. The Bills kicked a field goal. The heater shut off.

He walked over to the dresser and picked up the map. It was a standard issue National Park map. On one side, it had pictures of flora and fauna indigenous to the park, along with descriptions of them and a brief geology lesson. On the reverse side, it had a map of Grand Teton National Park and the surrounding area, showing roads, geographical features, ranger stations and visitor centers, hiking trails, and other points of interest.

Ray laid the map out on the table, the actual map facing up. He walked over to the nightstand and picked a Jackson Hole Inn pen off a similarly stamped notepad. He stood hunched over the table and scanned the map for various locations.

Jackson Lake Lodge was marked with a black square. Ray made a small X over it with the blue ink of the pen.

Just south of it, the two overlooks at the top of Signal Mountain were marked with black semicircles. He put an X through the lower one, where he and Lauren had spotted the triangular rock.

The Oxbow Bend turnout was similarly marked, but the one to the east of it was not. Ray booted his laptop and opened Google Maps. He used the satellite view to pinpoint the turnout, then compared the curvature of US 191 and the bends in the Snake River to identify where to place a third X on the park map.

Jackson was just a brown-shaded area at the bottom, with hardly any definition. Still, he put one X at the intersection of the main roads, where Highway 191 turned west, at the Town Square. He approximated the location of the Fairgrounds, using Google Maps for reference again, and placed another X on the map. He did the same thing for Teton Science Schools, in Coyote Canyon as it sliced through West Gros Ventre Butte.

Six locations. Six X's on the map.

With his finger, Ray traced Fish Creek Road, a spur emanating in the town of Wilson, at the base of the Teton Range along Highway 22. Somewhere was 2265 North Fish Creek Road. Another X? Somewhere was Woodrow Garner's ranch, shaped like a triangle, according to Audrey. Another X? Somewhere was Betsy Garner's grave, just another among many, again according to Audrey. Another X?

Nine total locations hinted at by Graham, either on the face of the postcards or in his writing on the back of the fifth. Nine X's on the map.

Find the triangles.

Ray studied the locations he knew. Two in Jackson. One just west of Jackson. Three well north of the town. Common geometry dictated that any three points could be connected to form a triangle. Six X's meant twenty possible combinations, if Ray was figuring it correctly. Add three more X's and the number went up beyond Ray's inclination to do math at eight p.m. on a Monday.

And, of course, it was possible to use various points multiple times, increasing the number of potential triangles even more. So where did that leave things?

The Dolphins punted.

Ray sat back, wishing he had some coffee. He thought about making a run to Jackson Hole Coffee Roasters, getting some fresh air in the process. Plus a walk might help him think. Not that it had yet.

He looked at the locations again. And a hunch hit him.

Middle school geometry—and Lauren's words over coffee the night before—came back to him once again. An isosceles triangle, if he wasn't mistaken, was a triangle with two or more equal sides. If all three were equal, it was called an equilateral triangle. An isosceles could be equilateral or not. Sort of like how a rectangle could be a square but wasn't always.

He looked back at the map, particularly at the three locations in the north. Jackson Lake Lodge, the overlook atop Signal Mountain, and the turnout east of Oxbow Bend that offered a view of Mount Moran. He stood and grabbed the notepad off the nightstand. Using it as a straightedge, he drew three lines connecting his three X's. Then he sat back. To the naked eye, they appeared to form an equilateral—and thus an isosceles—triangle.

Find the triangles.

First, he needed to identify the other three X's.

^   ^   ^

Ray slept fitfully and woke Tuesday with a desperate need for coffee. He went through the typical morning routine, then set out to get his morning brew. If he ever saw Graham again, he would ask him why he recommended a hotel without coffee makers in the room or coffee in the lobby.

The morning was clear but cool and crisp. He walked briskly, west, toward Jackson Hole Coffee Roasters. Some people liked variety and preferred to sample all the local offerings. Ray was content with good.

As he walked, he mulled what had been on his mind as he fell asleep the previous night, that "something" about Lauren that was bugging him. It wasn't her direct way, it wasn't her unsolicited help, and it wasn't anything spiritual that she'd said. In fact, it wasn't even her.

It was him. He'd realized, lying in bed, looking at the lights on the smoke detector, that he felt an attraction to her.

That in and of itself wasn't anything. He'd felt an attraction to lots of women over the years. But since meeting Annabelle, since falling for her, that attraction had been technical at most. Since Labor Day, he'd been in such a funk that he'd barely noticed other women. Now, he realized, he not only noticed Lauren but felt an attraction—one that was more than technical.

Somehow, that didn't seem right. Annabelle had been the love of his life. He'd been ready to spend the rest of his time on earth with her and only her.

So how could it be, less than a month after that relationship had ended, that he now felt something—whatever it was—for another woman? Did that cheapen the love he'd had for Annabelle? Was it a subconscious protective response to being dumped? Or was he making too much out of a common attraction to a woman he barely knew?

He really needed that coffee.

Jackson Hole Coffee Roasters delivered.

Ray walked back toward the Square, debating calling Lauren. She had said she'd call if inspiration hit. Did that mean he could return the favor? And at . . . ten till eight on a Tuesday? He thought for a few minutes, pondering what he knew of Lauren. He concluded she was not the sleep-in-till-noon sort of vacationer but the up-at-dawn-with-a-pot-of-coffee sort. At worst, he figured she'd be awake. So he crossed the street, passed through an antler arch, and pulled up her name on his phone.

The park was mostly empty. A couple others were enjoying their coffee there. A trio of women was doing yoga in one corner. A woman in layers of flowing clothes was reading a book on a bench.

Lauren answered after two rings. She did not sound groggy.

"Hey, Ray."

"Good morning. Not too early, is it?"

"Just pouring a cup of coffee."

He grinned.

"What's up?"

"I have an idea."

"Oh?"

"About postcards and triangles. I want to check out the other locations, and I'm wondering if you want to tag along."

Lauren said nothing.

"I don't want to intrude on your vacation, so you're more than welcome to say no."

"No, it's just—I mean, yeah, I do want to tag along. You caught me mid-drink."

He grinned again.

"Have you had breakfast yet, Ray?"

"No."

"Me either. You like waffles?"

He hesitated for just a second.

"Relax, I'm not inviting you over for waffles. I'm not that forward."

"Just generally curious then?"

"I think we should grab breakfast," she said, and he could hear the playfulness in her voice. "I know a place, and it's in the right location for where we have to go. If you like waffles."

"I like waffles."

"I'll pick you up in, say, an hour?"

"I can drive too."

"I don't mind."

"Okay. An hour."

"Bring your appetite."

Ray lowered his phone after saying goodbye. He told himself not to read too much into Lauren suggesting they grab breakfast. He told himself it didn't mean anything if she had. He told himself not to feel guilty having a good time while Graham was missing.

He didn't trust a thing he told himself.

FOURTEEN

Lauren was prompt. She was dressed in layers, a brown, partially unbuttoned Henley over a black undershirt, and jeans with a hole in one knee. Edgy design or the result of wear, Ray didn't know. Her hair was drawn back in a collegial ponytail and there was vitality in her eyes and smile. There were also two cups of coffee in her hands.

They left Jackson and drove west, past the twin buttes and across the Snake River. The riverbed was wide, and the water flowed in several channels that wound around sandbars and scrub- and brush-infested gravel beds. Driftwood was caught on the banks. It reminded Ray of the Platte River just west of Omaha, not an alpine waterway. Lauren noticed Ray's look and said that it had been a dry summer. When the river was full, most of what he saw was buried beneath one, wide stream.

Soon after, they turned north on a two-lane highway that, had it not been aimed at the protuberant Tetons, would have been commonplace, hedged by trees and bushes as it was. Houses and ranches broke the monotony, as did ranch headgates over gravel driveways. Ray and Lauren drove for six or seven miles, eventually breaking into more wide-open spaces. The mountains seemed close enough to touch.

While they drove, Lauren told Ray about her ladies' Bible study. They were deep into Deuteronomy. Not for the weak of heart, she said. The women at his church back home studied Beth Moore and Ann Voskamp books. Was that a Midwest versus mountains thing? He had no idea.

Just past the first golf course Ray could remember seeing since leaving Sioux Falls, Lauren turned left. Ahead of them, literally at the base of the mountains, was what looked like a ski resort community. Lauren confirmed it. "Jackson Hole Mountain Resort. Best skiing you'll find."

"This is all the resort?"

"The town of Teton Village. A census-designated place, technically. It's mostly the resort, hotels, restaurants."

"And this is where we're having breakfast?"

"More or less."

Lauren parked in a large lot that appeared to serve the resort and several surrounding properties, and they got out. "This is on me," she said.

"You don't have to do that."

"You haven't seen the prices yet."

"Expensive waffles."

"Not the waffles so much."

He frowned.

She smirked.

They walked toward a building with a clock tower and the words "Jackson Hole" affixed to it in the same script Ray had seen them elsewhere around town. The building had the same motif as most of them in the village. Ray didn't know the correct architectural term, but they looked like all the buildings in a typical ski resort. Very alpine chalet.

Lauren walked into the shadow of the clock tower and approached a ticket window. "Two tram tickets, please."

"Tram?" Ray asked.

She nodded.

He raised an eyebrow.

"Just trust me."

"Okay."

The tickets were $37 apiece, and Ray offered again to pay for his. Lauren shut him down as they climbed the stairs to the tram station, which Ray realized was the "building" with the clock tower. As they reached the platform, Ray examined the tram. Red and black paint, tinted windows, white decals of a cowboy on a bucking bronco and the words "Jackson Hole" in the same script again. The tram was suspended via a gray, steel arm from a series of cables that ascended from the station into the sky. Ray couldn't see the apex.

They waited five minutes before boarding the tram with a couple dozen other people and their "guide," Josh. He gave them a brief history of the tram, as well as some basic numbers—a twelve-minute ride would take them over four thousand feet to the summit of Rendezvous Peak. While he was talking, the tram began moving, so quietly and smoothly Ray almost didn't notice.

The trip was majestic, first coasting above grassy ski runs cutting through forests of pine, then floating over rocky crags befitting a back-country wilderness. The ride remained smooth except for when they passed one of the five towers supporting the cables. Then the tram swayed back and forth before resuming its steady climb. Rising nearly a mile, they went from early fall to winter as fields of snow filled in any valley, nook, or crevice. When they docked at the top and the doors opened, the cold air and mountaintop breeze cut through Ray's sweatshirt. The view was so stunning he barely noticed and certainly didn't mind.

Lauren led him toward Corbet's Cabin, a plain, boxy structure a short distance away. Plain, that was, except for the rows of skis attached to the wall. The interior was rustic but cozy, not dissimilar, Ray guessed, from any number of ski-hill eateries. Lauren recommended the brown sugar and butter waffles, and Ray followed her lead. The waffles were served in tinfoil, and they took them and coffees to a table by a window overlooking the valley.

"Good?" Lauren asked after Ray took his first bite.

"They are."

"But?"

"No but. I've just never spent forty bucks to ride to the top of the mountain for waffles."

"But you're glad you did?"

He took another bite and nodded.

"You heard anything new from Detective . . . What was his name?"

"Celek. No, I meant to call this morning. He promised to update me if he found anything out, so I'm guessing the trail is cold."

Lauren said nothing.

"But I may have found something last night."

"Oh?"

"Two things, in fact." He licked melted butter off his thumb. "Woodrow Garner married into the James family, one of the first families to settle in Jackson Hole."

"I've heard the name."

"You know anything about them?"

"Just the name."

"I did some basic research, a few names and dates. Nothing seemed to tie to Graham or to anything else we've discovered."

"It's data," she said. "You never know when something obscure might become relevant."

He nodded. "And second, I think I figured out the triangles."

"You did?"

"More or less."

She backhanded him. "Ray, you're kind of burying the lede."

"What?"

"You just let me ramble on about Deuteronomy and Tiffany's comparison of the old and new covenants when you had a breakthrough."

"I wouldn't call it a breakthrough."

"Then what?" she asked before jamming some waffle in her mouth. Without looking like a slob.

Ray recounted plotting the locations from the postcards on a map of the valley, in particular how three of them—Signal Mountain, Jackson Lake Lodge, and the turnout east of Oxbow Bend—formed an equilateral triangle. Lauren's eyes never left his face as he spoke, even though she consumed the rest of her waffle. When he was done, she swallowed hard. "So I was onto something about finding triangles?"

"I think so."

"You have the map with you?"

He reached into his back pocket and withdrew the map. He unfolded it and set it on the table beside their waffles. Lauren studied it for a minute, then lifted her eyes.

"It's not about finding triangles at the places but connecting the dots to find triangles on the map."

"Ostensibly."

"Even though there are triangles at the places, some of them imaginative and some staring you in the face."

He nodded and swigged his coffee.

Lauren tipped her head to the side. The ponytail flounced against the back of her shoulder. "So what happens when we plot the triangles?"

Ray shrugged.

"Three of them, ostensibly," she said with a demure look at him, "since there are nine points."

"Or will be when we identify all nine locations."

"Right."

"I did the math last night. You can connect any three points to form a triangle, so there are a lot of possibilities. But the equilateral triangle makes sense because of—"

"Isosceles," she said.

He nodded.

"The fourth."

Ray drank more coffee.

"I don't get it," she said after a minute.

"Get what?"

"Signal Mountain. It's one of the points of your triangle on the map, but there was also that huge triangular rock near the summit."

"Okay."

"The Garners didn't move it there. So is Signal Mountain special to them because it has that rock, or is it just a coincidence?"

"I never did much like coincidences."

"Me either. I hate them, in fact. They annoy me. But we've had to stretch to find triangles at some of these other locations. So what's the deal?"

"I don't know. And whatever the case, we still don't know what triangles on a map mean."

Lauren looked at her watch. "It's ten-fifteen. I've got to babysit at two. That gives us—"

"Babysit?"

"A lady from study. Something came up, I had the afternoon off . . ."

He nodded.

"That gives us a few hours to knock out a few more locations."

"I'm game."

"Another round to go?"

"If you let me buy this time."

"Sounds fair. Brown sugar and butter."

He ordered two more waffles, and they took them outside. The sun's intensity was strong two miles above sea level, and it offset the wind to keep the air from being too cold. Ray and Lauren enjoyed the panoramic view while waiting for the tram. In every direction, whether near or far, the horizon was a blend of white and purplish blue-gray. The valley was green speckled with shades of yellow, a little orange, a few dots of red. All but for where the Snake

River carved through the terrain like a blue ribbon tossed off its reel. Sioux Falls was going to be pretty boring by comparison.

The ride down was just as spectacular as the ride up, enhanced by a snack of waffles. They reached Lauren's Ford Focus at a quarter to eleven, and she guided them out of Teton Village and back south on the main road. Where it curved to the southwest, she exited onto a narrow, unmarked road.

"You know where we're going?" Ray asked.

"I called Audrey this morning."

"Planning ahead."

She nodded.

They made a series of turns, leaving one road for another and meandering through the trees, heading generally east.

"So what's the plan when we find Woody's ranch?" Ray asked. "Ring the bell and ask if we can look around the property?"

"Ring the bell?"

"Like an Old West chow bell."

"Aha."

He waited.

"We see what we can see from the road. Audrey said the property is triangular. Maybe it's not alone."

"Maybe that's the clue in and of itself."

She shrugged in concession. "Or maybe there's nothing to see. Maybe we just need to plot the location."

They made another turn, and Lauren hit the brakes. The road ended in a cul-de-sac. Two gravel drives veered off left and right. The one on the left was marked by a blue fire sign with white numbers. The one on the right was wider and spanned by a hewn timber headgate. Hanging from the crossbar was the word "Garner" in wrought iron. It was framed on either side by an iron triangle with a G circumscribed inside it.

"Or maybe that's our clue," Lauren said.

Ray squinted through the gate, following the driveway around and then over a slight hump in the ground. It was flanked by faded wood fencing that also ran perpendicular to the gate until swallowed up by trees on either side. Straight ahead, Ray could just see the rooftops of several buildings maybe two or three hundred yards away, over the hillock. It was twice that far again, if he had to guess, to where the sporadic trees stopped and he presumed the Snake River cut between the ranch and West Gros Ventre Butte. If Ray's geography was up to snuff. Woody Garner's ranch wasn't a big one, not by Wyoming standards.

"Can't see much from here," he said.

Lauren shook her head. "Not sure how they do things in South Dakota, but folks out here don't much cotton to trespassing," she said with a little twang. It made Ray realize that she didn't have much of an accent when she spoke normally. Then again, most of the women in Westerns didn't either, and they were from out west.

"They don't much cotton to it in South Dakota either," Ray said, sans twang.

"Put a pin in your map and move on?"

He nodded.

They backtracked to the main road and continued southwest, then due south. Lauren turned west on Highway 22, and a mile later back north on a small road in the town of Wilson. Two turns later, they were headed north again on Fish Creek Road, named for the meandering creek they had crossed twice. The small town was soon behind them. The foothills grew larger to their left. The sky stayed just as blue.

"We're getting close," Lauren said, pointing at fire signs. She stopped completely in front of one labeled 2265. They were the only ones on the road. The nearest building was a hundred yards back.

"This is it?" Ray asked.

The narrow driveway was little more than two dirt ruts through the grass. It led maybe two hundred feet to a grove of aspen trees on the bank of the creek. Set in the middle of a small clearing in the grove was a small building. Dark brown clapboard siding, green shingles—it was little more than a cottage. No vehicles were parked in the driveway. There was no sign of any human presence. There wasn't even, as far as Ray could tell, any electricity running to it.

Lauren turned in the driveway. The Focus bounced and jolted, and a couple of times Ray feared they might bottom out. The grove of trees was bigger than it looked from the road, as was the clearing. The cottage wasn't, roughly the size of a trailer home, albeit more square. There was no landscaping, just wild grass and flowers running right up to the walls and the front stoop. It was poured concrete, canted away from the door a few degrees. Two windows flanked the green door, both dark glass. Above the door, in space made available by a peaked roof, was a triangular window. An equilateral triangle, the sides approximately as long as the door was wide.

Lauren cut the engine, and they got out. The creek babbled in hushed tones, competing with the rustling of golden aspen leaves to be heard. Something small scurried amongst the fallen leaves and twigs. All else was lost.

"I guess it has charm," Lauren said. She looked at Ray. "You know, for the Jeremiah Johnson, live off the land sort."

"I guess."

"Should we knock on the door?"

"As opposed to standing here staring?"

"You make a good point."

They approached the door, again resembling very casual cops or feds, Ray thought. He knocked on the green door. Nobody answered. He didn't expect anyone to. The place was abandoned. He knocked again to be thorough. Nobody answered. They didn't even try the knob.

"So whose place is this?" Lauren asked, stepping around the side of the house.

"Could be Crazy Uncle Garner's place," Ray said, following her. "Could be their minimalist getaway cabin. Could be just a place with a triangular window that Woodrow thinks makes it special."

Lauren raised her eyebrows over her shoulder. She continued walking, now thirty feet from the back of the cabin. She stopped, looking down a gentle slope to the creek. Across it, a meadow stretched to another grove of aspen that began to climb the foothills.

"It does have charm," she said, looking back at Ray. "If you do want to get away, spend your day listening to the creek, looking for wildlife, cooking over a fire."

He shrugged.

"Assuming there's plumbing."

"That's a bit of an assumption," he said.

She took a deep breath of mountain air, as if she didn't inhale it continuously every day. "What are we at, seven down?"

"Eight if you count Teton Science Schools."

"No triangles there?"

"Not unless you get really obtuse."

"I see what you did there."

"Clever, huh?"

"Acutely."

He winked.

"It's on the way back to town," Lauren said. "We might as well stop and take another look."

"Okay."

They walked back to the car, walking around the other side of the cabin, just in case there happened to be an overgrown tombstone for Betsy Garner in the weeds. There wasn't. Made sense. Audrey said she was buried in Jackson.

They returned the way they had come and turned back toward town. Before reaching it, however, Lauren turned onto Coyote Canyon Road, as Ray had two days ago. This time, the parking lot near the cluster of buildings was nearly full. Several more cars were parked in the larger lot closer to the main road. Teachers? Students? Hikers? Other out-of-towners with missing cousins?

She parked, and they got out. A hiker, clearly identifiable by his apparel, was returning to the lot. A couple other people crisscrossed the commons between the two rows of buildings. Through the glass, others were visible inside. It was drastically different from Ray's first visit.

They walked the main path through the campus, pointing out corners of buildings and random points of geography and geometry. After the rock atop Signal Mountain, the iron triangles on Woodrow Garner's headgate, and the triangular window at the cabin on Fish Creek Road, Ray wondered about haphazard triangles like those he'd identified at the Jackson Town Square or Jackson Lake Lodge. Similarly, he was disinclined to believe there was anything "special" in Woody's mind—or thus in Graham's—about random triangles formed by the layout of buildings and sidewalks.

"Why would this place mean anything to the Garners?" Lauren asked.

"I don't know."

"I should say, the Manifest Destiny family legacy Garners."

"I still don't know."

"Maybe one of them went to school here?"

He shrugged.

"I mean, I get why the top of a mountain or the family ranch would be special or have high energy or whatever. But why here?"

"It's scenic."

"The entire hole is scenic."

"True."

They reached the northern end of the complex of buildings and stopped. They looked around. At the trees. At the brown hillsides on either side of them. At the wildflowers blooming haphazardly all around. And at a bed of red, white, and blue flowers near the base of trees east of the complex. Some sort of stone marker or plaque was in the middle of the flowers. Ray swept his eyes over it with mild curiosity. Lauren locked onto it, then cocked her head to the side and closed one eye.

"Ray."

"Yeah?"

She walked toward the flowerbed. Ray followed.

She stopped in front of the bed, then slowly walked around it until she was standing ten feet from Ray. The bed was wider on her side. It tapered to a point where Ray stood. And in two other places, which Lauren indicated by stretching out her arms.

"It's a triangle, Ray."

FIFTEEN

Ray nodded.

"An equilateral triangle," Lauren clarified.

Ray nodded again. And squinted to read the engraving on a brass plaque set atop a stone base, similar to a headstone, in the middle of the flowerbed.

"What's that?" she asked.

Ray said nothing, and she walked back around to stand beside him.

"'*In loving memory of Lincoln Nichols. Two thousand four to two thousand seventeen.*'"

"Huh," Ray said.

"Double huh. He's not a Garner."

"No."

"Have you ever seen a triangular flowerbed before?"

"Not that I've noticed."

"Me either."

"But I don't notice a lot of flowerbeds."

"I'm shocked."

He grinned.

"Coincidences really annoy me," she said. She tipped her head as she looked at him. "I don't suppose that name means anything to you. One of Graham's friends or something?"

"No. I can check with Heidi."

"His girlfriend?"

Ray nodded.

Lauren shrugged. "Might as well. My guess is this is what we were supposed to find here, for whatever reason."

"Me too."

They headed back toward the parking lot.

"Wonder why there's a flowerbed here," Ray said.

"Flowers are pretty," Lauren said with a hidden grin.

"Dedicated to a teenage boy?"

"A student?"

"Maybe."

"A donation made to the school?"

"Maybe."

"Why is it everything we find confuses us more?"

Before getting in the car, Ray got out his phone. He found Heidi in his contacts and tapped the call button. It rang just twice before she answered with a terse, "Heidi."

"Heidi, it's Ray Eastwood."

"What's up?"

Beside him, Lauren pulled the band holding her ponytail, then combed her fingers through her unbound hair.

"Wondering if the name Lincoln Nichols means anything to you," Ray said.

"Lincoln Nichols?"

"Yeah."

"He was a local teenager who died a couple years ago."

"Do you know how?"

"He fell off a mountain or something."

"A mountain?"

"I don't know. He was hiking or biking I think."

"Was he a friend of Graham's?"

Lauren leaned his way. "Where's that map?" she whispered.

Ray retrieved it from his pocket and handed it to her as Heidi answered.

"A friend of Graham's? He was like ten."

"You said he was a teenager."

So, for the record, had the plaque in the flowerbed. Or twelve going on thirteen at least.

"Whatever," Heidi said. "No, he wasn't Graham's friend."

"Would Graham have known him?"

"I don't think so."

Lauren had unfolded the map.

Ray pursed his lips. "What about the Garner Family? Any connection to them?"

"The who?"

"Woodrow Garner. He owns a ranch in the valley, owns a lot of business and properties in the area."

"I don't know. Why?"

"Just thinking," Ray said. "Thanks."

"Yeah, sure."

He ended the call and lowered his phone.

"Check this out, Ray," Lauren said. She had the map unfolded on the steering wheel of her Focus. She pointed as she spoke. "Woody's ranch is here." She traced an imaginary line with her finger. "The cottage in the grove of aspens—2265 North Fish Creek Road—is here." She traced another line. "And this is us here. I don't have a protractor app on my phone, but that looks like another equilateral triangle."

"Or pretty close," Ray said, eyeballing it with her.

"These people are weird. I've never heard of worshipping triangles."

Ray shrugged.

"What'd Heidi say?"

"Not much. Lincoln died in a hiking accident or something."

"Hmm . . . Yeah, I remember that now. He got separated from some buddies or his cousins or something. Fell down a mountain slope."

"She wasn't aware of a connection between him and Graham, and she's not familiar with the Garners, so doesn't know if there's one there."

"I wonder if Audrey would."

"Give her a call."

"You call. I'm driving."

He looked at her.

"At least dial. Put it on speaker."

Ray found the number of Panorama and dialed, by which time Lauren had folded the map, tossed it in his lap, and started the car and backed out of the parking stall.

"Panorama, this is Natalie."

"Is Audrey there?" Ray asked as he tucked the map back into his pocket.

"Just a sec."

It was more like a minute.

"This is Audrey."

Ray identified himself, and she remembered him from the day before. "I have what may seem like an odd question for you," he said, causing Lauren to look his way. She didn't turn back to the road for longer than he was comfortable.

"Okay," Audrey said.

"Are you familiar with the name Lincoln Nichols?"

Audrey was silent for a few seconds. "He was my cousin's son. He died two years ago. A hiking accident."

"I'm sorry," Ray said.

Another few seconds of silence passed. "Why do you ask?"

"One of the locations on the postcards we mentioned the other day was the Teton Science Schools. We found a triangular flowerbed there with a plaque dedicating it to Lincoln Nichols."

"That was Uncle Woody, I'm sure. He probably made a sizable donation, especially if he thought the school or the property had some intrinsic value."

"How was Woody related to Lincoln?"

"He was his grandpa. Lincoln was Woody's daughter Diane's oldest child."

Ray didn't know what else to ask, what wouldn't possibly upset her and what he couldn't find in public records. So he thanked her and reported to Lauren.

"So did Woody donate to the school because it was already important to him, or is it important because he donated there?" she asked.

Ray shrugged.

"And does it matter?"

He shrugged again.

"So what's that bring us to, eight of nine?"

"Only missing Betsy Garner's grave."

"Want to check out the cemetery?"

"Might as well cross it off."

The Aspen Hill Cemetery was located at the base of Snow King Mountain, between the ice rink, mini golf course, and landing zone for the alpine slide. It was not a typical cemetery with rows and rows of headstones dotting a closely mown lawn. Instead, the ground was sloped, the grass was long and blowing in the breeze, and trees and bushes cordoned off sections of grave markers. Lauren drove along a winding road as she and Ray discussed where and how to search for Betsy Garner's grave. Eventually, they settled on picking a spot and walking around reading names. The cemetery was, as far as they could tell, otherwise vacant. They wouldn't be disturbing anyone.

The search could have taken quite a lot of time. It took five minutes.

Lauren whistled, and Ray dodged a few plots to join her. She stood in front of a dark marble headstone, two and a half or three feet long and a little over half that high. The name Elizabeth "Betsy" Garner was engraved in gray, cursive script. Beneath it were the date of birth—June 4, 1933—and date of death—August 11, 1999. Beneath that was a short epitaph lauding Betsy as a "loving wife, mother, grandmother, daughter, sister, and friend." All the text was centered between an engraved likeness of an old woman and capital letter G inside an equilateral triangle.

"Nine for nine," Lauren said.

"Why her?" Ray asked.

"Why her what?"

"Why did Graham point us to her grave? There have to be other Garners here."

"Probably. Although I don't see any in the immediate area." Lauren stuck out her shoe, gesturing at the triangle on the grave marker. "Because of that?"

"Okay, so why does she have a triangle on her grave?"

Lauren shrugged.

"Is it possible Betsy was the one who started all this triangle business?" he asked. "Audrey did say it was after her death that Warren had a falling out with her dad."

"She also said the universe told him about the Garner Family's Manifest Destiny."

"Hmm."

They trudged back to her car.

"Can I see the map again?"

Ray pulled it from his pocket, and they opened it on the hood. Lauren quickly flipped it over. "No map of Jackson."

"No."

"The visitor center."

Ray looked at her.

"The Jackson Hole and Greater Yellowstone Visitor Center, on the north edge of town. They'll surely have a map."

"You have time?"

She checked her watch. "Yep. Let's go."

It only took a few minutes to drive across town, and Lauren parked in a mostly empty lot beside a large, grayish-brown pitched-roof building. A bronze grizzly towered over a male and female elk in a rock garden in front of the entrance. The elk refuge stretched to the north and east from the far side of the building. Ray squinted at the flat, green ground surrounding the serpentine Flat Creek. He saw no elk.

Lauren led the way inside. Straight ahead, a ramp led up to the second floor. Beside it, seven or eight stuffed elk were posed as if climbing a mountainside. Several of them were bulls, sporting six- or seven-point racks. Ray spent a few seconds admiring them, then turned to Lauren. "What do you know, there are elk here."

She whacked his arm.

Turning right, they entered what appeared to be a cross between a gift shop, a gallery, and an information center. T-shirts, paintings, and the usual assortment of souvenirs were for sale. In the center of the room, under a chandelier of elk antlers, was a desk staffed by two men in uniforms similar to the one Lauren had worn Sunday afternoon.

"Hi, Gary," she called to one of them, a young, thin man with a thick crop of black hair and a wiry beard.

"Lauren, how are you doing?"

"Good. This is Ray."

"Hello, Ray."

"Gary," he said as they shook hands.

"What can I do for you?" Gary asked.

"We need a Jackson map," Lauren said, leaning on the counter.

"Why, you get lost?"

"Ray's from South Dakota."

"Which part?" Gary asked, looking at Ray.

"Sioux Falls."

Gary winced. "Ooh. That's the middle of nowhere."

"Only two hundred and fifty miles from Fargo."

"Well, there you go. What kind of map?"

"As detailed as you've got," Lauren said. "Streets, landmarks."

Gary pointed to one of several maps lying flat on the countertop. "How's this?"

Ray and Lauren both shuffled a few steps to look at it. The map was printed on ledger-sized paper, not glossy or fancy. But it listed every street in town, or close, along with dozens and dozens of businesses and landmarks. Lauren raised her eyes to Ray.

"That'll work," he said.

Gary reached under the counter and pulled out a copy of the map. He handed it to Ray.

"Thanks."

"Anything else I can do for you?"

"Nope," Lauren said. "Thanks."

"Sure thing."

They went back outside, and Lauren pointed to a picnic table overlooking the elk refuge.

"You got a pen in your car?" Ray asked as he laid out the map.

"Let me check."

She was actually gone several minutes and came back carrying a short pencil. "All they'd give me inside," she said.

Ray had also unfolded the Jackson Hole map, the one on which he'd marked the triangle connecting Signal Mountain, Jackson Lake Lodge, and the turnout east of Oxbow Bend. Lauren used the pencil to mark the approximate location of Teton Science Schools, Woodrow Garner's ranch, and the cabin on Fish Creek Road. Spinning the map to use the grooves in the picnic table as a straightedge, she connected the three dots. There were now two equilateral triangles.

"Okay, here," she said, handing the pencil to Ray. He marked the Town Square on the map Gary had given them. Then he marked the approximate location of Isosceles IV's stall at the Fairgrounds. Then he approximated Betsy Garner's grave within the cemetery. Sitting back, he frowned.

"That's not an equilateral triangle."

"No, it's not." She tilted her head. "But it's close."

"A different corner of the Square?" Ray asked.

"Maybe."

"The postcard showed the Rodeo," he said. "And the Rodeo grounds are closer to Snow King Avenue than whatever this is."

"Karns Avenue."

"Should I move it?"

"Worth a try."

He made another point on the map, then emulated Lauren in connecting the points with lines. He looked up at her.

"Close."

"The Rodeo grounds are 'special,' not the stall where Isosceles is kept?"

"With these people, who knows," Lauren said.

"'*Find the triangles*,'" Ray said. "We found them. Now what? How does this help find or figure out what happened to Graham?"

Lauren said nothing.

Ray exhaled. "We're going on five days. It's like he disappeared into thin air. The police have nothing but dead ends. We're no closer than we were two days ago."

"We're closer."

He looked at her.

"We don't know how, but we've made progress."

He looked down at the two maps. "So Graham sends postcards to me with clues, it would seem to find these three triangles, right?"

"Right."

"He didn't wait until I got here, which suggests he had reason to think he couldn't wait. He didn't call or text me, which suggests he thought his phone was bugged or tapped."

"Or that yours was."

Ray narrowed his eyes.

"Just throwing out ideas."

"Fair enough. And he didn't come right out and write me a letter or tell me what I was supposed to determine from the postcards. He was cryptic. So he feared this might fall into the wrong hands?"

"Or he didn't have time?"

"He chased around buying postcards. He could have just as quickly written a couple paragraphs."

"I suppose."

Ray dropped the pencil he'd been twirling in his fingers. "Maybe I've been going at this wrong. Maybe I shouldn't have worried about the postcards but focused on tracking down his movements."

"How?"

"I don't know."

"You're not a detective. The detectives are stumped, like you just said."

"I know."

"I don't mean to be mean, Ray, but if they can't find anything . . ."

He looked up. "I know. And I'm not questioning them. Detective Celek seemed more than competent. But you know how people are. Some of them see a badge and uniform and clam up. Some of them don't respond well to interrogation-like questions. Maybe I should have tried more."

"Didn't you talk to several of his friends?"

"A couple. I ate lunch at Metro and made small talk."

"What else could you do, short of interrogating them?"

He conceded with a raise of his eyebrows.

Lauren placed a hand on his wrist. "Don't blame yourself, Ray."

He looked at her. "I'm not."

"Okay." She withdrew her hand.

"I just don't know what else to do."

"Unfortunately, I can't help you figure that out."

"I know."

"No, I mean, I've got to babysit."

"Right."

She grinned. "Where do you want me to drop you off?" she asked.

"It's a nice day. I'll walk back to the hotel."

"You sure?"

"Yeah. It'll give me a chance to think."

"Okay."

"Thanks for your help today, Lauren. And the waffles."

"You're welcome. You can't come to Jackson without taking that ride." She stood.

"Have fun babysitting."

"Little Libby is an angel. Don't drive yourself crazy over this."

"I won't."

She waved and turned for the car.

"Hey, Lauren."

She turned back.

"How long do you have to babysit?"

"Couple hours." A grin may or may not have been just below the surface. "Why?"

"You want to go with me to the Bar H-9 tonight?"

She looked at him a second, her jaw set. She took a few steps back to him. "Just to be clear, are you asking me on a date, or do you want a partner for some non-interrogation interrogation?"

Ray nodded for a second, thinking of how to phrase what he had to say. "I do enjoy your company. But the reason I'm going is because I want to poke around a little at the scene of the crime, maybe talk to some people who might know something. And I thought I'd stand out less and have a better chance of getting answers if I wasn't alone—if I had an affable female with me."

Lauren nodded slowly, appeared to be thinking too. "Pick me up at five-thirty. I'll text you my address."

"Okay. Thanks."

"Sure thing. I enjoy your company too." She turned, then spoke over her shoulder. "And nobody says affable anymore, Ray."

SIXTEEN

Ray returned to his hotel and ignored the sense that the walls were closing in on him. After spending the morning riding the tram into the mountains and traversing the wide-open valley, a standard-sized hotel room seemed lacking.

He fired up his laptop and did some brief research on the Bar H-9. It was billed as an authentic chuck wagon dinner experience, including a hearty cowboy dinner and colorful entertainment. Wagons left the ranch at six sharp, and the website recommended arriving ten to fifteen minutes early. Given its location a few miles south of town, Lauren's instruction to pick her up at five-thirty made perfect sense. Ray wondered for a moment how she knew when they should arrive at the Bar H-9, but considering everything else she seemed to know, it wasn't that surprising. Or maybe she'd picked it up in conversations with him about the times on the surveillance video showing Graham's disappearance.

He made reservations at forty bucks a head, which, while steep for dinner in Sioux Falls, wasn't all that expensive for several hours of what was tantamount to dinner theater. It also offset the price Lauren had paid for Top of the World Waffles.

"Are you asking me on a date?"

Lauren's words had echoed in his head as he'd walked back to the hotel. He wasn't sure why. Because of the clumsy way he'd asked her not to go on a date? Because part of him wished he had asked her on a date? Because he felt guilty even thinking about the possibility of dating someone? Twenty-two days ago he'd been engaged to the love of his life. Just a few weeks from now, they were supposed to be getting married, pledging their lives to each other till death. Could he legitimately be interested in dating another woman that soon after the breakup? He decided not to think about it because it wasn't a date. It was business. Business—finding Graham or figuring out what had happened to him—was the only reason he was still in Jackson Hole at all. So he told himself.

"I enjoy your company too."

That phrase rattled around in his brain as well. That and the memory of the hint of a smirk on her face as she'd said it. Maybe she was thinking about the corny way he'd put things. Maybe she was preparing to tease him about using the word affable. Or maybe she felt a little of what he felt too. And that made Ray want to smile as well, like a dorky teenager around a high-school crush.

He got out of the hotel. He walked south to the Teton County Sheriff's Office, where he asked to speak to Detective Celek. He could have just called, but he needed to clear his head and get some exercise.

Detective Celek was out, and Ray was given his cell number. He walked back toward the hotel, opting instead to find a bench in the Square. From there, he dialed the number.

"Detective Celek."

"Detective, it's Ray Eastwood. Graham Stoddard's cousin."

"Yeah, Ray. I'm afraid I don't have any news for you."

"No?"

"No. We double-checked the van taken from Jackson Hole Cleaners, and it was clean. No video surveillance there. A dead end. I also talked to a handful of people at the Bar H-9, none of whom saw or heard anything, noticed anything unusual about Graham. A dead end."

Ray sighed.

"And we checked out his apartment, talked to his girlfriend, everything we would normally do in this situation. Unfortunately, none of that turned up anything."

"Dead ends."

"Yeah," Celek said.

Ray thought about the postcards. About the connection to the Garners. But it was so inconclusive and so seemingly immaterial that he didn't know what to mention. It all seemed too absurd. Chasing around looking at various locations with Lauren was one thing; submitting their "findings" to a real detective was another. He also didn't want to besmirch anyone without a clear connection to Graham's disappearance. So he thanked Detective Celek, who promised to let him know if there were any developments. Ray didn't expect any.

It wasn't yet four o'clock. Ray had ninety minutes and change before he was to pick up Lauren. So he walked to his new favorite haunt in town, Jackson Hole Coffee Roasters. He went with the Kona blend again and walked leisurely back toward his hotel, popping in to check out a few shops offering handmade woodcarvings, leather goods, and less traditional souvenirs. He bought nothing.

Back at the hotel, he decided to shower and shave, as much to kill time as to look presentable on a non-date. Staring mindlessly at the intersecting lines of the acoustical tile above the bathtub, his brain suddenly clicked. He finished quickly, shaved, brushed his teeth, and dressed in a long-sleeve tee and the same pair of jeans. Then he retrieved the Jackson Hole map from the dresser and opened it on the table.

Six lines connected six dots to form two equilateral triangles, one just southeast of Jackson Lake and one straddling the Snake River west of town. Three more lines connected three more dots to form a third equilateral triangle on the map Lauren had procured from Gary at the visitor center. The lines, dots, and triangle would be too small to be identifiable on the larger map, but Ray had an idea.

He found the Gideon Bible in the nightstand and paused for a moment, remembering something else Lauren had said. *"If you want God to speak to you, Ray, read your Bible."* It was good advice, but for another time.

He set the Bible on top of the map and aligned the spine with the line connecting Jackson Lake Lodge to Signal Mountain. Using the spine as a straightedge, he extended the line south. It crossed the Snake River, then U.S. 191, and then ridge after ridge in the Gros Ventre Wilderness.

He used the same method to extend the line from the turnout east of Oxbow Bend to Signal Mountain. It just missed the edge of Jackson Lake before bisecting Jenny Lake and passing between Middle Teton and South Teton.

Ray turned the map and repeated the procedure with the lines comprising the triangle west of town. The line from the cabin on Fish Creek Road to Woody's ranch followed the Gros Ventre River for a while, crossed the highway, and eventually intersected with one of the lines from the first triangle east of the small town of Kelly.

The line from Teton Science Schools to Woody's ranch extended almost due north, just missing Teton Village and meeting the other line from the first triangle on the western slopes of the Tetons.

Ray sat back, looking at a quadrilateral. The lines intersected, but not at any obvious location. As he pictured the third triangle—the Jackson triangle—and its lines, he guessed where they would hit the others. Nowhere special, he didn't think. Then again, he was operating off estimates and guesses. Even so, he didn't know what to make of the intersections. In theory, he could extend all nine lines infinitely, and they would all ultimately intersect with each of the others at *some* point. But it might not be a point on the globe, much less in Teton County.

He sighed and looked at the clock. 5:14.

Ray folded up the maps and stuffed them into his pocket. Grabbing his Army zip-up sweatshirt and a baseball cap, neither of which he put on, he headed down to his truck. The sun was temporarily behind a cloud, of which there were now quite a few in the sky, and it made the evening air chilly.

Lauren had texted him directions to her apartment on the far west edge of town. Ray studied the sky as he drove, wondering if the clouds were fair-weather or a harbinger of rain. He was something of a failure as the son of a farmer in that he couldn't predict the weather by looking at the sky like all his buddies. Even so, this wasn't the prairie of South Dakota, so who knew what impact the terrain had on any prediction he might have otherwise had.

Lauren was waiting by the front door to her apartment when he pulled into the parking lot. She looked ready for a chuck wagon dinner. She wore a red and black flannel shirt, sleeves rolled to the elbows. It was tucked into distressed—naturally, it appeared, not by some high-priced manufacturer—blue jeans. Dark brown if not black cowboy boots completed the ensemble. Her hair was down, fluttering off her shoulder in the breeze. The only thing missing was a cowboy hat, and Ray had a suspicion that was by choice and not because she didn't own one.

"You look the part," Ray said after she had climbed into the cab and they had exchanged pleasantries. "I like the boots."

"This isn't my first rodeo, Ray."

He nodded and started driving. "How was the babysitting?"

"Mostly stacking and unstacking blocks. How was your afternoon?"

He omitted mention of her words about a date echoing in his head. "Okay. I thought I had a breakthrough regarding the triangles."

"Thought?"

He leaned to the side so he could extricate the maps from his back pocket. He handed them to Lauren, and she unfolded them. She frowned.

"I thought if I extended the lines, maybe they would intersect at some place of significance. But they don't."

"Unless there's a body buried in the mountains here," she said, tapping one of the intersection points. She looked up and winked.

Ray hung a left.

"You know where you're going?"

"I do."

"What about the third triangle? Square-Rodeo-Betsy?"

"Too small for this map."

"So we need a bigger map."

He shrugged.

"What?"

"Even if we connect all the lines, all we do is form a bunch more triangles and shapes. At best they give us more random locations to visit, and then what?"

Lauren sighed.

Ray hung a right.

She suddenly looked down at the map.

"Think of something?"

"On maps, what are triangles for?"

"Usually rest areas."

She stuck out her tongue.

He shrugged again.

"What else?"

"Mmm . . . north arrows."

She nodded. "They point."

"Okay."

"Did you try using the triangles as pointers?" ·

"No."

"Each could point three ways, but," she said, starting to speak faster, "only one way where they would intersect with the other two."

"Not if you extend the lines far enough."

"Okay, sure, if we want to drive to Utah."

She flipped open his glovebox and dug around. She came out with a Chevy Silverado owner's manual. "Ruler," she said, holding it up.

"I used the Gideon Bible."

Turning to use the window as a surface, Lauren pinned the owner's manual in just the right place on the map and used a pen, also from the glovebox, to draw lines extending from the point of the triangles.

"You sure that's a right angle?" Ray asked as she attempted to hold the owner's manual perpendicular to the opposite side of the triangle.

"Pretty."

He nodded. They were headed south out of Jackson, with an immediate slope on their left and the Snake River Valley on the right, stretching for a couple miles before the mountains rose up again. In the late afternoon/early evening sun, it was beautiful. Or would have been if a somewhat forward woman in flannel wasn't holding a map against the window to block most of the view.

Lauren had drawn a line pointing north-northeast from Woody's ranch. She now moved the owner's manual and drew a line extending southwest from Signal Mountain. They intersected a little bit south of Moose, not far from the Craig Thomas Discovery and Visitor Center where Ray and Lauren had met Sunday afternoon.

"The third one's tricky," Lauren said, lowering the map. She picked up the detailed map of Jackson, provided by Gary at the visitor center, and created a line extending almost due north from the Square. Still using the owner's manual as a square and straightedge, she extended the line in both directions to the edge of the map.

"Look square?" she asked Ray, holding the map toward him.

The line she had drawn intersected the line between the fairgrounds and the cemetery at what looked to Ray's eye like a perfect right angle. He nodded.

"If I extend the line, it runs through this peak," she said, referring to a place identified by darker shading on the map, "and the corner of elk refuge here." She swapped maps. "Now, if I can find that peak . . . Here. And the corner . . . Here." She held it up to the window and again used the owner's manual as a straightedge. She extended the short line farther and farther, then stopped.

"Ray."

He looked back from the road to her.

She lowered the map and turned it to face him. "They intersect."

"What?" he asked, focused on traffic that had slowed in front of him.

"The lines intersect. All three arrows 'point' to the same spot." She tapped the map for emphasis.

He looked briefly and saw that her rudimentary geometry had indeed produced a three-way intersection just south of the border of the park.

"These aren't just random spots and meaningless plots on a map, Ray." Her blue eyes were wide and bright. "They point us to a specific location."

SEVENTEEN

Ray followed a well-groomed gravel road off U.S. 191, down toward a riverbank, and then across a wooden bridge that spanned what a sign identified as Flat Creek. The gravel road split left and right. Right, it ran along the creek. Left, it passed under a headgate similar to the one at Woodrow Garner's ranch, only instead of wrought iron dangling from the crossbeam, it had the ranch name burned into the wood: Bar H-9. An old covered wagon was parked off to the side, its canvas top painted with the words "Chuck Wagon Dinner Here!"

The drive wound through a grove of mostly pines and ended in a gravel parking lot bound by a split-rail fence. A man in full cowboy gear—boots, chaps, vest, hat, and potentially a fake mustache—greeted vehicles and directed them toward a similarly dressed woman halfway across the parking lot. She guided Ray and Lauren into the back of a two-deep parking stall, two feet from the bumper of a silver Hyundai with Wisconsin license plates. Tourists.

Lauren unbuckled her seatbelt and handed Ray the folded maps. It had been five minutes since her discovery that the three triangles pointed to a common intersection. Of course, Ray had realized, put any three triangles anywhere on a plane, and they will point to a common intersection if the plane is large enough. Still, this felt like a breakthrough. It would feel more like one once he and Lauren had a chance to conduct more exact and precise measurements.

The night air was growing chilly, and Ray was glad for the sweatshirt he'd brought along as they trudged down a short path through the pines to a clearing. It contained a ticket office, a large seating area under a roof, a gift shop, and restrooms. Beyond the restrooms and through the boughs of several pines, Ray could see a stable and a corral where seven or eight wagons like the one by the entrance were waiting to be hitched to horses. He was a little disappointed to see rubber tires on the wagons, but otherwise, they looked authentic.

"So do we have a strategy for this?" Lauren asked after they checked in. They took a seat with seventy or eighty others.

"Not really. Play it straight. See what we see."

"See what we see?"

"For example, there were two parking attendants. On the surveillance camera, I only saw Graham."

"That was fifteen minutes after wagon departure too."

"True."

A barrel-chested man in full cowboy regalia called for attention from the front of the seating area, introduced himself as Chris, and spent a few minutes welcoming everyone, giving a brief history of the Bar H-9, and explaining how the evening would progress. He pointed out the gift shop, which would be open when the wagons returned, and the bathrooms. He directed everyone to check the "tickets" they had received during check-in for their wagon letter and table number. And he led a pre-meal prayer, which about knocked Ray off his seat. It wasn't the most spiritual of invocations ever offered, but given the politically correct climate and the fact that Jackson struck him as a bastion of liberalism, Ray half expected protesters to form a wall between the seating area and the corral. Instead, the barrel-chested man instructed everyone to head into the corral, watch their step, and find their wagon.

Ray and Lauren did so. They were two of ten riders, seated near the front on the left of two benches that ran along either side. The wagon's canvas sides were rolled up to allow for clear sight, revealing the wagon's metal frame. Technically not the most authentic experience, but Ray wasn't complaining. From what he knew, authenticity on a covered wagon ride was nothing to miss.

Two large, black horses were hitched to the wagon, and a short woman in checked purple and gray flannel and worn jeans held onto the reins. She had glasses, freckles, and reddish-brown hair flowing out in a ponytail from under a straw-colored cowboy hat. She welcomed everyone to the Bar H-9 and Wagon G and introduced herself as Nicki. She was young, Ray thought, probably a few years out of college. Close to Graham's age. He decided to wait until they had at least left the corral before grilling her.

The wagons exited in sequential order and formed a wagon train on a rutted path leading into the pines. Nicki introduced the two Percheron draft horses, Paint and Brush (named for the state flower), and gave some basic info on the breed. She explained they would have about a fifteen-minute ride to the campground, and told her riders to keep an eye out for coyotes, elk, moose, and bald eagles—among other animals—as they descended into the Snake River Valley.

As they came around a corner and the trees thinned to reveal the glimmering river in the distance, she pointed out several geographical features. That segued into a little more history about the ranch, how she had come to work there, and background about herself. That, in turn, segued to her asking her passengers to introduce themselves, where they were from, and what brought them to Jackson Hole. She started with those on her left and worked around to Lauren and then, next to last, Ray.

He gave his name, hometown, and said he had come to visit his cousin.

"She your cousin?" Nicki asked, pointing at Lauren. Her other hand still held the reins as Paint and Brush plodded along, keeping pace with the other wagons.

"No."

"Oh, I thought you two were together."

"Not today," Lauren said.

Ray looked at her.

She said nothing, gave nothing away with her face.

He turned back to Nicki, not wanting to pass on an opportunity. "He actually worked here."

"At the Bar H-9?"

Ray nodded. "Graham Stoddard."

"Yeah, I know Graham. Is he off this week?"

"No. He's missing."

Nicki frowned, enhancing the freckles. "Missing?"

"Nobody's seen him since last Thursday."

She continued frowning. "I'm sorry to hear that. Is that why you're here, at the ranch?"

"That, and for the cowboy supper."

"Well, you won't be disappointed there." She turned and urged the horses on, as one of them had dawdled to nibble on a bush by the side of the path. "You should talk to Jimmy," she said to Ray. "He and Graham were pretty close, I think. More than I was, obviously, since I didn't even know he was missing."

"Jimmy works here?"

"I think he's on the serving crew tonight. Long blond hair. You can't miss him."

"Thanks."

She nodded. After a moment, she turned to the last passenger, a middle-aged guy next to Ray, an author from Chicago who said he was in the area doing research for a novel. He was interrupted by a sudden whoop and the thunder of horses' hooves. From the trees to the left, a trio of white horses galloped onto the trail behind the last wagon. They were ridden by women with painted faces, long black braids adorned with feathers, and clad in buckskin jackets and pants.

It only took Ray a second to realize they were part of the act, and he watched with amusement as they raced up and down along the wagon train, whooping and hollering and waving streaming banners. It was hard to tell with the face paint, but if Ray wasn't mistaken, one of them was Diane, Heidi's friend he'd spoken to Sunday morning.

The "Indians" were eventually chased off by two cavalry soldiers in full military dress, who fired cap guns at them and then stopped to check on the passengers and doff their caps at several females. First a public prayer and now a skit depicting Native Americans as warriors. How did the Bar H-9 stay in business?

The trail again peaceful, the evening sun bathing half of the trees in golden light and shading the other half in gloomy shadows, Nicki resumed her role as guide. She talked more about area wildlife, provided further instructions about dinner, and warned her passengers not to approach the horses lest they get their feet stepped on. She finished just as they arrived in a wide clearing. There were hitching posts in the center, and the two cavalry soldiers and two other riders who had followed along with the wagon train tethered their horses. Meanwhile, the eight wagons halted around the round path while Nicki explained the purpose of circling the wagons. To drive her point home, the three Indians who had "attacked" the wagon train sat atop their horses on a small rise seventy yards in the distance, keeping watch. A little hokey, it was also mildly charming.

Ray, Lauren, and the other passengers disembarked and followed the crowd through a strand of trees to a large, open-air pavilion bordered by trees on two sides. On the far side, a few lone pines created a natural canopy for two long serving tables covered in steaming pots and stainless steel chafers. Beyond the "buffet line" were more trees. To the right, on the fourth side, the terrain sloped gently down to the Snake River some hundred yards away. A few trees broke the terrain, but the view was wide open. With the sun dipping toward the distant Wyoming Range beyond the river, the setting was idyllic.

As they approached the pavilion, Ray kept his eyes out looking for an unmissable guy with long blond hair. He didn't immediately spot him but did take note of a squinting cowboy leaning against one of the pavilion's support columns. He was the kind of guy who would have drawn attention from Louis L'Amour or Zane Grey, the dark-eyed stranger. Only in the old Western dime novels, he would have been smoking a cigarette. He was just standing there, ostensibly to direct patrons to their table.

Ray and Lauren found their way to Table 10, in the back right, where they were seated across from two elderly women adorned in layers of shirts, jackets, scarves, and shawls and down the table from half a dozen giggling teenage girls. Their chaperones were a woman in her thirties trying to look in her low-twenties and a man in his thirties trying to look as if he wasn't there at all.

Chris, the same man who had given them instructions back at the ranch, now gave instructions about dinner. It was a straight-up buffet line, so there wasn't much to instruct. He dismissed the tables in order, and Lauren made small talk with the two senior citizens across from them while Ray kept his head on a swivel looking for a man with long blond hair. No dice.

The smells were intoxicating, and when it was finally their turn, Ray loaded a plate full of salad with creamy homemade ranch dressing, dinner rolls, slices of roast beef and gravy, a thigh of barbecue chicken, mashed potatoes with more gravy, and corn on the cob. The corn on the cob was cut into three-inch sections and fished out of a steaming pot by a man wearing a thick black apron and holding a pair of tongs in each hand, enabling him to serve patrons on either side of the line simultaneously. It was busy work, and hot, standing over the steaming pot. Which was probably why his long blond hair was bound in a ponytail that hung onto the back of his flannel shirt.

Ray caught himself short of staring and took his plate over to the drink table, where he grabbed a cup of lemonade before heading back to Table 10.

"Did you see him?" Lauren asked as she slid in beside him.

Ray nodded.

"I don't even like corn on the cob," she said, holding up her three-inch section.

Ray looked at her.

"I had braces as a teenager. Stuff always stuck in my teeth. Some things just evoke bad memories."

The meal was delicious. The ambiance of the sun setting toward the mountains didn't hurt. And, Ray noticed, it cast Lauren in a very nice light. It also made it harder for her to inconspicuously toss her cob of corn into the nearby trees, but she managed.

After everyone had been through the lines, Chris got up on a stage at the far end of the pavilion and introduced the evening's entertainment, namely four cowboys with a trio of guitars and a fiddle. They sang "cowboy" songs, interspersed with a little banter disguised as a skit. It induced a few laughs and a lot of groans.

Ray cleaned off his plate and nudged Lauren so he could get out. He went through the line to pick up seconds of a few items, including corn on the cob.

The guy with long blond hair in a ponytail peered into his pot. "One or two?"

"Just one," Ray said.

He nodded and fished one out with the tongs.

"Are you Jimmy?" Ray asked.

"Yeah."

"Nicki mentioned you. She said you were friends with Graham Stoddard."

The guy's eyes narrowed slightly. "Yeah."

"I'm his cousin, Ray."

They looked at each other for a few seconds.

"You've heard?" Jimmy asked.

"I have." Ray looked over his shoulder. No one was in line. He looked at the stage. They were singing a soft ballad. "Could I ask you a couple of questions about his disappearance?"

The guy looked around too. "Yeah, sure." He nodded, and Ray followed him a short ways away from the serving line and around a corner of trees. It afforded them a small measure of privacy. "Did you come out here looking for Graham?" Jimmy asked.

"No, I came to visit for a week, but when I got here, he was missing."

"Yeah, he disappeared mid-shift Thursday," Jimmy said.

They covered a few of the particulars, realizing they both knew what the other knew about when and how Graham had disappeared. It was also what Detective Celek knew, and Jimmy said he'd spoken to him the day before.

"I'm sure he asked you this too," Ray said, "but did anything seem unusual or different about Graham lately? Was he acting suspicious or paranoid, or did he mention anything out of the ordinary?"

Jimmy took off his cowboy hat, revealing sweaty strands of blond hair straying all across his high forehead. He wiped his sleeve across his head, then replaced his hat.

"It's probably nothing."

"Okay."

"Graham has a girlfriend."

"Heidi."

"Yeah. They're kind of an odd couple. I've only met her once, but from what Graham tells me. You know that Katy Perry 'Hot n Cold' song?"

Ray shook his head. He didn't listen to Katy Perry. Didn't know anyone who listened to Katy Perry.

"Yeah, well, they're hot and cold. Break up, get back together, whatever."

Ray nodded.

"Couple weeks ago, he comes into work with one of those looks on his face, like he just pulled something off. Like he had a secret he couldn't wait to tell."

"About Heidi?"

"Not so much." Jimmy looked around. "Look, he didn't come out and say it, but he kept leaving hints that he'd hooked up with this other girl."

"He cheated on Heidi?"

Jimmy nodded. "He never admitted it outright, but he said it without saying it." He shrugged. "Like I said, they're hot and cold. Probably wasn't the first time one of them wandered into a different pasture, if you know what I mean."

"Yeah. Did he mention her name, give you any details?"

"No. A week later he was talking about Heidi again. It's like I said, he was acting like he got away with something."

Ray nodded. He was starting to understand why someone would want Graham to disappear. Perhaps someone in particular.

"Look, I don't know if you know Heidi, man," Jimmy said.

"We've met."

"Don't tell her, all right? It won't do her any good to know now. If Graham comes back . . . that's a different story."

"Yeah, sure." Ray probed with a few more questions, including asking about the Garners and triangles, but Jimmy's face was blank. Ray thanked him and took his quickly cooling plate back to Lauren. He was just in time to see the cowboys and cowgirls pass out ceramic pots containing blondies and serve Styrofoam cups of coffee.

"Get lost?" Lauren asked when they had been served.

"Talked to Jimmy."

"Oh?"

Ray explained in hushed tones what Jimmy had told him. Sort of hushed, considering the cadre of teenage girls down the table was giggling almost as loudly as the brief skit that had interrupted the singing on stage. Lauren digested the news right along with her blondie.

"You think Heidi had something to do with it?"

"Honestly, no."

"Don't think she found out? Women have a way of knowing."

"Speaking from personal experience?"

"Secondhand."

"No, it's not that. I don't think she knew, unless she was snowing me, and I don't know why she would have contacted me in the first place. I just don't think she could pull off a kidnapping. Or would. She'd stab him in his sleep instead."

"Hmm. And Jimmy didn't give you a name of this girl?"

"No, and I don't think he knew."

"Hmm."

"Yeah."

The skit ended and the four-piece band sang a rendition of "The Devil Went Down to Georgia," substituting Jackson for Georgia and replacing a few other of Charlie Daniels' lyrics. The fiddle player pranced through the aisles and jumped onto several tables, including right in front of the teenage girls. He was young, decent looking, and it played well. So did he. His fiddle was about smoking when the song concluded, and the emcee/lead singer announced a brief intermission while the crew cleaned up.

"I'm going to stretch my legs, try chatting up a few people," Ray said.

"Got someone in mind?"

"Not particularly."

Lauren nodded at the corner of the stage, where the bass player was setting his guitar on a stand behind the stool on which he'd been sitting for the last half hour. He was older than the rest, seventy, Ray thought, give or take five years. His gray hair was wavy and long enough to extend under a black cowboy hat that had aged right along with him. He had a walrus mustache, also gray, and looked as natural in a multi-colored flannel shirt, vest, and faded denims as any Western star. Speaking of Westerns, he bore a fleeting resemblance to Sam Elliott, only Sam was taller and thinner.

"Why him?" Ray asked.

Lauren placed a hand on his shoulder. "God is telling me you need to go talk to him."

EIGHTEEN

Lauren said it with such sincerity that Ray didn't realize she was joking until a half second before a mischievous smirk broke out. "Too soon?" she asked.

"No. Just too convincing."

Her smirk widened into a full-blown grin.

"Why him for real?"

"His eyes."

"They're kind?"

"They twinkle."

Ray squinted. "You can see that from here?"

She shrugged. "Call it a hunch. He looks like an old grandpa who sits back, says little, and sees a lot."

"You gonna tag along?"

"Why not?"

Ray took his coffee, and they got up. A handful of others were stretching, headed for dual portable toilets a short walk into the woods, or just walking around. The Sam Elliott ringer had left the stage and wandered a short ways toward the top of the slope. He stood with hands in his pockets, looking at the panorama of sunset. The sun had just dipped behind the mountains, and the sky was on fire. It was two-thirds overcast, but enough breaks allowed light through, and the clouds were dappled with oranges and pinks. It looked like the opening credits of a Western, only way better.

With Westerns on his mind, Ray pictured the man with the mustache sitting at a bar in the saloon and wondered how he should approach him. The out-of-town stranger was usually suspicious, but the best ones were straight-shooters. Ray emulated them.

"Good evening," he said.

The man turned. "Evening. How you folks enjoyin' the show?"

"Only half as much as we enjoyed dinner," Lauren said, a hand on her stomach for effect.

"Glad to hear it." He extended a hand. "Name's Sam."

Ray hid his surprise well.

"Sam Covington."

Lauren was closer and shook Sam's hand first, introducing herself. Ray followed suit.

"Where you all from?" Sam asked.

"I'm from Sioux Falls, South Dakota."

"I'm from Jackson."

He looked at them cockeyed. "You aren't together?"

"We are," Ray said as Lauren answered, "No."

"Uh-huh. Sounds like you all have some things to sort out."

"We are here together," Lauren said, "but we're not married or dating." She looked at Ray, who nodded agreement with her answer.

"I see. Well, didn't mean to make that awkward."

"No worries," Ray said.

"So what brings you to Jackson? Her?"

"Vacation, so to speak."

"You sure picked the right spot," he said, nodding toward the sunset. It was fading, but slowly. "I've lived in Jackson Hole since I was knee-high to a jackrabbit, and I can't think of a more beautiful place."

"I second that," Lauren said.

"How long have you worked for the Bar H-9?" Ray asked.

Sam chuckled. "I'm technically retired. A hitch in the U.S. Army and forty-three years working on various ranches and spreads around the area. That's how I met Chris, the owner of the Bar H-9. He lets me pick the bass and sing for them now and again. I like the surroundings, music, like the smiles on folks' faces, like the food." He leaned over, as if passing on state secrets. "They let us eat for free."

"Hmm, are they hiring?" Lauren asked.

"Every spring."

"How often do you play?" Ray asked.

"Once, maybe twice a week."

"So do you know Graham Stoddard?"

"Sure. Young fella that works here, right? Big beard?"

"That's him."

"Yeah. Haven't seen him the last couple nights, though, come to think of it."

"That's because he disappeared last Thursday."

"Disappeared?"

Ray nodded, then briefly explained. Sam hadn't heard, but then again, hadn't worked over the weekend, and the staff was somewhat transient. A few questions revealed Sam knew Graham, or rather, knew of him but didn't know him well enough or interact with him enough to offer any help. Namely, he hadn't seen Graham conspiring behind the stable with the criminal element, hadn't heard of his romantic exploits, and hadn't observed him acting paranoid.

"Sorry, I can't be of more help to you folks," he said. "And sorry about your cousin. But I do have to be getting back on stage."

"Of course. Thanks for your time," Ray said, offering his hand again. Sam's was rough and rugged, like an old cowboy's.

"Sorry," Lauren said when he was gone. A few other stragglers were out and about, even checking out the view, but they were essentially alone where they stood.

"No, it was worth a try."

She dragged the toe of her boot through the sand. Then she looked over her shoulder. "So how does Graham two-timing his girlfriend play into all this?"

"I don't know."

"And what is with three triangles intersecting at a piece of land in the middle of the valley?"

"I don't know."

"It's tied to the Garners somehow, clearly, but how?"

"I don't know." He looked from the panorama directly at her. "I also don't know how Graham knew any of this, why he sent it to me in code, or what we're supposed to make of any of it, or what we're supposed to do next."

She nodded back toward the pavilion. The breeze was doing nice things with her hair. "Listen to some music?" she asked.

Ray nodded. "Might as well."

The staff of the Bar H-9 passed out more coffee, and it was necessary as darkness crept over the valley and the temperature dropped. The four-piece band, including the decent-looking fiddle player who now had the teenage girls at Ray and Lauren's table screaming—and thus their male chaperone looking like he wanted to slide under the table—played half a dozen more songs, from Johnny Cash's "(Ghost) Riders in the Sky" to Roy Rogers' "Happy Trails." They concluded with "How Great Thou Art," which they claimed they did every night. The ACLU had to be about to shut this place down, didn't it?

Ray enjoyed the show, but he couldn't keep from pondering the questions Lauren had asked. Was Graham's "affair" with some other woman—if Jimmy was right and it had taken place—relevant to his disappearance? Ray wasn't a big fan of coincidences, but from what Jimmy said, from what Ray knew of Graham, and from what he knew of men in general—and, frankly, from what he concluded about Graham and Heidi's relationship from talking to Heidi—it wasn't like Graham having a one-night stand with another woman was all that surprising.

He also couldn't stop thinking—all night in fact—about the triangles on the map, the extended lines, or the "asterisk" where they intersected. He wanted to plot the lines out more carefully, not using a Chevy Silverado owner's manual as a straightedge and the window of a moving Chevy Silverado as a surface on which to draw lines on a small-scale map. He wanted to see who owned the land, what it looked like, and how—if at all—it was tied to the Garner Family.

Most of all, he couldn't stop thinking about how all of this was connected to Graham and his disappearance and how he, Ray, could do anything about it. And that made him feel a little guilty. Graham was missing—had been for the better part of a week—and all Ray could do was travel around the valley with a good-looking woman, taking in the scenery and attending cowboy dinner theater.

When the show finished, Chris directed everyone to head back to their wagons, with a reminder to stop in the Bar H-9 gift shop back at the ranch. Night had fallen, the crickets were chirping, and the stars that were visible through the clearing and in between the clouds were almost touchable. Ray fought off a shiver as they walked. He remembered on cool summer evenings or breezy autumn afternoons when Annabelle would scrunch her shoulders together and lean into him. He would put his arm around her, hold her close. Walking past snorting horses to Wagon G, he could still smell the shampoo in Annabelle's hair, see the love in her eyes as she looked up at him adoringly.

Before God spoke to her.

Ray and Lauren were almost back to the wagon when Sam Covington stepped away from the supply wagon that had carried the food, servers, and miscellaneous items from the ranch. He nodded in place of a wave. "You all enjoy the rest of the show?"

"We did," Lauren said as Ray nodded. "Especially the bass player," she said with a wink.

He grinned from under his mustache. "Say, I feel bad I couldn't help you earlier."

"Don't worry about it," Ray said.

"I got to thinking though, after we talked. You should talk to Jimmy. Seems I saw him and Graham together several times. Jimmy's been here several years, a regular."

"We spoke to him," Lauren said.

"Oh, you did, huh?"

"Our wagon driver mentioned him too."

Sam sighed. "All right. Thought it worth a mention."

"It was," Ray said. "Thanks."

Sam nodded.

And Ray had a hunch, maybe not unlike the one Lauren had had when she'd observed Sam's twinkling eyes.

"You said you worked on ranches in the area most of your life?" Ray asked.

"Yeah. Forty-three years."

"You ever work for Woodrow Garner?"

Sam shook his head. "Why?"

"It's a long shot and kind of complicated, but we think Graham's disappearance might be tied to the Garner Family and their fascination with certain plots of land in and around the valley. I thought with your experience, you might be able to shed a light on the mystery."

Sam looked at him for a long several seconds while other patrons headed for their wagons or posed for pictures in front of them. Then Sam looked at Lauren. His mustache twitched. "I never worked for Woodrow Garner. I never met him. Couldn't pick him out of a lineup and couldn't vouch for or against his character. But I do know there's quite a history of the Garner Family in the area." His mustache twitched again. "I tell you what, why don't you all head on back to your wagon, and I'll meet up with you back at the ranch."

"Okay. Thanks."

He nodded, and they hurried to their wagon. They were the last to board, and from the back, could only hear half of what Nicki said as Paint and Brush plodded back to the ranch. Several others in the wagon were inquisitive and kept a conversation with her going. It enabled Ray and Lauren to talk without being rude.

"What do you think of that?" she asked.

"I don't know. He seemed to perk up at the mention of the Garners."

"Perk isn't the word I'd use, but I know what you mean."

"I feel like every piece of the puzzle we get just has four more edges that don't fit, you know?"

"I do."

Lauren shivered. Ray thought about putting his arm around her. Not with any intention, but more like wondering what it would be like to do so. He didn't dwell on it.

When they returned to the ranch, the wagons all circled around the corral and parked where they had been a few hours ago. Ray and Lauren joined the throng funneling back to the main seating area and gift shop. In true cowboy fashion, Ray propped himself against a wood column supporting the roof over the seating area and waited for Sam. He'd been in the supply wagon, which had passed them on the way back. Nicki had explained, during one of the times she'd been speaking loudly enough for those in the back to hear, that the staff at the Bar H-9 had to feed and take care of the horses before they could eat themselves, which explained their hurry to get back. It made Ray wonder, then and now, how long they'd have to wait for Sam.

It turned out not that long. Within five minutes, he shuffled over to them, a cup of coffee in hand. He guided them around the gift shop and to a small fenced-in gravel area with a pair of picnic tables in the middle. It was poorly lit, only by ambient light from a window in the gift shop and yard lights around the seating area, parking lot, and corral. The din of people talking and walking and the hubbub of a ranch filtered in as well, but at least they had privacy.

"We're not keeping you from anything, are we?" Lauren asked.

"No," he said with a dismissive wave. "I'm retired, remember?"

"Well, thanks for taking the time to talk with us," Ray said.

Sam nodded. "Tell me more about why you're interested in the Garner Family."

With a glance at Lauren, Ray did. He saw no reason to be reticent around Sam, and as succinctly as possible, explained about the postcards, the locations he and Lauren had visited, and their deductions about what 'Find the triangles' meant. Sam nodded along, lips pursed. When Ray was finished, he nodded.

"Like I told you earlier, I've never met Woodrow Garner. Don't know him from Adam. But I've lived here for close to fifty years, so I know of the family, know of rumors, know of facts. I don't deal in rumors and speculation and gossip, but I will tell you what I know about the family. I'll let you decide if it's relevant at all."

"Fair enough," Ray said.

Sam nodded again. "The Garner Family, on its own, isn't all that interesting. They trace their lineage in these parts back about a hundred years, but I don't know that there's much to separate them from any other family in that. However, Woodrow Garner married a woman named Zora James, a descendant of Bret James."

"Who's Bret James?" Lauren asked.

"One of the original settlers in Jackson Hole," Sam said. "Arrived in 1890 with his wife and son, set about ranchin' and never quit. Also operated a freight company that birthed a modern company they sold off a decade or two ago for seven or eight figures."

Ray nodded. Sam's info, so far, matched what he'd dug up the previous afternoon.

"Bret's son Jeffrey had a couple of daughters and a son named Maverick. Zora was his daughter, which is how the James are connected to the Garners. But if you go back to Bret James, he also opened a trading post in Jackson Hole. His partner was his good friend and fellow rancher John Marion, who'd arrived in the valley a few years before James did."

Sam leaned forward and stroked his mustache. "John Marion had three sons, and the family tree grew into a forest. The original Marion Ranch passed down from generation to generation, and it's still in the family to this day. One of Marion's great-granddaughters owns it. Anyhow, James and Marion were the best of pals until Marion's death. The two families have had a falling out since, all based on a land dispute, if that isn't prosaic enough for you."

"A land dispute?" Lauren asked.

Sam nodded. "Way back when, it was occupied by Shoshone Indians. They disappeared around the turn of the century, and nobody knows where and why. There are all sorts of rumors, from a sudden disease to they went searching for ancient tribal treasure hidden in the Wasatch Mountains to John Marion chased them off to take the land." He shrugged. "Not sure if any of them hold much water, although Marion did end up getting the land. A lot of people speculate they just moved to Idaho, although it was awful sudden."

He sat back. "Anyhow, that's all rumor and I don't put much stock in any of it."

Ray nodded.

"Now, when the two of you mentioned interest in various pieces of land around the valley and mentioned the Garners—who are tied to the James Family and thus the Marion Family—well, I thought you might be intrigued by a little history."

"We are," Ray said.

"Do you know which piece of land?" Lauren asked.

"A place called Snake Island," Sam said. "If you follow the Snake River north from here," he said, gesturing toward it with his thumb, "it curves and heads in a pretty straight line, all things considered, a little east of north. Eventually, it forms the border of the park for a little while, then curves east before resuming northeast through the heart of the park. Before it turns east, it splits, and for a little more than a mile, runs in two channels about a quarter mile apart. In between those two channels is Snake Island."

Ray reached into his pocket and withdrew the Jackson Hole Map. He set it out on the table, and they all squinted in the dim light. Grand Teton National Park was shaded in green, covering more than half of the map. Projecting up into the park was an "isthmus" of white, private land that was not part of the park. The Snake River split, as Sam had indicated, with the left channel forming the boundary of the park and the right channel cutting through the isthmus of private land, which ended just short of where the two channels reunited.

Ray tapped the map between the two channels. "Is this Snake Island?"

Sam nodded. "Not marked on any map as so, but that's what all the locals call it."

Ray lifted his finger off the map, revealing the intersection of the three lines Lauren had drawn on the way to the ranch.

NINETEEN

Ray and Lauren weren't the last to leave the Bar H-9. They had talked for fifteen to twenty minutes with Sam Covington, which was long enough to outlast most of the patrons. But those who took their time browsing in the gift shop or waiting for restrooms were still around, leaving a few cars in the parking lot. One of them was parked behind Ray's Silverado and backed out as they approached the doors on opposite sides of the truck.

Ray stopped.

Across the hood from him, so did Lauren. "What is it?"

"The camera up there, on the light pole in the corner."

She looked up at it. "Yeah?"

"It's the only one in the lot," he said.

"Okay."

"It's the camera the footage of Graham's disappearance was shot on."

"That makes sense."

"Did you see that car back out?"

"Ray, it's getting cold out here."

"Sorry." He unlocked the truck, and they got in.

"Yes, I saw the car," Lauren said. "What of it?"

"It was a car, so obviously you could see the truck behind it from the camera. But if it had been a van, parked sideways, and my truck was a typical sedan . . ."

"It'd be hidden, at least partially, even though the camera is elevated."

"It was," Ray said.

"What was?"

"When the Jackson Hole Cleaners van pulled out, there was a car behind it, a little Honda or Nissan or something. I wasn't paying any attention because

I assumed the van was what was important. Detective Celek and I both assumed Graham got into or was forced into the van. But what if the van was a decoy? What if it blocked the Honda or Nissan so Graham could be loaded into the trunk? It could have left whenever later and nobody would have ever thought to look for it."

"That's possible," Lauren said. She shivered, and Ray got the hint and turned on the truck. "It makes sense," she said, "from a devious criminal's perspective."

"Yeah. That's what scares me."

They bounced back along the rutted path through the pines to the highway. As Ray turned left, back to Jackson, he turned to look at Lauren. She sat with hands in her sleeves, still shivering a little. He nudged the heater up higher.

"Thanks."

"A forward girl like you, I'd think you'd just take over the controls."

She gave him the evil eye.

"So what do you make of the Garners and James and Marions and Snake Island?" he asked.

"I think we need to do some digging into what makes Snake Island such a desirable plot of ground."

"First, I want to do a little more scientific projection of the triangles. I'm a little dubious of dots and lines and angles drawn on windows and using Bibles and owner's manuals."

"I was very careful, Ray."

"I'm sure you were."

"Well, at the risk of sounding forward, you want to come in for a little while when you drop me off? I have a huge map on my wall, a real nerd identifier. We could plot everything out on that."

"On the map on your wall?"

"Uh-hmm."

"Won't that kind of ruin it?"

"Not if we use pushpins and string instead of a Sharpie."

"That's using your head for more than a cowboy-hat rack."

"I also make pretty stinkin' good coffee."

"At this point, I don't even care if it's good just so long as it's hot."

Ray had no trouble finding his way back to her apartment, nor finding a parking spot. He noted the stars were nearly gone as they walked to the front door. He didn't think it was light pollution.

Lauren's was a second-floor apartment accessible from an external ground-level door. The apartment itself was small but cozy. It featured an open floor plan, with a living room at the top of the stairs and a galley kitchen to the left. The carpet was thick and soft, even under Ray's shoes, which made him think to check for mud and other elements tracked in from the ranch.

"Don't worry about it," Lauren said, flipping on recessed lighting over the counter separating the kitchen from the living room. It featured a pair of oversized chairs at right angles to each other and a glass coffee table in front of a corner fireplace. The mantle was topped with photos of Lauren at various ages. Most showed an older man with her, some showed groups of people, and some included Lauren, a younger version of the older man, and a slightly older "version" of Lauren. The walls held more photos, blown up into canvas prints.

"You take these?" Ray asked, looking at a quartet of photos of the Tetons taken from the Snake River Overlook, one in each season.

"Mm-hmm."

"They're beautiful."

"Thanks."

"You have a nice place," Ray said, smiling at a carved moose head on a table beside the hallway. Its antlers held several small photo frames.

"You haven't seen the best part," Lauren said, sidestepping a small, circular dining table on the far side of the living room. Ray joined her as she slid open a sliding glass door. They stepped out onto a small balcony that felt as if it was an extension of the boughs of a huge pine tree to the left. "Okay," she said, leaning on the cap of the wood railing, "so it's not much of a view now, but on a crisp autumn morning or summer evening . . ."

"I'll bet."

They went back inside, and Lauren set about brewing coffee while Ray checked out a map that covered most of one wall in the dining area. It was at least six feet by four feet, showing everything from the southern border of Yellowstone National Park to several miles south of Jackson, and everything in between the Idaho-Wyoming border and the Continental Divide. It was flat, but with such vivid topographic detail that it looked like a relief map.

With coffee brewing in a twelve-cup pot, Lauren announced she was going to use the restroom. She told Ray to make himself at home and disappeared down the hall. He took a deep breath and wandered toward the fireplace. He looked more closely at the pictures, having already concluded the man and woman in them were Lauren's dad and mom. The resemblance was strong, especially considering that twenty years ago, when the photos had been taken, Lauren's mom was probably about as old as Lauren was now.

"Isn't a day goes by I don't miss her."

Ray turned to see Lauren at the end of the hallway. She had shed the boots and rolled the sleeves on her flannel up to the elbows. Come to think of it, it was a little warm in the apartment, at least after being outdoors for several hours.

"You look just like her," he said.

"Thanks." She walked over and stood beside him. "You know, it just about kills me some days that I don't know Tania Waite the woman. I only know her as Mommy to a little nine-year-old girl. I don't know what moved her, what stirred her soul, what captivated her heart. I just know she made killer peanut butter and banana sandwiches and could kiss away owies."

Ray said nothing.

"Dad never talked about her much, not in those ways." She sighed. "Then again, Dad didn't talk about anything in those ways. He's a meat and potatoes guy, not big on huge emotional displays."

Ray said nothing.

"Kind of like you, Ray. At least, from what I know after three days." She grinned. "You want some coffee?"

"Yeah."

They headed to the kitchen, or in Ray's case, the counter. Lauren poured steaming coffee into two mugs, each bearing the National Park Service logo.

"Thanks."

"You see the map?"

"I did."

"I've got some string somewhere," she said. She set down her mug and rummaged through various drawers on either side of a range top in the counter. Ray tested the coffee. Hot and richly flavorful. He was glad she'd made a whole pot.

"Here." She carried her mug in one hand and a spool of string, scissors, and a clear plastic box of pushpins in the other. She set them on the table, and they stood and looked at the map.

"You're right," he said.

"What's that?"

"It is a bit nerdy."

She whacked his arm, and coffee sloshed out of his mug onto his hand and the floor. Lauren covered her mouth and stifled a laugh.

"It's not funny. You're wasting good coffee."

"I'll make more," she said, retreating to the kitchen to grab paper towels. "Is it hot?" she asked, handing him a paper towel so he could wipe off his hand.

"No, it's fine. I have multiple layers of skin anyhow."

She wiped the floor and tossed the paper towel on the far end of the table. Ray did likewise with his, and they again stood side by side, looking at the map.

"Okay," she said after a minute, "so how do we do this and make sure the lines are straight?"

"Your idea," he said.

She turned toward him, and he reflexively moved away from another whack that didn't come. In the process, he sloshed coffee out of his mug again.

This time Lauren couldn't contain the laughter and staggered back against the table. Ray put down his mug and wiped off his hand and the floor, then stood and smiled at Lauren. For whatever reason, it caused her to crack up even more, and she fell back into a chair.

"I'm sorry," she said when she finally had her laughter under control. "Is it late?"

"Nine."

"Shoot," she said, wiping the corner of her eye with the back of her hand. "I can't even blame this on being tired."

"Afraid not."

She pushed up from the table. "Okay, no more hitting your arm. Let's focus here, before it does get late."

"You have a yardstick?"

"Yeah."

"We'll still be somewhat imprecise, but on a larger scale."

"That works. Short of hiring a surveyor, I don't know what else we can do."

"Okay."

She retrieved a yardstick that bore the mark of a local hardware store and set it on the table. Then they began inserting pushpins into the map at the nine locations referenced in the postcards: the Jackson Town Square, the approximate location of Betsy Garner's grave in Aspen Hill Cemetery, the Teton County Fairgrounds, Teton Science Schools, the center of Woody Garner's ranch, roughly 2265 N Fish Creek Road, the Jackson Lake Overlook atop Signal Mountain, Jackson Lake Lodge, and the turnout east of Oxbow Bend. The pins formed three equilateral triangles.

"So far, so good," Lauren said. "Let me get you a refill," she said, taking Ray's mug. When she came back, she was carrying a ruler.

"What's that for?"

"This," she said. She balanced it on the pins at the cemetery and the fairgrounds. Then she placed the yardstick atop it, extending upward, and slowly slid the end of the yardstick along the ruler until it rested against the pushpin in the Town Square. "Forms a ninety-degree angle."

"More or less."

It stretched up to the east of Jackson Lake, and Lauren stuck another pushpin into the map at the top of the yardstick. "Yeah?" she asked.

Ray nodded and drank some more coffee.

They repeated the procedure, needing more than two hands for the other two triangles. When they were finished, a total of twelve pushpins were inserted in the map, nine forming three triangles and three more in positions such that a string from them to the tip of the triangle should be on a line to bisect it. More or less.

Using the yardstick as an approximate scale, they measured and cut three four-foot lengths of string. Lauren handed them to Ray. "You're taller."

After a gulp of coffee, he proceeded to tie the ends of string around the pushpins, essentially forming lines extending from the points of the triangles, perpendicular to the sides opposite the points, just as Lauren had done on the way to the Bar H-9. And just as her lines had, the three strings all intersected each other at the same point on Snake Island. More or less.

"Hmm," she said. "They're a little off."

"Pretty close," Ray said. The scale was such that one inch equaled one kilometer, and the strings intersected within an eighth of an inch of each other.

"Our method is inexact," she said. "If we had picked a different corner of the Square or a different part of the Lodge . . . Who knows, maybe whoever came up with these intersecting lines to begin with was a little off."

"Or maybe," Ray said, tilting his head, "if we had perfectly precise measurements, they wouldn't intersect but form another triangle."

Lauren tipped her head too. Ray was suddenly aware of how cute she looked staring at the map, a mug of coffee held dangerously in her hand, wearing socks, jeans, and red and black flannel shirt with sleeves rolled to the elbow. He focused on the map.

Lauren righted her head and looked at him. "I don't know why Graham sent you the message, I don't know why he sent it the way he did, and I don't know what any of this has to do with his disappearance, but I think we need to find out more about Snake Island."

"I agree."

She wrinkled her nose. "Sam didn't say anything about what caused the falling out between the Marions and James. I mean, what specifically about the land."

Ray shook his head.

"He started talking about the Indians that used to live on the land. Anything in that, you think?"

"I don't know." He sighed. "I guess I have more work to do."

"I'd help, but I've got a seminar tomorrow morning."

"A seminar?"

"For work. Cultural sensitivity."

"Sounds fascinating."

"Oh, don't you know it."

"Aren't you on vacation?"

"Not from this, apparently."

Ray frowned, then looked back at the map as he drained his coffee. He was about to suggest he get going when Lauren asked if he'd like one more cup for the road.

"Sure."

They took them into the living room, to the oversized chairs. "Can I ask you something?" Ray asked.

Lauren nodded.

"I've been thinking about what you said about how if we can't take what God said back to Scripture, we can't know that it was really God who said it."

She nodded.

"So what do you do with people who say God called them to be a pastor or told them which job to take or where to live?"

"Or who to marry?"

"For example."

Lauren pulled her feet up onto the chair and hugged her knees. She looked up at the ceiling for a moment, forming her words. "There's a difference between revelation and direction. You sound like a heretic if you tell people

God doesn't audibly speak to them. They tell you not to put God in a box, not to say what He can or can't do. And I generally agree with that."

"But not this time?"

"There's a difference between putting God in a box and recognizing the parameters by which He has revealed Himself. Talk about astounding, Ray. God has revealed Himself to us." Her eyes were wide with wonder. Then they narrowed. "Where was I going with this?"

He shrugged. "Something about boxes."

"Oh, right. God revealed Himself to us. Paul wrote in Romans that '*his invisible attributes, namely, his eternal power and divine nature, have been clearly perceived, ever since the creation of the world, in the things that have been made.*' It's what we call general revelation."

Ray nodded.

"Then Paul wrote in Hebrews that—"

"Paul didn't write Hebrews."

She raised an eyebrow. "You know that?"

"You know he did?"

"I have suspicions."

He shrugged. "Okay."

"*Somebody* wrote in Hebrews that '*Long ago, at many times and in many ways, God spoke to our fathers by the prophets, but in these last days he has spoken to us by his Son.*'"

"You have the whole New Testament memorized?"

"It's why I can't quote *MacBeth* verbatim."

He nodded.

"The days of God speaking to and through prophets are over. They were over in 66 A.D. or whenever *someone* wrote Hebrews. And Jesus isn't walking the earth anymore to speak to us, which leaves us with the words He did speak. Paul wrote that '*the gospel that was preached by me*' was '*received . . . through a revelation of Jesus Christ*' and that '*all Scripture is breathed out of God.*'"

Ray took a drink, listening.

"So we have God's general revelation in nature, and we have specific revelation—first through the prophets '*at many times and in many ways,*' and now through Christ and His Word. And that's all of God's revelation. It's not all of God. He hasn't revealed all of Himself, but He has revealed all we need to know of Him—all He wants us to know of Him. He has defined the box.

And to seek that which is outside of the box is to suggest that God's revelation is insufficient—that Scripture is insufficient. Paul warned against that when he wrote, '*if we or an angel from heaven should preach to you a gospel contrary to the one we preached to you, let him be accursed.*' Not exactly a light warning."

"You should be a preacher."

"Paul warned against that too," she said with a smile. She took a drink of coffee. "So when someone claims that God is speaking to them, that He is giving them revelation, I come back to these verses and say that no, He isn't."

Ray nodded. "I'm right there with you. I agree with everything you said, although I couldn't say it that well. But you said there was a difference between revelation and direction. So what about God prompting and guiding and convicting us?"

"Oh, He absolutely does that. But it's always through Scripture. '*For the word of God is living and active, sharper than any two-edged sword, piercing to the division of soul and of spirit, of joints and of marrow, and discerning the thoughts and intentions of the heart.*'"

"Seriously, do you have it all memorized?"

"Just parts. And like I said the other day, with Jesse, I do believe God told me to break up with him, not with some audible voice or mystical prompting, but through Scripture. That's the working of the Holy Spirit. Could He do that with an 'audible' voice or something else someone might call 'speaking'? Sure, I guess. But even so, He would only be reiterating what is in Scripture. And I think it's dangerous to start listening for God to speak instead of looking to where He has spoken."

"So what about things that aren't in Scripture?"

"Like what?" she asked, taking another drink. She set her mug back on the coffee table and hugged her knees again. "Marriage?"

"Yeah."

"I'll come back to what I said before, how does she know it's God speaking?"

"She would say she just knows."

Lauren nodded. "She's so familiar with God's voice that she can recognize it?"

"Something like that."

"I've heard people say that before, or something like it. But what is familiar? They may have 'heard' a 'voice' before, but unless they can compare that voice ultimately to Scripture, there's no way of knowing that voice is God's."

"Hmm."

"Not sold?"

"No, that makes sense. But I've got another one for you."

"Okay."

"We had a missionary couple in our church a couple years back, from the Middle East—they couldn't even tell us where exactly because it was too dangerous. But they said devout Muslims in their country were having visions of Jesus and hearing His voice, telling them they needed salvation or even in one case, to travel hundreds of miles across the wilderness to find this specific couple who they'd never met and ask them, 'Who is Jesus?'" He looked directly at Lauren. "What do you make of that?"

"I'd say I'm generally skeptical of people having visions and dreams, but I also think there are legitimate instances of what you just described. I have no other way to explain it."

"So God does speak to people?"

"In some dramatic instances, yes. But always to draw them to Jesus as revealed in Scripture. Never to reveal additional doctrine or teaching or some word of prophecy. We know from Scripture that such a vision or voice wouldn't be Jesus."

He nodded.

"As to marriage proposals, I guess I don't see those on the same level. Might God have spoken to Annabelle to draw her out of Islam and to faith in Him? Sure. To tell her to break off an engagement for no biblical reason . . ." She fluttered her hand back and forth. "And I don't mean to criticize Annabelle."

"No, I know." He sighed. "I've taken up too much of your time."

"No you haven't."

"Still, it's getting late. I should be going."

"Okay."

They stood, and she took his mug from him. Then she walked him to the door.

"Thanks for coming along tonight," he said.

She opened the door for him. "Thank you for dinner."

"My pleasure." He stepped out onto the sidewalk, then turned back. "Can I ask you something else?"

"Yeah," she said, leaning on the open door.

"This afternoon, when I asked you to go with me to the ranch, you asked if it was a date or not."

She nodded.

"Given everything we've talked about with Annabelle and Jesse, if I'd have said a date . . . what would you have said?"

"I would have said yes."

He nodded.

Lauren smiled. "Good night, Ray."

"Good night, Lauren."

She closed the door.

He stood there for just a moment, then headed for his truck.

TWENTY

Snow was flying when Ray opened his hotel room drapes Wednesday morning. Grass and tree branches and rooftops were glazed with a thin coating of white. The horizon was blurred in a haze created by flakes and maybe a hint of fog. It looked like January back in Sioux Falls. Ray hadn't paid attention to the weather forecast to know any precipitation was moving in. He also hadn't realized just how cold it really was.

He had fallen asleep thinking about Lauren and how much he'd enjoyed the evening with her, even if it had been "business." He awoke feeling somewhat guilty, considering he was still grieving the breakup with Annabelle. Or was he? he wondered as he stared out the window. Maybe this was what moving on felt like. Maybe it wasn't weird to be attracted to another woman so soon after being dumped by his fiancée. Maybe it was healthy?

This was too much introspection for early in the morning, before coffee. So Ray showered and dressed and hurried out to grab some breakfast. Walking past the shops in a resort town while it snowed might have been a romantic idea to some, but not to Ray. Especially not when the snow was coming in at a forty-five-degree angle. So he drove a couple blocks to Jackson Hole Coffee Roasters, ordered two coffees and a box of six donuts, and headed back to his truck. The snow wasn't sticking on the pavement yet, but it was making a slushy mess. Ray wondered if this was typical for Jackson in September.

He made another drive of a few blocks and parked in front of the Teton County Sheriff's Office. Detective Celek was in and willing to see Ray, and he eyed the box of donuts and drink carrier in Ray's hand as he welcomed him back to his cubicle.

"It's what you think it is," Ray said. "A shameless attempt to get into your good graces."

Celek took one of the cups from the extended drink carrier. "It worked. Why do you want in my good graces?"

He nodded at a chair and Ray sat down. He set the box of donuts on a vacant corner of the desk and opened it. "I don't mean to play the know-it-all amateur detective, but I had an idea and I wanted to see if you think it's valid."

"Shoot."

"On the surveillance video from the Bar H-9, we saw a van pull in front of Graham, and he disappeared, presumably in the van. But what if he didn't get into the van but into the trunk of a car parked behind the van?"

Celek paused with his hand poised over the box of donuts. He selected a glazed and sat back. He seemed set to speak, then pursed his lips. "What makes you think so?" he finally asked.

"I went out to the ranch last night, to the chuck wagon dinner."

Celek nodded as he took a bite.

"Some guy was backing out of the parking lot from behind my truck, and the idea hit me."

Celek swallowed. "Let's look at the tape."

It took him thirty seconds and a gulp of coffee to pull up the footage. Ray leaned forward to see the screen better. Like the first time, the feed showed approximately twenty cars in the lot. The timestamp in the corner was 18:13:04.

Like the first time, Graham walked into view from left to right. He wore jeans, a plaid shirt, and a cowboy hat. Ray studied a pair of cars in the center of the screen, a tan Toyota Corolla—the same color as Lauren's Ford Focus—and a Nissan Juke. Both were parked facing away from the camera.

Celek let the footage roll. At 18:13:44 the Jackson Hole Cleaners van drove into the picture and parked in front of Graham, and in front of the Corolla and Juke. For twenty seconds, nothing happened. Ray studied the grainy image, looking for anything telltale—a sudden reflection, movement where it shouldn't be. He saw nothing, to no surprise. If Celek hadn't seen it, why would Ray?

The van started moving again at 18:14:06. It disappeared out of the frame, leaving the Corolla and Juke, among others, where they had been in the lot.

Celek paused the video. He again leaned back in his chair. He pursed his lips again. Finally, he turned in his chair.

"Your theory is somebody jumped out of the van, stashed him in the trunk, got back in the van, and drove off, leaving Graham in the trunk?"

Ray nodded.

"They would have had twenty seconds or so. That could be enough time."

Ray said nothing.

"Of course, that's predicated on Graham walking along a certain path. If he goes down a different row, the van can still block him from the camera, but not use the trunk . . ."

Ray said nothing.

"Then again, that may not be that hard of a thing to figure out if they scoped out and planned ahead." Celek sat up. "It's a viable theory, at least." He looked back at the screen. "They wouldn't have used the Nissan . . . whatever it is. Joke? Juke."

"Because of the rear window?"

"Right. You don't kidnap a guy and lock him in what amounts to a hatchback. Even if you knock him unconscious, somebody could look in and see him. It's too risky. So that leaves the Toyota," he said before taking a large bite of the glazed donut.

"Do we have enough footage to see who got into it and when?"

"Let's see," Celek said, turning back to the screen. He ran the footage forward at high speed, stopping when he saw movement in the parking lot. False alarm. He went forward at a slower high speed, then stopped it again. He moved the scrubber back fractionally and let the video play at regular speed. The timestamp read 20:33:39. A man in a baseball cap, T-shirt, and jeans walked between the Corolla and Juke. He opened the door, got in, backed out, and drove away. Celek stopped the footage at 20:34:10.

"Eight-thirty," he said. "Two and a quarter hours later. That's nervy, if so."

"Not if they knocked him out, like you said."

He backed up the footage, paused it, and zoomed in on the guy. Tennis shoes with the jeans. They were preppy, tapered more than could be comfortable. The T-shirt was snug if not tight, and bore a logo and slogan Ray had seen at several of the shops around town. The hat was brown with a yellow cowboy riding a bucking bronco on it. University of Wyoming. The man's head was tilted down, maybe because he was obviously trying to avoid the camera or maybe because he was trudging along.

"Eight-thirty," Celek repeated. "How long's the show out there?"

"About two and a half hours."

"So this could be a guest or one of the staff."

"Most of the staff stay later," Ray said. "They take care of the horses, eat."

"So somebody who leaves at eight-thirty is a guest?"

"That's my guess. But who knows. Somebody could have knocked off early."

Celek shook his head. "Probably not. That draws attention. But a guest who goes on the wagon ride, has dinner, sees a show, comes back to the ranch and then drives off . . . I hate to say it, Ray, but that's cold-blooded."

"Very."

Celek bit into the donut again as he looked back at the screen. "Not much in the way of facial rec, but I'll see what the guys at the lab can pull off this. Maybe when the car arrives there's more, but I doubt it."

"License plate?"

"Yeah, we'll run it." He looked up at Ray. "It's worth a shot. It's local."

"How do you know?"

"The first one or two digits on all Wyoming plates correspond to the county. In this case, twenty-two is Teton County."

Ray nodded.

"Like I said, we'll run it. It's a good thought, Ray."

He shrugged.

"You hanging around town yet for a while?"

Ray shrugged again. "At least another day or two. I was scheduled to head out Saturday, so I might just stay till then."

"I'll call you later today and let you know what we turn up."

"I appreciate it, Detective."

Ray stood.

"Thanks for the coffee and donut."

"You're welcome."

The snow had abated and was just flurries as Ray exited the Sheriff's Office. He started his truck for the heat but didn't put it in gear. Instead, he got out his phone and called Heidi. She was her usual chipper self but agreed to meet Ray at Graham's apartment. Now that Ray knew about the Garner connection, he wanted to do a more thorough search through Graham's stuff to see if he could find anything more—research Graham had done, notes from a conversation, something. Heidi could get him in the door and maybe help him search. Maybe.

She agreed to meet him at ten, which gave Ray the better part of an hour to kill. He needed a refill, so he went back to Jackson Hole Coffee Roasters and purchased more coffee, ate a second donut, and tapped into their Wi-Fi. He looked up local real estate agents, compiling a list of people he could call to hopefully learn about Snake Island—who owned it, who had owned it, who was trying to own it. A little after nine-thirty, he returned to the privacy of his truck to make several calls. He left three voicemails, spoke to two agents who knew nothing, and received a no comment from a third.

Sputtering flurries melted on the windshield as Ray ended the last call. He checked the time and then drove to Graham's to wait there, in case Heidi was early. Sitting by the curb waiting, his thoughts turned to his conversation with Lauren the night before, by the door.

"If I'd have said a date . . . what would you have said?"

"I would have said yes."

Then or now, he wasn't sure why he'd asked her that. It had just sort of come out of his mouth. But now that he knew the answer, it behooved him to actually ask her. Lauren's eyes as she'd answered, then said goodbye, then shut the door, implied he should ask her too, recent engagements aside. But how was that practical, considering he was only still in Jackson to find out what had happened to Graham. Or was that not his only reason for remaining in town?

Heidi walked up the sidewalk at five till ten, which surprised Ray. She wore ripped jeans that looked a size too big and a huge, brown coat. He got out, and they exchanged head nods for hellos. Mumbling about the cold and snow, Heidi led him inside and back to Graham's apartment.

Nothing had changed. The place still looked ransacked. The sofa-sleeper was still unfolded. Two crusts still sat in a pizza box on the counter. Somehow, an overpowering stench had not yet pervaded the apartment.

"What exactly do you want to find here?" Heidi asked, shrugging out of her coat. She tossed it off her left arm in the general direction of a coat hanger on the wall. It missed. She wore several layers of pastel shirts—blue, lavender, a pale pink or white underneath them all. Her hair was nest-like on top of and behind her head. No makeup, no chance of a smile.

"He have a laptop, tablet?"

"Somewhere."

Ray nodded and concluded he'd have to find it himself. "Did Graham ever talk about the Garner Family?"

"The who?"

"Garner. Woodrow Garner especially."

She made a face as if Ray had just asked the dumbest question of all time. Considering the source, maybe he had.

He couldn't remember if he'd told Heidi about the postcards, so as he searched a bookshelf—void of books—next to the sofa-sleeper, he recounted receiving them, finding the locations they referenced, and extrapolating the intersecting triangles. He left Lauren out of it for the sake of brevity.

"Aren't you a mathematical genius," Heidi said.

Ray moved to a storage cubby in the wall. He concluded Heidi was not in the mood for further explanation. The cubby contained all measure of junk, but no electronics. He figured a file on a computer, tablet, or USB drive was the most likely place for Graham to have compiled any research he had conducted. He certainly wouldn't have written it down in a diary or journal.

Next, he looked at the console holding the TV, PlayStation, a DVD player, and an assortment of movies on DVD, video games, adapters, cords, and junk. No laptop or tablet. He got down on his hands and knees to check beneath the console, then laid down to look under the sofa-sleeper.

"Wouldn't recommend that on this floor," Heidi said.

"There's something under the couch."

"Probably a lot of things."

Ray stood and, after tossing a magazine and a pillow onto the bookshelf and back of the sofa, respectively, folded up the bed. It clanged and groaned into place, and he got down again and slid a laptop out from under the sofa. Ray frowned for a moment, wondering how thoroughly Celek's people had searched the apartment. Had they not looked under the couch to find the laptop? Had they not considered it relevant? He made a mental note to maybe check with Celek, at least if the laptop turned up anything.

Heidi shrugged as he got up, holding up the laptop. He sat down, flipped it open, and pushed the power button. It took less than a minute to boot and then prompted him for a password. Ray tipped the screen toward Heidi, who had come to stand beside the sofa. "Any ideas?"

"Hookem-oh-five."

"Do I want to know?"

"Something to do with Texas football."

"I didn't know Graham was a football fan."

"Have you seen the cheerleaders for the Cowboys and Longhorns?"

"Got it."

The computer logged on, and Ray spent ten minutes navigating to various folder locations. He knew just enough about computers to find his way around, including into hidden folders. Granted, if Graham knew more than Ray did, he probably knew a way to actually hide data. Or encrypt it. In which case, Ray would never find it. But it was worth a search.

Heidi sat down next to him. "What do you think's on here, anyhow?"

"Something to do with the postcards and the Garner Family."

"And that will tell you where he is? Because the cops don't have a clue."

Ray mentioned the Toyota Corolla and his theory that it had been the vehicle to abduct Graham, and recounted telling that theory to Detective Celek. "Hopefully that will lead them to a clue," he said.

"Just a genius of all sorts, aren't you."

"Not enough," Ray said, sitting back and sighing.

"Nothing?"

"No. Nothing much on here."

"He doesn't use it much."

"That would explain why it was under the sofa. I don't suppose you know his e-mail password."

"E-mail?"

"What, he doesn't use e-mail?"

"Does anybody anymore?"

"I do."

She huffed.

He closed the laptop and shoved it back under the sofa. He spent ten more minutes looking around the apartment, not really knowing for what, while Heidi wandered around and pouted some more. She was an expert. He was about done when his phone chirped. He pulled it out of his pocket, recognizing but not identifying the number.

"Ray Eastwood."

"Mr. Eastwood, Bob Bronson, Bronson & Sons Realty. You called me this morning."

"Yes," Ray said. One of the three voicemails.

"You have questions about Snake Island, is that right?"

"Yeah. I'm wondering if you can tell me who owns it."

"I have no connection to that piece of property," Bronson said. He had a cerebral sound, for what it was worth. "But it's a matter of public record. Technically, that land is owned by Jackson Savings & Loan."

"A bank?"

"That's right."

"You said technically."

"The land is in trust, and the bank is the trustee. And that's really all I can tell you."

"Well, that's more than I had. Thank you, Mr. Bronson."

"You're welcome."

Ray ended the call.

Heidi wandered in from the bedroom. She held up an iPhone.

"What's that?" Ray asked.

"Graham's phone."

"Seriously?"

"No, I thought now was the time for a practical joke." She handed it to him.

"Where was it?"

"Behind the bed."

"What?"

"Am I stuttering?"

"No. Why would it be behind the bed?"

"The same reason I once found it in the refrigerator. He's always dropping it, misplacing it, having it fall out of his pants. Old one fell out of his pants into the toilet when he was taking a dump."

Ray winced, then looked down at the phone. It powered on, but required a password. Ray turned it to her.

"One-seven-seven-six."

"Seventeen seventy-six?"

"He's a real patriot."

Ray was surprised Graham knew the year the United States had declared independence, but he tapped the code in. He was greeted with an Access Denied message, which he showed to Heidi. She took the phone from him, tapped it in, and shrugged when it gave her the same message. "Must have changed it. Are we done here?"

"Yeah, I guess so."

"Good," she said, picking up her coat.

"I do have one more question," Ray said, reminded by the apparent fact that Graham had changed his phone password, thus denying his girlfriend access.

Heidi's entire body participated in her sigh, but she waited for him to speak.

"There's no delicate way to ask this, so I'll just come out and ask. Is there any chance that Graham wasn't entirely faithful to you?"

"Who?"

He frowned.

"Who was he sleeping with?"

"I don't know that he was. I heard a rumor and thought, if credible, it could be connected to his disappearance."

"What, some former wannabe prom queen kidnapped him because he didn't hang around till morning? I don't think so."

"You don't seem surprised at the question."

"It's hot in here," she said, pushing past him and out the door. He depressed the lock button and followed her into the hall. Then down and out to the sidewalk leading to the street. The sky was still gray and the air still way too cold for September, but it had stopped snowing. What trace had accumulated on the grass or trees was mostly gone. It'd probably be sixty-five and sunny by mid-afternoon. Such was life in the mountains.

"Graham wasn't exactly celibate," Heidi turned and said. She shook her head. "We never promised each other exclusivity. We've been off and on a few times. I figured I wasn't the only girl he ever hooked up with."

"Any idea who it might have been?"

"Really?"

Ray shrugged.

"I got stuff to do, Ray."

"Okay. Sorry to have to ask. Thanks for your help."

She dismissed him with a wave and headed back the way she had come. It was too cold to stand around and think, so Ray headed for his truck, not sure what to do next.

TWENTY-ONE

Ray took Graham's phone to Detective Celek, explaining where it had been found. Celek said he would have his tech try to access it, but said it was possible the phone would reset if too many incorrect passwords were entered. They kicked around what finding it behind the bed meant—Had it been inadvertently left there? Had Graham hidden it? Ray wondered to himself how long his cousin had been without a phone, and could that explain why he'd sent Ray cryptic postcards instead of a text? He decided not to ask Celek about the laptop under the sofa—it had turned up nothing and there was no need to insult the detective's methods and thoroughness, neither of which Ray really doubted.

He left the Sheriff's Office and went to the Teton County Library, where he spent the rest of the morning doing research on land trusts, the history of Jackson Savings & Loan (it dated to the very early twentieth century), and Snake Island. He didn't get very far, at least in terms of uncovering who had put the land in trust, when, or why. He was distracted on several occasions by rain drumming against the windows (at least it was warm enough for it to be rain, although it sounded rather heavy, almost like sleet) and once or twice by something akin to loneliness. He wasn't sure if it was residual isolation from the breakup with Annabelle, a feeling of seclusion because Graham was missing, or simply the solitude of not having Lauren as his wingman.

Armed with a few basic facts, he left the library shortly after noon and set out to find something to eat. He recalled seeing a SUBWAY on the main highway, on the west side of town, and a toasted meatball sandwich was appealing on a cold and still occasionally wet day. He ate alone in a booth, oblivious to the sounds of the restaurant around him.

The way he had it figured, there were three possibilities for Graham's disappearance.

One, something he knew about the Garner Family, their affinity for triangles, and the apparent interest in Snake Island had placed him in a position of danger. What, why, and how was still a mystery.

Two, his tryst with someone had irked someone enough for them to cause him harm. Heidi? Ray didn't think so. The other woman's boyfriend or, he hated to think it, husband? Possibly. But that didn't seem to jive with a kidnapping, a snatch-and-grab job at Graham's place of work.

Three, the Garners and Graham's unfaithfulness had nothing to do with his disappearance. Ray found that the hardest theory to swallow. It required a lot of coincidences, was a theory with no evidence to back it up, and it failed to account for Graham's paranoia. That seemed tied to the postcards, the locations, the triangles, the Garner Family. Paranoia could have also been a result of an angry lover having it in for him. That, however, didn't explain the postcards, and angry lovers or exes didn't often resort to kidnapping, Ray didn't think. So was his affair or tryst or whatever the term was for cheating on one's girlfriend a coincidence too? If there was one, might there be two?

Ray was nowhere.

He had just finished and was balling up his sandwich wrapper when his phone chirped. He quickly exited the restaurant, depositing the wrapper on the way out and chucking his mostly empty twenty-one-ounce cup with it. The air was cool and the breeze nipping, but it was dry. Ray didn't recognize the number, so he answered with a frown.

"Ray Eastwood."

"Good afternoon, Ray. This is Angela Marion."

Marion. As in the Marion Family that traced its ancestry back to John Marion, one of the first settlers in Jackson Hole and good friend of Bret James? *That* couldn't be a coincidence.

"I wonder if I could have a moment of your time," she said. Her voice was neither masculine nor overly feminine. It was strong and steady. She sounded like a businesswoman who was five minutes late for her next meeting.

"Yeah, you can have a moment," Ray said.

"Good. I understand you've been making inquiries about Snake Island."

Ray had started walking toward his truck, but he stopped. "How do you understand that?"

"You contacted Walt Mitchum this morning. Mr. Mitchum is an old friend of the family and notified me."

"I take it you have an interest in Snake Island then."

It was possible she let out a breath before answering. "Why don't we discuss this face to face?"

"Okay."

"Come out to my ranch this afternoon. I'll put on a pot of coffee, we'll sit down and talk."

Ray wasn't sure if it was a question or a command. So he said, "I can do that."

"Head west out of town and take Spring Gulch Road all the way past Saddle Butte. You'll see the Circle M about half a mile ahead on your right. Drive up to the main house."

"Okay," Ray said. "When?"

"Four o'clock this afternoon."

Again, it wasn't a question. Ray had half a mind to say that didn't work, but he got the feeling Angela Marion was not the type of person to annoy for no reason. So he repeated the time in agreement.

"Bring your friend with you, if you'd like."

Ray stopped with his mouth open, about to ask how she knew about Lauren.

"Thank you, Ray. See you this afternoon at four."

The phone clicked before he could utter a reply. Ray lowered the phone into his pocket and looked around. Yep, he was just off the main drag in Jackson, a resort community in western Wyoming. He felt like he was in some mysterious, shapeshifting town on a cable-only paranormal TV show. He knew that was nonsense. He knew eyes weren't watching him from behind every window or an unseen drone up in the sky. And yet, Angela Marion seemed to have far more intel about him than she should.

He returned to his truck, wondering what she wanted. The Garner Family, so it would seem, had a special interest in certain places across the valley that, when the dots were connected properly, pointed to Snake Island. Woodrow Garner had married into the James Family, whose lineage went back to the nineteenth century and crossed paths with the Marion Family. Now Angela Marion had contacted Ray after he'd shown interest in Snake Island via local realtor Walt Mitchum. So what was the connection between the families? John Marion and Bret James had been business partners and friends, according to

Sam Covington. The families had also had a falling out over Snake Island. Was it as simple as that? Or was there something about Snake Island, something—Ray hated to say it—special?

He checked the time and called Lauren. She answered almost immediately.

"Hey," he said. "Your seminar finished?"

"Mercifully, yes."

"You have a minute?"

"A couple at least."

"I just received a very interesting phone call," he said.

"Who from?"

"Angela Marion."

"Who is Angela Marion?"

"If I had to guess, the great-granddaughter of John Marion."

"The one Sam mentioned last night, the one who owns the family ranch?"

"If the Circle M is the family ranch, yes." He relayed their conversation and her invitation.

"Are you going?" Lauren asked.

"I am."

"If this were the Old West, it would be an ambush," she said, and Ray could hear the smirk in her voice. And also, if he wasn't mistaken, an undertone of sincerity.

"I know that. Want to come along?"

"Me?"

"She said, 'bring your friend, if you'd like.' I don't have any other friends in Jackson."

"How does she know about me?"

"I don't know."

"Well, now I am intrigued. Count me in."

"It could be an ambush."

"It could," she said, "but in the Old West, no self-respecting cowboy or cowgirl could possibly turn down such an invitation. It's like she's calling us out."

"So I'm not reading too much into things?"

"No."

"She said four o'clock. I can pick you up about quarter to, maybe twenty to."

"That works. Gives me a chance to take care of a few things around the house."

Ray discarded a brief trace of disappointment that she hadn't suggested hanging out for the few hours between now and then.

"Okay. I will see you then."

"Angela Marion," she mused. "I've never heard of her."

"She's apparently heard of you."

"Who gave us up? Other than the real estate guy, I mean. You didn't mention me to him, did you?"

"Nope."

"Weird."

"Yeah." He paused, and when she said nothing, said, "So I'll pick you up later."

"Okay. Sounds good."

This time they ended the call. Ray looked at the clock on his phone. He had the better part of three hours to kill. He started by driving back to his hotel, where he laid out the postcards and maps and walked through all of his and Lauren's reasoning again. It made sense and led to the same conclusions. Then he reviewed what he knew about the Garner Family, "Trianglism," the James and Marion Families, and Snake Island. It all checked out the same. He tried fitting Heidi and Jimmy's allusion to Graham's cheating on her into the equation, but couldn't make the connection, same as before.

After concluding he wasn't making any additional progress, Ray gave up and called his sister. Cathy had just put the kids down for a nap and mixed herself a cup of instant hot chocolate to accompany her newest novel. But she made time for Ray, who updated her on the search for Graham. He did not mention "the lady park ranger," and she didn't either. That was good, for several reasons.

"Have you called Mom and Dad yet?" she asked.

"No."

"They're the closest thing he has to family."

"They are family, Cathy."

"You know what I mean. They should know."

"I'll call them when I know more."

"When will that be?"

He sighed. "I don't know. I'm supposed to head back Saturday. If I don't know anything by then, I'll let them know."

"Whatever you think is best," she said sincerely, not dismissively.

"I'll let you go. I know how you cherish naptime."

"Fleeting as it is," she said. "Bye, Ray."

"Bye."

He thought seriously about calling his parents right then and there but didn't. At work, Ray hated reporting back that he didn't know or didn't have a conclusive answer or set of data available. He'd rather delay the response until he could provide something concrete. The same was true in this instance, only Ray wasn't having much success analyzing this data.

For kicks, he Googled Angela Marion. His search generated several Facebook and LinkedIn profiles, none of which appeared to be this Angela Marion. The way this was going, if he did have the computer skills and knowledge to dig up information on the correct Angela Marion, she probably had protocols in place to notify her of the search. At least that's how it worked on the crime dramas on TV.

Detective Celek called a little after two. "We got a hit on the Toyota Corolla," he said.

"Oh?"

"Belongs to a woman named Margaret Lane. Or I should say, belonged. She died Christmas before last."

"The car belongs to a dead woman?"

"That's right. No known survivors. She was married once, a long time ago, and there's nothing on the ex-husband. No kids. No siblings. She was sixty-nine, so I doubt there's any parents."

"How did her car end up at the Bar H-9?"

"Working on that. So far, no records of it being sold or passed on, the plates being retired or anything of that nature. Seems like a dead end, but we're still following up."

"I appreciate the update."

"Sure thing."

"Hey, Detective?"

"Yeah."

"You know anything about a woman named Angela Marion?"

"Angela Marion . . . No, I can't say that I do. Who is she?"

"Local resident."

"She tied up in this somehow?"

"I'm not sure."

"How'd you come across her, if I may ask?"

"She called me."

"Out of the blue?"

Ray paused. He didn't want to drag the Garner Family's name through the mud if there turned out to be no connection to Graham's disappearance. And he didn't want to tell Detective Celek that he'd been holding back information, as inconsequential as it may have seemed. But his grandpa had once taught him, when you get in a hole, the first rule is to stop digging. So Ray explained about the postcards, the words on the back of one of them, his and Lauren's theories and conclusions about triangles, and Snake Island.

If Detective Celek was mad, he didn't let on. Instead, he shared Ray's confusion. He agreed it was odd, but that there was nothing "actionable" on the part of the Teton County Sheriff's Office. Nor did any of the people or places Ray had named trigger any connection in Celek's or the Sheriff's Office's collective memory bank.

Ray apologized, promised to update Celek if he came across anything actionable, and vowed to be careful. And Celek promised to let Ray know if there were any further developments regarding the Toyota Corolla or the investigation into Margaret Lane.

With still over an hour to kill, Ray went for a walk. He was pleasantly surprised at the uptick in temperature—he guessed mid-fifties—and the few rays of sunshine that penetrated the cloud cover. Ray thought as he walked, mentally rearranging puzzle pieces to see if any of them fit. Triangles, land disputes, unfaithful boyfriends. He tried plugging Angela Marion into vacant spots, thinking maybe she'd make a connection. She didn't, which wasn't a surprise. He knew nothing about her. She could fit anywhere or nowhere. But the fact that she had sought him out suggested she knew something of significance. He just hoped he could figure out what it was. And that Lauren was wrong about an ambush.

TWENTY-TWO

Lauren was not waiting for Ray outside her door this time. He parked the truck, killed the ignition, and got out. Then she opened the door.

She was dressed for comfort in blue jeans and a charcoal gray zip-up hoodie over a pink shirt. Her hair was down. Her smile was warm as she closed the door behind her. The air was also warm, compared to the morning. As much blue sky was visible as was not, and the winds had died down. It was still autumnal, but pleasantly so.

They exchanged greetings and got into the truck. As Ray turned the ignition, Lauren said, "She's divorced."

He looked at her. "Who, Angela?"

Lauren nodded. "Steve Carruthers, a tech startup guy originally from Los Angeles. Lasted four years, back in the mid two thousands."

"And you know this how?"

"It's public record. I did a little poking around this afternoon."

"Find anything else?"

"Not much. I even called a few people who know the who's who in the area. Nothing."

"I guess we'll find out when we get there," Ray said.

"Where are we going anyhow?"

"North on Spring Gulch Road about a mile south of the Gros Ventre River."

"That's where the Circle M is?"

"Uh-huh."

"I put that in the ol' Google search but got nowhere," she said.

"Me too."

"I guess we'll find out when we get there," she mimicked.

The drive took just over fifteen minutes, and he used the time to catch her up on what he'd learned that morning. It wasn't much. Spring Gulch Road hugged the base of East Gros Ventre Butte, also known as Saddle Butte Lauren said, before straightening out and running north through open fields of grass and sagebrush. The Teton Range was dusted with a fresh coating of snow, filling in some of the grays and purples and blues. The trees that lined the river were fiery yellow and orange, particularly as they caught the late afternoon sunlight, and Ray wished he and Lauren could be headed for a scenic overlook, a trek through the wilderness, or just a drive under God's blue heaven instead of a meeting with a mystery woman about his cousin's disappearance.

On the phone, Angela had said the Circle M would be about a half mile ahead on his right after he cleared the butte. He slowed as they approached a massive headgate that appeared hewn from sequoias. A giant iron circle with an inset M was mounted in the center of the crossbar. A brown metal gate was parted to allow entrance on a gravel road. As Ray passed through it, Lauren turned over her shoulder.

"Expecting it to clang shut behind us?" he asked.

"Uh-huh, sort of."

The gravel road ran straight east for a couple hundred yards, bordered by a field of brown corn on the right and by sagebrush on the near left. Beyond it, yellowing grass stretched for the better part of a mile to the distant tree line. Specks of dark brown or black were too far off to identify, but Ray guessed cattle. This was, after all, a ranch.

The first break in the corn and sage was a round pen on their left, adjacent to a corral. A woman with a long, blond ponytail flowing from underneath a Stetson galloped a white and brown spotted horse around the circle. Several other horses of different varieties stood in the corral. Two men leaned against the fence, watching the woman. Perhaps waiting a turn. Only one of them even cast a glance at Ray as he drove by.

Across from the corral was a single-story log and plaster building. Windows were evenly spaced at ground level and in the gable ends of a steeply pitched roof. The size of a small Cape Cod house, it was the smallest building in the complex.

Just beyond it, the driveway split to form a circle, roughly fifty feet in diameter. The center was filled with grass, inside of which was a rock-lined flower garden in the shape of an M. From between the two peaks of the M, a large flagpole towered at least thirty feet in the air, allowing ample room for Old Glory to flutter gracefully in the breeze.

From the circle, the driveway continued north, to Ray and Lauren's left. Right of the circle, a very modern three-stall garage looked relocated from a wealthy suburb. It was out of place, especially compared to the log and plaster building. One of the overhead doors was open, and the garage behind it was empty. A black Dodge Ram Laramie was parked just far enough around the circle that a vehicle could get into the garage. The Laramie was caked with mud and dirt, so much that the rear license plate was obscured.

Straight ahead, beyond the circle, was the main house. Recalling Angela's instructions to "Drive up to the main house," Ray veered right, around the circle, and parked in front of the Laramie. He killed the ignition, and, with a look at each other, he and Lauren got out.

The main house was not the new, fancy luxury home prevalent on many "ranches" in the area. It wasn't even worthy of the garage. It was white and square, two stories with dormers poking out of the black roof. While it was a poor match for the garage nearby, it fit on a "Western" ranch. It didn't take much imagination for Ray to see John Wayne strut out of the shadows on the porch, standing with his weight on one leg, hat a little askew, his eyes cast over his property. Instead, all he saw were shadows. The porch wrapped around all sides of the house, at least that he could see, and would be appropriately described as rambling. Maybe not luxurious, certainly not new, the house appeared well kept. Flowerbeds in front of the porch on either side of a short stairway had been dressed with cornstalks, pumpkins, and sprays of wildflowers. The paint was crisp and clean. The asphalt shingles sparkled in the sunlight. Myriad windows did too. Ray looked at them briefly, for signs that someone was watching him and Lauren. He saw no signs, but didn't doubt it nonetheless.

They met at the hood of his truck and stopped for a moment. His eyes followed the driveway north, past the corral to a grand, modern stable. Its wood was stained the color of honey, and the shingles on the roof were black as coal. It featured a porch all along the front—or east—end that parted in the middle to allow both human and equine access. On the near side, another opening emptied into the corral.

Beyond the stable, straight ahead, was a barn. Its gambrel roof reminded Ray of many back in South Dakota, only this barn wasn't painted red. It too featured stained wooden siding, only darker and clearly aged by the years and weather.

To the right, across the driveway from the stable, was a metal shed, its aqua green siding a stark contrast to the other buildings. It was a little too bright to match the sagebrush or well-trimmed lawn. It also failed to complement the dark green of a row of pines on the south side of the shed, presumably to hide it from the main house, separated from it by a seventy- or eighty-foot expanse of grass. Two large oaks, one on the northeast corner of the house and one due south of it, provided abundant shade for the lawn, even as their leaves had begun to change.

"I guess we knock on the door," Ray said. He'd gazed toward the two men leaning against the fence, watching the woman ride. Neither of them had made any move toward them. Nor was anyone else present in the compound. For some reason, he had a feeling the woman wasn't Angela Marion, but he couldn't identify the reason.

"I guess," Lauren said.

They climbed the steps and into the shade of the porch. The front door was black, like the roof, like the shutters. Ray couldn't remember ever seeing a black door before. The screen door was also black, little more than a wood frame to support a stretched screen. He opened it with a twang, and seeing no knocker—and no bell—he rapped his knuckles on the door.

He stepped back, unsure what to expect. Was Angela Marion a rough-and-tumble cowgirl, calloused hands, weather-beaten face, dressed for a rodeo? Was she a hands-off ranch owner, manicured nails, smooth features, faux Western? Was she young? Not too young if she'd been married and divorced over a decade ago. Old? She'd sounded young-ish on the phone, but that could be misleading.

Nobody answered. Ray knocked again, waited another minute, and checked his watch. Four o'clock on the button.

Lauren tapped his arm, and he turned to see her looking back toward the corral too. He saw one of the men who had been leaning on the fence walking his way. The other kept watching the woman in the Stetson who kept galloping her white and brown spotted horse around the circle.

The man approaching them was tall and lanky, with a crop of red hair under a faded Houston Astros baseball cap. A neatly trimmed beard was also red, almost matching the flecks in his checked shirt. He offered a thin smile as he reached the bottom of the stairs. "You looking for Angela?" he asked.

"Yeah," Ray said. "We're supposed to meet her at four."

The man climbed the stairs and offered a hand. "I'm Corbin, assistant foreman at the Circle M. You must be Ray?"

"Yeah," Ray said as he shook Corbin's hand. Strong and firm. "This is Lauren."

"Pleased to meet you," Corbin said, then reached for her hand. "Angela's just checking the herd. Let me radio her and let her know you're here." He reached for a walkie-talkie attached to his hip. He checked the tuner and squawked it twice. "Ang, it's Corbin."

Nothing but static came back.

"Ang, you copy?"

"I'm here, Corbin," her voice came through muffled.

"Ray and Lauren are at the house."

Ray couldn't interpret her response, but Corbin had no problem. "Copy that." He sheathed the walkie-talkie and looked up at Ray and Lauren. "Should be just a few minutes."

"Thanks," Ray said.

Corbin nodded and turned back toward the corral.

"Hard job," Ray whispered when he was out of earshot, "being the assistant foreman at the Circle M, I mean."

"Assistant foreman or butler?" Lauren asked.

After two minutes, she took a seat on the top step. Ray moved to the column supporting the porch and leaned against it. He watched the woman with the Stetson. She wasn't doing tricks, handstands or hanging off the saddle or anything. No jumps. Didn't appear to be taming a bucking bronco. Just riding in a circle. Ray supposed horses needed daily exercise too.

"Not a bad place to spend an afternoon," Lauren said.

"Them?" Ray asked.

"Anyone," she said. "Porch overlooking a stable with the Tetons in the background? All that's missing is a porch swing."

The cadence of clopping hooves changed, and Ray turned his head to see a horse and rider coming toward the house from the barn. The horse was a deep, rich brown color, like dark chocolate. It plodded straight ahead at a walking pace, in no hurry. The rider was a woman, sitting tall in the saddle. Her eyes were hidden under the brim of a charcoal gray cowboy hat. Her hair was not. Waves of dark brown not dissimilar in color from the horse's coat fell onto her shoulders. She wore a Kelly green and white checked shirt, the sleeves rolled up above her elbows. A dark vest, a windbreaker, was open halfway, making room for a kerchief the same color to hang loosely around her neck. Her dark blue denims were mostly covered by riding chaps, as were boots the same color as the hat, vest, and kerchief.

Ray stood up straight as she approached. Beside him, Lauren had risen to her feet. The woman gently pulled the reins, guiding the horse to a hitching post just in front of the porch. She swiftly dismounted and tethered the horse to the post. With a pat on its flank, she turned for the steps. For the first time, she let her eyes fall upon her company.

"I'm Angela Marion," she said as she climbed the stairs. She removed riding gloves and held them in her left hand while extending her right. "I'm sorry to keep you waiting. Ray."

They shook hands. Her grip was as strong and firm as Corbin's, but the texture of her hands was smooth and, well, feminine. No callouses, no leathery texture. Because she always wore the gloves, or because the hard-at-work cowgirl was a pretext? For what it was worth, the hands matched the rest of her skin. Unless she'd married straight out of high school, she had to be nearly forty but looked young enough to still get carded. Angela was handsome if not beautiful. Her cheekbones, chin, and nose were all angular, yet smooth, as if chiseled from marble. Instead of smelling like dirt or other, less aromatic ranch substances, she carried a citrus fragrance. She looked as if she should be kicking up her heels and breaking hearts at the Million Dollar Cowboy Bar on Saturday nights. For all Ray knew, she did.

"It's nice to meet you," he said. "This is Lauren." He stopped from saying her last name, although he wasn't quite sure why.

"Everything all right with the herd?" Lauren asked as she and Angela shook hands.

"Fine," she said. "Bear with me just a minute."

"Of course."

She stepped to the side and shed her chaps, draping them over the porch railing. She placed her gloves on top of them, then unzipped and removed her vest. Then the kerchief. Doing so revealed how well the Kelly green and white checked shirt fit her figure. She was only a couple inches shorter than Ray, who stood six-one. Her arms were tanned and muscular. Her stomach was flat, evident with her shirt tucked into the front of her jeans. They were held in place by a belt with a silver buckle that was somewhere between common and ostentatious. In Sioux Falls, the latter. Here, closer to the former.

Lastly, she removed the cowboy hat and ran the fingers of her left hand through her hair, drawing it back and away from her face. She left the rest of her gear on the porch, but carried the hat with her as she opened the front door and invited Ray and Lauren to follow.

The front door opened into a wide vestibule, two stories high with a gold chandelier hanging from the ceiling. The floor was old, dark hardwood except where a giant Persian rug lay in the center of the room. Hallways ran deeper into the house on either side of a wide staircase going up to a brief balcony that spanned the same width as the foyer. An open doorway led right, to what looked like a sitting room, and double pocket doors matched it on the opposite side.

Still carrying her hat, Angela led Ray and Lauren to the double pocket doors. One had a sensor built into it, and she placed her hand on the sensor. After just a second, the entire sensor glowed green, and a soft click indicated the doors were unlocked. High-tech for a house that Ray guessed—judging by the style, layout, and the floor and doorposts in the foyer—was at least a century old.

Angela pried the doors open, and Ray followed her and Lauren into a home office. Its floor too was hardwood, like the foyer, with another rug on the floor in front of a huge, sleek, glass-topped desk. A fancy office chair sat behind it in front of a window that looked out on the porch and down the driveway toward the mountains. On the far wall, one of two windows looked toward the stable, the corral, and the protuberant Tetons beyond them. Angela had picked the best spot in the house for her office.

A bookcase on the near wall to the left was filled half with books and half with photo frames and knickknacks. A black gun safe stood in the corner. The walls, painted a cross between burnt orange and brown, were decked with Western paintings—mountain landscapes, a cowboy on a horse, a barren and windswept desert panorama—and an overhead picture of the ranch. Ray glanced at it for a moment, judging it to have been taken recently.

Instead of guiding them to a pair of chairs in front of the desk, Angela gestured toward the other half of the room. It featured a wet bar, a small table and chairs in the near corner, and a comfortable-looking end chair and sofa in the far corner. In front of them was a bearskin rug, complete with head. It was aimed at Ray and Lauren, teeth bared. Not a coincidence.

"Please, have a seat," Angela said, nodding at the couch. She hung her hat on a pole coatrack by the door. "Would you like some coffee? It's freshly brewed."

"Please," Ray said as he sat at the end of the couch, nearest the chair.

"Thank you," Lauren said, sitting beside him.

Angela poured three mugs full of steaming coffee from a pot on the wet bar. She carried them, along with small pitchers of milk and sugar, on a tray that she set on a circular glass coffee table on the bear's back. Then she sat in the chair, adjacent to Ray. She crossed her right leg over her left knee, flexing her boot back and forth, almost like a tic. She took a sip of her coffee, black like Ray and Lauren's.

"So, Ray and Lauren, thank you for coming. I prefer to do business face to face."

"Of course," Ray said.

Angela set her mug on an end table between the chair and couch. "Why don't we get right to it? What is your interest in Snake Island?"

TWENTY-THREE

Ray was a bit taken aback by her bluntness, although he shouldn't have been. One look at Angela Marion told him she didn't beat around the bush. Out of the shadow of the porch and no longer under the hat, her brown eyes were narrow and piercing. She had the ability, it seemed, to look right through a person. She didn't waste words, or movement, or time. Ray decided to respond in kind.

"We aren't sure how," he said, "but we think Snake Island may be tied to the disappearance of my cousin, Graham Stoddard."

He watched Angela's face carefully. On the way over, he and Lauren had agreed that, not knowing who Angela was or how she was or wasn't tied to Graham's disappearance, they would be best served by putting their cards on the table. For all their earlier talk of an ambush, if Angela was a villain with evil intentions, inviting them to coffee at her ranch wasn't the most prudent way to carry out those intentions. And if they wanted to get answers, they couldn't afford to "pussyfoot around," as Lauren had said. So he went with the direct approach, mentioning Graham's name to see if it generated any response.

Angela's taut face didn't move. She said nothing. She just continued to stare at Ray, waiting for him to continue.

"I arrived Saturday from Sioux Falls," he said. "The plan was to spend a week here with Graham, but when I got here, I found out he'd been missing since last Thursday. He works at the Bar H-9 south of town, and their surveillance footage seemed to show him being abducted by a van."

"I assume you've gone to the police."

"Yes. They tracked down the van but found no trace of Graham. However, when I checked into my hotel, I had an envelope containing five postcards, presumably from Graham." He reached into his back pocket, where he'd stuck the envelope before leaving the hotel. He handed it to Angela. "It's easier to look at."

She took the envelope, pulled out the postcards, and sorted through them. Then she shook her head.

"There's writing on the back of that one," Lauren interjected.

Angela turned it over and read the writing. She lifted her eyes, her face still void of expression. "What does this mean?"

"We deduced that the writing on the back of that postcard revealed five locations around Jackson Hole," Ray said. "The other four postcards indicated four other locations. Nine total, forming three equilateral triangles."

"The Garners."

"You know about that?" Lauren asked.

"I do. Go on."

Ray reached for his pocket again, this time withdrawing the map, the one on which Lauren had drawn intersecting lines using the Silverado's owner's manual as a straightedge and the truck's passenger window as a level surface. He set his coffee down and unfolded the map. Then he turned it toward Angela.

"The three triangles point to the same location, as you can see. When we learned that piece of property was known as Snake Island, I made a few calls to real estate agents hoping to learn something more. One of those agents was Walt Mitchum, who you said this morning notified you and prompted your call. So if I may, Angela, to ultimately answer your question of what our interest is in Snake Island, what is your interest in Snake Island?"

She responded by slowly folding the map and handing it back to Ray. Then she stood. She paced to the wet bar and turned around. "Did you speak to any other agents other than Walt?"

Ray nodded. "A couple."

"And did you learn anything?"

"A man named Bob Bronson told me the property is held in trust by Jackson Savings & Loan. But that's all I know."

She nodded.

Then she walked across the room to the bookshelf beside her desk. She lifted a frame off it and carried it back to Ray and Lauren. The photo inside it was old, yellowed, worn. Black-and-white, it showed two men shaking hands. One wore overalls, a plain shirt underneath, the sleeves rolled to mid forearm.

The other was dressed in riding chaps, a long shirt, and a vest. Both wore cowboy hats, tipped back to show their faces.

"The man on the right is John Marion," Angela said, referring to the man in chaps and a vest. "He was my great-great-grandfather. He scraped this ranch into existence out of the dust of the earth. At one time, it spanned the Gros Ventre River and half of the land east of the Snake River." She took the frame back from Lauren and set it on the coffee table.

"He passed it to his son, John Jr., who then passed it to his brother Jacob when none of his children showed an interest in it. Jacob Marion passed it to his only son, Jacob Jr., who in turn passed it to his only son, Jake. My father. When he died in 2007, it became mine since he had no living sons." She looked straight at Ray, her face still a stone. "One hundred twenty years this piece of property has been in the Marion family, from generation to generation. We've scaled back over the decades, but we still run about five hundred head and a dozen horses. Some of them could trace their pedigree back almost as far as I can. All this to say, Ray and Lauren, the Marion Family is proud and strong."

She retook her seat. She crossed her legs again. She flexed her boot some more.

"The other man in the picture is Bret James, Great-Great-Granddaddy's business partner and best friend. The James Family was almost as prodigious in Jackson Hole as the Marions. Some of Bret's descendants still live in the area, although most have moved away. This photo was taken in 1917, five years before John died at the age of sixty-six. Bret outlived him by a dozen years, and they remained close until the day John died."

Ray said nothing, thinking of Sam Covington's words about a falling out over a land dispute. He had a feeling Angela was getting there.

"John was sick for the last year or so, and before he died, he sold off portions of the ranch to make sure his three sons had enough money in case the ranching business died out. He also made a special provision for future generations. As I told you, the Marion Family is proud, and that originated with John Marion. He wanted to make sure the Marion Family name lived on in Jackson Hole for years to come. So he took a plot of his land and put it in trust at the fledgling Jackson Savings & Loan with the provision that in one hundred years, that piece of land would become the property of his youngest male descendant. That piece of land is Snake Island."

They were a long way from tying anything to Graham's disappearance, but Ray was intrigued. He drank his coffee and waited for Angela to continue.

"John included a provision in the trust, in case he had no male descendants alive at the end of one hundred years. In that case, Snake Island would become the property of the youngest male descendant of his good friend Bret James. John figured if the Marion Family name couldn't continue, at least the James Family name would. That was in the fall of 1921, ninety-eight years ago. And the land has been in trust ever since, waiting for its owner."

Angela spoke smoothly and flatly, with a directness that fit her appearance and demeanor. But the way she spoke the last sentence, with a touch of hesitation and a slight tremor in her voice, almost sent shivers down Ray's spine.

He doused them with a drink of coffee.

Angela leaned forward. "In two years, the trust matures, and Snake Island will be awarded to the youngest living male descendant of John Marion. Assuming, of course, there is one."

"Is there not?" Lauren asked.

"No. John Marion IV died in 2000 of prostate cancer at the age of sixty-four. His nephew, Luke, died in 2009 from a drug and alcohol overdose. John's brother, George, died of pneumonia in 2012; he was seventy-one. George had one son who died in Iraq in Operation Desert Storm and two daughters, each of whom had a son. Ethan Thornton was killed in a car accident in 2015, and Isaac Marion committed suicide in 2007. They were both seventeen at the time."

"Wow," Lauren uttered.

"John Jr.'s daughter Justine's son Ricky was killed at the World Trade Center on 9/11 and his son, Will, died of colon cancer in 2010 when he was just forty. James Marion's lineage—John's second son, that is—died out after only one generation. And after my father, the closest relations are my brother Thomas, who died in the second Iraq War in 2004, and my cousin Cole, who died of skin cancer in 2012."

"My goodness," Lauren said.

"I have a sister, a niece, a cousin, and two first cousins once removed who are all female. There are another five sixth-generation Marions and five seventh-generation Marions, all female. My sister cannot get pregnant, my cousin is a lesbian, one of my first cousins once removed has had two miscarriages, and the other is unmarried and uninterested in children at least until she is married. And that's just this branch of the family tree. What that means is, barring something rather unforeseen, there will be no Marion male descendant to claim the land in two years."

"So it will go to the James Family," Ray said.

"In theory. Bret James' descendants have an uncanny ability to conceive predominantly female offspring. As of right now, there are no living male descendants in the James Family either."

"So what happens?" Lauren asked.

"There was a stipulation for that," Angela said. "In the case that neither family was able to produce a living male descendant, Snake Island is to be turned over to the National Park Service. This was prior to the forming of Grand Teton National Park, but Yellowstone had been founded for nearly half a century and had gained notoriety. John Marion was a lover of nature and believed that this picturesque valley could be home to a national park as well. At the time, he had no way of knowing that Snake Island would one day lie adjacent to Grand Teton National Park."

"So if neither family bears a son in the next two years, the land goes to the federal government?" Ray asked.

Angela nodded. "I don't know how any of this may tie to your cousin, but the postcards you showed me reference the Garner Family. Woodrow Garner married Zora James, Bret's great-granddaughter. The trust clearly states that the land must be given to a male descendant, not a relative by marriage. So Woodrow Garner can't inherit the land, but any descendants of his and Zora's could."

"But there are none?" Lauren asked.

"No. Their grandson was killed in a back-country hiking accident a couple years ago. The rest of their offspring are female."

"Lincoln Nichols?" Ray asked.

Angela nodded.

"Are there many candidates in the Garner or James family?"

"Bret's grandson Maverick had a son Zane in addition to Zora. Two of Zane's granddaughters have been cranking babies out as fast as they can in a desperate bid to inherit the land, largely I think because they believe it will be a windfall. They both live in the Denver area and have no real ties to the property. But so far, they've had three daughters and a fourth on the way."

"You keep pretty close tabs on this," Lauren said.

"I do. Bret's oldest great-granddaughter has several daughters with young kids so they could always have more, but I'm not aware of any immediate prospects. And Woodrow and Zora had four girls. The youngest had a daughter in 2005. The second youngest is unable to get pregnant. The second oldest is Lincoln's mom, and they have a daughter born in 2006, and the oldest has a girl who is eighteen or nineteen now, meaning of childbearing age."

"Wow, you really keep close tabs on everything."

"I'll make no secret of the fact that I want Snake Island to remain part of the Marion Family. I don't have the disdain for the James Family that some of my relations do, but I'd prefer the property stay in the family and I've kept abreast of both families. That said, it won't make or break the Circle M either way."

Ray nodded.

"What is so special about Snake Island?" Lauren said.

"Nothing, at least on the surface. But it was special to my great-great-grandfather, as was every inch of soil he possessed because every inch of it he had to work for. People look at someone with money, someone like John Marion or someone like me, and think because we're 'rich' we don't work hard. But I assure you that is not the case, either for John or myself—for anyone who's owned or worked the Circle M."

Angela uncrossed her legs and stood. "Snake Island comprises approximately 180 acres, most of which is forested." She walked to her desk as she spoke and opened one of the drawers. "The exact size and shape of the land changes over time as the river cuts and channels, rises and falls." She pulled out a sheet of paper and walked back. "Here's a satellite view of the property," she said.

Lauren took it and shared it with Ray. They'd viewed it before, but this image appeared to be higher resolution than what they'd seen. Angela's assessment was spot on.

"It's wild, it's rugged, it's a haven for wildlife. It fits with the Marion Family's history of environmental responsibility and stewardship. Conversely, others may not be as accountable with it."

"Do you say that with someone specifically in mind?" Ray asked.

"Bret's great-great-grandson, Willis, would have been—given the glut of females in the James Family—the youngest descendant had he not died of food poisoning while in the Caribbean in 2016. He had in mind to clear the land and turn it into a dude ranch. My cousin, Cole, talked about a hunting preserve before he died. And Woodrow Garner has long been rumored to be seeking a spot for some sacred site in the valley."

Ray and Lauren looked at each other. "What kind of sacred site?" Ray asked.

"Some sort of holistic resort, a place to channel energy or something. It all has to do with their fascination with triangles, I'm sure, which would be backed up by your findings. But that is only my speculation, as I've only heard rumors."

"And you think he envisions Snake Island for that purpose?" Lauren asked.

"I know he does."

Angela had retaken her seat and now leaned forward, resting her elbows on her knees. "I hesitate to mention this because there's no proof. But since Woodrow married into the James Family in 1976, there have been some suspicious circumstances surrounding the deaths of a number of Marions."

"Suspicious circumstances?" Ray asked.

"Luke McCandles had no history of drug use and only minor alcohol consumption when he overdosed in 2009. Isaac Marion's suicide came completely out of the blue, as many admittedly do. Ethan Thornton's solo car accident was unusual, to say the least. His sister, Jennifer, had two daughters and was talking about having more children when she suddenly divorced her husband Peter after finding out he'd been having an affair. Again," she said with a shake of her head, "there's nothing to link Woodrow or any of the Garners or James to these incidents, but with Snake Island hanging in the balance, nothing is out of the question."

Once again, the tone of her voice gave Ray chills. He looked to Lauren, whose facial expression suggested she felt the same way.

"Now, I apologize if I've bored you with too much family history," Angela said as she sat back in her chair, "but when you started asking around about Snake Island, it drew my attention and interest. I wanted to clear the air, so to speak, lest you draw any wrong conclusions. Unfortunately, I don't know what any of this might have to do with your cousin."

Ray sighed. "Neither do we."

"I won't keep you any longer," Angela said, rising. "Unless you have any other questions for me."

Ray and Lauren both stood as well. "I can't think of anything," Ray said.

"Me either," Lauren said.

Angela walked them back to the front door, which opened just as they reached it. Ray's eyes did a double take as the squinting cowboy he had seen leaning against one of the pavilion's support columns at the Bar H-9 walked into the house. He may or may not have recognized Ray, but his focus quickly turned to Angela.

"Sorry to interrupt, Miss Marion," he said, "but Norman's fever is still up."

Ray noted that he called her "Miss Marion" whereas Corbin had referred to her as "Ang" on the walkie-talkie. He also tried to figure out if there was some connection to be made between him having been at the Bar H-9, presumably working, and also being at the Circle M now. He couldn't think of one—unless he drove off in a Corolla.

"Norman's one of our horses. Had a fever for a few days now."

"You want me to call the vet?" the man asked.

She shook her head. "No, I'll do it. Thanks, Ben."

He nodded and backed out the door. Angela, Lauren, then Ray followed. Ben was already down the porch and striding back to the stable. Ray noted that the corral and riding area beside it were empty of horses, women with blond ponytails under a Stetson, or redheaded and red-bearded men observing her.

Ray, Lauren, and Angela shook hands. Ray thanked her for taking the time to meet with them, and he and Lauren walked down the steps.

"If there's anything else," Angela said, still standing at the top of the stairs, "give me a call."

It was a friendly gesture, and yet as Ray nodded in response and Lauren said, "We will," he couldn't help but feel it was as much of a command as an invitation. Angela Marion had been open and forthcoming, but through it all, Ray couldn't overcome the feeling that she was somehow manipulating the situation. Maybe that was just her nature, a Type A, an Alpha, always in command. Or maybe it was because she viewed Ray and Lauren as outsiders meddling in family business, an incursion. Or maybe it was because she was hiding something, although Ray couldn't figure out what.

Whatever the case, he and Lauren were no closer to finding out what had happened to Graham.

TWENTY-FOUR

Ray and Lauren were halfway down the driveway before either of them spoke.

"How much of that was theatrics?" Lauren asked.

"Theatrics?"

"You really think she was out 'checking on the herd' when we arrived?"

"As opposed to . . . ?"

"Waiting just off stage to make a dramatic entrance, a nice slow ride from the barn while we stand and watch, then she dismounts, dusts herself off . . ."

"Sort of like the marshal riding into town while the Clanton Boys stand outside the saloon chawin' tobacco?"

"Something like that."

"Only I don't recall her dusting herself off."

"It was still meant to intimidate, I think."

"Did it work?"

Lauren smirked. "What do you think?"

Ray smiled as he turned onto Spring Gulch Road.

"You know the question I didn't dare ask?" she said.

"*You* didn't dare ask a question?"

She stuck her tongue in her cheek.

"What's that?"

"Why Angela hasn't had any children."

"Maybe she can't."

"Maybe."

"She is divorced. Maybe she doesn't want to have a child outside of marriage."

Lauren shook her head. "When she talked about one of her once removed cousins not having kids until she was married, she said it with disdain in her voice."

"I wasn't sure if that was disdain or frustration."

"Little of each, I think."

"Anyhow, maybe it's not a moral thing, but maybe she doesn't want to be a single mom."

"So why doesn't she get a husband?"

Ray looked at her.

"She's good-looking, clearly well-off. She could have any man she wants."

"You sound like a man," Ray said. "What about falling in love, what about finding Mr. Right?"

"I'm not talking about falling in love," Lauren said. "I'm talking about continuing a lineage, about procreation, and I'm trying to think about it from Angela's perspective."

Ray nodded.

"Then again, maybe any potential husbands got scared off when they realized she'd eat them immediately after conception."

He chuckled.

"But we're getting off topic," Lauren said. "What do you think about all the Marion Family genealogy?"

"It's complete, that's for sure. I feel like with everything she told us, there must be something relevant. I just don't know what."

"You need to let it filter down, like you're panning for gold."

"Something like that."

She sat back and turned her head out the window. Ray followed her gaze, out the window, over the northern end of West Gros Ventre Butte, at the mountains, splashed now in late-afternoon sunlight. He alternated between looking to his right and looking at the empty road ahead. And he waited until Lauren turned back his way.

"I know it's a little early," he said, "but do you want to grab some dinner?"

There was a twinkle in Lauren's eye as she said, "Are you asking me on a date, Ray?"

He looked at her until doing so would have been dangerous, given that he was still driving. "I don't know," he said. "I was engaged a month ago. I'm not sure I'm ready for a 'date.' But I am asking you to dinner, with no plans to interrogate the wait staff this time. Make of that what you will."

Lauren nodded. "Fair enough. Yes, I'd like to grab some dinner."

He nodded back with a smile.

"You have a place in mind?"

"It's your town."

"Okay, what are you in the mood for?"

"How about a good steak?"

"Mmm, sounds good. The Gun Barrel."

"Yeah, I've seen it. On the main drag."

Lauren nodded. "Can we swing by my place first?"

"Sure."

"In fact," she said, "it is a little early for dinner. Why don't you drop me off and pick me up at, say, six?"

"Okay. Will we have any trouble getting a table then?"

"If we do, it's a nice place to hang out."

"All right."

They drove mostly in silence back to her apartment. As she opened her door to get out, Ray said, "Lauren, thanks for coming along this afternoon."

"Of course." She smiled. "I'll see you at six."

"Six," he repeated, then watched as she walked to her door, waved, and went inside.

Ray drove back to his hotel, feeling butterflies in his stomach that he hadn't felt in a very long time.

^   ^   ^

Ray and Lauren were seated next to a stone fireplace in the shadow of a mounted moose head. It was not alone. The Gun Barrel Steak and Game House was the epitome of a western steakhouse. Mounted heads—everything from elk to water buffalo—graced the walls, and a full-size bison stood by the entrance. Murals and landscapes depicted panoramic vistas and a variety of wildlife. Logwood railings cordoned off sections of seating, and more logs formed the siding on the walls and ceiling. The décor included everything from saddles with stirrups hanging on support columns to the trademark crossed rifle barrels.

The food matched the atmosphere. Exceeded it, in fact. Both Ray and Lauren had ordered steaks and were content to savor slowly while talking about their childhoods, life in Sioux Falls compared to Boise or Jackson, and various aspects of their work. They hadn't agreed to avoid discussing Graham's disappearance, but they might as well have.

"And that is why I am never having a roommate again," Lauren said, concluding a story about her senior year of college.

"Not even a husband someday?"

She gave him a side-eyed look as she reached for her iced tea.

"What, too forward?" Ray asked with a hint of teasing.

"No, it just felt like the supposedly casual reference to a boyfriend to see if someone's single."

"Sorry."

Lauren grinned as she sliced into her steak. Medium rare, a hint of juice. She'd changed into a navy blue sweater over a collared shirt, leaving the shirt untucked under the bottom of the sweater and over her jeans to maintain the informality. She had perhaps teased her hair a little, maybe added a touch of makeup. It was subtle. She also wore silver hoop earrings. She hadn't worn earrings before that Ray recalled. They looked good. She looked good.

For his part, he'd changed into a clean shirt and fixed his hair. It was something.

"It was actually one of the things Annabelle was the most worried about," he said, setting down his knife and reaching for his iced tea.

"Living together?"

Ray nodded.

Lauren cut a bite of steak. "Why's that?" she asked before depositing it into her mouth.

"The little things like how different people from different families and different backgrounds do things differently."

"That's a lot of differents."

He conceded the point with a bob of the head. "You know, how they organize the kitchen counters, what they keep on the bathroom sink and what goes in the medicine cabinet, who does what chores, when and where you eat. But more than that, two people used to living alone moving in together, sharing space all the time, being around each other constantly. And then when it's two people of the opposite sex, who are so different to begin with . . ."

"Careful, Ray, implying there are differences between the sexes. You'll be labeled a backwoods Bible-thumper or something."

"I've been called worse."

Lauren smiled and dipped her fork into her garlic mashed potatoes. She eased them onto her tongue as if savoring a delicacy. She chased them with a drink and turned her head. "If you don't mind me saying so, maybe it wasn't God telling her to break up with you so much as her . . . fearing commitment."

"The woman being afraid of commitment?"

Lauren shrugged.

"Hmm." He thought through a bite of his own garlic mashed potatoes. "And I don't mind you saying so, by the way."

"No?"

"No. Talking about it doesn't hurt quite as much as it used to. That's good, I think."

And so for a while, they talked about Annabelle—how she and Ray had met, what she was like, why she had appealed to him. He wasn't sure if Lauren was asking specific questions for a reason—it almost felt like it—or just making conversation. Nor was he sure why he, though usually reserved, had no qualms about baring his soul to Lauren. He only knew the longer they talked, the less it felt like ripping the scab off an old wound and the more the detached and impersonal it became.

"Was she the first girl you loved?" Lauren asked after a brief lull. They were almost done with their entrées.

Ray looked at her.

"Too personal?"

"No. Just trying to figure out why you're asking. You don't strike me as the kind to get weak-kneed about something like this."

"I'm not. Just curious."

He nodded. "Yeah, she was the first."

Lauren took a drink.

"What about you?" he asked before she could continue.

"What about me?"

"You mentioned Jesse, said it wasn't all that serious between you. There ever been somebody with whom it was serious?"

"Sort of," she said at length. "When I was a freshman in college, I met a guy, and we became good friends. It wasn't romantic between us, but there was a connection, something that felt like more than friendship. Almost . . ."

He looked at her, waiting for her to continue.

Instead, she turned her eyes toward something on a faraway wall. It took a few seconds for her to bring them back to him. "He transferred after one year.

I never saw him again." She looked back to her potatoes, and Ray sliced off another hunk of his steak.

The conversation lulled, and in fact, ended. Lauren was quiet for the rest of the meal, something clearly bothering her. Ray hadn't seen her like that before, in something of a funk. Still a broken heart over a close friendship her freshman year of college? He didn't think so. He didn't know what it was, even though he felt like he should have known. And that bugged him.

They were both too stuffed for dessert, so Ray picked up the check, and they headed out to his truck. The sun had set, but the sky above was still light blue, nearly cloudless. The air was cool and crisp.

"I know we just passed on dessert," Ray said, "but you wanna grab a coffee, maybe figure out what we learned from Angela."

Lauren's smile was as thin as the mountain air. "Thanks, but I should get back home. Today was . . . long, and I've got the second half of the seminar tomorrow morning."

"Oh, I didn't know. I'll drive you home."

Lauren looked as if she'd been stabbed in the gut as they got into Ray's truck. He spent the five minutes driving back to her apartment wondering how a fun, relaxed evening had turned sour. Something in their conversation had led to Lauren's taciturn attitude, but what? It was one of the reasons Ray wasn't into talking about feelings and emotions.

Lauren said nothing on the ride back, just stared out the window. When Ray parked in front of her building, he dropped his hands from the wheel. "At the risk of sounding stupid, are you upset?"

She turned her head his way. "I'm not upset."

"Because it seems like something's b—"

"How long are you going to be staying in town?" she asked.

He frowned. "I . . . I don't know." He shrugged. "The end of the week, at least."

She nodded. "I'll give you a call tomorrow after the seminar."

"Okay."

"Thanks for dinner, Ray."

He nodded.

With another thin smile, she reached for the handle and let herself out of the truck. She entered her apartment without looking back.

Ray was not a genius, but he wasn't a dunce either. He knew something was off. Something had changed mid-conversation, somewhere along the lines of Lauren's guy friend the freshman year in college. Ray should have known what, and why. Not a genius, and maybe closer to dunce.

He drove back to his hotel, via Jackson Hole Coffee Roasters, and took his mind off Lauren by replaying what he had learned that day. His theory that Graham had been taken not by a Jackson Hole Cleaners van but the Toyota Corolla parked behind it in the lot at the Bar H-9. Heidi's admission that she wouldn't be surprised if Graham had "hooked up" with another woman. The news that Snake Island was held in trust by Jackson Savings & Loan. Angela Marion's call, invitation, and explanation about family origins, the history of Snake Island, the trust, and potential benefactors. He added the postcards, Woodrow Garner's interest in triangles, and other tidbits of information he had gleaned over the last several days. He felt like he should have known something more, been able to put pieces together, figured out the riddle. It was a recurring problem.

He eventually gave up and flipped on the TV. He watched absentmindedly, thinking about Lauren, about their conversations, about the way she had grown distant. He remembered asking her to dinner, the smile on her face as she'd said yes, the way she'd looked in a navy blue sweater and silver hoop earrings. He thought about Annabelle, about the things he and Lauren had discussed, how the hole in his heart seemed to be shrinking.

Then he thought about going back home, leaving Jackson and Graham and Lauren behind. He thought of the empty house waiting for him, void now and forever of Annabelle.

Maybe the hole wasn't shrinking after all. Maybe it was just temporarily covered. Maybe it was about to be exposed all over again.

It took Ray a long time to fall asleep.

TWENTY-FIVE

Thursday dawned in stark contrast to the day before. The sun was shining when Ray pulled back the blinds to his room, and forty-five minutes later when he headed down to his truck, the air was cool but pleasant.

He'd slept fitfully and, as he'd showered and dressed, been unable to shake his final minutes with Lauren the night before. He remembered verbatim her words about the guy she'd met while a freshman in college. *"It wasn't really romantic between us, but there was a connection, something that felt like more than friendship. Almost . . ."*

She hadn't finished the sentence but instead explained how her relationship with the guy had ended. And then she'd grown distant. He still didn't know why. Or more like he did know but couldn't recognize what he knew.

She had said she'd call after her seminar, and maybe then she'd offer some explanation. Until then, he was on his own. He'd concluded the night before that, for everything he'd learned regarding Graham's disappearance, he was still missing something. The reason he couldn't fit the puzzle together was that he didn't have all the pieces. So he'd done some old-fashioned sleuthing—he'd looked in the phone book—and found the number for someone who might be able to supply a missing piece.

Sam Covington had agreed to meet Ray for breakfast, since he was retired, and had suggested a place called The Virginian Restaurant. Now, as Ray got into his truck in the parking lot behind his hotel, he noticed a man sitting in a gray sedan two spots away from him.

There was nothing distinct about the guy, and Ray couldn't make out many details anyhow, what with having to look through two car windows to see him. But something about him was out of place. His posture? His presence in the car by himself in a tiny parking lot? It was probably nothing. In fact, it was nothing. And yet, Ray had noticed the guy and thought something of it, as opposed to every other person he saw or spotted in the course of his day. What it meant, he had no idea. That was becoming a tiresome refrain.

The Virginian Restaurant featured a large, spacious dining room. The vaulted ceiling was supported by open trusses. They formed triangles. Sam Covington was sitting at a table by the front window, holding a mug of coffee. He nodded as Ray joined him. The table was square, but turned at an angle, with a white tablecloth and the standard condiments—salt, pepper, sugar and its substitutes, jam, ketchup, Tabasco sauce, along with two glasses of water and one upturned mug.

"Appreciate you seeing me," Ray said as he sat down.

"My missus is still somewhat torn when it comes to my retirement. Says I'm underfoot all the time. She appreciates me seeing you too."

Ray grinned. A waitress appeared, and Ray said he'd take a coffee. He consulted his menu and asked, "What's good?"

"Everything," the waitress said.

Ray nodded. Two minutes later, he'd settled on the biscuits and gravy with a side of eggs. Sam ordered corned beef hash. The waitress was gone, and they both sipped coffee.

"I got a call from Angela Marion yesterday," Ray said. "The owner of the Circle M."

"Out of the blue?"

"Sort of. I asked some questions to a realtor, he tipped her off, and she called me."

"What kind of questions?"

"Who owns Snake Island?"

"Nobody."

"You're talking about the trust?"

"I am."

"How much do you know about it?"

Sam set down his mug. "Why don't you tell me what you know, and if I know something you don't, I'll change that."

"Sounds fair," Ray said. He took a drink of coffee, then related what he'd learned from Bob Bronson, the real estate agent, and from Angela Marion. As he was finishing relating his and Lauren's visit to the Circle M, the waitress brought out their breakfasts, ample portions of steaming hot food. It looked and smelled great.

She topped off their coffees, and they were alone again.

Sam cut into his eggs, causing runny yellow yolk to spill out. He proceeded to stir his corned beef hash into his eggs. "It sounds like Angela gave you a pretty thorough rundown."

"That was my thought too," Ray said, unable to look away as Sam lifted a forkful of eggs and hash to his mouth. Most made it inside. A little hung to his mustache.

"She was direct but forthcoming."

"I've never met Angela, although I am technically related to her."

"You are?"

Sam nodded as he scooped more egg and hash onto his fork. "My sister Melissa married Johnny McClintock. His mother was a Marion, but I don't know how you connect the dots from her to Angela."

"Do your sister and Johnny live in the area?" Ray asked.

Sam shook his head as he swallowed. "Johnny killed himself back in 1977. Melissa moved to New Mexico and married a Baptist preacher."

Ray hadn't touched his biscuits and gravy, but he now cut into them. His taste buds were rewarded. So he tried the eggs next.

"A couple of years ago, there was a huge Marion Family reunion. Johnny's mother turned ninety-five, just a few months before she died. Pretty much every Marion that is or ever was was invited, including Melissa, even though Johnny'd been dead for forty years." He paused for a bite of toast. White, lots of jam. Some of it stuck to his mustache too.

"Melissa's second husband, the Baptist preacher, couldn't make it . . . or wouldn't make it, I don't know. So I accompanied her. There were so many folks there I don't know that I'd have been able to find Angela in the crowd had I wanted to. But I did talk to a young woman . . . What'd she say she was?" He looked up at the ceiling. Ray took the opportunity to have some more biscuit.

"Jacob Marion's great-granddaughter, I believe it was. No, Jacob Jr. Whatever the case, we started talking, and somehow or other the trust came up. Sounded like she'd done her homework. I don't know much more than what you know, than what Angela told you. Especially nothing factual. But if you got questions, she might have the answers."

"Do you remember her name?" Ray asked.

"I was afraid you was going to ask me that," Sam said, leaning back in his chair. He closed his eyes for a few seconds. "Becca or Rebecca. Maybe Elizabeth . . . No, Bethany."

Ray waited.

"I'm almost positive. Bethany Cahill. I used to know some other Cahills, no relation, I don't think, so I remember that." He nodded. "Bethany Cahill."

"You know if she lives in the area?"

"Pretty sure she was a student at Montana State, maybe Montana. But that was a couple years ago."

Ray nodded. It was worth looking into, at least. Maybe.

"Afraid that's about all I know," Sam said, cutting into his eggs again.

"Angela mentioned several 'suspicious' deaths of potential Marion benefactors. Luke McCandles and Ethan Thornton. She said it with an almost accusatory tone, as if the Garner or James Family had something to do with it. Do their deaths ring a bell to you? Anything strike you as suspicious?"

"Refresh my memory on what happened to them."

"Luke was a drug overdose, and Ethan had a solo car accident."

"Ethan Thornton, you say?"

Ray nodded.

"I remember reading about Ethan. Killed out in Nebraska, I think. Some small town outside of Omaha. Granite or Greta or something unusual. No drugs or alcohol was all I remember. It's usually drugs or alcohol."

Ray nodded. Angela hadn't mentioned the accident taking place in Omaha. Cathy had lived there for six years. He wondered if she remembered it. Then again, it wasn't like one car accident was going to stand out in a city the size of Omaha.

"I told you the other night I don't do rumors," Sam said, "but as far as rumors and suspicion go, my understanding is it's not just the Marion Family complaining."

"Oh?"

"Elizabeth—I mean Bethany—can probably fill you in more. But what I've heard is both families have leveled accusations. Mostly frivolous, from what I hear. But what I hear ain't all that much."

Ray didn't bother to contradict him. They finished their breakfast and second and third cups of coffee. Ray filled in a few more details about Graham's disappearance, and Sam talked a little more about working at the Bar H-9, dealing with tourists and customers all the time. He wasn't complaining, at least much. When they were done, Ray thanked Sam for his time and picked up the tab. Sam said, "Much obliged," just like the cowboys in the movies always did.

The temperature had warmed, but the air still contained a slight nip, especially in the breeze. Ray returned to his truck, checking his phone. He saw he had a text message from a familiar number. Lauren.

My seminar ends at noon. Wanna grab lunch after? Say 12:30.

Ray stared at it for a moment. It was very straightforward, very direct. Because that was Lauren's style or because she was distant? She'd gone informal, using "wanna" instead of "want to." That was casual and approachable, wasn't it? He shook his head and sighed. Playing *CSI* with a text message.

He quickly thumbed back, *Sure. Name the place.*

He got in and started the truck, thinking about calling Cathy to check on Ethan Thornton's accident. He decided to wait until he got back to the hotel. Good thing, too, or he would have missed Detective Celek's call.

"Remember I told you we found the Corolla's owner?" Celek said after they exchanged pleasantries.

"Yeah, Margaret Lane."

"Turns out it wasn't *that* Corolla that was hers."

"Come again?"

"Margaret Lane, up until her death in December of 2017, owned a 2004 Toyota Corolla and those were her plates on the Corolla at the Bar H-9."

"But not the same car?"

"Correct. We dug a little deeper and found a record of a donation of the car from her estate to a charity that takes used car donations. We contacted them, they checked their records, and confirmed taking possession of Margaret Lane's Toyota Corolla. VIN number matched what was on file with the DMV. It was the same Corolla."

"So somebody took her old plates and put them on their Corolla?"

"That's the theory. Without renewing them, so the plates are expired and the car's illegal. But at a glance, the plates are on a Corolla, the same general color, same model and year, or close to it by the looks of things."

"That's not a coincidence," Ray said. He happened to look in the mirror and saw a gray sedan two cars behind him. A sedan very similar to the one he'd observed in the parking lot outside his hotel. Not a coincidence either, he didn't think. Someone was following him. Who? And why? He considered taking evasive maneuvers but decided against it. Too hard in the confines of Jackson and, besides, the guy knew where Ray was staying. Assuming he was being tailed and his imagination wasn't acting up on him.

"You there?" Celek asked.

"Yeah, sorry. So where does that leave us?"

"Still nowhere on who got the plates. The guy I spoke with at the charity organization said there was no record of any plates being on the vehicle when it was donated, which is standard. And they immediately return them to the owner if there are. So someone presumably took them prior to that, but who is a mystery."

"Hmm."

"There's one other thing. We also uncovered where she bought the car, back in 2009."

"Where's that?"

"From a guy named Ben Pyle. He lives over in Wilson."

Ben. The name rang a bell, but Ray couldn't figure out why. He was back to the hotel and pulled into the parking lot. The gray sedan did not. Maybe he was imagining things.

"Ran a background on Pyle, just to check, and he's clean as far as we can tell. Seems to be a dead end."

Ben. The ranch hand who had interrupted their meeting with Angela—the same guy Ray had seen leaning and squinting by the pavilion at the Bar H-9—had been named Ben. Possibly a coincidence, but worth checking.

"How old is Pyle?" Ray asked as he parked the truck.

"Uh, I don't recall exactly. Fifties or so."

Too old to be the Ben at the Bar H-9 and Circle M. Way too old.

"He have any kids?"

"Yeah, I think so. Let me check a second. Why?"

"Maybe nothing," Ray said.

He heard mouse clicks and fingers on a keyboard.

"Two kids. A girl and a boy."

"What's the boy's name?"

"Ben Jr."

"Age?"

"Let's see, born in '94 would make him twenty-five. Twenty-four, I guess. His birthday's next month."

"There was a ranch hand at the Bar H-9 who I also saw out at Angela Marion's place. Worked for her too. His name was Ben."

"Ben Pyle?"

"I don't know. But he was about twenty-five. Or thirty. Or twenty. Hard to tell. And it's certainly nothing more than circumstantial evidence."

"Evidence of what?" Celek asked.

"Nothing, as of yet." Ray sighed. "That's the problem."

They again thanked each other, promised to keep each other in the loop, and ended the call. Ray headed up to his room. Lauren had texted him back: *You like Mexican?*

He wrote back a, *Sure.*

While waiting for her reply, he called Cathy. He heard screaming children in the background, but she assured him it was a good time to talk. He gave her a brief update, then asked about Ethan Thornton. "It was about four years ago, and he was killed in a solo car crash outside Omaha."

Cathy paused. "Oh, and you thought I was Alexa."

"Who?"

"Oh my goodness, Ray. Alexa. Like Siri or Cortana. Google?"

"Should we start this conversation over?"

Cathy sighed. "Why are you asking about this anyhow?"

"Word is the crash was suspicious."

"Suspicious how?"

"I don't know. That's what I'm hoping you might remember."

"A four-year-old car crash? Bobby, stop screaming."

"It was some suburb of Omaha. Greta maybe?"

"Gretna?"

"Could be."

"When exactly did it happen? Bobby, this is your last warning."

Bobby screamed a death wail that resounded through the phone.

"Do you need me to call back?"

"I need a representative from Sandals to call," she said with a sigh.

"It was four years ago."

"I mean when in the year. Was it Thanksgiving night?"

"I don't know."

"There was a crash Thanksgiving night on Highway 6. A kid flipped a pickup into a tree. He was going like a hundred miles an hour."

"That takes away the suspicion as to why."

"He was in intensive care for a couple weeks before he died. Somebody who knew him went to our church, so it was on the prayer chain. But I could have sworn his name was Nathan."

"Nathan. Ethan?"

"I suppose. Leah! Put that down! Ray, I gotta go."

"Okay, I'll—"

She had already hung up.

Ray sat in the chair and looked out the window. Angela Marion's ranch hand's father sold a car to Margaret Lane, and ten years later, her expired plates were used on a similar-model car to, presumably, kidnap Graham. The maybes and could haves were endless. A male descendant of John Marion—and thus a potential benefactor of the Snake Island land trust—had died after rolling a car going triple digits on a Nebraska highway. Tragic but not really suspicious unless Cathy was confused or missing part of the story.

His phone buzzed. He looked down.

Merry Piglets on N Cache

He frowned. And typed. *Merry what?*

Lauren's reply came in just a minute.

Merry Piglets. Walls are creepy but food is great.

Ray replied, *Food's what matters. Okay.*

Great.

He thought for a moment, then sent another text: *Are you paying attention to your seminar?*

Another minute passed.

[Sticking out tongue]

Ray grinned, then wiped it off his face when he realized he was text-flirting.

TWENTY-SIX

Lauren had been right about the walls. They depicted a variety of beach scenes with pigs instead of people. Pigs swimming. Pigs surfing. Pigs having cocktails. Pigs on a picnic. Creepy to say the least.

Ray had taken advantage of the nice weather and walked the few blocks to The Merry Piglets, just north of the Square. He had not spotted a tail but wasn't sure he could spot one in the first place.

Lauren had met him at the front door. She wore distressed and torn blue jeans and a raglan shirt, white with orange sleeves and a blue horse outlined in orange—a Boise State Bronco—on the front. Her face was bright and her smile warm, a one-eighty from when they'd parted the night before.

They'd passed through an imitation of a Spanish cantina, complete with a thatched roof and accented by skylights that made it bright and warm too. Almost as bright and warm as Lauren's face and smile. They'd been seated in the back, with the pigs. Ray ignored them and studied the menu, which offered a wide assortment of Mexican options. He settled on several varieties of street tacos.

"So, I'm sorry about last night," Lauren said when they had ordered. Other than saying hello, brief talk about her seminar, and "what's good?" questions about the menu, they had said little. She leaned on the table, elbows spread wide. Her blue eyes searched Ray's, waiting.

"You don't have anything to be sorry about," he said.

"I was kind of cold, not properly grateful for dinner."

"You were grateful."

"Not properly. And you can't deny I was cold."

He shrugged.

"So you did notice."

"I didn't say I didn't notice. Just that you had nothing to be sorry for."

Lauren stared at him.

"Was it something I said or did?" Ray asked.

"Yes." She sat back. "And no."

Ray raised an eyebrow.

"It's complicated. I'm a woman. Let's not talk about it now."

"Okay."

"But you don't have to feel bad, okay?"

"Okay."

She smiled, and it was warm again.

"What'd you do this morning?" she asked after a drink of her ice water. So Ray told her, starting with his conversation with Sam, then Detective Celek, and then—because their food hadn't arrived yet—his call to Cathy.

"So, ultimately, we're nowhere," Lauren summarized.

"More or less."

Ray's phone vibrated, and he dug it from his pocket. Cathy.

"Sorry," he said to Lauren, "it's my sister."

"Go ahead."

"Hey, Cathy."

"I thought of something else. About that Ethan guy."

It was silent in the background. Early afternoon naps?

"What's that?" Ray asked.

"I mentioned he was in the hospital for like two weeks, in intensive care. From what I remember, word on the prayer chain was he was getting better. Then he died, all of the sudden."

Ray said nothing.

"Maybe that's the suspicious part," she said.

Ray frowned as their waitress brought their meals.

"Was it suspicious?" he asked.

"I don't know. It was sudden."

Ray thought about pushing. He could ask her to call people on the prayer chain who might remember. But he didn't want to tear open old wounds, and likely over nothing. If there was anything really suspicious, the Omaha cops would have found it, wouldn't they?

"Anyhow, thought you'd like to know."

"Thanks, Sis."

"Say, what's going on with that cute lady park ranger you mentioned?"

"She's sitting across from me, and our tacos just came."

"You're out to lunch? I hope you're paying at least."

"TBD."

"Where'd you go?"

"Cathy, this isn't the time."

"Come on, you know how I like eating out in different towns, and seeing as how I probably never will again . . ."

"Someplace called The Merry Piglets."

"Ooh, Graham liked that place."

"What?"

"The Merry Piglets. Graham liked that place."

"How do you know?"

"It was on Facebook."

"Graham's on Facebook."

"Everyone's on Facebook, Ray."

"When were you on Facebook?"

"All the time."

"I mean to see what Graham liked."

"After you mentioned he was missing. I was putzing around one day."

"Did you see anything else?"

"Sure, lots of stuff."

"Anything about triangles or places around Jackson? Anything about a girl not named Heidi.?"

"Whoa, Ray, calm down."

"Sorry. Look, can I call you back?"

"Yeah. Enjoy your tacos. And your lady ranger."

"Bye, Cathy."

He sighed as he lowered his phone.

"Where do I start with that?" Lauren asked, nibbling on a tortilla chip.

Ray raised an eyebrow.

"Who's sitting across from you?"

"What?"

"You said 'she's sitting across from me.'"

"I meant you."

"Of course, but who am I to your sister?"

"I mentioned you to her a while back. After all, when a stranger comes up to you and asks to help you find your missing cousin . . ."

Lauren gave him a playful glare.

"Can we eat? This is going to be cold soon."

They did, and Lauren had been right about the food at The Merry Piglets too. It was delicious. Ray's combination of tacos hit the spot, and as he ate, he related what Cathy had said. "It never occurred to me to check social media—is that what they call it?"

Lauren nodded with a grin.

"Maybe there's something we can find there, something to tell us who this other woman is or to tell us why Graham disappeared. It's a shot."

Lauren shrugged.

"How's everything tasting?" their waitress asked.

They both approved.

"I'm sorry," she said, crouching down as she spoke, "I didn't mean to eavesdrop, but did I hear you mention Graham's disappearance?"

Ray swept his eyes across Lauren's face before nodding.

"Graham Stoddard?" the waitress asked. Ray took note of her nametag—Raquel.

"Yeah. You know him?"

"We worked together at Metro before I came here. I heard that he had disappeared. Do they know what happened yet?"

"No," Ray said. "I'm his cousin, by the way. Ray."

"Raquel."

They shook hands.

"I came to visit, and when I got here, he was gone. We're scrambling to figure anything out."

"When was the last time you saw or spoke to him?" Lauren asked.

"Let's see . . . He was actually in here with Caitlin about two weeks ago, maybe? No, closer to three, I bet. Time flies, let me tell you."

"Caitlin," Ray said. "Someone you know?"

"Yeah, sort of. I mean, I know who she is, but we're not BFFs or anything."

"Do you know her last name?"

"Garner."

Ray and Lauren's eyes were drawn to each other like magnets.

"Caitlin Garner?" Lauren asked.

"Yeah. You know her?"

"No. The, uh, name's familiar."

"I'm sorry, but could you tell, were they together?" Ray asked.

"Looked like it. I thought he was dating someone else, but that's been a while."

"Can you remember specifically when it was?" Lauren asked.

"Oh, gosh, let me think . . . It was a Friday afternoon, I think. It wasn't Friday the thirteenth because that day was just weird. Must have been the week before that."

"Thanks, Raquel," Ray said.

"Sure. Can I get you guys anything else?"

"Not now."

"No," Lauren echoed, and Raquel departed with a smile.

Lauren leaned forward. "So this whole Garner connection suddenly takes on a new complexion."

Ray nodded.

"Jimmy tells us Graham bragged about hooking up with some other girl. Heidi admits to you the two of them weren't exactly the picture of fidelity. And now Raquel places Graham here with another woman and said it looked like they were together. Safe to say he was cheating on Heidi."

Ray nodded again.

"Also safe to say it was with Caitlin Garner."

"Agreed."

Lauren reached for a chip. Before snapping half of it off in her mouth, she said, "How much you want to bet Caitlin has no connection to the rest of the Jackson Hole Garners?"

"Not very much."

"Me either."

Ray had all but forgotten his street tacos, as good as they were. Now he picked one up, eating absentmindedly as he pondered this new development. "It still doesn't explain what Graham knew about the Garners," he said at length, "but it does explain how he knew. At least if Caitlin is one of those Garners."

"Which neither of us is betting against."

"Right."

"I'll call Audrey when we're done and find out."

"Okay."

"Otherwise, we could just pay a visit to the source."

"Who? Caitlin?"

"Well, if we can find her. But I was thinking Woody."

Ray raised an eyebrow.

"Drive out to his ranch, actually enter it this time, and ask him what the H-E-C-K is going on."

"It's direct, I'll give you that."

"I'll call Audrey first. No sense in wasting a trip if they're not related."

"If she doesn't answer, maybe we should just get an ancestry.com account. It'd come in handy with all these family trees."

"I know, right? Angela had me dizzy yesterday."

"Hey, Lauren . . ."

"Yeah."

"I'm not all that down with modern slang—"

"No," she said with heavy sarcasm.

"But does 'hooked up' convey what I think it does?"

"Well, having never hooked up myself, I'd have to go off what I've heard, but I'd say yes."

"So if Graham and Caitlin hooked up, and nature took its course . . ."

"She *could* be carrying the legal benefactor of the Snake Island trust," Lauren finished.

"And if someone knew about their relationship, knew where it was prone to lead . . ."

"It could be a motive for someone making Graham disappear."

^   ^   ^

Ray rode shotgun in Lauren's Focus as they headed west out of Jackson on Highway 22. Both of them had been quiet during the rest of lunch, contemplating the possibilities. If Graham got Caitlin Garner pregnant, and the baby was a boy, he would be the youngest male descendant of Bret James and thus in line to inherit Snake Island. But it was too soon for Caitlin Garner to more than guess that she was pregnant, too soon to know the sex of the baby, and too soon—quite possibly—to know the father. Let alone for anyone else to know. And in that case, it would be too *late* for anyone to want to make Graham disappear.

But, if someone—and out of fairness Ray was trying not to picture Angela Marion—had known of Graham and Caitlin's relationship but not its duration, and had considered the propensity of their relationship leading to sex, it would not have been too late to make Graham disappear as a form of birth control. Speculation, at the most.

After lunch, Lauren had called Audrey Garner. She had confirmed that Caitlin was one of "those" Garners. She was Woodrow's granddaughter, by way of his oldest daughter Amber. She was eighteen and thus, while ten years younger than Graham, legal. He almost deserved to disappear.

Audrey also informed them that Caitlin lived with her grandpa Woody. Amber Garner worked in Yellowstone National Park as a custodial supervisor, traveling more often than not, and Woody provided Caitlin a permanent place to stay. Given that information, Lauren had again suggested going to visit him. Ray had agreed. They had nothing to lose at this point. Now, as they turned north on Highway 390, toward the impressive Tetons, Ray began to wonder. Angela Marion had extended the invitation to them. Would Woodrow Garner be as welcoming to uninvited guests?

They followed the familiar route off the main highway and soon were at the cul-de-sac with two gravel drives, one going left, one going right. Lauren turned right under the hewn timber headgate adorned with the word "Garner" in wrought iron and flanked by triangles inscribed with G's.

"Wanna turn around?" she asked.

"Yes," Ray said.

She let her foot off the gas.

"But don't."

She smiled and reaccelerated. The driveway wound around a pair of small, grass-covered hillocks and opened to a trio of buildings. They were all made of log, stained dark, like some of the National Park Service buildings. There was a house on the right—a cozy log cabin on steroids—along with a garage in the middle and a stable on the left. No barn. No shed. No riding circle. No vehicles out. No sign of anyone. And not what Ray had expected for someone worth seven or eight figures.

Lauren parked in front of the house. She cut the engine and turned to Ray. "Well, at least if they're wary of uninvited guests, a grandpa-gold Ford Focus is about as innocuous as it gets."

"True."

They got out. All was calm. They climbed the steps. The front door opened.

"Can I help you two?"

The voice belonged to a short, somewhat potbellied man in an ivory-colored collared shirt and blue jeans. He sported a Santa Claus beard, albeit shorter. Maybe Kenny Rogers. He wore a dark brown cowboy hat on his head, of course, and the stub of a cigar extended from his mouth. It did not affect his speech at all, which was twanged like a good ol' boy's.

"Are you Woodrow Garner?" Lauren asked. She and Ray had not discussed their strategy with any specificity, but Ray was content to let her talk. A good-looking woman could be as disarming to a potentially inhospitable rancher as a "grandpa-gold" Ford Focus could be innocuous.

"I am," he said. He puffed on the cigar. "Who are you?"

"My name's Lauren Waite. This is my friend, Ray Eastwood. We're wondering if Caitlin's here."

Ray glanced at her. Definitely a bold opening move. He liked it.

Woodrow Garner puffed on his cigar some more. "Why do you want to see Caitlin?"

"It's sort of a long story," Lauren said.

"Well, she's not here. But I do like stories." He didn't smile, but his face softened. "Would you like to come in?"

"Thank you," Lauren said. Ray let her go first, sweeping his eye once more over the garage, stable, and driveway. Something had bothered him about it, and he now realized what. No triangles.

Woodrow led them down a hallway with several rooms on either side and into a massive living room that featured a vaulted two-story ceiling and a bank of windows looking toward the river valley and West Gros Ventre Butte. A six-foot-wide stone fireplace was built into the opposite wall, its chimney rising to the ceiling. Two moose-antler chandeliers lit the room, or at least would have in darkness. The furniture was rustic, with gnarled wood arms and legs. The coffee table was made to look like a carved-out riverbed, complete with a stuffed salmon "swimming" upstream, all beneath a glass top. An old, long, rifle hung above the fireplace. It reminded Ray of the décor at the Gun Barrel, which reminded him of something he had said or done to make Lauren distant. He tried to forget it as Woodrow offered them seats.

"Thank you for seeing us," Lauren said.

Woodrow nodded. Puffed his cigar. Didn't offer them one, or a drink. Angela won points for hospitality.

Lauren looked at Ray. He nodded. She'd gotten them in the door.

She left out a lot of details. She didn't mention postcards or triangles or various locations across the valley. Instead, she explained that they were looking for Ray's cousin, that they had reason to believe he was "friendly" with Caitlin, and that they hoped she could shed some light on where Graham was or what had happened to him. She was soft-spoken and non-accusatory. Woodrow listened while smoking. His face gave nothing away. Ray was watching.

"I appreciate your candor, Miss Waite. And yet, I suspect that isn't all of the story."

"It's not. And in all candor, we also have some questions for you."

Woodrow pursed his lips. Sucked on the cigar. "Caitlin has gone to visit some old friends of hers in San Diego. She's going to be there for quite a while."

Convenient, Ray thought. He said nothing. Neither did Lauren.

"As far as her being 'friendly' with your cousin, I don't know anything about that. Caitlin has her own social life, and I try not to meddle."

Ray nodded.

"But I can assure you she had nothing to do with his disappearance."

"I didn't mean to imply she did," Lauren replied. "We thought she might know something, however, that would prove relevant."

"I can't imagine what that would be."

"When did she leave?" Ray asked.

"I drove her to the airport Saturday morning," Woodrow answered.

Ray wasn't sure what the timing meant, if anything.

"You said you had some questions for me?"

Lauren again looked to Ray. This time, he took the cue. "Before he disappeared," Ray said, measuring his words carefully, "Graham mentioned to me a number of locations around Jackson Hole." He watched Woodrow's face carefully as he began listing places. "The Jackson Lake Lodge, Signal Mountain, the Jackson Town Square, your ranch."

At the mention of his ranch, Woodrow's eyes' narrowed slightly. His brow furrowed. He took a drag on the cigar.

"He also referenced finding triangles, which we understand are significant to your family. We plotted these locations on a map, nine in all, and found they seemed to point to a piece of property in the center of the valley. Snake Island."

Woodrow crossed his ankle onto his knee, grabbed his boot with one hand, and sat back. He removed the cigar from his mouth with his other hand. "What do you know about Snake Island?"

"Not very much," Ray said. "We know it's held in trust for the youngest male descendant of the Marion Family, or the James Family if no Marion males are alive. And we know as of right now, neither John Marion nor Bret James has a living male descendant."

"Sounds like you know quite a lot."

Ray shrugged, said nothing.

"Do you also know about the lengths the Marion Family has gone to in order to make sure no James—or Garner—has a male descendant?"

"What sort of lengths?"

"My grandson Lincoln was killed while hiking in the Tetons. Supposedly, he got separated from his friends and slipped. But Lincoln was not a careless hiker."

"We're sorry for your loss," Lauren said.

"Thank you. The authorities said 'accidents happen,' even to accomplished hikers. And I suppose that's true. But Lincoln's friends also reported seeing a man in camouflage on the trail, shortly after Lincoln was separated and shortly after they heard his scream. They couldn't identify him, and no one else in the area reported seeing him. All very mysterious."

Lauren was ever so delicate. "That doesn't implicate the Marion Family."

"On its own, no. There's also Willis Moran, Bret's great, great-grandson. He died from food poisoning three years ago. He had very specific allergies and was incredibly careful about what he ate. Of course, 'accidents happen.' Never mind that either Lincoln or Willis, were they alive, would stand in line to inherit Snake Island."

Ray looked at Lauren. It sounded like the Garner/James side had as many fingers to point as the Marion side.

"Another of Bret's descendants, Miriam, lives in Loveland, Colorado. She had a girl a few years ago and was planning to marry the girl's father. Their relationship ended when she caught the man in bed with another woman, a former employee at the Circle M Ranch, owned by the Marion Family."

"You think that was a ploy to keep them from having more children?" Lauren asked.

"I think it's certainly suspicious."

"That I'll grant you."

"Mr. Garner," Ray said, "you mentioned the Circle M. Just to be clear, when you say the Marion Family has gone to great lengths, are you referring to Angela Marion?"

He removed the cigar from his mouth. "I am." He reinserted it and puffed away.

Ray nodded. "With all due respect, Mr. Garner, we don't care about the trust or which family gets the land. Our only interest in any of this is Graham. And we don't mean to accuse you in any way, but do you have any idea how he knew about these locations, the triangles, Snake Island, or what his interest in them was?"

"I do not," Woodrow said. "I've never met your cousin, that I know of. In fact, until a quarter of an hour ago, I'd never heard his name. I can't imagine what connection might exist."

"Is your . . . belief in triangles common knowledge?" Lauren asked.

He winced at her choice of words but didn't correct her. "I don't believe so, but it's not something we keep secret either."

"Would those be things Caitlin might have talked to Graham about, assuming a relationship between them?" Ray asked.

"You're making an assumption I'm not, Mr. Eastwood," Woodrow said. "But were I to make it, I don't know what Caitlin may or may not have discussed. But I will say this, I can't imagine any reason for her to bring up Snake Island or our 'belief in triangles' with him unless he led her to it."

Ray nodded. He looked at Lauren. She looked back.

"Mr. Garner, thank you for your time," Ray said.

"Of course."

The trio stood. Woodrow walked them back into and through the hallway and out to the porch. He stood at the top of the stairs and watched as they descended the stairs. He watched as they got into Lauren's car. And he watched as she turned the car around and drove out of sight around the grass-covered hills.

Twenty-Seven

When they passed back under the headgate and thus exited Woodrow Garner's property, Lauren turned to Ray. "You think there's any chance Caitlin's actually in San Diego?"

"No."

"Me either."

"I think he sent her somewhere or stashed her somewhere, but I doubt he'd give us the location."

"Yeah."

"Thing is, I can't figure out why."

"Why he'd stash her or why he'd lie?"

"Stash her. Unless . . ."

She waited.

"Forgive me," Ray said, "I'm not a real expert in these matters, but how soon might a girl know she's pregnant?"

"Depends," Lauren said.

"On?"

"On timing, for one thing, and what you mean by 'know.' Be a few days or a week late and suspect, take a positive pregnancy test, or have it confirmed by a doctor?"

Ray thought for a moment. "Know enough to tell your grandpa you think some guy's stupid cousin got you pregnant."

"Such that he'd hide you away for the better part of nine months in case you're having a boy who would inherit a much-coveted piece of land?"

"For example."

Lauren nodded. "Back to the timing, depending on Caitlin's cycle and when she and Graham may or may not have . . ." She whistled. "Potentially by last Saturday."

Ray nodded. "So assuming Woodrow Garner is that desperate for Snake Island and assuming he believes an unborn baby inside his granddaughter would be in danger from Angela Marion, it would give him a motive to stash her in San Diego, the upstairs attic, or somewhere."

"It would. But there's another possibility."

"Go."

"Caitlin had something to do with Graham's disappearance, and her grandpa's hiding her in case the hammer falls on her."

"Hmm."

"No idea what that something would be, but it's a possibility."

"Or," Ray said, "she could have disappeared too. Maybe Grandpa Garner is responsible and made them both disappear, and gave us the San Diego story for cover."

"So why'd he make them both disappear?"

"No idea. There's no motive on his part to do anything to Graham."

Lauren slumped, leaning on the steering wheel, waiting for traffic on the main highway. When it cleared, she sat up straight again and turned south, headed back for town. It was two-thirty on the button.

"Did you notice something weird about Garner's place?" Ray asked.

"What's that?"

"No triangles."

She stuck her tongue into her cheek.

"I mean, sure, vague triangles you'd see in any building or room, but nothing obvious."

"No shrines you mean."

"I expected his living room to feature a skylight with a sundial in the middle or something. It was just a big cabin."

"The house, garage, and stable sort of formed a triangle."

"Sort of."

"That is weird."

"There's just way too much here that doesn't make sense. Angela hints the Garners are responsible for suspicious deaths in her family. Woodrow hints she's responsible for suspicious deaths and happenings in the James Family. Neither has proof. Caitlin is missing either for the same reason Graham is, because she's hiding from the cops because she killed him in a lover's spat or something, because she's pregnant with his male child who could inherit a timber-covered piece of land in the middle of a river, or because she's catching up with her girlfriends she hasn't seen since graduation. And nobody has any definitive answers a week after Graham's disappearance, and I'm running out of vacation time."

Lauren said nothing. They drove in silence, back to Highway 22. She turned east.

"Are you on Facebook?" Ray asked.

"What?"

"Are you on Facebook?"

She frowned. "Sort of."

He waited.

"I have a Facebook account, but I check it about once a month. Why?"

"My sister said she's friends with Graham on Facebook. I thought maybe if you had an account, you could see what she sees."

"Depends on his security settings. At least I think."

"Wanna try it out?"

She shrugged. "Sure."

They stopped at her apartment, which was light and airy in the mid-afternoon. She retrieved a laptop from her bedroom and opened it on the counter between the living room and kitchen, then asked, "You want a cup of coffee?"

"No, I'm good."

"You feeling okay?"

He grinned. "Fine."

Lauren logged into her Facebook account. "This goes back like ten years, so if you judge me for anything you see here, I will smack you."

"Am I going to be seeing judgment-worthy things?"

"I was in college once, remember. I had a bunch of girlfriends. We didn't skinny-dip in the Snake River or have toga parties or anything, but . . . Why am I explaining myself to you? Do you want me peering into your life as twenty-year-old Ray?"

"I don't mind," he said with a shrug. "Besides, I was smart enough not to put pictures of anything on the internet for the whole world to see."

"Neither did I, but those girlfriends . . ."

"No judging," Ray said, and she turned the screen toward him. They found Graham's page. He didn't post much. He loved his coworkers at Metro, several of whom were pictured. He hated the president, who was depicted in caricature. He liked half a dozen bars and restaurants, including The Merry Piglets (he'd also gotten street tacos). He'd shared half a dozen videos, several of which weren't appropriate for Ray or Lauren's virgin eyes. He'd made a handful of random comments on other people's posts, none of which seemed in any way relevant to his disappearance. There were a couple pictures of Heidi, one with Graham, one without. There was no mention of Caitlin Garner. He wasn't friends with Caitlin Garner, or with anyone else that drew attention. Facebook, as Ray had always believed, was a waste of time.

"It was worth a shot," Lauren said.

"I suppose."

"Maybe we should try talking to Audrey again," Lauren said. "See what she makes of Woodrow's comments."

"Worth a try."

They got back in Lauren's car and onto the main highway. As they did, Ray turned around to look through the rear window.

"What's up?"

"Nothing, I guess."

She raised her eyebrows.

"I thought we had a tail, but he turned the other way."

"A tail? And your response is to twist all the way around in your seat and stare him down?"

"Sorry, my spycraft is a little rusty."

"What makes you think we've got a tail anyhow?"

"This morning when I came out of my hotel, there was a guy sitting in the lot in a gray sedan. Small lot, and he looked . . . I don't know, intentional in being there."

"What'd he look like?"

"Couldn't see him that well."

"But you could see he was intentional?"

"It was a hunch, a gut instinct, something about the way he was sitting in the vehicle. I can't define it."

"Sure your gut instincts aren't rusty too?" She smirked.

"Then after breakfast with Sam, I see a gray sedan behind me. Could have been the same car, could not. I didn't get a great look at it from two cars in front. He followed me back to the hotel."

Lauren raised an eyebrow. "Could be coincidence."

"Or paranoia or somebody watching me. Then when I see a gray sedan just now, same general make as the one in the parking lot this a.m., I got suspicious."

"Why would someone be following you?"

"Well, if this was a spy novel, because I was getting close to something."

"So why would someone be following you?" she asked, the smirk threatening to break out again.

"I don't know. But nobody was following me the last four days. We talk to Angela, and suddenly I'm seeing gray sedans like they're black helicopters."

The smirk did break out. "Maybe they've been following you all week, and your spycraft is really rusty."

"Yeah, maybe."

The afternoon was as beautiful and crisp as the rest of the day, and the Square was festooned with autumn colors. It also seemed alive and full of energy, and busier than it had been before. Then again, it was Thursday, the start of a long weekend, perhaps? Lauren parked as close to Panorama on Center Street as possible, and the duo got out.

Audrey was not sitting behind the checkout "counter" in the gallery. A young man with cuffed skinny jeans, a very thin sweater over a V-neck T-shirt, and a beard that looked painted on was. At least he wasn't wearing one of those Smurf caps.

"Can I help you?" he asked, standing. He wrapped the sweater around him.

"Is Audrey in?" Lauren asked.

"No, she's out for the day. Sick, I think. It's going around."

"It?" Ray asked.

"Flu. Fever, cough, you know."

"Yeah."

"Okay, thanks anyhow," Lauren said. They ducked back out of the gallery. "She sounded fine when I talked to her earlier. I guess it came on suddenly."

"Cell phones make everybody sound half sick, what with the bad connections. It'd be hard to tell."

"Whatever you say, Grandpa. Okay if I walk across your lawn here?"

It was his turn to give her a playful glare.

"I can call her," Lauren said. "At least, if I can find a phone with a good connection."

"Don't bother. If she's sick, I don't want to disturb her with conspiracy theories about her uncle and second cousin or whatever Caitlin is. We'll figure something else out."

"Wanna walk while we figure?"

"Sure."

They wandered along the sidewalks, strolling slowly, fitting in with the crowd. They ducked into a few shops on Lauren's suggestion. It was the sort of thing Ray usually had no patience for—window shopping. But the sun was warm, Lauren was in a good mood, and he was on vacation.

As they walked, in between her admiration for various pieces of artwork or kitschy knickknacks that would look good in her apartment, they tried to figure out what they were missing and what next steps to take. They didn't get very far. Then Lauren bought some salt water taffy, and they busied themselves guessing at flavors.

"How else could we find Caitlin Garner?" Ray asked as they exited a T-shirt store. He'd been there already and had followed Lauren around for five minutes while she shopped for unknown persons.

"Find her?" She reached into the bag of taffy he was holding.

"Not necessarily in person, but find her to talk to her."

"You think she'll tell us anything?"

"Maybe, maybe not. But she's the key to all this."

"Cherry," Lauren said, holding up the wrapper from the piece she had in her mouth.

"Noted."

"What are you going to do, call up and ask if she's pregnant?"

"I might lead into it a little."

Lauren reached for another piece of taffy.

"What does your dentist say?"

"That I have a beautiful smile."

He nodded.

"You figure out the orange?"

"Orange," he said.

She shook her head at him.

"What?"

"I thought it was peach."

"Peach has yellow stripes."

"What are you, a taffy connoisseur?"

"Just been around the block."

"Speaking of," she said, pointing to the right. They turned, waited for traffic, and crossed the street. "I don't remember this place," she said, pointing to a gallery. They ducked inside.

It was upscale, like Audrey Garner's, featuring a lot of bucolic and Native American pieces and paintings. Ray scoped out some woodcarvings of various animals, thinking about buying one for his dad. The price tags gave him pause. He figured he could always come back, and browsed some more, stopping in front of a painting that drew him in.

More than a dozen Native Americans were depicted, all in various stages of panic and flight, judging by the expressions on their faces and their posture. One rode on a horse. Several ran. A few more crawled. Several more were splayed on the ground, dead. The ground was tinged with blood and water. It appeared to be a streambed. The trees in the background disappeared into a fog, or maybe smoke. It was a graphic painting, and realistic. Haunting, even, in the style it was done.

"Mesmerizing, isn't it?"

Ray turned to see the gallery proprietor, a middle-aged woman with spiked black hair. She was dressed elegantly, a far cry from Audrey and her festive skirt, peasant blouse, and trendy sandals.

"That's another word for it," he said.

Lauren had also drifted over. "What's the subject?"

"No one knows. The artist never said."

Lauren bent closer, reading the small gold placard beneath the painting. "'Driven.'" She looked up at the proprietor.

She shrugged. "There are several theories, mostly that it depicts a First Peoples tribe being driven off their native land."

"Hmm."

"Can I show you any other works or pieces?"

"We're just browsing," Lauren said. "But thanks."

The woman smiled perfunctorily and left them.

Lauren made eye contact with Ray, and they headed for the door. He took a last glance at a wood bison on the way out. His dad was already getting a coffee mug . . .

Lauren stopped on the sidewalk, smiling up into the sunlight. She turned to look at Ray. "I feel like coffee."

"Okay."

"Something on your mind?"

"If it were only one thing . . ."

"What in particular?"

"That painting."

"It was powerful."

"More than that. Remember what Sam told us the other night, about Snake Island being populated by Shoshone Indians who suddenly disappeared?"

"Yeah."

"One of the theories, he said, was that John Marion drove them off their land."

Lauren looked around. A few pedestrians passed by them, and she took Ray's arm and turned him the other way. "Are you suggesting John Marion massacred an Indian tribe to get Snake Island?"

"No."

"Good, because that's a stretch."

"Admittedly. That painting could have been of one of hundreds of incidents. Or none at all. It could have been a general statement." He made eye contact with Lauren. "But it looked specific. It felt personal."

"I didn't know you felt art so deeply."

"I don't."

Lauren nodded.

"It just makes me wonder if there's any truth to any of the particular rumors. Maybe that's why Snake Island is so important."

She raised an eyebrow. And reached for more taffy.

They stopped at the corner.

"I feel like coffee," Lauren said again.

"Well, you need something to wash all that taffy down."

They walked a block south, to the corner where the highway jogged west. The Wells Fargo-like stagecoach wasn't there.

"Grab a cup?" Lauren asked.

"Better idea," Ray said, reaching into his pocket. He came out with his wallet. "You go buy us coffee, and I'm going to make a few calls."

"I can pay for coffee," she said.

"So can I." He handed her a ten.

"Who you going to call?"

"Bethany Cahill, for one."

"And for two?"

"My brother-in-law."

She raised an eyebrow but didn't ask.

"I'll fill you in when you get back, if there's anything to fill."

"Okay. Back where?"

He nodded at the Square, and they split. He crossed the street and found a bench in the shade. It took a few minutes of searching the internet on his phone to determine there were no Bethany Cahills in Missoula, home of the University of Montana. There was one in Bozeman, home of Montana State University. Ray called her, got no answer, and decided to leave a voicemail. He identified himself, explained the situation as briefly as possible, and asked her to call back when she had a chance.

Then he called Cathy. The kids were up and screaming, so he made it short, asking for Jason's number. Ray had his brother-in-law's cell number in his phone, but Jason never answered his cell. Seldom replied to texts. So Ray asked for his number at work. Cathy had to look it up on her phone, and Ray memorized it and dialed it quickly before forgetting.

"Jason Ross."

"Hey, Jason, it's Ray."

"Brother-in-law Ray?"

"The one and same."

"Everything okay? You don't usually call me at work."

"Yeah, everything's fine. I'm calling because I have a favor that might be up your alley."

"Lay it on me."

"There's a legend in Jackson Hole about a Shoshone Indian tribe that disappeared from the valley somewhere around the turn or early part of the twentieth century. From a place called Snake Island. Nobody knows what happened to them. Some say the tribe moved away voluntarily, some say they died out from disease, some say they were killed or forcibly driven from their land. I don't know if this is anything you have the sources to find out about, but I know it's something I don't."

"You want to know what happened to them?"

"Especially as it pertains to something violent happening. Were they murdered, conquered, something like that?"

"I can look into it. What else do you know?"

"You've heard it."

"Wow, a real lay-up, Ray."

"Yeah, well."

"I'll see what I can find. I know some people who might be able to point me in the right direction."

"I appreciate it."

"Why the interest?"

"It's a long story. Short of it is they may have something to do with Graham's disappearance."

"Yeah, Cathy told me about that. I'll see what I can do and let you know."

"Thanks. Don't make Cathy a research widow over it. It's not that big of a deal. But if you have some spare time."

"I'll find it. I'll call you, Ray."

"Thanks."

He disconnected the call and sat back, taking in the park—the people, the trees, the blue sky above. It felt as if he'd been in Jackson for weeks, maybe months. South Dakota felt light years away. So did his life there, his work, his ex-fiancée and the pain she'd caused him.

"Here you go," Lauren said, walking up to the bench. She extended a cup of coffee—Jackson Hole Coffee Roasters, of course—and sat down.

"That was fast."

She shrugged.

"Thanks."

"You paid. I've got your change in my pocket."

Ray waved. "Just pass me the taffy."

"Oh, did I sneak off with that?"

He winked at her faux confusion and nodded at the bag. "I'm just surprised there's some left."

"I can only chew so fast."

Ray opened a piece of brown taffy, sure bet to be chocolate, and scanned the Square again.

"You get ahold of Bethany?"

"Voicemail."

"Do I get to know about call number two?"

"My brother-in-law. He's a research assistant at UNO, specializes in American history, and I asked him to dig into this legend of the Shoshone Indians that were driven off Snake Island. Maybe he can find something somewhere."

"I should know this, but UNO . . . ?"

"Nebraska-Omaha."

"Aha. Are they Cornhuskers too?"

"Mavericks."

She nodded.

"We're missing something somewhere," Ray said. "Caitlin, the suspicious deaths, Angela's ranch hand Ben's dad selling Margaret Lane a Toyota Corolla with plates used to take Graham."

"It's like one of those old murder mysteries where everybody's got a motive and opportunity. An Agatha Christie novel."

Ray shook his head. "I feel like it's there, but I'm just not seeing it."

Lauren looked at him for a minute. "I have an idea."

"About what we're missing."

"No. I think we should get out of here."

"Out of here?"

"You've been chasing down leads all day. Pressing. And it's wearing on you."

Ray said nothing.

"So let's go for a drive, or a hike. Take your mind off things for a while. Maybe it will give all the jumble in your head the space to sort itself out."

"Think so?"

"Worth a shot. Besides, you haven't been to Mormon Row yet, have you?"

"No."

"So what do you say?"

He looked at her. "Okay."

Lauren tipped her coffee cup into his. "Besides, I need to talk to you."

TWENTY-EIGHT

For reasons she kept to herself, Lauren suggested they take Ray's truck. So they did. Leaving her car parked in the Square, they walked back to his hotel and retrieved his Silverado. Ray drove. Lauren controlled the CD player. Switchfoot's "Fading West" was an appropriate soundtrack as they cruised north out of Jackson. No gray sedans were spotted.

The late afternoon sun was vibrant as it shone down on the rugged Tetons, the snow that mostly blanketed the peaks colored anywhere from bright white to light and medium tones of blue. Slabs of granite still poked out in numerou places, their colors much darker on the blue-purple-gray spectrum. The sage was grayish green, tinged with gold, as was the brownish grass around it. The trees were dark green in the case of the pines, and yellow turning to orange in the case of the aspens and cottonwoods. The beauty was beyond words.

Lauren turned up "When We Come Alive."

Ray looked at her, smiling contentedly.

"What?" she asked.

"Surprised you're not singing along."

"I can't sing a lick."

"No?"

"No. My daddy once said I couldn't carry a tune in a five-gallon pail."

"Ouch."

"He said it kindly."

"Still."

"Besides, it's rude."

"To sing?"

"Would you grab a brush and start painting alongside Van Gogh? Add a stanza to one of Kipling's poems?"

"Point made."

They kept going for a while, then pulled off to get a closer look at a small herd of elk out in the sagebrush. A couple of bulls, but a ways off.

Back on the highway, they passed the airport, then the turnoff to Moose and the park entrance. Blacktail Butte rose up on the right, then fell off. Lauren pointed to a road branching off to the right, and Ray slowed to turn.

"Antelope Flats Road," Ray said, referencing the sign at the turnout. "Any chance we'll see antelope?"

"More likely buffalo."

They drove for a mile, and Lauren had Ray make a right onto a narrower road. Still paved, but he was starting to see why she'd opted for his truck.

After a thousand feet, they came to a small turnout, and Ray followed Lauren's outstretched hand and turned into it. She was already reaching for the door, and he put the truck in park, killed the ignition, and followed her out. Across the road and a little south of them was an old, brown barn. Its gable-style roof flexed halfway down, its slope flattening to accommodate lean-tos built onto either side of the barn. They formed one structure, surrounded by tall grass and little else. A narrow, serpentine creek wound through the foreground, and a copse of tall trees was off to the left. More trees in the distance blocked the line where the base of the mountains met the prairie.

"Mormon Row," Lauren said across the bed of Ray's truck.

"This is where all the pictures are taken," he said, recognizing the barn from numerous photographs he'd seen over the years. The old barn would have drawn photo enthusiasts by itself, but the backdrop of the Tetons made it truly picturesque.

"T.A. Moulton Barn," Lauren said. "Built in the early 1900s. His brother's place is just north of here. They were part of a Mormon settlement that chose this spot, in part, because the alluvial soil was more suitable for farming. But they had to dig miles of ditches to get the Gros Ventre River's water here." She looked at him sheepishly. "Sorry, didn't mean to go all tour guide on you."

"No, it's fine."

"I don't know what it is," she said. "The Tetons are magnificent enough by themselves, but throw an old barn in front of them, and people flock the world over to see it."

"I can see why."

They lingered for a few minutes, then got back in the truck, and drove back to the intersection where they had originally turned south. There was another parking area there, a little larger, and occupied with a sporty SUV. Ray parked beside it, and they again got out.

Beyond the parking lot, a gravel drive continued north, somewhat ill-defined as it ran through grass and dirt, flanked by sagebrush. As they walked, Lauren informed him that this was John Moulton's homestead. First came a pink stucco house behind a small grove of aspen trees, and then a gambrel-style barn, also flanked by attached lean-tos. It was surrounded by old wood fencing and, on the north side, a cattle chute. This barn was even more familiar from photographs, and even more picturesque. Accordingly, the sporty SUV's driver—presumably—stood behind a camera on a tripod and snapped pictures.

"Quite a view," Ray said.

"See the buffalo in the distance?"

"I do now," he answered, scanning the fields of sagebrush behind the barn. "Wish I had a camera."

"Here," Lauren said, reaching into her back pocket. She retrieved her phone and turned around, extending her arm to take a selfie. "Get in here," she said, pulling Ray over. They smiled into the phone's display, and she snapped several pictures.

"Probably not as high quality as his," Lauren said, nodding at the guy with the tripod who had packed up and was trekking back toward his sporty SUV.

"You going to post those on Facebook now?"

"Ha."

Ray retrieved his phone as well. As he lined up a picture, Lauren chuckled aloud.

"What?"

"I just figured you more for the flip-phone type."

He looked at her.

"I'll even bet that was your first selfie."

"Not even. It wasn't mine."

"You know what I mean."

"And you're wrong. My sister's a millennial. If she doesn't have a selfie of it, it didn't happen."

Lauren grinned, then leaned on the fence while Ray took a few pictures. When he was finished, he put his phone back in his pocket and leaned on the fence beside her. For several minutes they stared silently, the barn dominating their view, but the Teton Range still clearly visible beyond it. There was maybe another hour before the sun sank behind the mountains. Maybe less. It was golden hour, as they called it.

Tires crunched on loose gravel as the guy with the sporty SUV finally drove off. Ray and Lauren were alone. They kept looking at the view, feeling the sun, hearing the breeze in the leaves of the nearby aspens.

"I don't want you to leave, Ray."

He looked at her.

"That's what last night was about," she said, looking back at him. "And you don't have to look at me like that because I don't mean anything more by that than what I said."

"Look at you like what?"

"That," she said, turning to face him. "Wondering what you're supposed to say next, wondering if there was a subtext or something deeper. Wondering if this is about to get weird."

"Was I looking like that?"

She nodded. "Don't read between the lines."

"Okay."

"Anyhow, when we started talking about Kevin—the guy I met freshman year?—it got me thinking about how much fun I've had with you the last few days, and by Monday, you'll be gone, and I'll be talking about the local flora and fauna to a bunch of tourists from Minnesota."

Ray started to speak. She cut him off.

"And I love my job, but you know what I mean?"

"I do."

She turned and leaned back on the fence, dangling her arms over the top log in it. "So what do I do, instead of maximizing my time with you and enjoying a nice dinner, I go into a shell and have you take me home so I can mope."

"I never pictured you as a moper."

"And I don't want you to, which is why I went home to do it." She looked up and grinned.

"Well, you want to get dinner tonight, make up for it?"

Her grin widened. "Yeah. But not yet." She turned back to the vista—the barn, the mountains, the grazing bison in the distance.

"For what it's worth," Ray said, "I don't really want to leave either."

"Nobody wants to leave Jackson Hole, Ray."

He thought it. He wasn't sure about saying it. Wasn't sure what it would mean to her. Wasn't sure what it would mean to *him*.

He took a breath, and said it anyhow.

"I don't want to leave you, Lauren."

She turned, waves of hair sliding over the orange of her sleeve. She looked at him with a peaceful smile but said nothing.

He said nothing.

They stared at the mountains until the sun set behind them.

^   ^   ^

Bethany Cahill called back while Ray and Lauren were eating burgers at Liberty Burger in Jackson, right next door to The Merry Piglets. They had said nothing more while watching the sunset, letting their statements stand without clarification, without addition or subtraction. They had driven back into town listening to more Switchfoot, watching the post-sunset colors play out in the sky and the mountains south and east of the valley. It was one of those moments Ray knew he was going to want to relive when he returned home. He also knew his memory of it would be only a fading glimpse, like the vanishing daylight.

They ate bison burgers while talking about nothing—sports affiliations and memories of home and books they'd read or movies they'd watched. Then Ray's phone vibrated in his pocket. He fished it out, looked at the display, recognized the number, and looked at Lauren.

Her eyebrows went up.

"Bethany," Ray said to Lauren as he swiped his phone. He put it to his ear. "Ray Eastwood."

"Mr. Eastwood, it's Bethany Cahill."

"Thanks for returning my call," he said. He motioned to Lauren that he was going to take the call outside, where it was quieter. "Did you get my message?" he asked as he stood and headed for the exit.

"I did. I'm sorry to hear about your cousin."

"Thank you. I know it's an odd request," he said, now outside, leaning on a wood railing separating the boardwalk from the street. "But, I'm wondering if my friend and I could ask you some questions about the Marion Family, its history, the trust. Sam Covington mentioned speaking to you a few years back at a reunion, like I think I mentioned on the voicemail, and we're at a dead end, so I'm willing to try anything—even being a little uncouth."

"It's not uncouth," Bethany said. "I remember Sam. Big guy, big mustache?"

"That's him."

"You and your friend, you're in Jackson?"

"We are. We could set up a Skype session, or we could come to you up in Bozeman."

"That's a long drive."

"But scenic," he said. He and Lauren had discussed the possibility briefly, and neither had anything else to do on a Friday. Plus, it seemed a shame to come out here and not even see Yellowstone National Park.

"What if I met you halfway?" she asked. "I don't have classes on Friday, and can juggle a few things on my schedule."

"I don't want to impose on you."

"Oh, it's not," Bethany said. "Besides, I've been meaning to get into the park again before the snow falls. I'd make a day of it."

"That would be great," Ray said. "If you're sure you don't mind."

"I'm sure. Let's see . . . how about Old Faithful?"

"Okay."

"I think it's about equidistance, pending traffic and bison crossings," she said with a chuckle. "Should we say noon?"

"That's fine."

"There's a little café there called Geyser Grill. Great place to grab a bite. Want to meet there?"

"That's fine too. Geyser Grill at Old Faithful at noon. I appreciate it very much, Bethany."

"No problem. I'll see you tomorrow."

Ray lowered his phone. He looked at the tree-shielded park across the street. He shushed the voice that said he and Lauren would be wasting a trip into the park, that Bethany would be another dead end. Then he shushed the voice that said it wasn't possible to waste a day with Lauren. He went back in and finished his burger.

"Not that I'm not with you," Lauren said, "but what are we hoping to learn from her?" She dipped a French fry in ranch dipping sauce and looked up at him.

"I don't know. I'm gathering information. Anything to fill in some blanks."

She shrugged. "I like Old Faithful. And the Inn. Why not?"

When the check came, Ray just beat Lauren reaching for it.

"It's my turn," she said. "You paid last night."

"You bought taffy."

"You bought coffee."

"You kept the change," he said with a grin. "And you can get breakfast tomorrow."

"Breakfast? Now who's being forward?"

Ray shrugged. "I figured we have to eat on our way out of town."

"I know just the place."

"Okay."

He settled the bill, and they headed out. Ray drove back to his hotel, and they took their time walking back through the Square to Lauren's car. They didn't linger too much, because nighttime had brought a chill to the air, and Lauren hadn't brought a jacket.

"You want my flannel?" he asked, tugging at the sleeve of his shirt.

"No, I'm fine."

They stood beside her car, between it and another in the next parking spot.

"Thank you for dinner, Ray."

"You're welcome."

She leaned in and gave him a hug. A quick one. Still, it was the first time they had touched, other than a slap to the arm or poke in the ribs.

"I'll pick you up at eight," she said.

"You're driving?"

"You drove today."

He smiled. "Okay. I hope this all balances out when it's all said and done."

She narrowed one eye. "Eight," she said, then opened her door and ducked inside. Ray stepped up onto the curb, waved, and watched her back out.

Eight. It was about eight o'clock now, by no means late, and yet neither he nor Lauren had suggested hanging out longer. He'd expected her to invite him to her place and was both disappointed and glad she hadn't. He wasn't quite sure what was going on between them, but it felt prudent not to hang out in her apartment at night. Maybe that was weird, maybe that was a memory of past temptations, or maybe it was just that, prudent. But having vocalized it earlier, Ray also couldn't deny what he realized he'd been feeling for several days—he was dreading no longer having Lauren's company.

He walked back to his hotel, thinking about her, thinking about Graham, thinking about everything they'd learned over the last few days. An idea began to form in his mind. It wasn't much of one, but it was an idea. And he had nothing else to do with his night. So instead of going up to his room, he got into his truck and headed out of town.

He drove south from Jackson, on U.S. 191, until he came to the turnoff for the Bar H-9. By now, it was twenty after eight, about the time the wagons would return to the ranch. It was a long shot, Ray realized, but he wanted to scan the parking lot for a Toyota Corolla. It was unlikely the person responsible for taking Graham would return the vehicle to the scene of the crime. Unless it was their only vehicle, unless they had no reason to think anyone was onto them, and unless the scene of the crime was their place of employment.

Ray followed the well-groomed gravel road to the riverbank, across the wooden bridge spanning Flat Creek, and past the covered wagon marking the entrance to the Bar H-9. When the drive emerged from the pines and into the parking lot, Ray scanned for an open space. Mindful of the security camera, he didn't take the time to go up and down the rows of cars. Instead, he parked in the corner, facing the majority of the parked cars. If anyone was watching the security feed in real-time, Ray figured, they would conclude he'd come to pick someone up. He was safe.

The lighting was poor, despite a half moon sinking in the western sky, and Ray was unable to identify a Toyota Corolla from where he was parked. He waited as patrons began streaming into the lot. He checked vehicles as they left. No Corollas. He scanned the lot again as it thinned. Eventually, a dozen or so remained. The lot quieted. Only the staff was left, Ray assumed.

Ray waited, watching the clock. At ten, a few people straggled into the lot. They were dressed like cowboys and cowgirls. A couple more cars arrived in the lot, picking up people or parking and waiting, like Ray.

One of them was a tan Toyota Corolla.

Ray was too far away to read the license plate, or to confirm it was the same year and precise model as the one on the security feed from a week ago, but this was too much of a coincidence. Especially when a familiar-looking cowboy walked down the trail and got into the passenger seat. Ben Pyle Jr.

The Corolla made a sharp U-turn and headed for the exit. Ray started his truck and followed, grateful for another car that got in between them, lessening the likelihood Ben or his driver would get suspicious they were being followed.

The Corolla and the intermediate car both turned north on 191. Ray followed. Both turned west on Highway 22 in Jackson. Ray followed. The intermediate car kept going on 22 while the Corolla branched off onto Spring Gulch Road. North. Toward the Circle M.

Ray stuck to the Corolla, drawing as close as he dared. Close enough to make out the license plate. It was not a match. Not the same plate as on the Corolla on the security footage. So was this just a coincidence? Ben Pyle Sr. sold a tan Toyota Corolla to Margaret Lane. When she died, she donated the car, but the license plates ended up on another tan Toyota Corolla that had been at the Bar H-9 the night Graham disappeared. Now Ben Pyle Jr., who worked for Angela Marion, was picked up from the Bar H-9 in a tan Toyota Corolla with a different set of plates. Granted, it was a popular car, but this was too much. Wasn't it? And yet, Ray couldn't make the connection.

They continued north on Spring Gulch Road, beyond East Gros Ventre Butte. Then the Corolla slowed. Signaled. Turned into the driveway of the Circle M Ranch.

Ray blew on past, hoping to alleviate any potential concern on the part of Ben that he had been followed. He looked in his mirror and saw the taillights continue on up the driveway and eventually disappear. Ray slowed without braking, then cut his own lights. He made a careful Y-turn, then very slowly drove back south, pulling off the side of the road a few hundred yards north of the driveway to the Circle M. If the Corolla belonged to one of Pyle's friends, someone giving him a ride, Ray could follow it when it left and see where it went next. Maybe that would provide him a missing link. That is, if he could avoid being spotted.

Ray waited for an hour.

The Corolla never came back out the driveway.

TWENTY-NINE

"About time."

Ray stopped in the doorway to his hotel, letting his heart start beating again. Heidi sat on the edge of his bed, watching TV in the dark. She was fully dressed in ripped jeans and a T-shirt with Che Guevara on it. Probably had no idea who he was or what he stood for, but it was trendy. The least of Ray's concerns.

"What are you doing here?" he asked, letting the door close behind him.

Heidi stood. She was in socks, her shoes kicked to the side by the dresser. Hanging off the bed beside where she'd been sitting was a zip-up hoodie. She'd made herself at home.

"Waiting for you," she answered. "You want to turn on the light before this gets creepy?"

Ray stared at her. "You're watching TV in my hotel room with the lights off, and I'm the one who's making it creepy?"

"Whatevs, just hit the switch."

He did. And waited.

"I need to talk to you."

"Why didn't you call me?"

"I did. You didn't answer."

Ray pulled out his phone and looked at the screen. It was black, and no button pushing changed it. His battery must have died. He vaguely remembered seeing earlier that it was low.

He looked back at Heidi. "How'd you get in here?"

"I know Dylan downstairs. We went to school together."

"Great security."

"I was going to wait outside, but it got cold. Where were you?"

"Nowhere." He sighed. "Okay, what do you need to talk to me about?"

"Graham. He was cheating on me."

"How do you know?"

"Corbin told me."

"Corbin?"

"You know him?"

"If he's the same Corbin who's an assistant foreman at the Circle M, I do."

Heidi shrugged. "I don't know what he does. I just know him from school."

Ray raised an eyebrow.

"It's a small town, Ray."

He nodded. "What's Corbin look like?"

"Red hair, red beard, tall, good-looking."

"That's the same Corbin."

"Okay. I told you I don't know where he works. We aren't that close."

"But he told you Graham was cheating on you."

"I ran into him at Albertson's, and we said hey and caught up. I mentioned my boyfriend was missing. He asked who it was, and when I said Graham Stoddard, he frowned. I may not be a shrewd detective, but I knew something was wrong. I pressed him, and he said he'd heard that Graham was dating someone else. Anyhow, I thought you would want to know he mentioned her name. Caitlin Garner. Weren't you wondering about Garners or something?"

"Yeah. You know her?"

"No. Never heard of her."

Ray nodded.

"I'd like to meet her. Maybe punch her in the neck."

Ray looked at her.

"Relax, Ray, I didn't kill Graham and dump him in a river because he cheated on me."

"I didn't say that."

She sighed. "I'm actually kind of over him already."

Ray said nothing. After all, he was less than a month from being dumped by the love of his life and already not wanting to leave the company of another woman, so who was he to judge the expediency of a healed broken heart.

"Anyhow, thought you'd want to know."

"Yeah, thanks. Uh, when did you say you talked to Corbin?"

"Tonight. You need a time stamp?"

"No, just wondering." Caitlin Garner had been gone for a week. There was no way Heidi had done something to her. It was just a fleeting thought anyhow, not an actual suspicion. Heidi might punch Graham or his "girlfriend" in the neck, but Ray didn't think she'd do anything worse than that. They weren't worth her time, the way she acted.

"Sorry to intrude," Heidi said, scooping her sweatshirt off the bed. She stepped into her shoes. Stomped, more like it.

"You need a ride home?"

"I can walk."

"It's cold, and late."

"What are you, the last gentleman in America?"

"Just offering."

She sighed. "Sure. Thanks."

Ray drove her home and returned to an empty hotel room. He locked the door behind him and crashed, still dressed, on the bed. Two people could now identify Graham's girlfriend as Caitlin Garner. More significantly, one of them was Angela Marion's assistant foreman, meaning she theoretically knew. Not that Ray could figure out a motive. It didn't do her any good to try to keep the Garner Family from having a male child. The Marion Family had precedence. Unless . . . she just wanted to keep them from getting the land out of spite. But he was a long way from being able to make that connection.

He sighed, undressed, and went to bed, hoping the following day would bring some answers.

^   ^   ^

Lauren's "grandpa gold" Ford Focus was warm and inviting when Ray got in the next morning. That was partly because she had the heat cranked up in contrast to a frosty but sunny morning. It was also in part to a beautiful smile as she said hello. She wore a flannel shirt, black and charcoal gray squares, over a black shirt. Her jeans were untorn. She did not have coffee for him, but presumably, the place they were eating would.

"How was your night?" she asked.

"Interesting," Ray said.

"Oh?"

252

He explained about going out to the Bar H-9, waiting, seeing Ben get into a tan Corolla, then tailing it to the Circle M. Lauren listened with rapt attention. So rapt that she missed the restaurant. She circled the block again, giving Ray time to finish his story before parking in front of a small grassy courtyard. It was next to a Ripley's Believe it or Not, just down from The Merry Piglets and Liberty Burger, across from the same park as they were. A sign in front of the courtyard advertised The Bunnery Restaurant and Bakery.

Ray read the name.

"Trust me on this one, Ray."

He nodded and got out.

They bypassed the outdoor tables and were seated inside, next to a window looking out at the courtyard and the street. A TV in the corner showed The Weather Channel's coverage of a hurricane bearing down on the Gulf Coast. The waitress was a petite Latina girl who took beverage orders—coffee and coffee—and provided them menus.

"You not get much sleep?" Lauren asked.

"Huh?"

"You're staring."

"Hurricane Cheri is a cat 4."

She turned in her seat. "So it is."

"And no, I didn't. Heidi was waiting in my room when I got back."

"In your room?"

He nodded. "She's friends with the guy working the front desk, apparently. Anyhow, she'd heard too that Graham had, uh, been with Caitlin Garner."

"Oh?"

"From Corbin."

Lauren looked up from her menu. "The Corbin we know? Assistant foreman Corbin?"

"According to her description."

"Hmm."

"That's what I said."

They ordered—a ham and cheese omelet for Ray and something called The Glory Bowl for Lauren. They drank their coffee. It was delicious and perfectly warm on a cold morning.

"Any other breakthroughs?" she asked.

"No. Well, sort of."

She looked at him.

"I read my Bible this morning."

"Oh?"

"First time in a while. Used to be regular, but . . . I slacked off. Anyhow, what you said got me thinking. It was the kick in the pants I needed."

"Good."

"I fell into a funk, when people like Annabelle and her dad would talk about hearing God and being in tune with God, and I felt like I was missing something. Then when she broke up with me because God told her to . . . it rubbed me the wrong way, and I took out my frustrations in the wrong place." He met her eyes. "So thanks for helping me see things a little differently, reorienting my thinking."

"That's what we're all here for, Ray. It's why the church is called a body."

He nodded. "Okay, that's all I've got."

She nodded too. "Then it's my turn."

"You do some late-night sleuthing too?"

"Well, I don't have cable, and I'm between books."

He waited.

"I was thinking last night, about Snake Island, the Garners and Marions, missing people and suspicious deaths, and whatnot. And it occurred to me, the trust stipulates the land goes to the Marions if there's a living male descendant, right?"

"Right."

"And if not, it goes to the James Family, which Woodrow's descendants are through his marriage to Zora James, if they have a male descendant."

"Right," he said again.

"So, it would make sense for the Garners or James to want to eliminate any Marion descendants since they would be next in the pecking order, if they had a male descendant alive."

"Yeah."

"But the Marions have no motive. If they have a descendant, he gets the land. If they don't, it does them no good to off any James or Garner descendants. All they need to do is have a baby boy, and it's theirs again."

Ray nodded. "Yeah, I had a similar thought last night."

"Which stinks, because it seems like we've been leaning toward Angela being a suspect. She has means and opportunity, just no motive."

"That we know of," Ray said.

"Right. Anyhow," she said with a flick of her head to get her hair out of her eye, "that put me back on Woodrow Garner's trail, especially when I heard back from Marty."

"Who's Marty?"

She frowned. "Didn't I tell you about him?"

"No."

"He's an old friend—acquaintance, really. I called him yesterday morning between texting you. I didn't mention that?"

Ray shook his head.

"Hmm. Well, Marty works for the planning and zoning commission, and I asked if he'd heard anything about a certain—ahem, ahem—parcel of land. Any rumors, any scuttlebutt, anything."

"This town seems to be rife with rumors and scuttlebutt."

"Not just this town, but yeah. And Marty had some."

Ray waited.

"Remember what Angela told us, about Woodrow wanting to turn Snake Island into some sort of holistic resort? Well, Marty told me Woodrow Garner has already hired an architect. He's going full-bore ahead, expecting to get that property."

"How?"

She shrugged. "Apparently Woodrow's been greasing the wheels on the chance he does get the land, and he wants to break ground the day the trust matures."

"Never mind it wouldn't be his but his grandson's or great-grandson's."

"At best. I also called Audrey again."

"Oh?"

"She's feeling better, by the way. And she has no idea where Caitlin is or why she would have gone to San Diego or anywhere. She thought it sounded like a load of cattle cookies from Uncle Woody."

"So that's unanimous."

"Yeah. I also asked her for Woodrow Garner's full family tree, anyone who could possibly have a son and inherit the land as a James-slash-Garner."

"And?"

"Some of this I think we've heard before, but it's worth a refresh. Woody and Zora James had four daughters, Kelsey, Diane, Stephanie, and Nicole. Kelsey is Caitlin's mom, never married Caitlin's father, and is in her late thirties, so still of childbearing age, but that didn't sound like a possibility according to Audrey."

The petite Latina waitress brought Ray's omelet and Lauren's Glory Bowl—fried eggs covered in Swiss cheese, mushrooms, and hash browns. She also refilled their coffee.

When she was gone, Lauren continued. "Diane Garner is married to Marcus Nichols. They had two kids, Lincoln—who died in the hiking accident in 2017—and Mackenzie, who's 13. Stephanie Garner married Keith Doyle in 2012 but is unable to have children. Audrey said it was some sort of medical condition, but wasn't sure on the details. And lastly," Lauren said, stirring up her bowl, "Nicole Garner is only twenty-nine, has one daughter, Karissa, who's fourteen, and isn't married or seeing anyone that Audrey knows."

Ray nodded along, thought, tried his omelet. It was good.

"So basically," he said, "we have five women who could, in theory, get pregnant."

"In addition to Caitlin."

"Maybe Woodrow knows something we don't know."

"Maybe." She shrugged. "It's, what'd you say the other night, gathering information and filling in blanks?"

"More like creating more blanks."

They ate breakfast, and found the food at The Bunnery was as good as the coffee. And the service. Lauren picked up the check, and while she paid, Ray eyed pastries in the glass display counter at the front of the restaurant. The idea of grabbing a couple for the road was appealing, were he not already stuffed.

He lifted his eyes to Lauren, and in the background, saw two patrons in a table tucked in the corner, in a separate section from where he and Lauren had been eating. The man had his back to them, but his red hair and beard were still apparent, and his lanky build was evident even though he was sitting. Corbin. And the woman was his and Lauren's waitress from The Merry Piglets the day before, Raquel.

"Ready?" Lauren asked.

"Yeah."

Ray followed her outside and told her what he'd seen.

She stopped walking. "Corbin and Raquel?"

"Yeah."

"This *is* like an Agatha Christie novel. Everybody is connected to everybody else. You're not really a constable undercover, are you?"

"How'd you guess?"

She resumed walking, circling her car when she got to the street. "You think they're an item?" she asked over the roof of the Focus.

Ray shrugged. "Hard to tell from breakfast."

"Yeah, we had breakfast."

She ducked into the car, and Ray frowned over the roof for a moment, then got in as well.

"Raquel sees Graham and Caitlin together," Lauren said as she started the car. Ray buckled his seatbelt. "She tells Corbin, who is either her boyfriend or breakfast pal or clandestine co-conspirator, and he tells his old friend Heidi when they bump into each other at Albertson's." She looked at Ray. "Why?"

"I don't know. Small towns gossip? But there are a lot of webs interlaced together here."

"Yeah."

"I just wish we could see the connection."

"Yeah." She whacked his arm. "Let's go see some water shoot out of the ground."

THIRTY

Albeit cool, the day was clear and crisp, and the drive north was another scenic marvel. Ray still couldn't get over the way the Tetons carved into the pristine blue sky. The leaves on groves of aspen trees were brilliant yellows and golds, if anything a little more vibrant after the midweek cold spell.

They continued north, past Moran, and past the turnout to the Jackson Lake Lodge. Ray was now in uncharted territory and kept a wary eye out for scenery and wildlife. Lauren, meanwhile, tuned the radio, hopping from station to station looking for good music. She concluded they had time, and pulled into a turnout at the Jackson Lake Overlook. It was a unique perspective, viewing the range from the north. Grand Teton had lost most of its distinctiveness and appeared like just another far-off mountain. Still a good view.

It was another dozen miles north along the John D. Rockefeller Jr. Memorial Parkway to the southern entrance of Yellowstone National Park. Both sides of the road were heavily lined with trees north of the entrance, offering little in the way of scenic views. Many of the trees had fallen and were left in place. Lauren explained the rationale of the Park Service was to be as unobtrusive as possible.

They drove beside the Snake River, gradually rising on the west slope of a canyon it carved. It took them a little over thirty minutes after entering the park to arrive at West Thumb, on the shore of Yellowstone Lake. As they drove, Lauren explained how much of the park was part of a massive caldera, or land depression, that was actually a volatile volcano. The park's numerous geothermal features—hot springs and bubbling mud pots and steaming vents—were evidence of the instability beneath the surface. Experts predicted another cataclysmic eruption was imminent. She then clarified "imminent" meant within the next thousand years. Ray felt better until she added that thousands of small earthquakes were reported annually in Yellowstone. Maybe they should have just Skyped with Bethany after all.

From West Thumb, the road split and essentially formed a crude figure 8. The Grand Canyon of the Yellowstone River, including Upper and Lower Falls; the picturesque Tower Fall; and the road to Cody were all to the right, following Highway 20. Mammoth Hot Springs, Grand Prismatic Spring and most of the other geothermal features, and the west entrance to the park were straight ahead, ultimately west. So was Old Faithful, situated on the bottom left corner of the figure 8, just across the Continental Divide.

"Where are all the bison herds?" Ray asked as Lauren continued straight. He'd been periodically studying the map they'd picked up at the entrance, so he knew the general layout of the park. But the map did not have wildlife locations listed on it.

"Hayden Valley," she said. "Or the Lamar Valley, way up north."

"There's nothing here but trees," Ray said. "Where they haven't been burned."

"You'd prefer South Dakota, where you have to drive twenty miles to find a tree?"

"The open prairie has its charms."

It was another half hour, going at park speeds of forty-five miles per hour, before they reached the turnout to Old Faithful. It was an actual exit ramp, with an overpass spanning the highway. Ray hadn't seen an overpass since leaving I-25 in Casper on Saturday afternoon.

Lauren followed a one-lane road through the trees, looping back around to approach the Old Faithful complex from the east. The road led to an expansive parking lot that was about half full. The air had warmed considerably, and Ray shed his outer shirt as he got out. Lauren rolled up her sleeves. They headed out on foot.

A service station, the Old Faithful General Store, and the Old Faithful Snow Lodge (including Geyser Grill) were immediately on the left. Across the parking lot to the right was the Old Faithful Lodge, along with numerous cabins, cottages, and yurts. Directly ahead was the massive, modern Old Faithful Visitor Education Center. It served as a gateway to the large, semicircular boardwalk that surrounded the actual geyser known as "Old

Faithful." Beyond the center, on the other end of the compound, was the historic Old Faithful Inn. A person could spend a day at this one spot alone.

"We've got about twenty minutes," Lauren said, checking her watch. "Wanna run over and see when Old Faithful's due?"

"They know that?"

"Why do you think it's called Old Faithful?"

"I didn't think they had it down to the minute."

"They don't, but ballpark."

He shrugged, and they hiked to the visitor center, which was far more than just an information stand. It contained a bookstore, several exhibits, and a theater. It also had posted the approximate time of the next eruption, plus or minus ten minutes.

"Just missed it," Lauren said, noting the next time as roughly ninety minutes in the future.

"After lunch, then."

Ray reached into his pocket as his phone buzzed. It was a text from Bethany, saying she was running half an hour late and could they meet at 12:30 instead? He typed back a quick reply and informed Lauren.

"Want to check out the general store?" she asked.

"Why not?"

They backtracked to the Old Faithful General Store, which contained every imaginable souvenir. T-shirts, sweatshirts, hats, mugs, shot glasses, photo frames, stuffed animals, and a multitude of huckleberry products. Not to mention tasty-looking ice cream and other novelties. Lauren found a Kelly green T-shirt with "Yellowstone NP est. 1872" emblazoned on the front. She held it up, and Ray approved. He saw some huckleberry jam that he thought Cathy might like. Or that her kids might like to smear on the wall.

At twenty after, they took their purchases back to the car, then headed over to Geyser Grill. They climbed the front steps between a pair of American flags and benches on either side of the door, their backs made of skis. A woman was sitting on the one on the right, her legs crossed, texting. She was young, not unattractive, but a little overweight. She had straight blond hair flared just above the neck, a trace of makeup, no jewelry. She wore a long-sleeved white T-shirt with "Montana State" scrawled on the front in blue and gold. Ray was about to ask if she was Bethany when his phone buzzed from his back pocket.

He took it out and looked down from the woman to his screen.

Waiting out front, the text said.

He looked back up. "You're Bethany," he said.

"Yes," she said, standing and smiling. "Ray and Lauren?"

They nodded, shook hands, and thanked her for meeting with them.

"I'm happy to," she said. "I haven't been to Old Faithful in ages."

"Me either," Lauren said.

"Should we grab something to eat?" Ray asked.

The women agreed, and they headed inside. Several minutes later, they were seated in the cafeteria-style dining room around trays of burgers and sandwiches, fries, and soft drinks. Mostly Ray, with a few comments from Lauren, gave Bethany a detailed explanation of their quest to find out what had happened to Graham, from unraveling the meaning of the postcards he'd sent to discovering the trust instituted by John Marion to their recent discovery that Graham had had some kind of relationship with Caitlin Garner that seemed germane to their investigation. Bethany hardly touched her food while she listened, waiting patiently for Ray to ask the ultimate question.

"We feel like we have a hundred puzzle pieces, but they don't fit together. We're hoping you know something more that will help us make sense of it all and help us figure out what happened to Graham and why."

Bethany nodded and finally took a bite of her fish sandwich. She continued to nod as she chewed, swallowed, and dabbed her mouth with a napkin. "I can tell you that Angela is obsessed with that piece of land. Has been ever since she became the unofficial head of the Marion Family."

"Head?" Lauren asked.

Bethany nodded. "When her dad died from a heart attack in 2007, the Circle M was passed to her, and with it, the mantle of leadership in the family. Her brother, Thomas, died in Iraq three years before that, leaving no male heirs at the time. So it was hers."

"And she's been obsessed?" Ray asked.

Bethany swallowed another bite of her sandwich. "She and I aren't that close. Even though we're family, there's an age difference, and we have some major philosophical and ethical differences. I've made an effort to keep a relationship going, but she doesn't seem particularly interested. That said, I've tried to visit her once or twice a year, when I know other members of the family are going to be in the area. And I've heard her talk about it."

"What specifically?"

"Well, for starters, she's never understood the nature of the trust in the first place, why it would ever pass out of the Marion Family. She complains that John Marion was a chauvinist and rants about male dominance and suppression. She's something of a feminist."

Ray nodded.

Bethany ate a fry. "She's also upset that the trust stipulates that, right now, technically, Snake Island is public land. It's held in trust by the bank, but hunters or trappers or hikers or fishermen can use the land if they want. That gets her goat."

"Any idea why?" Lauren asked.

"No. She's never said."

"Does she use it for anything?"

"No. No one in the family does, that I know of. That's why I don't understand why it's such a big deal." She sipped soda through her straw. "But what really irked her last time I was there was when she found out about Woodrow Garner's plans if one of his descendants inherited the land. Apparently, he has some scheme to get the land from a grandson or great-grandson if one were to be born."

"Would that even be legal?"

"Oh, I'm sure the Marions would fight it, but the trust deeds the land to a male descendant. What he does with it after that is entirely up to him. I don't know much about the legal matters, especially if that descendant is a minor, which he would be, but I don't think Angela could do anything to fight it."

"Me either," Ray said.

"So his resort upset her?" Lauren asked.

"No," Bethany answered, covering her mouth with her hand as she finished downing another bite of sandwich. "She's known about that for several years, and didn't approve. But what set her off last time was some addition to the original plan—some new terrace or veranda or something. She was enraged."

"Odd," Lauren said, looking at Ray.

"How long ago was this?"

"Back in the spring," Bethany said, looking up at the ceiling. "Before Easter. But Easter was late. Early April, I want to say."

The general date didn't mean anything to Ray, at the moment, but he was gathering information.

"I tried asking her about it, last Thanksgiving when we were together, why the land was so important to her." Bethany picked up her sandwich. "She just glared at me, as if I ought to know or something. I haven't talked to her about it since."

"But she ranted to you about this addition to Woodrow Garner's resort?" Lauren asked.

Bethany nodded.

"Do you put any credibility into the rumors about suspicious deaths in either family?" Ray asked.

"No. Not that I can't imagine someone having such wickedness in their hearts, such greed, that they'd do it, but because from what I've heard of the rumors, there's nothing to them. Nothing substantial anyhow."

"I didn't mean to cast aspersions," Ray said.

"You didn't."

"We figured Angela would have no motive anyhow," Lauren said, "since any Marion boy would trump a James or Garner boy, and if there isn't a Marion, no elimination of any James or Garner would change anything. Unless it was out of spite."

"That's not entirely true," Bethany said.

Ray and Lauren looked at each other, then at her.

"For one thing, and I don't mean to throw stones, but I wouldn't put spite past Angela. She holds a powerful grudge. But she also has an ace up her sleeve."

"How so?" Ray asked.

"According to the trust, if there's no male descendant of John Marion after one hundred years, the land passes to the youngest male descendant of Bret James. If there's no living male descendant of Bret James, the land passes to the National Park Service. The Marion Family has a long tradition of environmentalism and ecological stewardship, so I'm sure John Marion's thought was that if his family or his best friend's family couldn't benefit from the land, the public at large could. He had no way of knowing that Snake Island would eventually be adjacent to Grand Teton National Park."

She paused to take another drink.

"So it would seem that, in that case, both families are out of luck. However, Angela's grandfather—my great-grandfather—Jacob Marion Jr. was the youngest of five children and the only boy. It's how he inherited the Circle M. And his youngest sister Wendy's granddaughter married a man named Jeff

Cogburn who is, according to what I've heard from several sources, a bigwig with the National Park Service."

"What kind of bigwig?" Lauren asked.

"Deputy Director of something. I heard Angela confiding in her sister Kelly a couple years ago that Jeff has the pull to see that the Marion Family has a say in what happens to the land. Maybe even enough pull to have the land donated or sold back to them after the Park Service receives it via the trust."

Ray and Lauren looked at each other again but said nothing. For several moments, the trio ate in silence. Ray finally broke it.

"So you're saying that the Marions get the land if there's a male descendant of John Marion, but also if there isn't a male descendant of Bret James?"

"I don't know if they get the land. That was a possibility. But they certainly would have a say in what the Park Service did or didn't do with the land. At least according to Angela."

Ray stroked his jaw. Thinking. The pieces were sliding together, but he couldn't see how yet. Not quite.

"I don't mean to cast aspersions either," Lauren said, "but are you sure Angela wouldn't . . . act to keep the Garner or James Family from getting the land?"

"Oh, she'd act all right. Or rather, have somebody else do it. She has minions to do everything for her, and she has eyes and ears out everywhere— town councils, county and state employees, at least one police department, probably some federal agencies. I'm not kidding, I think she could give you name, date of birth, and home address for every single descendant of Bret James, male and female. Everything short of what they had for breakfast, and that's only because it isn't relevant."

"But you don't think the rumors are credible?"

"Not the ones I've heard. Lincoln Nichols had a hiking accident, and the investigation turned up no signs of foul play. The only argument for foul play is Lincoln's friends saw another person hiking in the vicinity. And Willis Moran's food poisoning occurred in Barbados. I really doubt she'd send someone all the way to Barbados to kill him if she intended to."

"That does seem far-fetched," Lauren agreed.

"You said she'd act," Ray said. "How far do you think she would go to get Snake Island?"

Bethany looked him in the eye. "As far as she had to."

He left his follow-up question unasked, considering it to have already been answered. If Angela Marion had reason to believe killing or kidnapping or somehow harming Graham would help her get Snake Island, she would go "as far as she had to."

THIRTY-ONE

Old Faithful erupted while they were finishing lunch, so Ray and Lauren learned after thanking Bethany for her time, her information, and her candor. They really couldn't come to Old Faithful and not see Old Faithful, Lauren argued, and Ray agreed. So they wandered around, killing time before the next eruption, scheduled for approximately ten till three.

They spent half an hour admiring the Old Faithful Inn. Its towering brown exterior and steep roof topped with a row of flags—the United States flag along with the state flags of Idaho, Montana, and Wyoming—was nothing compared to the interior. With a five-hundred-ton, eighty-five-foot-tall stone fireplace as the focal point, the lobby of the inn featured four levels of balconies, all constructed out of lodgepole pine logs and limbs. The inn was 115 years old, and standing in front of the hearth, looking up at the construction, it was not hard to imagine they were back in the early twentieth century.

"It almost burned down in 1988," Lauren said.

"Really?"

"A third of the park was burned, and the fires were close enough to Old Faithful that they feared the inn might go up. They had crews out watering the roof to protect against flying ash and embers."

"That'd be a shame," Ray said, turning his head again toward the nearly hundred-foot-high pitched ceiling.

They wandered and milled around a little longer before eventually making their way back outside. It took a few moments to acclimate to bright sunshine after the dim interior of the Inn.

"What are you thinking?" Lauren asked as they trudged slowly toward the Old Faithful boardwalk. They still had half an hour to forty-five minutes to wait.

"How this all ties together."

"You think it does?"

He nodded. "Angela wants Snake Island, right?"

"Yeah. She said so."

"And Bethany said she'd go to almost any length to get it?"

"She did."

"And we now know that the trust has a provision that could get the land for her, at least possibly, if no member of the James Family stands to receive it."

Lauren nodded.

"Which means it does benefit Angela to keep any James babies—or Garner babies—from being born."

She nodded again.

"Angela's assistant foreman knew that Graham was having a relationship or a tryst or whatever with Caitlin Garner. Bethany told us Angela has eyes and ears everywhere, so it's reasonable to assume she knows what he knows."

"Reasonable, but not a given."

"Fair enough. It's also reasonable for her to assume that two people having a romantic relationship are going to sleep together, potentially conceive, and fifty-fifty odds say it's a boy."

"Making Graham a potential liability to her."

Ray nodded. "It gives her the motive we've been lacking. Factor in one of her ranch hands working at the Bar H-9, where Graham disappeared, and was picked up in a car the same style as the one in which Graham disappeared, and that that ranch hand's dad sold a car to a woman who registered it with the plates that were used on the car in which Graham disappeared . . ." He looked into Lauren's eyes. "Means and opportunity to go with the motive."

She shook her head. "That's not proof, though."

"No, not even close. And while she admitted she wants the land, there has to be more of a reason before it's even logical to assume she'd kill for it or make someone disappear over it."

"Does there? People do pretty awful things. They shoot each other over parking spaces at the grocery store, for crying out loud. Bethany gave less than a glowing review of Angela, and we both found her somewhat domineering. The tipping point to do something horrible may not be that far."

"Fair point."

"My question is, if she's guilty—and we're saying 'if' here—"

"We are."

"If she's guilty, why have us out to her ranch in the first place? Why tell us all she told us? Just to 'clear the air' or whatever it was she said to us?"

"Yeah," Ray said. "To control the situation. Get out ahead of any potential suspicions we might have."

"I suppose."

"I just don't get why the land is such a big deal."

"Family," Lauren said. "Angela's sentimental, in her own way."

"True. But it's a flood-prone piece of timberland. There's no real value to it. I'll buy that she just really, really wants it and I'll buy that she's willing to go to any length to get something she wants without there being some bigger motive behind it, but I'm not sure I'm willing to buy both. We're missing something yet."

Lauren nodded.

They wandered to the boardwalk and camped out southeast of the geyser. At present, it was little more than a bubbling hole in the ground, like someone had propped a hose to shoot upward and not turned off the water. "It gets better," Lauren said with a wink.

A crowd began to grow. Ray got tired of standing. Tired of waiting. Tired of not being able to figure out what had happened to Graham. More than that, he was consciously becoming aware, even if he did solve the riddle or make a deduction as to what had happened to him, it didn't mean Graham was coming back. If Angela was as desperate as Bethany claimed, and if she'd had reason to do something to Graham, Ray doubted it was send him on a round-the-world cruise. Graham had been gone over a week, and signs were turning toward foul play—maybe even murder.

The bubbling heightened marginally, eliciting several murmurs in the crowd. False alarm.

"What's your gut tell you?" Ray asked Lauren.

She squinted at him. "That I want to get ice cream for the road."

He nodded once.

"Bad timing?" she asked.

"No."

She nodded once. "Honestly?"

"I'd expect nothing less."

"I think Angela killed Graham. She got wind of his relationship with a Garner, feared he'd father a child, and took him out before he could do it. At least, before he had any more chance to do it. For all we know, he did, and Caitlin's in hiding until the trust matures." She winced. "Sorry, that was blunt and honest."

"That's fine. It's my gut feeling too."

"But what do we do about it?"

"And how do we confirm it?"

She looked at him but said nothing.

This time Old Faithful did erupt, sending a rocket blast of water up into the cerulean sky. Ray had seen the pictures before, so he knew what to expect. And it met his expectations. It was water shooting out of the ground. It was neat, but he wasn't going to lose his mind over it. What impressed him most was the noise. That he hadn't expected. That he hadn't seen in pictures. That, and the faint odor of sulfur.

It lasted only a couple of minutes, dying down as quickly as it had started. The crowd cheered. Some clapped. Good job, water. Then they dispersed.

"I work for the Park Service, so I really shouldn't say this, but . . ."

"Overrated?"

"A little. I mean, seeing a bull moose grazing in a riverbed with the purple-tinged Tetons behind it is way cooler for a park experience."

"Yes, but you can't schedule your watch by bull moose."

"True."

"Ice cream?"

She smiled. "It is a long ride home."

They stopped off in the Old Faithful General Store to get ice cream in waffle cones. This time Ray went with some version of extra, sinfully dark chocolate and Lauren opted for huckleberry.

"You want me to drive?" Ray asked with a nod at her cone as they walked back to the parking lot.

"Why, are men better equipped to drive while holding ice cream?"

"Just in general, I've always thought," he said, smirking as she glared at him. "You're savoring more than I am," he said. "I'll be done quicker."

She dug into her pocket and flipped him the keys. The afternoon sun was warm, and they kept the windows down as they drove slowly back toward the highway, then east on Highway 191, winding and climbing.

They crossed the Continental Divide at an elevation of 8,262 feet above sea level. Shortly after that, as they were climbing again out of a small valley, Lauren pointed to the side of the road. Her ice cream was down below the top of the cone, and she had just licked a glob of purple from the side of it. "Turn in here," she said, and Ray braked and coasted into a turnout high over a valley. Tall pines blocked much of the view, but there were several vantage points overlooking a wide valley with a lake in the distance. And, as he squinted through the windshield, distant white-capped peaks.

"Are those . . . ?"

"The Tetons," Lauren said, reaching for her seatbelt. The door handle was next, and Ray followed her. A low rock-and-mortar wall separated the sidewalk and parking lot from a drop down into the valley. Ray and Lauren approached it, he inhaling the tip of his cone, she continuing to lick and bite off sections.

"You knew about this place?" he asked.

"A friend of mine who works for the park's food service vendor recommended it. I've never stopped."

"It's nice," Ray said, turning his eyes down to a brown wooden sign with white letters, like all those in the parks. It announced they were overlooking Shoshone Lake.

And suddenly, the tumblers in Ray's head began to fall.

Lauren sensed it. She looked at him. "What is it?"

"I don't know yet."

She waited.

"Something with Shoshone, with the Indians that used to inhabit Snake Island." He thought for a minute, hearing the breeze in the boughs of the pines and cars on the highway behind him. Lauren ate her ice cream.

"What if . . ."

Lauren turned her head.

"Your friend Marty said that Woodrow hired an architect, that he has plans to go forward with this resort."

"Uh-huh."

"But according to Bethany, what really angered Angela wasn't the plans but an addition to the plans. So what would have changed with those plans that would have made her desperate not to let Woodrow get his hands on Snake Island?"

Lauren shrugged. "You think it's something with the Shoshone tribe?"

"Maybe it's a product of me watching too many crime dramas, but there's a rumor that John Marion was involved in their disappearance. What if there's evidence on the land that would link him to it? Or maybe it's not that sinister. Maybe Angela has Shoshone blood and knows this land was sacred to them, a burial ground or something?"

"I suppose either's possible."

He sighed. "Yeah, possible. More conjecture and theory."

"At any rate, we should find out what that addition was."

"Bethany said a terrace or veranda."

"Seems innocuous, but depends on the specifics—what exactly it was, where . . ."

"Let's check it out."

"How?" Ray asked.

"I'll call Marty and see if he can give me the architect's name. Maybe he'll let us look at the blueprints."

"You think so?"

"Can't say no unless we ask."

They got back in the car, Ray driving again, and headed through West Thumb and back south out of Yellowstone Park. Lauren called her friend Marty again, who gave them the name Mark Bruce. Lauren tried calling his office but got no answer. Mid-afternoon on a Friday, that wasn't surprising.

As they entered Grand Teton again, Lauren tried Mark Bruce again. This time she left a message, saying it was urgent and asking for a call back if and when he got the message. Then she tried Marty again, wondering if he had a cell or home number for Bruce. He didn't but did have the cell for his secretary. She was the source, he said, of the scuttlebutt. Lauren tried that number, got nothing, and left a voicemail.

They came to Moran Junction, reminding Ray that he was scheduled to leave via the road heading east tomorrow. Leaving Graham. Leaving his disappearance unsolved. Leaving Lauren. He turned his attention instead to the scenery, and then to the bison herd on the east side of the highway. Traffic had slowed to a crawl to observe the herd, and he crept along, wary of bovines straying into the highway or gawkers stepping in front of traffic. He avoided them both.

Lauren's phone rang. "This is Lauren. . . . Yes." She turned to Ray with a nod and mouthed something he couldn't discern. As she continued to speak, however, Ray concluded she was talking to Bruce's secretary. Lauren mentioned Woodrow Garner's resort, under the guise of being associates of his who were interested in investing but wanted to conduct an unbiased investigation first. To that end, they wanted a look at the plans for the resort but were flying out of town in the morning. Could they somehow stop by yet today to look at them?

She looked at Ray with a hopeful wince on her face as Bruce's secretary spoke. Then Lauren replied, "Uh, we're about half an hour outside of town right now. . . . You'd do that? . . . Great, thank you so much." She tapped the phone and dropped it to her lap.

"Suzanne Bening, Bruce's secretary, is going to meet us at the office. She's willing to stay late."

"Is it late?" Ray asked.

"Going on five already."

He raised his eyebrows.

"Big country out here. It takes a while to get anywhere."

"Yeah. So, we're investors?"

"I thought it made sense. The truth was too crazy to try."

"Slippery slope."

"You want me to call her back?"

"No."

"Okay. Bruce's office is about a block off the highway just into town."

Ray nodded.

"Also, I think we should get married."

He snapped his head to her.

She winked. "Makes more sense as married investors, right?"

He took a breath and nodded.

"Relax, Ray," she said, punching his arm.

"No, I'm good."

"Uh-huh."

"Just wasn't expecting a proposal this trip."

She grinned and sat back. "Also, we're probably hippies."

"Even better."

THIRTY-TWO

Mark Bruce shared a small office building with a chiropractor and a tax attorney. It was a modern, sleek, glassy building, with a tip of the cap to the rustic lodge style. His secretary, Suzanne Bening, was young, blond, good-looking. Her blouse and skirt blurred the line between professionally modest and flirtatiously suggestive. Her lipstick was red as blood, matching nail polish Ray observed when she shook their hands in the lobby of Bruce's half of the building.

"Thank you for making time for us," Lauren said. "We really appreciate it." She looped her arm inside Ray's and smiled up at him. She was enjoying this.

"It's nothing," Bening said. "I've been working sixty and seventy hour weeks for the last few months, so I have no social life anyhow."

She led them into a conference room with floor-to-ceiling windows looking out at tall pines and the brown grass of East Gros Ventre Butte. Frosted glass skylights let in all the light that was needed. A long mahogany table was in the center of the room, surrounded by plush, reclining office chairs. In the middle of the table was a thin ream of poster-board-sized paper and a 3-D model. Bening invited them to sit down and asked if they wanted anything to drink.

"No," Ray said. "We won't take up any more of your time than absolutely necessary."

"Well, here are the blueprints for the Garner Property," she said, turning the ream of paper toward them. "And this is a scale model Mr. Garner asked us to print for him."

"Print?" Lauren asked.

"Yes, we have a 3-D printer."

Ray focused on the model. It showed not only the main building but also the surrounding property, including what was marked as the west branch of the Snake River. Hundreds of pines and aspens were even depicted in miniature. Nestled amidst them was a triangular building, oriented so that one of its equilateral angles pointed almost due northwest. The roof of the building was steeply pitched such that the northwest corner was, if the model was indeed to scale, six to eight stories tall. The other two angles were one or, at most, two stories tall. The effect was that two of the three sides were also triangular.

"These two sides," Bening said, "are to be glass panes, letting in as much natural light and ambiance as possible. The roof is a mix of skylights and solar panels that will power the resort exclusively."

The building was surrounded on all three sides by a sidewalk. The exception was around the northwest corner, where the ground fell away, and the sidewalk was replaced by a deck. On the southeast side, a carport extended from the shortest wall, covering a circular end to a driveway that snaked through the pines to get to it.

"There's no parking," Lauren observed.

"No. To cut down on emissions, traffic noise, and to save space, Mr. Garner's plan is for all guests to be serviced by a shuttle."

"How do they get there?" Ray asked. "There's no road to Snake Island."

"No, there isn't. Mr. Garner is working on that, I understand."

Ray nodded.

"The plans here will show you a variety of details about the overall property, elevations, cross-sections, as well as the plans for every floor."

Ray and Lauren flipped through them, looking in detail both to satisfy Bening that they were investors and in case something should prove relevant. The resort featured a minimal number of guest suites, an opulent spa, several dining options, a library/study, a few lounges, and something tabbed as a Meditation Chamber. Triangles were everywhere in the design, to no surprise.

"We heard something about an addition to the original plans," Ray said.

"Yes. That would be . . ." Bening flipped through the plans, back to one of the preliminary pages. "Here. Not depicted on the model or the plans are a number of hiking trails around the property and 'sacred spots,' as I believe Mr. Garner referred to them. His last revision called for a terrace to be built here." She pointed to a spot west of the main building. "He's working on getting the various permits to build an actual wall on the side of the river so that the terrace can extend right up to the edge of the river, but that may prove difficult, from what I understand. In which case, these plans would place the terrace here."

"And it's just a terrace?" Ray asked.

"Mr. Garner describes it as a place of extremely high energy. I think he mentioned something along the lines of an altar—triangular, of course—to be placed there, along with seating options. He was also discussing making it something of an amphitheater, but I'm not sure he's decided one way or the other."

"An altar?" Lauren asked, her eyes wide.

"Yes, for incense and oils."

"I see."

"When was this last revision made?" Ray asked.

"Early this year. February, March maybe?"

He nodded.

"Is there anything else I can show you?"

"No," he said, looking up from studying the page—particularly the terrace—one last time. "Thank you so much for your time."

"You're welcome. Mr. Garner has been one of our best customers over the years, so anything we can do to help his friends or co-investors, we're happy to do."

They got out while the getting was good. Ray, since he'd been carrying the keys all along, got back in the driver's seat. "Where to?" he asked.

"The Answer Store," Lauren said, exhaling. "What did we learn?"

He shrugged. "Nothing, really."

"Why is Angela upset about an incense altar on a terrace?"

"The only thing I can think of is the old real estate fallback: location, location, location."

"So what's at the location? Why is that part of Snake Island so important?"

"That is the question."

He drove back to the Square. He parked. They got out.

"What are we doing?" Lauren asked.

"I don't know."

"Okay."

"I need to walk, think."

"Okay."

"Plus, I'm going to miss this place."

She nodded. They walked. And talked. They had a theory, one that made sense. They had some circumstantial evidence. But that was it. Theories and thin circumstantial evidence didn't bring people back, didn't bring about justice.

They circled around the Square, then walked west past the shops, Jackson Hole Coffee Roasters, and Friday crowds. The sun was low, and the temperatures were dropping.

At Millward Street, they turned back, still kicking around ideas. They could take what they had to Detective Celek, let him run with it. It would be a very short sprint. They could drive back out to the Circle M and confront Angela. But she would have no reason to tell them anything, and they may end up buried under the corral.

Ray's phone rang as they returned to the Square, and he extracted it from his pocket. The number on the display was familiar. Jason.

"Hey," he answered, stopping. Lauren took a step past him and stopped too.

"I did some digging on that Shoshone tribe you mentioned."

"Yeah. Can you hold a sec?"

"Sure."

Ray motioned for Lauren to follow, and walked quickly back to her car. Once inside, he put the phone on speaker. "Jason, I'm here with my friend Lauren. You're on speaker."

"Lauren," he said with an odd tone.

She raised an eyebrow at Ray. "Hi, Jason."

"Hello. So, yeah, I was telling Ray, I did some digging into the Shoshone tribe he asked me about. Turns out there's quite a bit of information on the Jackson Hole tribe, but it was hard to sort fact from fiction."

"Could you?" Ray asked.

"More or less. The facts are there was a tribe in the Jackson Hole area until the early twentieth century. They did disappear rather suddenly in 1907 or 1908. And they were never heard from again, at least not in any documented, verifiable way."

"So they were heard from again?"

"No. There are rumors and legends, but nothing more."

Ray said nothing.

"So those are the facts. They existed. They disappeared. They weren't seen again. I'll spare you all the rumors and speculation, because I found quite a few theories and I have a feeling I've only scratched the surface. I quit when I saw the word 'alien.'"

"Prudent."

"But I did cull the herd, so to speak, and came away with several accounts I think are the most credible and thus the most likely explanation for what happened."

"Let's hear them."

"About ten years after they disappeared, there was a pretty significant flooding of the Snake River. Permanently changed its course in several locations. As is the case with most floods, it uncovered some interesting things. One of those was a human body with what was believed to be a bullet hole in the back right portion of the skull."

"Believed to be?" Lauren asked.

"Well, they didn't have CSIs back then, but it was pretty conclusive from what I've read." He paused for a moment. "The skeleton was Native American."

"How do you know?" Ray asked.

"Couple of things. Size, shape, bone structure. It also had a few tatters of fabric and beads attached to it, all distinctly Native American. Shoshone in particular."

"And they determined this in the nineteen-tens?"

"No. The body was on display for a number of years at the University of Utah as part of their History Department. There's also an article from *The Salt Lake Tribune* back in 1963 that quotes an old Shoshone woman who claimed she survived, and I quote, 'a massacre between the river' when she was a young woman. The details were pretty thin, but she claimed the white man had killed her tribe."

Lauren shifted in her seat. "'The white man' as in it wasn't other Indians, or 'the white man' as in a specific white male?"

"I assume the former. She didn't name names. Probably didn't know names. Like I said, the details were pretty thin."

"No mention of where the massacre was, what river it was?" Ray asked.

"She didn't remember."

"Hmm. Anything else?"

"A lot else, but not much that I deemed credible. I could give you a dozen rumors, but they would only muddy the waters, I fear."

"Probably," Ray said. He looked to Lauren, who said nothing. "Thanks, Jason."

"Sure, Ray. You take care."

"I will. Say hi to Cathy and the kids."

"You got it."

Ray ended the call and looked at Lauren. He waited. Finally, she said, "I'm hungry."

"Me too."

"What are you in the mood for?"

"Honestly? Pizza."

"Pizzeria Caldera or Pinky G's."

"Your town. You pick."

"Both good. I'll say Pizzeria Caldera."

"That's on the strip, right?"

"The strip?"

"Whatever."

"Yeah, just around the corner."

"Walk?"

"Sure."

They hiked back past the Square and turned west on Broadway. Pizzeria Caldera was on the second floor, above the Mangy Moose Emporium, where Ray had looked for postcards similar to the ones Graham had sent him and bought an elk-antler frame for his mom. On a Friday night, the place was packed, and Ray and Lauren opted for outdoor seating on the balcony. White Christmas lights lined the railing, and six-foot-high patio heaters kept the canopy-covered balcony warm despite the evening chill.

They ordered drinks and scoured the menu. Pizzeria Caldera served Napoletana-style pizzas, and Ray and Lauren picked a pie with white sauce, chicken, mozzarella cheese, and Applewood-smoked bacon. As they waited, they discussed what they'd heard from Jason.

"You buy that lady's story?" Lauren asked.

"I do because he did."

She nodded, bent her straw down to her mouth. She spoke before sipping. "You think she's talking about the Snake Island tribe?"

Ray nodded. "As soon as Jason said the word 'massacre,' I thought of that picture we saw at that gallery the other day."

"'Driven.'"

"Yeah. I think the Shoshone tribe here in the valley was driven off their land, killed, and scattered. And I think John Marion did it."

"Why's that?"

"Because it explains why Angela is so intent on making sure Woodrow Garner doesn't get the land and doesn't get to build his resort on it. I think she's afraid when he starts digging and excavating, he'll find more skulls with bullets in their heads."

Lauren said nothing.

"The land itself isn't anything spectacular. Sure, she might want to keep it because it has family history or because she's into land conservation, but she already has the Circle M, and there's plenty of conserved land around here. One uninhabited, inaccessible piece of land can't be worth that much."

"Woodrow Garner thinks it is."

"But only because he's got triangles on the brain."

"True." She tipped her head. "If you're right, then it might not be about her getting the land but keeping Woodrow off it. She admitted it wouldn't make or break the Circle M if she didn't get it. But if Woodrow did . . ." She tipped her head back the other way. "On the other hand, if the land goes to the Park Service, maybe Angela can pull strings to get it back in the family or maybe just pull strings to keep it from ever being disturbed, under the guise of the Marion Family's long tradition of conservation and environmental responsibility."

"Flex your boot when you say that."

Lauren leaned on the table. "It's a theory again."

"Yep."

"So the theory is she found out about Graham and Caitlin via Corbin and Raquel, and took drastic steps to keep the two of them from procreating?"

"Uh-huh. I think Caitlin found out about it and told her uncle Woody, or maybe he found out about it and had her sent away somewhere where Angela couldn't reach her."

"Because she thought she was pregnant?"

"That or he feared what had happened to Graham would happen to her."

"Hmm."

"You disagree?"

"No," she said, reaching for her straw again. "Just thinking." She sipped. "So Caitlin is the one who told Graham about the Garners and triangles. Pillow talk."

"Something like that. It seems like he was paranoid before he disappeared. Maybe a gray sedan was following him, or maybe he sensed something at work like Angela's people scouting their snatch strategy. He never knew about the trust, about the danger being seen with Caitlin could cause, and figured Woody was a threat to him."

"But why?"

"I don't know."

"Who knows how much Caitlin told him? Maybe she mentioned the trust, left out the Marions, and mentioned the resort. Then if Graham sees people following him, he thinks it's because he suddenly knows too much about a pending land deal . . ."

Ray shrugged. "That could be it."

"Or maybe we're missing something yet," Lauren said.

"That could be it too."

The pizza came. Ray was typically a pepperoni, sausage, cheese, and red sauce pizza guy. He didn't go in for frills or trends or artisan toppings. But the "Campo" pizza at Pizzeria Caldera was delicious. Add another item to the list Ray was going to miss—Jackson Hole's tasty food.

They pondered other theories and loose ends as they ate. They kept coming back to the same basic theory. Angela had made Graham disappear to keep him from impregnating Caitlin Garner and potentially giving Bret James a male descendant. They also kept coming back to the fact that they had no proof.

Lauren snatched the check from under Ray's fingers. "My turn."

"I've honestly lost track."

When she had paid and the waitress had boxed their leftovers, they headed back down to the street. Absent the patio heaters, it was getting cool.

"The night's young," Lauren said. "Grab an after-dinner coffee?" She nodded down the block to Jackson Hole Coffee Roasters.

"Yeah. Why not."

"I'm going to run this to the car first."

"I'll take it."

"I need to work off dinner. And warm up."

"Okay."

He checked his phone while she headed toward the Square. He tried to think of someone else he could call, one other pump he could prime for information. It felt like they'd been stringing their investigation along for several days, finding one more clue or one more person who could give them information. Now there was no one left. And as many times as he replayed what he'd heard from Suzanne Bening, Bethany Cahill, Sam Covington, and a host of others, he couldn't find that missing piece that would substantiate his and Lauren's theory. Even so, it wouldn't bring Graham back. He agreed with Lauren's "blunt and honest" assessment that Angela had killed Graham. That cold reality was setting in, and it—along with his pending departure—left Ray feeling depressed.

Lauren returned. She stuck her arm in Ray's, as she had when greeting Bening a few hours earlier. This time, she wasn't acting.

They walked leisurely toward Jackson Hole Coffee Roasters. Ray enjoyed having Lauren "on his arm." He enjoyed her being close. He enjoyed what their relationship had become, whatever it was, in a few short days. He didn't even feel twinges of guilt at memories of Annabelle anymore. He'd somehow gone from getting by to moving on in the span of a week. And there was one person responsible.

That person stopped suddenly. Ray stopped too, looking back at Lauren. She was staring straight ahead, almost catatonic.

"Lauren?"

She turned her head toward him. "I think . . . Yeah." Her eyes suddenly blazed. "Ray, I think I may know how we can uncover the truth about what happened to Graham."

THIRTY-THREE

Ray and Lauren stood on the bank of the Snake River, watching the water churn and roil as it raced southward in the darkness. The night was quiet, but for the rushing water. The night was still—almost no breeze to speak of. And the night was cold, causing Lauren to shiver despite the added layers she, like Ray, wore.

"Are you sure about this?" he asked.

"Eighty, eighty-five percent."

He looked at her. A half-moon made it possible to see the sparkle in her eyes, and instead of objecting, he nodded. "Okay then."

Over coffee at Jackson Hole Coffee Roasters some three hours earlier, she had laid out her plan to Ray. They had no proof that Angela was the person ultimately responsible for Graham's disappearance, even though they believed it to be true. And as much as they wanted the person responsible for his disappearance brought to justice, what they really wanted most was to know the truth of what had happened and, if possible, to rescue Graham.

"If our goal was to convict Angela," Lauren had said, "we'd need evidence. Proof of her guilt. And not just a couple of circumstantial maybes thrown together. Rock-solid proof. But if all we want is the truth, maybe there's another way of getting it."

Ray shook his head. "I'm not following."

"What is Lauren most afraid of?"

"Losing Snake Island to Woodrow Garner."

"So let's play on that fear."

"How? Convince her Caitlin Garner did indeed get pregnant?"

"No. I don't know how we'd do that convincingly, and plus, it'd put Caitlin in danger."

"So what then?"

"I've been thinking about the Shoshone angle, and if your theory is right—that John Marion drove them off the land and killed them—and if that's the secret that Angela wants protected more than anything because it would damage her family name, then we threaten to reveal that secret."

"How?"

"By finding evidence that John Marion massacred the Shoshone tribe."

Ray raised his eyebrows while Lauren took a slug of her coffee.

"Bethany said Angela blew her top when she found out about the new altar-terrace thing. What if that's because she knows that's where the bodies are buried?"

"That would make sense, but how does that help us?"

"We beat Woodrow Garner's potential excavation crew to it."

Ray leaned forward. "You want to dig up bodies?"

"All we need is one bone, one piece of fabric or a bow or anything that could be tied to the Shoshone Indians. If there's any possibility that Snake Island is the site of an Indian massacre and thus a burial ground, there's no way anybody will get a permit from the government to do anything there."

"Isn't that what Angela wants?"

"Yes, but she doesn't want the scrutiny that would come with it, the archaeologists and college interns and history hunters who would dig—pun not intended—to find out what happened to the Indians in the first place. Who's going to be suspect number one?"

Ray sat back. "So you want to find something and then blackmail Angela with it?"

"A little quid pro quo. She gives us the truth about Graham—she gives us Graham if he's still alive—and we keep our discovery quiet."

"Assuming we make a discovery," Ray said. "It's not like we can just dig a six-inch hole and strike a grave."

"No, but if there were hundreds of Indians—if there were even dozens, there will be quite a few bodies buried. Especially if they were dumped in a mass grave, such that an add-on terrace would be devastating whereas the original temple to triangles wouldn't."

"That makes sense, but we're still talking about a large swath of land. That terrace was fifty feet in diameter."

"You got a better plan?"

"Than digging up a potential Indian burial ground on private property?"

"Technically, I think it's public. That's what Bethany said."

Ray sighed.

"It's your call," Lauren said. "But my guess is the bodies aren't buried too deep. The flood disturbed one of them, and I doubt whoever committed the massacre would have done more than drop them in a shallow grave."

"We could dig all night and find nothing."

"We could."

"All weekend."

She nodded. Drank some coffee.

Ray thought good and hard for a minute, weighing pros and cons. Finally, he said, "How do we even get onto Snake Island?"

It had taken them two hours to compile everything they would need, starting with a two-person kayak rented from a local outfitter, shovels and other digging implements, several camping lanterns, and a few miscellaneous items. They had taken turns first at Lauren's apartment then at Ray's hotel adding layers—long johns, multiple shirts, jackets, hats, gloves—and set out for the south bank of the south/east branch of the Snake River. They had eyeballed maps and identified a public "road" that would take them close enough to the river and provide them a place to insert the kayak.

"Well," Ray said, "let's get moving."

Lauren grabbed his sleeve. "Wait. Ray, is this a bad idea?"

"You ask me that now?"

She shrugged. "Sorry."

"Let's go."

They ported the kayak down to the bank and got in, one at a time. The water was dark and loud and seemed to be rushing a hundred miles an hour. They had chosen an insertion point right where the southbound flow turned west. The plan was to row with the current as much as possible, crossing the fifty-foot-wide river to the bank of Snake Island. Avoiding driftwood and sandbars in the process could prove tricky, but Lauren was confident. Or, at least, had been until recently.

She sat in front. Ray sat in back, a backpack containing the majority of their supplies on his back and two shovels interlaced in the webbing of the backpack. They pushed off from the bank until the current caught them, and the kayak wobbled back and forth. It didn't tip.

Working off the moonlight and a strap-on headlamp Lauren wore, they guided the kayak into the water. She shouted directions, and Ray paddled according to them. They avoided a large felled tree protruding into the water, then steered for a sandy bank beyond it. But the current was too strong, and they sailed past it.

"Left!" Lauren hollered, and they both steered left, around more driftwood, back toward the middle of the river.

"Ahead, one o'clock."

"I see it," Ray hollered.

The river began to curve south again, and another sandy bank was directly in front of them. Steering against the turning current, they aimed the kayak directly for the center of the bank and ran aground with a soft thud.

"Nothing to it," Lauren said with a smile as they hauled the kayak up onto the shore.

"Nothing to it," Ray echoed, shrugging out of the backpack. He then extricated the shovels so he could carry them.

"Want me to take the backpack?"

"I'm good. You lead the way."

She did, following a compass north and west. They did not have access to Mark Bruce's blueprints again, so they were working off memory of where approximately the terrace had been depicted in them. The very northern portion of the landmass between the two branches of the Snake River was actually incorporated in Grand Teton National Park. Thus the northern boundary of the Snake Island Property was a straight line, and the north/west branch of the Snake River only bordered a small portion of the property. In that portion, the river's bank cut at an almost forty-five-degree angle, running northeast to southwest. The terrace had been centered due south of another small island in the midst of the river, and the altar in the center of the terrace had been marked at thirty-two feet from the southeast bank of the river. That much Ray remembered from the blueprints. The rest would be guesswork.

The terrain was largely flat but uneven, covered with tree roots and rocks. There were a couple meandering streambeds or estuaries of the river that cut through the property too, evidence of the most recent flood. Ray wondered how Woodrow's relatively large resort building would be supported. He couldn't imagine this was the sturdiest of foundations. Then again, they built skyscrapers on Miami Beach, so . . .

Lauren stopped when they reached the west bank of Snake Island. The ground dropped off a dozen feet down to the edge of the river. Small whitecaps and wave crests reflected in the moonlight. The trees on the far bank blocked out the light from several ranches and houses Ray knew were there. More trees on the island north of them blurred where it ended and the far bank behind it began.

"What do you think?" Ray asked.

"Lot of trees."

"Uh-huh."

"Makes it easier," she said.

"How's that?"

"We can't dig where there are trees."

"No." He again shrugged off his backpack, setting it on the ground at his feet. He withdrew a thermos of coffee, which he handed her, and then a laser-based rangefinder. It was the same sort of thing weekend golfers used to figure out the distance to the flag or hunters used to gauge the distance to big game. Ray had no use for such a thing on the rare occasions he played golf because he had no clue how far the ball might go on any given swing of this or that club, and if he had to use some third-party device to know how far away the animal in his sights was, it was too far for him to make the shot. But for concluding the distance to a piece of driftwood, for example, it came in handy.

"I've been thinking," he said.

"Yeah."

"This altar Woody was planning to build. Think there's any chance he knew about the massacre or suspected it at the least?"

"I don't know. Maybe."

"Maybe there's a reason he picked to have his terrace altar in the exact place that would upset Angela."

"Why?"

Ray shrugged. "Maybe the Great Triangle told him to, Charlie Brown."

She raised an eyebrow.

"At any case, unless you've got a better idea, I say we start digging as close to that proposed altar location as possible."

"I'm game."

They spent ten minutes approximating and estimating and ultimately concluded that a patch of open land about ten feet square between a submerged boulder and a trio of pines corresponded to the altar marked on the blueprints. Or rather, corresponded as closely as they would be able to approximate without a survey crew. The fact that it was a path of open land sold them on the idea. After more coffee, they got to work.

Whether it was growing up on a farm, just growing up in the Midwest, or growing up as his parents' son, Ray had inherited a strong work ethic. However it had come to her, Lauren had the same work ethic. Ray had also been blessed with a strong back and the physical ability to maximize that work ethic. Lauren, though smaller and not his match physically, lacked nothing else and kept up with him as they dug a hole two feet deep and five feet wide. They shed several layers each, perspiring and breathing heavily, their breath visible in the cool night air. Two LED camping lanterns lit their work. The river and the occasional creaking of pine boughs combined with a distant—very distant, Lauren assured—coyote's howl to serenade them. And coffee and some granola bars Lauren had packed sustained them.

"Wider or deeper?" Lauren asked as they both leaned on their shovels.

"Figure they'd have to go several feet deep at least to lay the foundations of the terrace. Not to mention how much deeper they'd go with machinery, moving dirt around before moving it back."

"Deeper."

He nodded. "A little."

"Plus the terrace was below the level of the main sidewalk, wasn't it?"

"Yeah, and we don't know the elevations. We might be there already."

"Deeper," she repeated, and they got back to work.

The soil was sandy and shoveled easily, but both of them were slowing down. They went to three feet deep, then worked to widen the hole. They ran up against the boulder on one side, and multiple pine tree roots on two others. They had yet to unearth anything even remotely human, and before giving up or moving on, Ray wanted to widen the hole a little in the one direction where they were unencumbered. So he nodded in that direction and began digging again.

"Wait," Lauren said.

He chucked a shovelful of earth and stopped. "What?"

"Did you hear something?"

"No."

Lauren stepped around the hole and grabbed one of the lanterns. She darkened it. Ray looked at her, then grabbed the other lantern and turned it off. He looked at her again, and she returned his intense gaze.

Slowly, Ray shook his head. "What's going on?" he asked in a muted voice.

"I heard . . ."

A distant drone reached Ray's ears. He looked at Lauren, and her eyes flashed in the moonlight.

"What is that?"

It grew louder, coming from across the river. Or maybe up the river. It grew even louder.

Ray strained his eyes to see the water upriver, sensing the sound was coming from that way. In a valley, with all the trees and the riverbank, his ears could be playing tricks on him.

He thought he sensed movement, a distinction in the darkness, but he wasn't sure.

Then Lauren grabbed his arm, pulling him back behind a tree just as a floodlight snapped on. It emanated from the middle of the river, and its potent beam knifed into the trees just to Ray and Lauren's right.

The drone had grown into a steady growl, as from an outboard motor. The light was blinding, but as it turned to pan over the shoreline, Ray got a look at its source. It was mounted on the bow of a small rigid-hulled inflatable boat (an RHIB) closing quickly on the shore just down from where they had been digging.

The light turned their way, and despite crouching behind the trio of pines, they were unable to avoid it.

A shout echoed through the night. Squinting against the brilliant light, Ray saw motion. Several dark-clad figures, disembarking from the RHIB.

Lauren seemed to be processing a step quicker than Ray. She stood, flailing at his hand.

"Run!" she said, and crashed into the underbrush as the figures from the RHIB clambered up the bank.

THIRTY-FOUR

Ray's mind was a blur. Who were these guys? Where had they come from? Why?

Despite the lack of answers, he didn't disagree with Lauren's sentiment and chased after her. He darted around pine branches that attacked his face and arms and stumbled over tree roots and through underbrush that was hesitant to give way. He heard Lauren blazing a trail in front of him and heard the pounding of feet and shouts from behind him. At least no gunshots. Yet.

He was gaining on Lauren, and suddenly she was a blur of blue in front of him, flailing her hands at tree branches. Then she went down.

Ray caught up to her, lifting her by the arm and dragging her to the side until she got her feet beneath her. They ran side by side, weaving around tree trunks and ducking under branches. They were moving southeast, directly away from the river. The noise behind them had died down slightly. Had their pursuers lost pace? Were they fanning out to choke off alternate escape routes? Had they merely wanted to run Ray and Lauren off?

Lauren turned them into a thick strand of trees, and they stopped, secluded for the moment. They were panting heavily.

"Who are . . . these guys?" she asked.

He shook his head.

"And what do they want?"

"I don't intend to find out."

"Yeah. We should split up."

"What?"

"Two are easier to track."

A twig cracked in the distance.

"I'll go this way," she whispered. "Meet you at the kayak."

"No. You get there, you get across the river."

"But—"

"No buts. Go." He gave her a light push to one side and immediately took off in the other direction, running as loudly as possible, hoping to attract attention. Pine boughs slapped at his arms and legs and swiped at his head. He and Lauren had covered maybe two hundred feet before stopping. He'd made another hundred since. The altitude, the cool night air, several hours of exertion, an old knee injury reintroducing itself—they all sapped his strength. But he ran on.

He heard footsteps in the brush behind him and quickened his pace. Then he heard a scream.

Lauren.

It sounded like fright, an outburst, something she couldn't control. He turned and stopped behind a tree, looking over both shoulders. The moon was obscured by the trees, and his vision was next to nothing.

He heard another exclamation, then an outright scream.

Instinct took over, and Ray ran toward the scream. He stopped when he saw the beam of a flashlight. He dropped to the ground, feeling it cold and hard beneath him.

Two flashlight beams converged, and the crunch of leaves and twigs and pinecones increased as a crowd assembled fifty feet in front of Ray. He was lying on the edge of a slight slope, and groundcover kept him further obscured. Yet he was able to see clearly as four men gathered. Two of them held Lauren's arms, marching her between them. All of them held rifles. They had come hunting.

Ray didn't move. Lauren wasn't in immediate danger. She was their prisoner, but they were making no effort to harm her. And all he would do by revealing himself was get captured as well. For now, he remained where he was.

The four men conferred briefly in hushed tones. One of them withdrew a walkie-talkie from a holster on his hip. His back was to Ray, so he couldn't hear much of what was said. He thought he heard the words "woman" and "shovels," but that was about it. The reply was so cloaked in static that Ray could discern nothing.

The man turned and approached Lauren. "Get down on your knees."

Ray tensed.

Lauren stared defiantly.

One of the men holding her stepped on the back of her leg and, with a groan, she fell to her knees.

Ray tensed even more, ready to make a suicidal dash into the fray if what he thought was about to happen happened.

It didn't. Instead, the man who had spoken directed one of the men to bind Lauren's arms behind her back. She resisted, but they overpowered her, eventually knocking her face-first into the ground, like a cop making an arrest. Only so much different.

Ray tensed yet again when the man directed the other three to "fan out," ostensibly to search for him. He was protected by the brush if they didn't come his way. But despite his dark jeans and black shirt, he would be spotted almost instantly if they walked directly toward him. So he shimmied backward, down the side of the embankment, and under a large sage bush. It gouged and poked and scraped him, but at least it wasn't home to a family of raccoons or a rattlesnake.

The search lasted five minutes, during which one of the men came within twenty feet of Ray's hiding place but failed to spot him. The leader whistled, and the man turned back up the hill. When he had crested it, Ray sneaked back to his original spot.

Lauren had been pulled back up onto her knees, her arms bound behind her. Her blue pullover was caked with dirt, evidenced by the flashlight beams that illuminated the four men. Ray couldn't make out enough of their features to identify any of them, and yet one struck him as familiar. He wore a baseball cap, low over his eyes. Was that it? Had Ray seen someone wear a cap like that? Was it his general build, albeit cloaked in a heavy, hooded sweatshirt? His posture as he leaned against a tree trunk?

Ray was interrupted from thinking about it further when one of the men lowered a backpack off his shoulder and pulled out a black cloth. Lauren struggled when she saw it, but two of the four held her steady while the man lowered the cloth—actually a hood—over her head.

She struggled some more, thrashing her head. Ray nearly puked when one of the men jabbed her head with the butt of his rifle. It was far less than a vicious blow, but enough to send a message. With a whimpered moan, Lauren stopped resisting.

Two men jerked her to her feet, and the group turned and marched her back into the trees. In thirty seconds, their light was gone, and the night was silent again.

Ray lay in the dirt, paralyzed. He had done nothing.

There was nothing he could have done.

That was debatable and would be debated internally later. But now, Ray had to find a way to get Lauren back. And that started by figuring out who had her and where they were going.

He got to his feet, looking warily around to make sure the group had all cleared out. Then he started walking in the same direction they had gone, back toward where he and Lauren had been digging. They would get back into their RHIB, and Ray would be powerless to track them, other than to see the direction they went. But maybe he could overhear something, or see something that would give—

A twig snapped.

Ray stopped.

Out the corner of his eye, he saw the rifle butt coming at him, and he ducked. Just in time. The butt of the rifle grazed the back of his head and swung through the air harmlessly. Ray plowed forward into his assailant, driving his shoulder into the man's midsection and driving him back into a tree. That movement took Ray just out of the reach of a flying tackle from a second man.

Both assailants were off balance, and Ray stood and ran back in the direction he had come. He heard them behind him. He waited for the sound of a gunshot. Or maybe for the hot, searing pain of a bullet tearing through flesh and then the echo of the gunshot.

Neither came, but he heard the two men behind him. It had been a perfect ambush. Instead of hunting all over for Ray, they had taken Lauren prisoner and expected him to follow. And he had walked right into it. Now, not only did he have no idea where she was being taken, but also was threatened with his own survival.

He ran in a straight line, dodging trees where necessary, not gaining much ground. If any. He paid little attention to direction, just running as fast as the terrain and his waning supply of energy would allow. They remained in close pursuit, and Ray seriously thought about giving himself up. At least then he would know where Lauren was. At least then he wouldn't be alone.

Survival instinct kept him running, and gradually, he began to put distance between himself and the two men. He kept running, his lungs burning, his muscles screaming for a break, his knee throbbing. He pounded on.

He could still hear them, behind him, and he chanced a look back. In doing so, he lost his balance and began to pitch forward. He realized he had come to the bank of the south/east channel of the river, although he didn't know precisely where. But his glance back had revealed several flashes of movement, indicating the two men had not called off the chase. So instead of trying to regain his balance, Ray used his forward momentum. He pushed off with two more ungraceful steps and leaped into the black, foaming river.

∧   ∧   ∧

Ray was numb as he drove back to town. Physically, because he'd been so exhausted when he'd jumped into the river that he'd been able to do little to fight the current and had been carried half a mile downstream before he'd managed to swim and float and stumble to the south bank. He'd been lucky to avoid cracking his head on driftwood, and in that his pursuers had decided not to follow him into the river. The way he'd been dragged downriver, they probably had figured he was a goner. Then he'd hiked back to the truck, stripped off his soggy clothes, and put on extras he and Lauren had brought just in case they dumped the kayak. He'd been totally spent, so much so that the aches and pains of digging and running and playing flotsam in the Snake River were only background observations at most.

Mentally, Ray was even more exhausted. He'd let them take Lauren. He hadn't put up a fight. He'd run away. His brain told him it had been the prudent play. The men were armed. They could have killed him. Or her had he put up a fight. It would have been suicidal. His heart told him only a coward lay in the dirt while thugs dragged a woman off into the woods with a hood over her head. His heart reminded him that he should never have let it get to this, that his obsession with proving Angela's guilt had let Lauren talk him into the search in the first place.

His heart was loud, much louder than his brain, but he forced himself to listen to his brain anyhow. It was what he would have to rely on if he was going to get Lauren back.

First things first, he reasoned as he drove south, the heat blasting on his Silverado, he had to figure out who had her. There were several suspects. Angela, if she truly was guilty. Woodrow, if he'd somehow gotten wind—say from an architect or his secretary—that Ray and Lauren were interested in his resort. Some unknown villain who wanted the land for their own reasons. Or was Ray's thought earlier that the four men had come hunting closer to the truth than anything? Bethany had said hunters and trappers used Snake Island. Could it be that Ray and Lauren had been caught on a hidden trail cam and alerted poachers or black-market hunters, who had come to drive them off prime hunting ground?

Now that he was thawing out and his adrenaline was ebbing, Ray was starting to think more clearly. All were viable options, but Angela still made the most sense, if his and Lauren's suspicions were right and she was trying to keep buried secrets buried. She could have been the one on the other end of the walkie-talkie, giving instructions to her henchmen. She easily could have had an RHIB stored in her big green shed, and she could have had trail cams on Snake Island to keep tabs on who "trespassed" on it. Had she seen Ray and Lauren digging and deployed four of her ranch hands to stop them? It made sense.

Especially when Ray realized he *could* identify one of the four men. The one with the baseball cap who'd been leaning against the tree. It was his posture that was familiar. Ray had seen it before, when he'd leaned against a pavilion support column at the Bar H-9. Ben Pyle Jr.

He braked as he reached the edge of town. Angela had Lauren. So what would she do with her? Try to blackmail Ray into leaving town to gain her release? Set her loose after a stern warning or some not-so-friendly persuasion to leave things alone? Do with her what she'd done to Graham?

Ray headed due south, planning to go to his hotel. But as he passed the very empty, very dark Town Square, he thought better of it. His dashboard clock told him it was 2:47 a.m. It had been at least an hour since Lauren had been captured, meaning her captors had likely brought her to Angela—assuming it was Angela behind it, which Ray was assuming. That meant Angela would have already had time to identify Lauren and conclude that Ray was also involved. It was a good chance his hotel was staked out.

So he turned west on Broadway and drove until he came to a Loaf 'N Jug gas station with a minimart that looked open. He parked, checked his appearance in the mirror—it could have been worse—and went inside. He made a pit stop, then returned to the minimart. He filled the largest cup that he could find with coffee, grabbed the least dubious of sandwiches under a heat lamp, and scoured the aisles until he found a cheap pay-as-you-go cell phone. He purchased everything, drawing a bored look from the cashier, and returned to his truck.

Chugging the coffee to gag down the hours-old sandwiches, he got back on the road. He didn't know where he was going. He was hardly thinking about it. His mind was more focused on the plan cementing in his head. It was not a good plan. In fact, it bordered on being a bad plan. But it had been there since he'd returned to his truck soaked and shivering, and it was still the best he could come up with.

He looked for a place where he could park and not draw attention at three in the morning. He found it in the form of a Super 8 on the south side of town. He parked as far away from the lights as possible and finished his second sandwich and most of the coffee while extricating the phone from its package and figuring out how to activate it. It was not just that he wanted the anonymity of a "burn phone." His was waterlogged.

With the phone ready to go, Ray lowered his head onto the steering wheel. He'd been mumbling "Lord, help" prayers since crawling out of the Snake River but hadn't taken the time to further petition the Almighty. Not that an official, well-formed prayer would suddenly behoove God to save Lauren. But despite Ray's spiritual questions and struggles of late, and even though he couldn't explain how it worked, he believed there was power in prayer. Or rather, in the One who answered prayer. So he spent a few minutes asking God to protect Lauren—to save her. And to give him wisdom in his efforts to do so himself.

Then he lifted his head and the phone and set about his plan—wise or otherwise—to do just that. He realized he didn't know the number he needed. The Super 8 was set back from the road a little way, and its parking lot serviced several other commercial properties, including a small strip mall across from the hotel. None of the stores looked open, but Ray spotted a payphone under the porch in front of them and hurried to it.

On TV—at least, on the old TV shows Ray watched—when private eyes availed themselves of a payphone's phonebook, they found the page they needed and ripped it out. Ray always found that distasteful, but he wasn't in the mood for memorization. With the crinkled page in hand, he hustled back to the truck, took a look around to confirm that he hadn't been spotted, and dialed.

The phone rang four times before a male voice answered. "Hello?"

"I need to speak to Angela Marion."

The voice hesitated. "It's the middle of the night."

"I have a feeling she's awake."

"Look, I don't know who—"

"Tell her it's the ghost of a Shoshone Indian. Trust me, she'll want to take the call."

Ray was answered with silence for two and a half minutes. He was starting to wonder if the man had simply left the phone hanging or sitting on a table and gone to bed. Then the timbre changed.

"Who is this?" Angela Marion asked.

"You have something that I want."

"Mr. Eastwood, I presume."

"Where is she?"

"I have no idea what you're talking about."

"And yet when I said you had something I want, you knew who I was. Let's cut the banter and get down to business."

"What do you want?" she asked.

"You let Lauren go, you let Graham go if you have him or tell me the truth about what happened to him if you don't, and I will leave Jackson Hole, and you'll never hear from me again."

"I have no idea what you're talking about," Angela said again. "Even if I did, what makes you think I would do what you want?"

"Because I have something you want."

"Oh, and what's that?"

Ray set his jaw and stared through the windshield. "A small human skull. Probably a child's. I'm guessing if experts were to analyze it, they'd conclude it's Native American. I'm also guessing the two holes in the back are bullet holes."

Angela said nothing.

"And I'm guessing you know where I found it."

"I think you're lying. I don't think you found anything."

"Then hang up the phone and go back to sleep. I'll take my find to the police or the nearest university's research department or maybe I'll just YouTube myself holding the skull and talking about exactly where I found it and what I think it is," he said, raising his voice. He took a breath. "You sure you want to call that bluff?"

Angela said nothing.

"Especially when it costs you nothing to buy my silence?"

"Nothing?"

"I just want Lauren back and to know what happened to Graham. I don't care about your land or your desires to keep it. I don't care about rumors about your ancestors or this or that Indian tribe. I don't have enough evidence to go to the cops, or it'd be them calling you right now. And if you're smart, you can give me what I want without giving them any evidence, so they won't be able to touch you."

Ray could hear her breathing over the phone.

"Theoretically speaking," she said finally, "how would I know you wouldn't double-cross me?"

"The same way I know you won't double-cross me. Because I give you my word."

Angela said nothing.

"Do we have a deal?" he asked.

"Why don't you come out to the ranch in the morning and we can talk about this face to face instead of over the phone in the middle of the night?"

"There's nothing to talk about. Lauren and Graham for the skull and my silence."

"You're playing a very dangerous game, Mr. Eastwood."

Ray waited.

Ten interminable seconds passed. Then five more.

"Come to the ranch at dawn."

"Do we have a deal?"

"We have a deal."

"Good."

"But know this, Ray. I still think you're bluffing. If you are, you might be able to inconvenience me, but that is all you can do. I can destroy you. And if you are bluffing, that's exactly what I'll do. Do you understand me?"

"I understand."

"You take a shot at somebody like me, Ray, you'd better not miss."

"I'll see you at dawn."

Ray punched off the phone and dropped it in his lap, then gripped the steering wheel with both hands to keep them from shaking. He took several deep breaths, willing himself to calm down. He still had one more call to make. He was bluffing. Angela knew it.

His only chance was to rig the game and deal himself an ace in the hole.

THIRTY-FIVE

"Would you like some more eggs?"

Ray glanced up from his plate to look at Sam Covington. He stood against the doorpost, holding a cup of coffee, his mustache clean. His eyes were dark and sober. He nodded. "She'll be offended if you say no."

"Well, that isn't at all true," Sam's wife said, shooting him a fussy look.

Mary Covington was at least as old as he was, gray-haired, wrinkled, seemingly frail but, Ray suspected, tough and scrappy in a way only a woman who'd spent her life as the wife of a ranch hand could be. She wore what Ray assumed would be called a bed jacket. Ivory, with flowers. Her black-tinged gray hair was tied in a bun behind her head. Glasses—just readers, she'd said—were perched on top of her head. For the last half hour, she'd darted around the small farmhouse kitchen in a manner that belied her age, fixing a middle-of-the-night breakfast of scrambled eggs, bacon, toast, orange juice, and coffee.

It was all delicious, so Ray nodded. "Please."

Mary smiled and spooned the remainder of the eggs from the skillet onto Ray's plate. Two more bacon slices followed, and before he could thank her, she'd topped off his coffee for at least the second time.

Sam took a step forward. He took a long drink of coffee, then held his mug out to Mary when she gestured with the pot. When she'd filled it for him, he sat down opposite Ray at the old wood table.

"So let me get this straight," he said, "so there's no confusion."

Ray nodded and scooped some eggs onto his fork with the last of his toast. He had explained the events of the day to Sam and Mary while she had made breakfast. This after calling them in the middle of the night (after a second run to tear a page out of the phonebook) to ask for help. He'd briefly explained on the phone and been invited to their house outside of town, by which time Mary had already been up brewing coffee. The full explanation—laying out his and Lauren's "evidence," recounting their actions that night, and summarizing the current predicament and Ray's barebones plan—had lasted until Mary's breakfast was served.

"You're blackmailing Angela with evidence you don't have," Sam said as Ray ate, "planning on making an exchange when you have nothing to exchange, and you want me to provide you cover so you can effectively 'stick up' one of the most powerful persons in the valley?"

"That about sums it up," Ray said. "Believe me, I never would have come to you and involved you in this if there was any other way or any other person I could think of. And I won't be the least bit upset if you say no."

Sam waved him off as if he was offended Ray would even think he might be turned down.

"Why not go to the police?" Mary asked.

"Because I don't have any evidence," Ray said. "Not really."

"Speculation, rumor, hearsay," Sam said. "Even if they believed you, they'd have no probable cause to search Angela's property or means to persuade a judge to issue a search warrant, so they'd be hamstrung."

Ray nodded. "Bethany Cahill also implied that Angela has sources in law enforcement that could tip her off."

Mary frowned.

Sam drank his coffee. "One of the first rules of the West is you don't get involved in other people's business."

Mary started to object, but Sam cut her off. "But an even more primary rule is you help somebody what's in trouble. And you, Ray, are in trouble. So's your lady friend."

Ray didn't quibble over terms and titles.

"So I'll help you." He leaned on the table. "But first, I want you to look me in the eye and tell me you think this plan of yours can work."

Ray squared him up. "I believe it can work. I think we can get Lauren back without firing a shot. But we will be walking into an unknown, to some degree, and I can't guarantee how Angela or her people will respond, so all I can say is, yes, I think it *can* work."

Sam didn't break the stare.

"It could go south," Ray said. "I know this is a huge ask, and I hate that I'm putting you in this position."

"Life is full of being put in untenable positions. You can't avoid them. Best to focus on finding the best way out of them."

Ray nodded and scooped more eggs.

"You know you took a big risk coming to see me in the first place," Sam said.

"How's that?"

"Did you forget I'm technically related to Angela?"

"His sister married a McClintock," Mary said, "one of Angela's distant relatives."

"I know that," Ray said. "But you've never given me reason to doubt you."

Sam nodded and lifted his mug again.

"Besides, Lauren trusted you too. That first night at the Bar H-9. She said your eyes twinkled."

Sam raised an eyebrow.

Mary stood behind him and patted his shoulder. "I always thought so too."

Ray grinned for the first time in a while.

"Well, I'd better get changed," Mary said.

"Wait, you're not . . ."

"Coming with you? You bet I am."

Ray shook his head. "I can't ask you to do that."

"You didn't ask. I volunteered. And if the situation's as dire as you claim, you'll need all the help you can get."

"I'd take her up on it," Sam said. "Ask the local varmint population. They'll tell you she's a sharp shot."

"Also four-years-straight runner-up at the Teton County Fair's women's trapshooting competition."

"No age restrictions," Sam said.

"I'm grateful," Ray said. "But if something were to happen—"

"Oh knock it off, sonny. I'll be fine, and I'm not taking no for an answer. Sam, see those dishes get rinsed off."

"Yes, ma'am."

With Ray's help, he made quick work of cleaning up. Then they spread a detailed county map out on the table, honing in on the Circle M. Ray also sketched a quick map of the ranch from memory. "Last time," he said, "Angela had me come up to the main house."

"You go inside, you lose any advantage of having someone hiding in the bushes."

"I know. I won't go inside."

Sam poked a meaty finger down at the circular driveway. "So I need a clear shot to here."

"Right."

"What's this over here?"

"About a hundred feet of grass, then a field of corn."

"Still up?"

Ray nodded.

"How far's it go?"

"As far south as her property goes. Quarter mile?"

"Okay. I'll hide out here. Gives me line of sight around the garage and down the driveway as you approach and also toward the stable and barn."

Mary had emerged from the hallway. She wore blue jeans over boots, a denim jacket over a hooded sweatshirt, a kerchief around her neck for good measure, and a cowboy hat perched forward on her head to make way for a gray ponytail that fell halfway down her back. "Where do I go?"

Ray looked up at Sam.

"Either as a second sniper here," he said, pointing to a location west of where he would be, on the other side of the garage, "or in the bed of Ray's truck. She can give you cover as you leave, if need be, or just serve as a second gun to help get the draw on Angela."

"And how do you make your escape?" Mary asked.

"I'll hike back through the corn to the four-wheeler."

"Mm-hmm," she said with a nod.

"You don't like that idea?" Ray asked.

"No, it's fine. As long as Sam here doesn't keel over from a heart attack," she said, patting his stomach.

"I haven't yet."

"Not exactly proof of future vitality."

Ray grinned again at their good-natured bickering. It was odd that it popped into his mind at such a time, but he could see him and Lauren being the same way someday. Assuming they both lived through the current day.

"It's not exactly the D-Day Invasion," Sam said, "but I think it's our best bet. And dawn's coming."

They headed outside. The night was still perfectly dark. Cold. Ominous. While Sam made sure their four-wheeler was gassed and ready, Mary checked their cache of weapons.

"I assume you know how to handle a rifle," she said, loading cartridges into a Henry repeater.

"I do. Is that for me?"

"Nope. This is my varmint rifle. Holds seventeen .22 rounds. Ain't a possum or jackrabbit on the property."

Ray nodded.

Mary slid the rifle bolt into place.

"Four years straight, huh?" Ray asked.

"Yep." She winked at him. "Lost each year to Angela Marion."

∧ ∧ ∧

Ray pulled off the side of Spring Gulch Road about a mile south of the Circle M Ranch. East Gros Ventre Butte—also known as Saddle Butte—rose up to the immediate right. A few yard and porch lights from properties on the hillside failed to do much in terms of lightening the roadside. Neither did the stars overhead. The moon had long set. The sun was an hour from rising. Dawn was twenty-eight minutes away. Assuming Angela defined dawn the way Ray did, as the beginning of civil twilight.

Sam's Honda ATV had just barely fit into the bed of Ray's Silverado. Using a series of two-by-six planks, they carefully backed it down and out of the bed. They stowed the planks back in the truck. Sam would ride the ATV as close to the ranch as possible, then hike in still under cover of darkness and take an "overwatch" position.

He carried his Henry "Long Ranger" rifle, complete with a scope. He was good from a couple hundred yards, he claimed. The Long Ranger held five .223 rounds, plus one in the chamber. Sam also had strapped in a harness on his back a Remington 870 tactical pump-action shotgun with six shells loaded. He carried extra ammo for each gun.

Since he had a long ride and hike to get in position, he said quick goodbyes. They included a handshake with Ray, accompanied by a confident nod, and a quick hug with Mary. Then he got on the ATV and, with a wave, headed down the road.

Ray and Mary got back inside the truck, where it was warm. Ray did as he'd been doing for several hours, praying and going over options, scenarios, contingencies. They had worked out an abort code with Sam—three quick shots into the air. But as much as Ray hated bringing the Covingtons into this mess, the only way he could abort is if he thought of another way to save Lauren. And for all his efforts, that was one thing he couldn't think of.

"You like this girl, don't you?"

Ray turned to Mary, who had sat silently looking straight ahead for several minutes. "I do," he said.

She nodded. "You feel guilty about not being able to save her."

"I'm not sure it was a matter of ability."

"So, what, you're a coward?"

Ray shrugged.

"Bah. You're no coward, Ray. Wouldn't do what you're doing now if you was."

"Sam didn't tell me you were a retired psychologist," he said with a good-natured smile.

"Spend half a century with that man, and you'll become one by default." She reached over and patted his arm. "We'll get her back."

"I hope so."

They sat for a while. Ray watched the dashboard clock tick toward 6:48, when civil twilight officially began. His eyes alternated from the dash to the sky north and east, around the tip of Saddle Butte. The sky had turned from pitch black to very dark blue, the first indication that daylight was on its way.

Ray was riddled with doubts. What if Angela anticipated his ad-hoc plan and had him outflanked? What if she had a plan to double-cross him as he did her? What if she'd done something to Lauren? What if she *did* something to Lauren in response to Ray's actions? What if his plan got Sam or Mary hurt or killed? The questions were enough to paralyze Ray, but he had no recourse. He had to do something.

"You look like an expectant father," Mary said.

"Yeah."

"For what it's worth, I like your plan."

"You just saying that?"

"I am," she said, and they both laughed. The finer points of Ray's plan had been discussed in the yard outside Sam and Mary's farmhouse just before they'd loaded into the truck. Sam had said a prayer, a simple prayer for safety and success, and they'd headed out. That had been when Ray's confidence had been the highest. Now, it was nearing the lowest.

He sighed. "You know, I was engaged a month ago."

"To Lauren?"

"No. A girl named Annabelle."

"Well, this should be an interesting story."

"Not so much. She broke up with me, said it wasn't God's plan for her."

Mary nodded. "So you mad at her or at God?"

"Neither. Anymore."

"Um-hmm. Because of Lauren?"

He looked at her. "In part. She was . . . a breath of fresh air when I needed it."

"Was?"

Ray lowered his head, conceding her point.

"We're going to get her back," Mary said again. "We have to. I'm looking forward to meeting this young lady."

Ray smiled as the clock ticked to 6:44. "She'd like that too, I'm sure."

"Then let's get it done."

"You sure you're okay climbing in back?"

"Ray, I've slept on the cold, hard ground, on a church pew, and in the front seat of a Buick that wouldn't recline. I can certainly handle the back of a truck for a few minutes."

"Okay then."

They got out, and with a hand from Ray, the spry septuagenarian climbed into the bed of the truck. She retrieved her .22 rifle and lay down on a blanket. Ray then covered her with an old tarp and gently placed a couple of sawn-off two-by-fours at an angle across the tarp, to complement the two-by-six planks.

"You good, Mary?"

Her voice was muffled but sure as ever. "Let's roll."

THIRTY-SIX

Saturday dawned over Jackson Hole.

Ray turned into the driveway of the Circle M Ranch and through the open gate. The eastern sky in front of him was a glowing amber color that bled into darkening shades of blue higher in the sky. The headlights of the Silverado still cut a swath through the gloom, revealing the ever prevalent sagebrush on his left and a cornfield on his right. The cornfield that Sam Covington was hiding in with his Henry "Long Ranger" rifle and a Remington shotgun. In case things really went south.

Ray glanced into the rearview mirror, toward the bed of his truck, where Mary Covington lay under a tarp with her "varmint rifle." His eyes caught the Teton Range in the background, the snow atop the mountain peaks on fire as the sun drew close enough to the eastern horizon to shine upon them. Under any other circumstances, the view would have been mesmerizing. Instead, to Ray, it was just a reminder of how wrong things were right now.

He drove past the bunkhouse on the right. It was unlit. Potentially filled with armed ranch hands willing to do Angela's bidding. Ray could almost see the rifle barrels poking out the windows, like in the livery and saloon windows on a Western. Then it—and any potential armed ranch hands—was behind him.

On his left, the riding pen where the woman with the ponytail and Stetson had been riding on their previous visit was empty, as was the corral behind it. Ray coasted to a stop in front of the garage. All doors were closed. No Dodge Ram Laramie parked outside. No sign of anyone inside.

The Silverado's headlights brightened the front porch of the house, revealing nothing. Ray cut the lights, and the house was again shrouded in darkness, rimmed by the amber sky in the east. No lights on inside. No signs of human presence.

"All's quiet," Ray said. The rear window of the truck was open so he could communicate with Mary in the bed, under the tarp. "I'm getting out."

He did, leaving the Remington Model 783 rifle loaned him by Sam on the passenger seat. His shoes crunched on the gravel. The night breeze still carried a chill.

Ray turned from the house and looked down the driveway toward the barn. Green shed flanked by pines on the right. Stable and corral on the left. Forty feet of dirt and gravel between them. The barn was two hundred feet from Ray. Two windows on either side of generic barn doors. Another in the mow up above. Any of which could conceal a sniper who could kill Ray before he knew what hit him.

All was silent.

Ray waited. He heard nothing. Saw nothing.

Then a shrill chirp blurted into the stillness. It lasted several seconds, then went silent. It took Ray until it sounded again for him to identify it as a cell phone. Not his; it was soaked and likely dead. Not Mary's—it wasn't coming from the truck bed anyhow.

It rang a third time, and Ray turned his head toward the front porch. He looked around again, still spotting nothing, and took a few tentative steps toward the house.

A fourth ring.

Ray walked to the steps. Climbed them.

A cheap, black cell phone sat on the top step. It looked very similar to the one he'd purchased at the Loaf 'N Jug a few hours earlier. Its LCD display glowed green as it vibrated and rang again.

Ray scooped it up, looked around again, saw nothing again, and opened the phone and pushed it to his ear.

"Hello?"

"Come to the barn." The voice was Angela's, crisp as the morning, all business.

"Where's Lauren?"

The line had gone dead.

Ray dropped the phone into his pocket. Was she playing games? Being extra careful? Leading him into a choke point?

Because it offered protection, hid his rifle, and concealed the fact that he didn't have a Native American child's skull to exchange—and because it contained his backup in Mary—Ray got back into the truck. He passed word to Mary of the change of plans, hoping Sam would be able to adjust his position to still have an angle to shoot. They had no way to communicate, so Sam would have to react to what he saw. Ray trusted the former soldier to know what to do. It was executing it in time and unseen that could be a problem.

Ray followed the contour of the driveway around the circular grass area with the flowerbed M and flagpole. He crept north, past the corral. He stopped even with the south end of the stable and shed, announcing to Mary where he was.

He put the gearshift in park but kept the engine running. He again got out. The truck's sensor dinged, alerting him the keys were still in the ignition. He closed the door, and although it latched softly, it sounded like thunder rolling across the valley.

He realized too late that he'd left his gun on the seat. He hadn't been sure about wielding it, whether that would send a message that he was in control or would spook Angela and her people. This was his first hostage exchange, and despite all the TV dramas and Westerns he'd watched over the years, he was unsure of protocol. But it was too late now.

Ray ran his eyes over the compound. Left at the stable, with its porch cloaking the entrance in darkness. It was the perfect place to set an ambush. Or stash a captive.

His eyes caught a flicker of movement. The swishing tail of a horse in the barnyard beyond the stable, adjacent to the barn. He couldn't see much of the barnyard, but he saw at least two horses. A red bar gate separated the barnyard from the dirt and gravel square between the buildings.

Ray turned right, to the aqua green shed. A large white panel door hung on a slider. It was closed. Beside it, on the far side, a white standard door was also closed. Between the shed and the barn, another gate barred access to the yellowed grassland that served as pasture for the Circle M's cattle. Just visible in the twilight were the ruts of a path cutting through the grass.

Ray turned back to the barn. Dark-stained wood, aged and weathered over the years. Dual sliding doors. Gambrel roof with minimal overhang. The windows were paned glass on the lower level. The one in the mow had no glass. A pair of shutters were wide open, which explained the cooing of pigeons Ray heard. Everything else, save the soft purr of the Silverado's engine, was quiet. Everything, but his pounding heart.

He waited again. The seconds felt like hours.

The right door of the barn slid open a few feet, squeaking and groaning on its tracking.

Angela Marion stepped from the darkness. She wore brown and white flannel under a dark buckskin jacket. Denims and boots. The same dark cowboy hat as last time. No kerchief. No gun in her hands, but a holster was strapped to her thigh. Delta Force, not Old West.

She looked straight at Ray and walked straight toward him. Ray waited a moment. Spotting no one else, he walked to meet her.

They stopped three feet apart in the center of the yard. Her face was hard as granite.

"Where's Lauren?" Ray asked.

"Where's your skull?" she asked.

"In the truck."

"Let me see it."

"Let me see Lauren."

Angela glared.

Ray didn't blink.

"In the stable."

"Let me see her."

She glared some more.

Ray waited.

Angela extended a hand toward the entrance to the stable.

"After you," Ray said.

She frowned.

"I'm unarmed," Ray said, extending his arms. He nodded at her thigh. "Unless you want to unstrap your little sidekick."

Angela murdered him with her eyes. Then resolutely strode toward the entrance to the stable. Ray followed with wary looks around.

The wood-slats of the porch creaked as they stepped onto them. Angela's boots thudded as she walked through an unbarred entrance, flicking a switch as she did so. Bare bulbs in the ceiling flooded the stable with light. A main hallway ran left and right, the length of the building, opening to the grass corral left and the barnyard right. On either side of the hallway, stalls were segmented by eight-foot-high walls, leaving open air above the stalls beneath a pitched roof. There were five stalls on the far side of the building, four on the near, making room for the entrance.

Angela stopped in the middle of the hallway, straight in from the entrance. "Ben. Bring her out."

Ray's heart was a jackhammer as he followed Angela's gaze to the far stall on the back left. The door opened, and Ben Pyle Jr. stepped out, wearing a dark hooded sweatshirt and ball cap, same as on Snake Island. He held a pistol in one hand. He held Lauren's arm in the other as he pulled her from the stall.

She was okay. Still in the same clothes as before. Caked with dirt and straw. A small cut above her left eye—from the rifle butt while under the hood—had dried. Her hair was unkempt, as expected. And she looked exhausted and scared. But she was okay.

"Lauren."

"Ray."

"I'm going to get you out of this."

She nodded, biting back tears.

Angela stepped into his line of sight. "Now your turn."

He looked over her shoulder as Ben herded Lauren back into the stall.

"Show me the skull."

Ray forced himself to breathe. "It's in the truck."

"After you," she said, and this time Ray took the lead. They walked back out of the stable.

Ray stopped five paces from the truck. He wasn't sure on Sam's line of sight. Had he moved? Had there been enough time for him to do so? Was he in position now? He decided to stall.

"How does this work out?"

"You tell me," Angela said. "You were the one who called me."

Ray nodded. "I show you the skull. Then you have Ben bring Lauren out. No gun. She walks to the truck while I walk to you with the skull. She gets in, I give you the skull, and we all part ways."

"Whatever you say."

Ray didn't trust her, didn't trust the look on her face. That was okay. He wasn't being trustworthy either.

He nodded and turned, back toward the truck. He reached up and removed a faded old Denver Broncos baseball cap from his head. It was a loaner from Sam, and its removal was to be his signal. He was supposed to fire his Long

Ranger rifle in Angela's general direction, a scare shot, an announcement that Ray had a sniper concealed somewhere. It was supposed to give him leverage over the exchange, as Ray had figured Angela would value her own wellbeing above anything else.

But as Ray tossed the cap onto the passenger seat and made to reach for his rifle, no shot rang out. Sam did not own a suppressor. He hadn't fired.

Ray waited.

Still no shot. The possibilities ran through his head. Sam didn't have an angle. Sam was hurrying to get in position. Sam had been caught by Angela's people. Sam had succumbed to the heart attack Mary had teasingly mentioned.

"Well?" Angela asked.

He was out of time. He slid his fingers over the walnut barrel of the rifle but didn't pick it up. If he got the drop on Angela, there was nothing to stop a concealed sniper of hers from blowing his head off. Nothing but the knowledge that she was in the sights of a second sniper, one they couldn't neutralize.

Still no shot.

Ray stood, scrambling to stall.

He poked his head around the door. "I'm going to go around to the other side," he said to Angela.

She frowned, opened her mouth to speak.

Before she could, rustling from the back of the truck drew both her and Ray's attention.

Mary Covington stood in the bed, her .22 varmint rifle tucked against her shoulder, the barrel pointing directly at Angela's chest.

She slowly cut her eyes from Mary to Ray. "What are you doing?" she asked.

"Call for Ben to bring Lauren out here."

"This isn't what we agreed to."

"Call. Now."

She licked her lips. Mary did not cock her gun for emphasis. She didn't need to, Ray figured. It was already cocked.

"Ben," Angela called, her voice echoing off the buildings. "Bring Lauren out."

"No gun," Ray said.

"Holster your gun," she called.

Thirty seconds passed. Then Lauren shuffled out onto the porch. Ben still held her arm, but his gun was holstered.

When Lauren's shoe touched down on the dirt, Angela held up a hand. "Stop."

"What?" Ray asked. He jerked his head right, to where the standard door in the shed had opened, and a man had stepped out. Dressed like a cowboy, black hat. Wielding a rifle.

Another emerged from the barn door, still cracked a few feet. He wore a dark gray sweatshirt, no hat. Both leveled their rifles.

"Back inside, Ben."

"No," Ray said.

"Your old lady shoots me, you both die in an instant, and Lauren watches it before eating a bullet herself."

"You willing to die?" Ray asked.

"Are you willing to, with her blood on your hands?" Angela asked, looking at Lauren. She nodded. "Back inside."

Ben pulled Lauren. Ray felt Mary tense behind him. But he said nothing.

"Now that we have the theatrics out of the way," Angela said. "Let's get down to business."

A rifle shot reverberated through the morning stillness, like a sonic boom shattering the dawn. In its wake, Ray heard a soft but audible groan and turned in time to see Mary Covington collapse backward in the bed of the truck.

THIRTY-SEVEN

Instantaneously, Ray raised his eyes to the window in the mow of the barn. He saw a man perched on one knee, his rifle barrel aimed at Ray's truck. Peripherally, Ray saw Angela dive to her right and to the ground. He also saw the two men—one from the shed, one from the bottom door of the barn—taking aim.

He dove into the truck as his door window shattered and another boom cascaded down from the mow and across the property.

Ray's first thought was to grab the Remington 783. But he would be limited in his ability to maneuver it inside the cab of the truck. He would also be outgunned severely. Mary was down, maybe dead. Sam was an unknown. Lauren was back in the stable. His ad-hoc plan had been blown to bits.

So Ray improvised. The truck was still running, and he used the steering wheel to pull himself farther into the truck, at the same time stabbing his foot toward the pedals. One hand on the wheel, he used the other to shift into drive. His foot scraped the top of the brake pedal and found the gas as another shot rang out. Ray expected the windshield to shatter, maybe the engine to seize, else the gas tank to explode. None of those things happened.

While reaching for the gearshift selector, he had fleetingly considered putting the truck in reverse, using the rearview mirror to back out of the driveway and to safety, like the action heroes did on TV. But that meant abandoning Lauren, and he wasn't ready to do that.

So with the transmission in drive, Ray mashed his foot on the gas pedal. Gravel and dirt spraying, the Silverado launched forward. Ray peeked over the dashboard, now gripping the wheel with both hands.

Another shot rang out.

The man kneeling in the mow pitched forward and plummeted to the ground, directly in Ray's path. He veered a little right, unintentionally taking aim at the man who had come out through the barn door. He hurried to his left, away from the truck's path, as several shots from Ray's right pinged into the truck.

Then the Silverado tore the right barn door off its tracking as it slammed into the barn.

He had no idea what to expect. Horse stalls or cattle stanchions? Old farm equipment? Vintage automobiles? A meth lab? A shrine to circles or squares?

Hay bales.

Ray plowed into them, bringing the truck to a sudden stop and deploying his airbag. He felt for the rifle on the seat, kicked open his door that had never latched, and slid out from behind the airbag.

He whirled around, peering through the darkness out into the yard, where Angela and Gray Sweatshirt looked his way. He leveled the rifle and fired a shot between them. It had the desired effect, as they both turned and ran toward the shed, where Black Hat had presumably also retreated.

Safe for at least the immediate future, Ray leaned over the side of the truck bed. "Mary!"

She had propped herself up on one elbow. The sleeve on her other arm was stained with blood.

"Here, don't move," Ray said, reaching a foot for the rear tire to hoist himself into the bed.

"Aaah, I'm fine," Mary said. "Just grazed me."

"You're bleeding."

"Well, that's 'cause it done grazed me." She looked back toward the door as she reclined herself against the far panel of the truck bed. She reached with her uninjured arm to undo the kerchief around her neck. "What about the guy in the mow?"

"You saw him?" Ray asked as he took a rapid survey of their surroundings. He had made it to the middle of a forty- or fifty-foot-long barn before hitting a stack of hay that filled the back half of the barn. The hay stretched from one side to the other, including under balconies that ran the length of the barn on either side. They were connected by a balcony at the front of the barn, from which the sniper had fired down at Mary. Where there wasn't hay, there had been, as evidenced by loose pieces and dust on the floor. There was little else in the barn. A pitchfork and a coiled length of rope on one wall. A few old, rusty tools. Some rusty cans and barrels.

"As I fell back," she answered. "Darn carelessness."

"He fell from the window. Here, let me help you." She leaned forward with a grimace, and he tied the kerchief tight around her arm to stem the blood flow. "Somebody shot him," Ray said, making eye contact with Mary.

"Sam?" she asked.

"My guess."

"Took his sweet time. Where's Angela and her friends?"

"Three of them ran for the shed. Ben's still in the stable with Lauren as far as I know," he said, helping her down from the truck bed. They scurried to opposite sides of the open door. All was still, and Ray swept his eyes from the stable to the shed. He saw nothing.

"Are you okay to shoot?" he asked Mary, already knowing the answer.

"Of course."

"Switch with me."

They did. "Cover me," he said, and she nodded. He spent two minutes arranging a barricade of hay bales in the barn door opening. As he stacked the last bale in place, he was startled by Mary firing several rounds in succession. He ducked down behind the hay, and she turned back behind the barn door.

Several shots plugged into the door and the hay. Ray clambered to his left, to one of the windows that flanked the door. He and Mary were at an advantage, being in the dark barn, in that even the faint morning light would reflect off the windows and block Angela and her goons from seeing inside. But the windows did provide him a portal to see they had opened the main shed door, behind which they had constructed a makeshift barricade of an old door and sheets of plywood stacked against something. Sawhorses, maybe.

Mary took two more shots, then ducked down.

Ray crept to the corner of the doorway.

"We stuck in here?" Mary asked.

"I'll check. Can you hold them off?"

"All day and half the night."

Despite the circumstances, Ray couldn't help grin. As Mary stood and shot again, he ran back into the barn. The entire north end was full of hay bales, stacked in such a way that Ray was able to clamber to the top of them. From the top, he had access to the balconies that spanned either side of the barn, and also to peer down at the back wall of the barn. There was a closed door in the west wall, near the corner. As Mary traded more gunfire with Angela, Black Hat, and Gray Sweatshirt, Ray scrambled over the bales and looked down. It was too far to jump, but if he tipped over some bales, he could make a rudimentary staircase.

He returned to Mary, who had ducked down behind the bales.

"How many rounds you have left?" he asked.

"Six, seven."

He returned to the window, peeked out, and came back. "Let's give them a salvo. Save a couple so you can cover me while I reload."

She nodded.

He raised his rifle. "Go."

She stood, and he spun around the edge of the opening. He'd killed before with a gun. Deer, mostly. A coyote once. Some birds. He'd never taken aim at a human being. But he squeezed off three quick shots, aiming through the opening of the shed at the makeshift barricade. He didn't know how many bullets a stack of hay bales could absorb or how many shots an old door and plywood could take. One thing he was confident of was that his bales weren't going to tip over because of concussive force. He didn't know that about Angela's fortification.

Three spent shell casings ejected from the gun, and Ray ducked down.

"Reloading," he said as Mary continued sporadic firing. He had eight spare rounds in his pocket, with a box of more shells in the truck. He finished reloading, then nodded at Mary, who dropped down and did likewise. For the moment, the trio in the shed was quiet. Sam was nowhere to be seen.

"I'm going to sneak out the back," Ray said. "Try to get to the stable and Lauren."

Mary nodded.

"You be okay here?"

"As long as nobody sneaks up on me."

"I'll make sure they don't."

"Then get moving."

He stopped only to pick up more shells from the truck, then climbed the bales again. Behind him, Mary fired intermittently. Angela's people wouldn't know she was alone, and thus wouldn't be likely to try to storm the barn if her fire died down. Even so, Ray hoped to be in position to cover her by the time she had to reload again.

He quickly analyzed the bales at the back corner of the barn and began tumbling them down into the narrow crevice between them and the back wall. Satisfied that he could safely get down, he jumped/slid/climbed to the floor, then briefly destroyed his path so that one of Angela's people couldn't sneak in the back way and get the drop on Mary.

Ray had counted seven shots from her "varmint rifle." She had ten remaining.

His gun ready, his heart at a constant strobing beat, he pushed open the door into the barnyard. It was maybe fifty feet by fifty feet, with a fence forming the two edges not framed by the barn and stable. A red bar gate was immediately to his right, matched by the one opening between the barn and stable. In the middle of the barnyard was a steel hay trough. Four horses stood scattered around the yard. Their ears were pricked and their heads high and attentive, but they didn't seem spooked by the gunfire. Or by Ray.

The stable entrance was empty. And dark. The lights had been turned off. Ben, and presumably Lauren, had likely retreated to the stall on the far corner.

A sudden barrage sounded, coming from the shed, Ray figured. He crept along the edge of the barn, envisioning getting to the corner and shooting back to the shed from an unexpected angle. Maybe he could catch Angela and her people unaware and take one of them out. The fact that he was thinking in such terms sobered him, but he didn't have time to worry about it.

He also didn't have time to get to the corner. He caught a flash of movement in the yard. Angela and Gray Sweatshirt were running for the stable. Mechanically, Ray raised his rifle and took aim. Angela was gone before he had a chance, but Gray Sweatshirt had turned with a pistol to fire several shots back toward the barn. It slowed him enough for Ray to get off a shot. His aim was bad, low, but the bullet still found a mark in Gray Sweatshirt's leg, as evidenced by a red mist exploding from just below his knee and a loud growl of pain as he stumbled and dove for the cover of the porch. Ray quickly chambered another round but was too slow, and his bullet sailed through the porch just after Gray Sweatshirt crawled into the opening.

He was down but not out, and now Ray had given away his position.

He hurried to the corner of the barn, peeking around toward the shed. The entrance was empty and dark. But Ray spotted movement to the left of the shed, behind a fencepost and a rusting fuel drum surrounded by overgrown weeds. An olive green army jacket beneath a dark stocking cap. Sam, taking up a position. He must have circled all the way around the house and the shed, presumably getting there in time to take out the man in the mow. Now, he'd crept to another vantage point, closer to the action.

Ray gestured to get his attention and began to signal where the other players were. He saw the movement to his right just as the wood six inches above his head splintered. He dove down and back behind the barn as another bullet clipped the edge of the barn.

A volley rang out in reply, sounding like Mary's .22. Then shots from the stable entry. Ray chanced a peek around the corner and saw the makeshift barricade had fallen. A sheet of plywood lay reclined on top of a fallen sawhorse or support. A black hat lay in front of it. And a body lay crumpled beside it.

Sam was firing at the stable, and Ray turned his attention to the entrance. He hoped Lauren was safe, that no ricochets or stray bullets somehow got to her. He sensed things were heating up. Two of Angela's people were down. She, Gray Sweatshirt, and Ben were pinned down in the stable. But they had a hostage and a rear escape, into the grassy corral. The time was now.

Ray stood, carrying his rifle in two hands, like the little green army men he used to play with. He reached the stable wall and turned to signal to Sam that his plan was to enter the stable. But Sam was busy alternating between shooting and hiding behind the drum. Mary was continually firing as well, and Ray wondered if they had been able to communicate with each other.

He didn't have time to think about it. He edged toward the door. The sun had peeked over the horizon, at least far enough to color everything in Ray's vision a brilliant orange. It also put him at a distinct disadvantage peering into the dark stable. He thought about trying something action-hero-like, spinning around the corner and diving into the darkness, gun drawn and ready to fire from the floor. But his eyes would be unable to adjust, and he'd be at the mercy of whoever was inside.

Unless . . .

He tried to picture the stable from his brief time inside. The stalls ran along the east and west walls, but he thought he'd spied a gap between the end stalls and the north wall. A place to store equipment or tack? More to the point, a hiding spot? He could whip around the corner and duck in between the northernmost stall and the north wall. If he could do so unseen, he could let his eyes adjust and then go hunting in the dark.

The thought filled him with terror, like every scary scene from a movie he'd ever seen. Only one thing scared him more: the thought of something happening to Lauren.

Psyching up his courage, Ray took a deep breath. Then he hurled himself around the corner of the opening.

Right into Ben Pyle.

THIRTY-EIGHT

Ray had gone low, and he crashed into Ben's waist and midsection. But Ben had been coming with some momentum, and it carried Ray back into the corner of the stable and ultimately out into the barnyard.

Ray stood, the rifle still in his hands. Ben had rolled to the side and to his feet, brandishing the pistol he had earlier aimed at Lauren. Before he could bring it to fire, Ray used the rifle like a pugil stick and swung the barrel at Ben's hand. He succeeded in knocking the gun loose, but his two-handed maneuver left him susceptible to Ben's left arm.

Instead of throwing a punch, he looped his arm around Ray's neck, pulling him into a headlock. At the same time, he chopped down with his right hand, getting a hand on the rifle barrel. Ray tried to jerk it free while struggling against the headlock, but Ben was wiry and strong, and his arm felt like steel.

They staggered back into the hay trough. The gun was jostled and fell. Then they stumbled to the side and into the hind legs of a horse who had stood calmly during the fight thus far. It now spooked, jumping to the side, its hooves missing Ray's arm by inches.

The combination of the fall and the interaction with the horse loosened Ben's grip. Ray threw an elbow and shoulder that knocked him back into the trough and allowed Ray to get away. He looked for the rifle, saw it closer to Ben, and reacted by throwing his whole body into a right roundhouse punch that caught Ben square in the jaw as he regained his footing.

Both men again fell over. Ray felt like his punch should have knocked Ben senseless, but he actually got to his feet first. As Ray got up, Ben's shoe drilled him under the ribcage. Ray fought to keep his breath as he rolled over.

He was thankful Ben wasn't wearing boots as he kicked down at Ray a second time, a shot directly to the side of the head that stunned him.

Instead of kicking again, Ben reached down and jerked Ray to his feet. He threw him against the side of the trough and, before Ray could recover or defend himself, threw a punch packed with every amount of pop that Ray's had been. Only it didn't throw Ben off balance, and he was able to follow it up with a left jab to the nose that drew blood and watered Ray's eyes.

He dodged another punch by stepping to the side, but lost his balance and toppled back into something solid. The flank of a horse, he realized, as Ben pivoted and threw another lightning quick punch. Ray reacted by jerking his head to the side. The punch grazed his ear with enough force that it felt like it had taken it clean off. But instead of Ben's knuckles colliding with Ray's skull, they smashed into horseflesh.

The horse whinnied and pranced to the side. Ray fell back, expecting to have his head stepped on at any moment. Instead, Ben tripped or lost his balance and fell on top of him.

Ray's head pounded, blood was dripping into his mouth, and he feared Ben's kick may have broken a rib. But he still had plenty of fight in him, and as they grappled and rolled looking for an advantage, it was Ray who found an opening and the opportunity to throw an uppercut that rattled Ben's jaw.

This time it was Ray who picked Ben up. Remarkably, Ben shook the cobwebs from his head and dodged Ray's next punch. He returned it with a hard right that staggered Ray back, his bad knee buckling under him. He was aware of horses left and right of him, and of gunshots reverberating from the barn, shed, and stable. But he was focused on Ben, who charged again.

Instead of blocking the punches, Ray stumbled backward and fell intentionally. Ben's punches at air left him off balance, and he fell into the side of the barn. Anticipating that, Ray got to one knee. Grabbing Ben, he rammed his other knee into Ben's stomach. The air went out of him with an "oof," and he slumped back against the barn.

Ray again pulled him to his feet. Unable to catch his breath, Ben could do little to defend himself as Ray again used his knee, this time driving it up between Ben's legs and into his groin.

Ben's body reflexively bent forward, his chin up. Ray pushed him back and swung a right, left, right. Each punch spun Ben's jaw, the last one dislodging several teeth and sending Ben into the barn with a thud. He slumped to the mud, unconscious.

Ray turned and spat a stream of blood that had dripped from his nose into his mouth. He took two slow steps, his body shaking in the wake of the fight. He grabbed a steel bar of the trough for support. A horse snorted.

The distant gunshots were a little less frequent but had been replaced by a grumbling hum. Ray took another uneasy step forward, past the flank of a horse, and saw an old, red tractor emerge from the shed. Sam sat behind the wheel, a dirty yellow bucket raised as a shield. As bullets plinked off the metal bucket, Sam accelerated and made a charge for the stable.

Ray exhaled, trying to think. He wanted to shout to stop Sam. Lauren was in the stable. Or maybe she wasn't. What had gone down during his fight with Ben? Where was Mary? Where were Angela and Gray Sweatshirt?

Amid shots from the stable and barn, Sam barreled toward the stable, bucket raised. Ray watched, frozen in place from shock and from the effects of his fight with Ben, as the tractor bucket crashed into the porch roof. The roof buckled but also slowed the tractor's progress. Sam mashed the gears. A belch of black smoke shot out the exhaust stack, and the tractor surged forward. Sam adjusted the bucket, no longer using it to shield bullets but as a wrecking ball to demolish the stable.

Ray wiped his sleeve across his nose and mouth, smearing blood away. He had dropped the rifle early in his fight with Ben, on the other side of the trough. Ben had also dropped his pistol, which may be more advantageous in close quarters. And with Sam playing demolition derby, quarters were getting closer.

Ray took two steps forward and stopped.

Lauren appeared in the doorway of the stable, still unharmed. But that was in jeopardy. Angela stood behind her, gripping Lauren's neck and shoulder with her left hand and a black pistol with her right. The bright morning sunshine reflected off the pistol's polymer barrel, emphasizing the fact that it was pointed into Lauren's side, in front of her arm, just above the elbow.

"Get down," Angela said.

"There's nowhere to go," Ray said, even as the hydraulics on the bucket squealed and more of the porch collapsed.

"Get. On. The. Ground." Angela emphasized her point by jabbing Lauren in the ribs with the gun.

"Okay," Ray said, hands extended. He dropped to a knee, then two. He glanced at the tractor. Sam was getting down, his shotgun in his hand. A shotgun was the last thing they needed, with its wide spray pattern. They needed a sniper rifle.

"On the ground," Angela growled, and Ray prostrated himself.

"Where is the woman?"

"I don't know."

Angela turned the gun and fired it into the dirt six inches to Ray's side. Mud and dirt shot up into his face, and he blinked against it. By the time he opened his eyes, the gun was back in Lauren's ribs.

"Where?"

"I left her in the barn."

A shotgun blast shook the air. Angela looked over her shoulder, then backed up against the outer wall of the stable. She was protected from all angles by the building and by Lauren's body.

"Marcus!" Angela shouted.

No answer.

"Two of your people are dead," Ray said. "Another two hurt. All you have to do is let us go and this ends."

"Shut up."

Another shotgun blast.

Angela leaned forward and peeked around the corner. As she did so, Lauren used her right arm to shove Angela's right hand—and thus the gun—away from her.

Angela spun back, trying to turn the gun back on Lauren, at the same time pinching her neck and spinning her. Lauren had a grip on Angela's wrist, and for several seconds, they struggled for leverage and position. Angela dug her hand deeper into Lauren's neck. Lauren growled, then took a chance.

She released her grip on Angela's wrist, in the process pulling her arm back and launching her elbow upward. It was a gamble, but it paid off when her elbow cracked into Angela's jaw, snapping her head sideways and backward. Her grip on Lauren's neck loosened, and Lauren spun out of it, clawing at the gun. She knocked it loose and dove away from Angela's grasp.

Ray had watched it all from his prostrate position on the ground, unable to move for fear that Angela would shoot Lauren. Now that she had dropped the gun, however, Ray rose to his feet.

Angela's gun was twenty feet from him, but only a few from her. She had staggered back against the stable but seemed coherent. She would get to it before him. His rifle was only ten feet away, just around the trough. He ran for it as Angela pushed off the stable and bent for her pistol. Ray's fingers grabbed the rifle's walnut handle and lifted it from the mud.

"Uh-uh-uh," Angela said.

Ray turned his head to see her rising from a crouch, the pistol back in her hands. It was aimed at his head but swiveled slowly toward Lauren, who sat to her side eight feet away.

The tractor was still idling, so it muffled the gunshot into a pop. Angela spun around as a bullet plugged into her right shoulder. A second pop sounded, and a second spray of blood exploded from just above her wrist. She fell back against the shed, dropping the gun as her wrist clacked against the vinyl siding.

Ray stood as Sam emerged from the shed, the shotgun in his hands. He nodded, which Ray took as a signal that Marcus/Gray Sweatshirt had been neutralized. Ray looked left, across the red bar gate and out into the yard where Mary Covington stood, her hat off and her gray hair mostly out of a ponytail, a blood-stained kerchief around her left arm, and her "varmint rifle" lowered but still pointing in his direction.

Ray turned to Lauren, who had started to get up. He extended a hand, pulling her to her feet. She then crashed into him and embraced Ray in the tightest hug of his life.

THIRTY-NINE

Ray turned his head at the sound of tires on pavement. A "grandpa gold" Ford Focus coasted to a stop and parked beside his rented car. He glanced at the Tetons, towering against a blue sky decorated with pink and purple-tinged wisps of clouds, then looked back to the parking lot.

Lauren got out. She wore dark, distressed jeans with a hole in the left knee that looked more Abercrombie than the result of wear and tear, and a white button-down shirt, tucked in at the front, half open over a black undershirt and worn under a brown leather jacket. Her hair was down, waves and curls flowing around her shoulders. She looked good. Really good.

And she held a drink carrier with two cups of coffee.

Ray smiled and waited as she walked, first past the pink stucco house behind the grove of aspen trees, then to where Ray stood against the fence in front of John Moulton's gambrel-style barn.

"Thanks for coming," he said.

Lauren grinned and extended the drink carrier. "Hard to turn down a cryptic invite like this."

"Cryptic?" He took a cup. Jackson Hole Coffee Roasters, of course.

"Meeting here instead of in town or somewhere not half an hour away."

"Sorry."

"Don't be." She dropped the drink carrier in the grass by her feet, which were clad in boots. "But I am curious. Why here?"

"Because here's my favorite memory of you."

She smiled the serenest smile he'd ever seen, then sipped her coffee.

"How are you doing?" he asked.

"Same as last time you asked."

Last time had been mid-afternoon, when Lauren had come to the Teton County Sheriff's Office to conduct a full debriefing with Detective Celek. She and Ray had shared a moment in the hallway, as he had been on his way out. He'd gone back to his hotel to sleep for the first time since Thursday night. He'd awakened at six, showered, and called Lauren, leaving a voicemail and asking her to meet him at Mormon Row to "watch one last sunset."

He didn't know what Lauren had told Detective Celek but doubted it mattered. Ray had spent several hours with him, the Jackson Police, and an FBI agent via Skype. He had gone through everything—everything—from his arrival in Jackson a week ago to the shootout at the Circle M. He'd taken full responsibility and accepted all consequences for everything he, Sam, and Mary had done.

The authorities had arrived at the Circle M just moments after Mary had shot Angela. Someone had apparently heard the shooting and called 9-1-1. Before they reached the corral where the gun battle had come to a conclusion, Ray had gotten some answers, breaking away from his hug with Lauren and kneeling down by Angela.

She lay in the mud and against the shed. Her left hand held her right shoulder, blood seeping through her fingers. Ray wasn't a medic, but he doubted it or the wound in her lower arm were life-threatening.

"You . . . never had a skull," Angela said, coughing then moaning.

"No."

"I knew it."

"Where's Graham?"

She swallowed.

"Is he dead?"

Angela nodded.

Ray turned his head, clamping his lips together. He rubbed his sleeve across his face again, wiping away residual blood from his nose. It took almost a minute before he could ask his next question.

"Did you kill him?"

"No."

"Did you have him killed?"

Angela closed her eyes.

"Did you have him killed!"

She opened them and nodded.

"Why?"

"I couldn't let him have Snake Island."

"Woodrow?"

She nodded. "He was . . . he was dating Caitlin G . . ."

"Caitlin Garner."

She nodded.

"Did you kill her too?"

"No. I don't know where she is."

"You had my cousin killed over a piece of overgrown, flood-prone land. When you have all this?" he said, gesturing around.

Angela closed her eyes.

Ray had stood, his eyes catching the strobe of red and blue lights in the driveway. He'd held Lauren again and waited for the cops to arrive. They had then taken over, initially taking everyone into custody or to the hospital. Black Hat and the mow sniper were both indeed dead. Marcus was nearly so, having been shot with Sam's Remington 870 shotgun. Ben Pyle was concussed and would be eating through a straw for a while. He was also quite possibly unable to father children. Angela needed surgery. Mary Covington did not. And Lauren, despite having been through an ordeal, had checked out medically in the back of an ambulance. She'd insisted she was fine then, and when Ray got a chance to talk to her at the Sheriff's Office between interrogations. And now.

Ray and Lauren leaned on the fence. They watched the sky and the mountains. They drank coffee.

"How are Sam and Mary?"

"They're good," Ray answered.

"Sam's not going to kill you for getting his wife shot?"

"No."

"They're not in any legal trouble?"

"No. None of us are."

"What about Angela? Detective Celek was so worn out, and I was so worn out, I didn't bother to ask him for many details."

"Apparently she confessed to everything. She must have known it was over. She admitted to having Graham snatched and killed. She outed her people, came clean about it all."

"I'm sorry for your loss, Ray."

He nodded.

"Have you told Heidi?"

"No, the cops spoke to her."

Lauren took a drink.

The cops had done a lot. They'd gotten a full confession from Angela, including the details of Graham's death. One of Angela's henchmen had driven the Jackson Hole Cleaners van. Two others had jumped out, grabbed Graham, knocked him out, and stuffed him in the back of the Toyota Corolla. They had then gotten back in the van, driven off, and left the Corolla for a fourth henchman—who'd been riding to a chuck wagon dinner during the actual kidnapping—to drive off in later. He'd driven back to the Circle M, where Angela had interrogated Graham to learn all that he knew, then had him shot and buried under a rock pile on the back forty.

Ben Pyle had played no role in the actual kidnapping. The details of the Corolla and the license plates and Margaret Lane were still undetermined, and somewhat unimportant in lieu of Angela's confession. Detective Celek had vowed to speak to Woodrow Garner about Caitlin's whereabouts, her relationship with Graham, and any connection to any of the events that had played out recently.

Ray didn't care much about any of that anymore. Whether or not his theory was right that Woodrow had hidden her away didn't matter. Whether or not her and Graham's relationship had been sexual or not didn't matter. Whether or not she someday bore a son who inherited Snake Island didn't matter. In fact, Ray had no idea what would happen to Snake Island now. Did Angela's actions affect the trust? He doubted it. Would Jeff Cogburn, Kristin Marion McClintock's husband with the National Park Service, still pull strings to get the Marion Family the land or a say in what happened to it? Would it ever be excavated, revealing the remains of slaughtered Indians? He wasn't sure.

And he didn't care. Graham was dead.

"So," Lauren said after several minutes of silence, the sun now long gone, the colors fading, and the temperature starting to drop, "is this 'one last sunset'?"

"Yeah. I have to head out tomorrow, be back at work Monday, assuming the mechanic can get my truck fixed in time." He shrugged. "Anyhow, I wanted to remember it like this."

"It?"

"Jackson Hole. Somehow, I can't help but think that whenever I think about Jackson Hole, I'm going to think about Graham, about his life being snuffed out over a piece of land, a cover-up of a massacre."

"Is that for sure—the massacre?"

"From what Detective Celek told me about Angela's confession."

"I can't believe she came clean about everything."

"Yeah. Apparently, this morning was a clarifying moment." He shook his head. "All this beauty, and it's tainted by death and blood and . . . I almost killed a guy with my bare hands today."

She took his free hand with her free hand.

He looked at her. "And the worst part is, when I think of what they did to you, what they threatened to do to you . . . I don't even regret it."

Lauren said nothing.

Ray tried to speak several times, but couldn't formulate his words. He finally nodded back at the mountains. "That's why I wanted to come here, to try to replace those images."

She let go of his hand and leaned over the fence. "It's kind of a microcosm of life."

"How's that?"

"We live in a beautiful world, from vistas like this to the sweet laughter of a little child, from wildflowers in bloom to a stirring piece of music to random acts of charity and kindness. And yet it's a fallen world, tainted by evil and sin and people like John and Angela Marion who would commit murder to get a piece of property."

Ray said nothing.

"But this world isn't the end. There's a promise of redemption, that one day all the wrongs will be righted." She looked his way. "And while you will always have bad memories of Jackson Hole, you'll always have the good memories too. Like this," she said with a nod at the barn, the mountains, and the last vestiges of the sunset.

Ray looked at her. "That's a pretty good analogy."

"Yeah, well, it's a pretty good promise. Eternal life, new bodies, no more pain and suffering."

He nodded. "Yeah, it is."

They drank some more coffee.

"Anyhow, that isn't what I meant about 'one last sunset.'"

He looked at her.

"I meant, is this one last sunset with you and me?"

Ray sighed. "I don't know, Lauren."

She nodded.

"I'll shoot straight. I like you. I don't mean the way I like Sam and Mary Covington. I mean the way I wondered if I'd ever like a woman again."

Her eyes were dark and deep.

"And this is all too weird for me. I was engaged a month ago. I didn't know you a week ago. This morning I confronted my cousin's killer, and I've been obsessed with solving this mystery since I got here. I'm not entirely sure what I'm feeling, why I'm feeling it, or what I should be feeling."

Lauren nodded.

"And I live eight hundred and seventy miles from here." He shrugged. "I don't know what that means."

Lauren was slow to reply. "I like you too, Ray. And after what happened this morning, I really like Sam and Mary Covington, but not the way I like you. And I agree this has a junior high summer camp feel to it. Or a freshman at Boise State feel to it. And I don't want to be a rebound girlfriend, for your sake or mine."

Ray nodded.

"I'm tired. I slept an hour last night in a horse stall and about two hours today while you were with Detective Celek. I can't tell if I'm thinking clearly or not. But I have a thought."

"I'm listening."

"I'm going home for a couple days over Thanksgiving. To Moscow, I mean."

"The one in Idaho."

She fought off a sly grin. "*Da.* For Christmas break, I was looking at visiting a couple of old friends who live in the Chicago area. What if I stopped in Sioux Falls on the way there or back?"

"You're driving?"

"Hadn't decided, honestly."

"Okay. You stop in Sioux Falls . . ."

"And we see where we're at three months from now. Maybe those three months will be agonizing, and we'll realize we're madly in love. Or maybe we'll realize this is like summer camp, and by then I'll have fallen for a cute park ranger with a beard or Annabelle will have heard another message from God and realized what a mistake she made."

Ray grinned.

"What do you think?"

"Christmas in Sioux Falls?"

"Yeah."

"And if in three months I still like you and you still like me . . . ?"

"We figure something out then. But at least it won't be based on a week of s'mores and campfire songs and longing looks by the lake."

"You sound like you're speaking from experience."

She winked. "Focus, Ray."

"Yeah. Okay. Christmas in Sioux Falls. I can spend the next three months anxious about what sort of gift to get the girl I like but who may not still like me and who may or may not become my girlfriend."

"That's the spirit."

"You know how many good views there are of the Tetons?" he asked.

She frowned at the change of direction. "A lot?"

"Yeah. But this is the one I wanted to remember. And that's because of you."

Lauren smiled. "You eat dinner yet?"

"Snacked."

"Hungry?"

"Kind of."

"How about I buy you dinner at the Gun Barrel, make up for last time? 'One last' meal together?"

"You got a deal."

She nodded and turned toward their vehicles.

Ray stopped her by grabbing her hand.

She looked at him.

"Just in case things don't pan out at Christmas, I'd be remiss . . ." He pulled Lauren close and leaned in. He paused for just a second, giving her a chance to withdraw. She didn't, and he kissed her, slow and soft and yet relatively short.

They stepped apart, and Lauren's face began to morph into a smirk. "And here I thought I was the forward one."

AUTHOR'S NOTE

I have been to Jackson Hole three times, on two different trips out West, each time for only a day. I love it more each time I visit. This last trip, I realized I had to set a novel there, as much because writing and researching the book would "take me back" as anything. As always, I tried to keep the descriptions as realistic and accurate as possible, but I had to use artistic license in a few places. I hope those who know better don't mind and those who don't know better can't tell.

The usual cast of characters again merit a thank you. My wife, Sierra, supports not only my writing but also my existence. I couldn't do either (write or keep going) without her. My parents have been equally inspiring and provide a valuable second and third eye to my stories. Mark and Tiffani Robinson add advice and correction and let me ramble about my ideas. Chris Hembel faithfully and enthusiastically proofs and encourages.

A special tip of the cap also goes to Chris Baker, whose encouragement has buoyed this writer's spirit in general, and whose shared experiences in Jackson (shared over social media from across the globe, by the way) helped ignite the spark of *Broken Trust*. I hope when you read this, it takes you back too.

And lastly, thanks to my readers, who spend their hard-earned money on and take the time to read the words I write. I am forever grateful that you consider my books worthy of your time.

Also by Nathan Birr

The Last Resort Series
Fire & Ice

The Douglas Files
Overnight Delivery
Three's a Crowd
All an Illusion
Shot List
Chasing the Wind
Blood and Treasure
One Life to Lose
Golden Key

Douglas Files Shorts
Black Male
WinterKill
Short Sail

God, Girls, Golf & the Gridiron
(Not Always in That Order) . . .
A Love Story

All is Calm? – A Christmas Novella

The Book of Levi

Augusta Whispers

www.nathanbirr.com